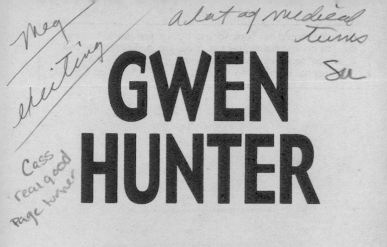

GWEN HUNTER

DELAYED DIAGNOSIS

MIRA®

ISBN 1-55166-803-3

DELAYED DIAGNOSIS

Dedicated with love to
Mary Anne "Mare" Hoffman,
dear friend in Seattle.

Though I drew on Chester County, S.C., and its hospital for inspiration and information, Dawkins County, its citizens, its employees, its hospital and patients are entirely fictional. I have tried to make the medical sections of *Delayed Diagnosis* as realistic as possible. Where mistakes may exist, they should be ascribed to me, *not* to the able, competent and creative medical workers in the list below.

John Saunders, M.D.; Susan Saunders, friend and fellow writer; Kim Livingston, M.D. neurosurgeon, for advice on the aftereffects of penetrating head trauma!; Mary Anne Hoffman, friend; Tamar Myers, fellow author and friend—who never gives up; the local chapter of SCWW...for the critiques and the encouragement; Joyce Wright, my mom, for...well...everything; Rod Hunter, for everything else.

In Chester County, S.C.

Laurie Milatz, D.O., for the final medical revisions. You could not have been more helpful!; Chase Manhattan Owens, M.D.; Richard Hughes, M.D.; Isom Lowman, M.D.; Darlette Stanley, R.N.; Barry Benfield, R.N.; Tammy Taylor, R.N.; Sherry Minors, R.N.; Susan B. Jacobs, R.N.; E. C. Chrisler, doctor of radiology; Kenn Cruise, M.T.

In Rock Hill, S.C.

Susan Prater, O.R. Tech; Susan Gibson, equipment manager; Eric Setzer, DVM; Mike Fedele, Jr., Physical Therapist at Catawba Rehabilitation Services.

_____ Prologue _____

I always wanted to be a hero. Another part of me, almost as strong, almost as needy, wanted to be kept safe and protected by a hero of my own. The two sides of me were in constant contradiction, an internal discord I thought I had resolved by attending medical school. I had thought that being a doctor would provide a way out of my miserable, ugly-duckling youth. I thought that I could save the world and make a good living, finding friends, a husband and children along the way. That I would blossom in the rarefied atmosphere, a Florence Nightingale-like M.D. in mink and diamonds, copies of _How To Win Friends and Influence People_ and Dr. Spock under my arm. That was youth dreaming, egotistical and idealistic. Some parts of it worked out well enough, though I wear scrubs instead of mink and diamonds, and having the M.D. hasn't meant kids and love ever after.

My first year as a med student squashed my ideas of my own superiority, and residency took care of the rest. I lost John—my fiancé—most of my compassion, and am still in hock up to my armpits for medical school. But I have friends. It was a talent

I always had, the making of friends. Real friends, not the casual, speak-to-you-if-I-get-time, forget-you-if-you-move-away-or-get-transferred-to-another-department kind of friends, but lasting friends. The lifelong kind...

And because of my best friend, because of Marisa, I accomplished the first dream of my youth, only to discover that being a hero wasn't all it was cracked up to be. It could, in fact, make my second dream impossible to attain.

1

Cowardice

I had never been a coward, but it took all the courage I ever had to walk into Marisa's room. She was just sitting there, slightly slumped, her face and form in silhouette, framed by the window and rising sun. Unmoving. A mannequin in shadow.

I reached for all the instincts created by four years of medical school and three years of residency. All the cool, dispassionate calm and impersonal stoicism pounded into me by impossible hours of study and other people's heartache and pain. That professional calm had deserted me. Everything I had learned, everything I thought I knew, vanished like low-lying fog in the face of dawn.

Marisa didn't rise to greet me. Didn't lift her head. Didn't move at all except for the slow rise and fall of her shoulders. The usual scent of Chanel No. 9 she had worn for years had been replaced with the faint scent of sickness—feces and the ammoniac smell of urine in diapers. I clutched the door frame, a weakness in my knees that had nothing to do with the lack of sleep or the long night in the E.R.

"Marisa?"

She didn't move. I crossed the room to the rocker where she sat beside the bed, bundled into an afghan in the too-warm room. Knelt before her, eye to eye. She blinked. Tears gathered at the corners of my eyes, making her waver with motion not her own.

Her face was bruised, the left orbit purplish and green, the lid puffy with fluid. Her hair, only two weeks past so gloriously thick and blond and always perfectly secured with pins in some elegant version of a French twist, was lank, hanging parted in the middle. Her breath stank from teeth left unbrushed.

"Oh, Jesus, Marisa."

It was true. All that the E.R. crew had said when I walked in from my two weeks in the Appalachians, still covered with the sweat of our last, cold hike up some well-traveled tourist path, still carrying the anger of John's last words, our last goodbye. It was all true. Marisa had had a cerebral vascular accident. A stroke, just thirteen days past. And her prognosis didn't look good.

Steven Braswell, Marisa's husband and my immediate supervisor in the emergency room, had taken her home from the hospital, making it clear that Marisa was to receive no visitors. She needed rest, interspersed with bouts of intensive therapy, not socializing. But even after all I had heard last night, all the horror stories of the morning Marisa had been found and brought in by ambulance, I hadn't expected this…this…

I tried to position my eyes so hers would fall on mine, so she would recognize me, come back to me, show me that she was going to recover. Marisa only blinked. When I did the same, my tears fell, and God knows I hadn't cried in years.

Angrily, I knocked back the tears with my wrist. Doctors learned early not to put fingertips to eyes. Contagion. Viruses left beneath the nails. My hands shook. My breath was too fast, coming up from my lungs in quick little gasps that sounded somehow like sobs. I lifted my hand to touch her, shake her, slap her awake from her stupor, as in some old movie.

Marisa blinked again. And that was when I saw the small drop.

My hand paused in midair. Fingers curled, I focused on the drop leaking beneath Marisa's nose. Odd little drop of...

Slowly I reached forward, touched the single drop of bloody fluid below Marisa's left nostril. It was cold. Startled, I jerked back my hand and started to rise.

I stopped, the motion arrested, the drop of fluid caught on my finger, trembling in the sunlight that struggled up over the horizon and in through the window. I took a deep breath. It, too, trembled as I stared at the fluid. Slowly the drop rolled down my fingertip into the shadow of my hand.

Standing, my knees groaning like a grandmother's, I carried the fluid to the window and the pallid Friday-morning sun. Outside the house, scudding clouds took on a golden hue. A bird sang off somewhere, a warbling throaty tune. Leaning into the dawn, my back to Marisa, I touched thumb to the drop, dabbing it gently, swirling the fluid.

"My God," I whispered.

It wasn't mucus. Or even serous fluid, the clear, yellowish fluid often secreted from a wound.

It was something else entirely.

I turned my back to the morning and looked at Marisa, struggling against the tears that clogged my throat and thinking processes. Drawing upon the medical detachment that allowed a doctor to see a patient as no more than a series of symptoms pointing to a diagnosis, I looked at her again, breathed deeply and forced calm into my system as I observed her. Studied her not as a friend but as a patient.

I brought the drying drop to my nose and sniffed. It was scentless.

Marisa was pale and nonresponsive, staring sleepwalker-style at the corner of the room. There was nothing to stare at. The corner was empty.

I recrossed the room and knelt again at her side, touched her skin. It was cool and dry. As I measured her respiration, I took her pulse through the thin fabric of her nightgown. Twelve and shallow. Eighty and steady.

The January sunlight was strengthening by the moment, brightening the cheery yellow room, highlighting the bruises that marred her flesh. In medical school, while my complexion grew sallow and dull from the long hours and stress, Marisa's had remained vibrant, lovely. The traditional peaches and cream of a plantation owner's daughter. No longer.

Bruises stained the skin beneath and above the left eye, a hematoma circling the orbit. A small circular wound was healing just beneath the brow bone, where the flesh was puffy and swollen, edematous.

When she blinked, that lid moved a fraction of a second after the right one and opened sluggishly.

There was a healing scar above her left eye, the pale white and pink puckered irregularities of recently removed stitches in sharp contrast to her skin.

Even with the presence of the strange fluid, nothing I was seeing was, by itself, abnormal for a stroke patient who might have fallen and hit her head. But taken together...

The small wound above Marisa's left eye was oddly circular—too regular, too symmetrical—one centimeter in diameter, as though she had landed on an upturned unsharpened pencil and the rough end had penetrated the skin, creating an abrasion. She had a subconjunctival hemorrhage in the inner corner of the eye, the white of the eye stained a bright crimson. And the pupil was blown, dilated to its full width. Marisa was blind in that eye.

I lifted her wrists, which resisted slightly, the pressure equal in both sides. When I dropped them, they fell slowly, settling into Marisa's lap. Marisa had some motor function left....

"It just don't seem right, Dr. Missy Rhea."

I whirled, my heart slamming painfully in my ribs. It was Essie. Only Essie. My co-conspirator and Marisa's long-ago nanny, standing in the doorway wearing a housedress and slippers.

"She always so smart and all and beautiful as that Princess Diana was. And now she sit and stare. Just don't seem right."

"It isn't right, Miss Essie. I need my bag."

"No reason, Dr. Missy Rhea. Dr. Steven done all he could to bring her back. I seed it with my own eyes.'' Essie shook her head slowly and shuffled into the room. Nearly eighty, Essie did everything slowly. But she had been with Marisa's family for over seventy years, and was as much family as Marisa's blood. She had kin in Charleston, a daughter here in town and other family up north somewhere, but neither Marisa nor Essie would have thought of parting.

"That man done holler and weep and all going on. Fell out hisself when he brung her home. I seed him, fell out in the floor. I bring a dab of ammonia like Missy Marisa done showed me how to do. Wake him up after a while it did. And him cry like a baby.'' Essie shook her head. Which matched my judgment about the situation perfectly. I didn't believe it, either. Steven Braswell never displayed emotion in public and seldom in private. And certainly not in front of the *servants*. He was an iceberg.

"Miss Essie, I need my bag. I'm going to the car and come right back in. Okay?"

Essie eyed me, her mouth in a tight line, arms crossed over her chest as she considered. "You got to be gone before that nurse come. Dr. Steven say no visitor, not even family, exceptin' the nurse, and the muscle man.''

"Steven hired a physical therapist?"

Essie nodded. "That the one.''

"I promise I'll be gone before they get here.''

"Well, you hurry then, Dr. Missy Rhea. I too old to be standin' in line for unemployment. And too old to be huntin' me a job.''

"You get fired and I'll hire you myself. It'll be the best move I ever made.''

"That the truth, that pigsty you live in.''

"I love you, Essie." I kissed her on the cheek, turned and ran for the back door and the brand-new BMWZ3 I had left in my drive, a quick run through the woods.

Three minutes later I was back, breathing deeply from the exercise. Essie was sitting in her favorite overstuffed chair by the gas logs in the keeping room, knitting piled on her lap. Pointedly she looked up at the clock as I passed.

Flipping on all the lights in the bright yellow room, I dispelled the last of the gloom left by the night and checked my watch. If I pushed it, I could do a thorough exam in ten minutes. A quick one in five flat.

The room was silent around me as I worked, black bag at my side, instruments clicking, whooshing and pumping, tapping rubber on flesh. Normal. Everything was normal. Slipping the stethoscope from around my neck, I inserted the earpieces and unrolled the blood pressure cuff, rolled up the sleeve of Marisa's nightgown. And stopped.

The bruise was fading, bluish green around her wrist bones, pale pink over the artery that pumped steadily beneath the surface. It was about five inches long and circled Marisa's wrist. And it had the un-mistakable shape of a large hand.

2

Assault and Battery

A car in the drive announced the registered nurse Steven had hired to look after Marisa. It was 7:00 a.m. and I was out of time.

I jerked down Marisa's sleeve, dumped my tools into the medical bag and snapped it shut before Essie appeared again in the doorway. Slipping to the window, I unlocked it and slid it up and down to make sure it wasn't painted shut or too tightly sprung. I didn't want it sliding open after I left.

A car door opened and shut, a controlled sound. I needed more time. I had spent too long grieving and not enough time being a physician. With a last look at my best friend in the world, I left the room.

In the hallway a shadow moved and I jerked, thinking it was Steven. Fearing I was caught. It was a boy, too tall, too thin, staring at me with his face in shadow, peering out of a doorway. "Eddie?" I asked.

After a moment he nodded. "Yeah. She's not getting any better, is she?" he asked tonelessly. His voice was hoarse, as if he had been crying or screaming.

I wanted to lie to Marisa's stepson, tell him things would get better, ease the pain I saw in his face, but experience had taught me that lying to family members was foolish. "No. I don't think so." Outside, a second car door slammed, softer than the first. I had to get out of here. "Do you want to talk about it? About Marisa?"

He laughed, the sound hollow. "What good would that do? What good does talking ever do?" He stared at me a moment longer, turned and slipped back through the hallway. He entered his father's study and closed the door.

In the flicker of brightness from the room beyond, I saw him clearly for an instant as the door shut. His form was painfully thin, as if he had not eaten in a long time, the kind of slenderness achieved by adolescent growth spurts, or by long illness, or by prolonged drug use. I had a feeling drugs were the cause of Eddie's weight loss. Now seventeen, Eddie lived with his mother in Florida and I hadn't seen him since he was a kid, riding horseback, short legs rapping against the sides of the horse.

Footsteps ground against the walk out front.

I wondered for a moment if Eddie would tell Steven that I had been in Marisa's room. His relationship with his father had never been loving and close, and I hoped I would be safe.

Whirling, I entered the kitchen. "What time does the RN eat lunch, Miss Essie?" I asked as I headed past her for the back door and escape.

"Noon on the mark. Whatchoo got planned, Dr. Missy Rhea?"

"She eat with Marisa or in the kitchen with you?"

Essie crossed her arms, her eyes suspicious.

"With you or with Marisa? It's important, Miss Essie." I stopped and gripped Essie's upper arm, staring down into her dark brown eyes. There was sorrow there, timeworn and bone-tired...and a wisdom that said acceptance was the hardest part of maturity. It was a lesson I wasn't ready to learn.

I shook her arm slightly with impatience. "I'm not Marisa's doctor, and I have a feeling that Steven wouldn't let me treat her even if I was. Help me help her, Miss Essie. Please. Before it's too late."

"I can make her eat with me if I cook a good meal."

"Good. Cook something *great* today, Miss Essie. And seat her facing away from Marisa's door with the door shut."

A knock sounded, a steady, controlled, three-beat knock. I slid open the sliding glass door, stepped out into the cold and the soft dawn light. "Please, Miss Essie."

"You and Missy Risa always up to no good," Essie sighed. "I cook some chicken soup and homemade yeast bread. You come in at ten after and be gone by twelve-thirty. Earlier, if I drops me a pan on the floor. And don't you be stepping on my sage I got planted under that window. You hear?"

"I hear. I really do love you, Miss Essie," I said, closing the door. She grumbled something under her breath and headed for the nurse waiting on the front porch.

Running lightly through the winter-crisp grass, I entered the woods and slowed my pace, glancing back once. In the still air my breath left little puffs of mist along my path, dissipating as I watched. The sun reflected yellow-gold on Marisa's windowpanes, as bright and cheery as the paint on her walls. The bird I had heard earlier warbled again, a happy morning song.

A heaviness, part exhaustion, part grief, seeped into me like the cold. Marisa used to sing in the mornings. In medical school I had wanted to throttle her when she started each day with a Sunday school melody. Her favorite had been "The Old Rugged Cross." It had been my wake-up call for two years.

I jumped the creek between the Braswells' property and mine, following the well-worn trail home.

My back door stuck, unopened as it had been for two weeks. The air inside was stale and cold and dank, a musty odor that meant I needed to Clorox the bathroom again. It had been only nine months since I cleaned it last. How could one small damp room turn black and fuzzy pink so fast?

Just as I had left it, the place was a mess. Clothes piled in corners, dust a thick layer over everything, dishes in the sink. Food had been dried on the stoneware so long it would have to be chiseled off. I ignored it all.

I had been up for twenty-four hours, going strong, with almost no rest. I had a great deal to do and no time for inconsequentials.

I turned on the gas heat, lit the hot-water heater and proceeded to unload my new little toy of a car. Moving fast, I filled the unlit back hallway with knapsacks, a camp stove, sleeping bag, a sack of dirty laundry, a bear bag, various camping supplies for the camper who likes a bit of civilization in the wild, and my small telescope. As I crawled over the pile of camping supplies, I was vaguely surprised that I had managed to get all of it into the sleek little roadster without having to leave the convertible roof open.

John had laughed at the car and pronounced it desperately impractical; but then, John wasn't around anymore, so I don't suppose his opinions mattered.

There was no stack of mail waiting. It was all stuffed into my P.O. box downtown in Dorsey City. DorCity to the locals. I could worry about that later. More inconsequentials.

I turned on the answering machine, which had been off for two weeks, kicked a path to the bathroom and relieved myself. Digging through a pile of folded clothes in the far corner of my bedroom, I found a clean purple sweatshirt and a pair of navy sweatpants, an old pair of undies with a little elastic left in the waistband and a good pair of socks. Checked my watch.

It was seven-fifteen. The local Wal-Mart didn't open for two hours. I couldn't see Marisa for five hours. I needed a bath desperately. I needed to wash my sheets and clean up this place. I needed to be clearheaded in a very few hours.

Setting the alarm for eleven, I crawled between dirty sheets and fell instantly asleep.

I didn't really wake up until I stepped beneath the scalding shower and grunted with the pain. I had lived in this rental house for nearly a year and never gotten totally accustomed to the steamy central heat or to the boiling-hot water.

In my mind I was still living in Ohio, in the sixty-year-old, four-hundred-square-foot duplex of my residency. Amenities there included a small space heater in one corner of the living room, tepid hot water, no insulation beneath the warped hardwood floors and a closet the size and shape of a small coffin standing on end. The place came furnished with mismatched furniture in several shades of brown and bile green.

Because John was there with me, laughingly suffering the discomfort, I thought it was grand. It was even better three years later when we moved together to Charleston, bought a small house with new furnishings, hired a decorator and sealed it all with a proper South-of-Broad engagement, with its formal parties, announcements and balls. All over now. Gone like the steam that billowed up around me.

I leaned against the mildewed tile and forced John from my thoughts, letting the viciously hot water bring my blood back from death-warmed-over to simmer, then almost alive. Oil of Olay liquid soap did the rest. While I rinsed, I considered Marisa.

Ethically speaking, I should go right to the hospital, track down Steven and admit that I bullied my way into his house. And then, in my most professional, casual manner lay out my concerns about Marisa. But what if I was wrong?

According to hospital gossip I picked up last night, Steven was on duty when Marisa was brought in. He had done everything he could to save her. A CT scan—more commonly called a CAT scan—to diagnose the location, extent and cause of her symptoms, blood work and quick admittance to the ICU under the care of Percy Shobani, a London internist of Indian descent whose office was located across the hospital parking lot. He had administered drugs for four days—antibiotics and a barrage of medications to combat swelling of the brain—until Marisa stabilized and Steven took her home for around-the-clock care and rehab.

I hadn't checked the blood work, though. I hadn't pulled the CAT-scan films, either. I was no specialist but I could have looked for trauma. Bleeding. A clot. With a little maneuvering, I could have had access to her chart. And unlike Steven, who ruled the E.R. through intimidation, a fierce outlook and a glacial disposition, I had friends who would help me discover what I needed to know.

And if I was wrong, Steven would never know that I had gone behind his back, in clear breach of ethics, looking into the care of his wife. And that was the problem. I had no legal right to do what I clearly intended to do.

I shut off the water, dried off on my last clean, fluffy, oversize towel, and shaved my legs. By eleven-thirty I was dressed in my colorful sweats, had on enough makeup to keep people from thinking I was celebrating Halloween early this year and had dried my hair. Without bothering to sort anything, I tossed all the dirty laundry into the back seat, stripped the sheets off the bed and grabbed up my medical bag. Breaking the speed limit with impunity, I headed for Wal-Mart.

Dirt bikes flying over bumps and ridges on the trail that paralleled the road in front of my house raced my car down the long straight stretch until I pulled ahead and left them behind. Rural kids used to ride horses on the trails through the woods and along the roads. Now they rode dirt bikes and wore shiny helmets. And the injury ratio of kids-to-ride had stayed the same. I turned my attention back to the unmarked black ribbon of asphalt beneath my tires.

When John and I split up, he took the house, most of the furniture, the copper cookware, the electronics and Beca, the dog. I got the silver, the good china and a cash settlement. The only thing I really missed was the dog. Beca was irreplaceable—a large, long-haired golden retriever who came into the world so wise we had chosen the Spanish word for scholarship as her name.

Occasionally I also longed for the big-screen TV, when a Hornets game was on or the Panthers were playing. John, I had refused to think about for twelve months. I could find that indifference about my former fiancé again, but I would always miss Beca. I was sure of it.

Wal-Mart was packed with after-Christmas shoppers taking advantage of the year-end sales. Hundreds of people all in frantic haste, fierce expressions on their faces, shopping as if that meant life itself.

Marisa and I had planned to splurge when I got back from my camping trip. She insisted it was time for me to furnish the house I had occupied for nearly a year, especially once I made a final decision about John and our future together. She had known even before I that I would not be going back to Charleston and the life we had designed there.

She also wanted to organize a better wardrobe for

me.... That was the word Marisa used—*organize*—
as if this were a campaign of war or a charity function. She had always bewailed the fact that I dressed
in what she called ''thrift-store castoffs.''

Marisa loved to shop. Treated each expedition to
a mall as a hunter-gatherer survival course-cum-
pleasure spree. She made a list of necessities, gathered swatches for color comparisons, packed shoes
for the all-important ''heel height test'' and set out
to purchase and conquer. And she loved every minute.

Except for the time of my engagement to John,
when my wardrobe was obtained in couture shops, I
shopped at Wal-Mart, Kmart and consignment shops.
When I bothered to shop at all. Marisa thought me
a heretic.

As a part of my conversion, now that I had the
kind of money that came from a doctor's salary, she
was going to take me to Charlotte and force me to
buy out all of South Park Mall's better fashion
stores. I wouldn't have to face that now, and I wondered why I was lamenting that fact. Straightening
my shoulders, I entered the electronics department of
the oversize store.

By five of twelve I had made my purchases,
dropped off the laundry and was back home. Emptying out one of the knapsacks I had dumped in the
hallway only hours before, I stuffed in my new toys
and strapped it shut. I was moving fast but I did take
time to grind beans and start a pot of coffee. I would
need it before the day was through.

At ten after twelve, I pushed open the window of
Marisa's ground-floor room, looked to make sure

that I missed stepping on anything green, as I didn't know what sage looked like, and lifted in my two bags. I was breathing hard, finding it more difficult than I had expected to face my friend again. My best friend. Closer than family.

Moving quietly, I closed the window, stripped off Marisa's nightgown and went to work. Speaking softly into the small, handheld tape recorder I propped beside Marisa, I took her pulse—72, checked her blood pressure—118 over 69, listened to her heart, chest—front and back, her abdomen. Normal, clear, nonremarkable all, essentially unchanged from this morning. I checked her reflexes, which were equal but perhaps a bit slow.

And the whole time, I watched Marisa. Twice her eye followed my hands moving on her body, I could have sworn it. But when I paused and tried to attract her attention again, she had vanished, withdrawing behind the vacant-eyed stare of a vegetable. Her good eye refused to track my finger passing before her face.

Putting aside my disappointment, I pulled out the cameras I had purchased at Wal-Mart and put them on the bedside table beside Marisa's latest mystery novel. It was the new paperback by Tamar Myers, open facedown on the table. The prized autographed copy I had found for Marisa for Christmas. There was a light covering of dust on the bright cover.

Still speaking softly, I photographed Marisa's face, the back of her neck, her wrists and legs, each place where fading blue bruises appeared. Placing a one-foot plastic ruler over each bruise, I photographed again with another camera, giving exact dimensions so nothing would be lost.

And then I moved to Marisa's head.

Her ears were clear, no drainage, no swelling. Her blind eye ignored the light I shined deeply into it, which allowed me to determine that the nerve in the back of the eye looked healthy. Marisa's blindness wasn't caused by damage directly to the eye itself, which meant it could be caused by pressure from within the cranium. As in a closed head wound. Or a stroke.

As I worked, I kept a pediatric-size sterile test tube by my side. Three times during my exam, a small drop of clear, blood-tinged fluid appeared at the opening to Marisa's left nostril. Each time, I unstopped the tube and collected the fluid. I guesstimated the total volume at less than 0.5 milliliters.

Marisa's throat was fine except for a trace of clear, bloody exudate on the back wall of the pharynx. The fluid resembled the fluid draining from Marisa's nostril. I collected a drop on a sterile swab and broke the swab off into another sterile tube, though I had no idea what I would do with it.

Capping the tube, I pulled out two micro blood-collection tubes, a sterile lancet, a 1×1 alcohol swab and gauze. I lifted Marisa's hand and checked my watch. Twenty-five after.

In the silence of the room, I could hear my heart thud, too fast, a bit irregular. The enormity of what I was doing struck me suddenly. It was, technically speaking, breaking and entering and assault. I looked at the lancet. Assault and battery if I continued. I could lose my license. Go to jail. I paused, the small test tube, shorter than my pinkie, in one hand, Marisa's cold fingers in my other.

"Damn. This is stupid. Really stupid," I whispered, not caring that my words were on tape.

"Damn," she said, the word slurred.

I looked at Marisa. "What? What did you say? Marisa?"

But she was as blank as ever, lips parted now, eyes glazed.

"Jeez, I know you talked. You always did hate it when I cussed." With no further hesitation, I tore open the alcohol wipe and cleaned Marisa's fingertip. Stabbed it with the lancet. Marisa tried to pull away.

"Good girl," I whispered again as I collected blood. "React. Fight. Just don't give up until I figure out what's going on. Please. Just don't give up." Applying pressure to the small wound, I placed everything I had brought back into the medical bag, every scrap of paper, every instrument, my pen, the ruler. The cameras went into the knapsack. Marisa went back into her clothes. I straightened the bedcovers.

From the kitchen a horrendous clatter sounded. A pan dropped onto the floor. Voices. I thumbed off the little cassette player and rechecked my watch: 12:33. Bless Essie. I kissed Marisa's hand, tossed the tape recorder into the knapsack and grabbed up both bags, running for the window, praying the little wound in Marisa's fingertip was clotted over and wouldn't seep on the bedcovers, giving it all away.

Opening the window, I dropped my bags over and leaped through, remembering only at the last moment to watch for sage. I hopped once to avoid a small green plant, pulled the window down and squatted in the noonday light. When I was certain the neighboring yards were clear, I slipped the bag straps over my shoulders and ran for the woods and the safety of my house. As my feet pounded the path, I could hear the sound of my own voice in my mind, replaying the last comments I had made about Marisa's wounds.

"Patient has a one-centimeter circular, sharply demarcated wound over the left supraorbital notch. And what appears to be CSF rhinorrhea from the left side only. Confirmatory glucose and chloride to follow."

CSF. Cerebral spinal fluid. Draining from Marisa's nose. CSF rhinorrhea did occur in some otherwise-normal patients, and was treated with bed rest, but it was not a symptom that was usually consistent with the diagnosis of stroke. It pointed to something more frightening. I felt a tingling in my fingertips, a reaction half fear, half excitement.

3

Breakdown

I had been in Dawkins County for nearly a year, since my initial breakup with John. I moved here in the spring, into the middle of one of South Carolina's poorest, largest counties, at the invitation of Steven Braswell, who needed a warm body to handle the E.R. at night. Marisa had undoubtedly pushed him into the invitation and job offer, as Steven and I had never really meshed on a personal level. And I had come for the same reason, because Marisa had pushed.

Risa usually got her way in our relationship, not because she was dictatorial, but because she was always right. Even as a kid, she knew I needed to spend the summer in Dawkins the year we met. Knew I needed proper food, a good hug, a real friend and a real family, even if it was hers and borrowed for a few months. Because she claimed to be lonely—which she never was—her parents invited me to the Stowe farm in Dawkins County the summer I turned eight, an invitation that instantly became a standard in our lives.

Summers notwithstanding, I was a city girl at

heart, raised in Charleston and its elegant outlying districts until I was twelve, and in its less-than-elegant districts thereafter, as Mama drank her way through her trust fund. And though the summers at the farm had been my salvation, I hadn't thought I would like it here as an adult, stuck in the middle of almost nowhere, with the closest city of any size nearly an hour away, in a locale populated with more cows and pigs than people. But I had. Marisa said it was my innate ability to make friends quickly that cushioned the move. I planned to make use of those friendships now. For Marisa's sake.

Though my brain felt as if it had been stuffed with cotton and I was fighting exhaustion that my short nap hadn't been able to erase, I was sitting in the hospital laboratory by 1:00 p.m., having entered through the kitchen and delivery doors. I slipped in the back way to minimize my chance of being seen by another doctor who might waste my time with chitchat or mention my presence to Steven. There was no reason why I shouldn't be in the hospital, but I was feeling guilty after skulking around Steven's house and poking around on Steven's wife. Steven had that effect on people. Making them feel guilty.

Straddling a poorly padded vinyl lab chair, I watched as Bess, a lab tech, ran Marisa's blood through the Coulter STKS, called the Stack-S in lab lingo. Bess was testing a micro-sample of whole blood for a complete blood count, a CBC, which could tell me all sorts of interesting things about Marisa's health—or tell me nothing at all. A CBC was one of the most basic diagnostic tools; the values might be instantly significant to a patient's condition, or might simply point the way to the next stage of testing. A signpost of sorts.

There would be no record of the test results. Bess would simply hand me the values, treating the sample as a control or random duplicate that was run every few hours to test the sophisticated machine's reliability.

Bess had no idea whose blood she tested. She hadn't asked and I hadn't volunteered. Bess had three kids all under the age of six who had shared a respiratory virus just after Thanksgiving. Knowing her shaky financial situation, I checked her kids for free one night in the E.R. and wrote out prescriptions. Saved her several hundred dollars and gave her peace of mind.

In the next department, Amanda was running a series of twenty-five chemistry tests on the serum portion of Marisa's blood and testing the clear fluid from Marisa's nose for glucose and chloride values. Amanda had chronic migraines, and I had done her a favor or two in the past year as well. Quid pro quo. Sometimes it paid to be nice.

After spending my youth with my mother, Tammy Annette Lynch, née Rheaburn—of *the Charleston Rheaburns*—I knew all about being nice. The methods and modes of high society had been pounded into me, sometimes literally, for years.

It would be after seven this evening before I could get a look at Marisa's CT films. And obtaining Marisa's hospital chart could be tricky, depending on which RN was supervising this evening. Tricky, but not impossible.

"Here you go, Dr. Rhea-Rhea," Bess said, using the diminutive of my name—the name I used with my pediatric patients—and pulling me from my weary reverie. "The white count's up some, so I made a slide. It's staining, but I can count the differential in a few minutes."

"Thanks, Bess," I said, taking the CBC results. Normal. Totally normal except for the white blood cell count of 13.2. "Mind if I take a look at the slide after you finish the count?"

"Help yourself, Doc."

I fingered the CBC, my thoughts drifting between the small wound above Marisa's left eye to ways of obtaining a copy of her chart. Around me machines clicked and whirred, groaned and gurgled. It was a wonder all the lab techs weren't partially deaf from the constant unpleasant hum. I shivered.

"You guys keep it cold in here," I said, knowing my body could usually handle cold temperatures well. It was the exhaustion creeping up on me.

"Not my idea. We get by in winter wearing long johns under our uniforms. Yet and still, I stay sick 'cause 'a the cold in here and how dry it is," she said in her mill-hill dialect.

Bess stepped behind me and I swiveled my chair to follow her movements. She opened a lid to the slide stainer, a compact little machine as noisy as all the rest, and then opened a circular lid beneath. She removed six slides and answered the phone at the same time, speaking softly into the mouthpiece. A moment later, she spoke to me.

"You in a big hurry, Doc?"

"Not really," I said, thinking of my bed and a hot

shower in my moldy shower stall. Heaven waiting for me at home.

"Well, Dr. Braswell ordered three CBCs, stat from the E.R.," she said apologetically, a diffident expression crossing her face. "And he gets kinda—"

"I'm in no hurry at all," I said, putting visions of bed and a good snooze aside with what grace I could muster in my fatigued state.

"Thanks." A grin flashed across Bess's round, freckled face. "He comes first 'lessen we want him kicking in the file cabinet again. Wednesday, maintenance had to bring up a rubber hammer and bang out the dents just sozat we could get the bottom drawer open."

I focused in on her chin as she turned away, not certain I had understood her mill-town vernacular correctly. "You're joking."

"Nope," she murmured, her eyes peering into the dual eyepieces of the microscope, her fingers dancing over a keypad to one side.

"He does this often?'

"Only since his wife... Well, I guess you heard about Mrs. Braswell."

"Yes," I said softly, crinkling Marisa's illegally obtained CBC in my fingers. "I heard."

"He ain't exactly been his usual emotionless self since. I heard—well, never mind."

"Gossip?" I shivered again. My fingers were like icicles.

Bess glanced away from the vision of stained blood cells she was counting. "Lots of it. And some of it might even be true."

"You want to tell me? Off the record?"

Bess hesitated. I could see that she wanted to tell me—perhaps any interested body would have sufficed—but I was a doctor, after all. It was part of the "us against them" internecine war of every hospital, doctor against personnel, that made me a kind of enemy.

Bess glanced over at the lab manager's office, which was dark, the door shut and locked. Mike wasn't back from lunch yet. His absence was the reason I had appeared in the lab at one, myself. He could be a stickler about his employees doing favors, though he was never loath to ask for them when he needed something.

"Well...I heard he hit an X-ray tech."

I raised my eyebrows, feeling some of the exhaustion fade away in surprise. "Steven Braswell hit someone?"

"With his fist." Bess leaned closer, the stat test forgotten. "Cracked Dora Lynn's jaw. It's just gossip, but it's strange that Dora Lynn's been out of work since the—" Bess's tone changed, becoming deep and dramatic "—alleged incident occurred. *And* the hospital lawyer paid a visit to X-ray for over an hour the next day, and *then* spent nearly two hours in Dr. Braswell's office. With the door closed." Bess nodded her head knowingly before returning to the microscope and the field of vision only she could see.

"When did the, ah, the alleged incident occur? That Ste—Dr. Braswell hit Dora Lynn?"

"A day or so after his wife was brought in. It was really sad and I reckon everyone understood, but it's kinda hard satisfying him now. If you're one minute late getting him a test result he just loses it. He even yelled at me in front of a patient yesterday. Used the F word.''

I gulped back the shocked comment I was about to make. ''I see,'' I said softly, instead, trying to tie this latest information in with the picture I was developing of Marisa's situation.

Steven was older than Marisa by thirteen years, married—if one could call it that—at the time they met. His South-of-Broad, high-society wife had been a closet drug addict, stoned on Demerol twenty-two hours out of the day. A marriage like that could make a man cold and unfeeling, but Marisa claimed she could see past all the frozen barriers into the warm heart of the man; this claim made within minutes of seeing Dr. Steven Braswell for the very first time at the head of the classroom in our sophomore year of medical school. He'd been filling in for a professor of microbiology who was out on maternity leave. Marisa was smitten.

From day one all I had seen was the cool, dispassionate exterior. Risa had seen something else entirely. She and Steven had fallen quickly in love. Steven's divorce, Marisa's first pregnancy, and marriage following shortly. For Marisa, the sun rose and set on the man. She and Steven, Mama Braswell, Steven's mother, and Eddie, Steven's son, had seemed blissful that next summer when I visited Dawkins, where they all settled. A real family, Steven even seeming a degree warmer whenever his eyes lighted on his young, happy wife. But the thaw hadn't lasted long.

I had attended Steven's mother's funeral that following autumn. Steven had been a mama's boy, closer to his mother than seemed normal or even healthy, to my way of thinking. He sat through the funeral without a single change of expression. No grief, no anger, no loss of control. And no change in his attitude in the weeks that followed. It was much the same when Risa lost the baby before Christmas. Cold and unfeeling. And when Chessie, their daughter, died of SIDS a year later, he was even worse. Marisa had thought him amazingly strong and self-controlled. I had thought him abnormal, but kept the judgment to myself.

And now he was falling apart.

Without looking up, Bess said, "And what with his kid being in jail an' all, it really has been unpleasant around here."

"I just saw—" I stopped myself. I couldn't exactly admit to seeing Eddie only hours ago. I wasn't supposed to have been at the Braswells' home. I leaned forward, making the chair squeak, and settled for, "Eddie's in jail?"

"Probably made bail by now. Rich kids' daddies don't like sonny-boy to rot in some cell with the lowlifes." She gave me a quick grin over the microscope eyepieces. "You didn't hear about him?"

"No. I didn't. Too much gossip to catch up on in one night."

"Humph," she said, going back to her scope. "Him and a pal from school assaulted a teacher. Tried to rape her in the parking lot after a game. I wasn't working the night EMS brought her in, but I hear they banged her up pretty dang bad. She got away by pulling a little .38 she kept in her glove box and emptying the chamber at 'em. It was in all the papers.''

I shuddered. Eddie, the only child of Steven's first marriage, the troubled child Marisa had helped to raise, had tried to rape a teacher? Eddie had been the perfect kid till age thirteen. Then, a summer spent with his mother and her new family had triggered something and Eddie changed. He had become rebellious, angry. Started smoking cigarettes and dope, experimenting with harder, more lethal drugs. He'd been caught shoplifting, arrested for petty theft and not-so-petty vandalism. But he'd never been violent against a person. And now, suddenly, he tried to rape a woman?

I remembered the bruises on Marisa's wrists and ankles. ''I'll...I'll read the back issues,'' I said softly.

''Page one. Can't miss 'em.'' Bess turned to the computer keyboard at her side and typed in the differential of white blood cells she had counted. Seeing the computer screen hum to life gave me an idea, one that should have occurred to me already. Exhaustion was clogging my brain, hiding the simple answers from my conscious mind.

''You guys print up a cumulative report on every patient in the hospital once a day, don't you?'' I asked, knowing it was true, but wanting to lead into my request with a bit of finesse.

Bess nodded, returning to the microscope, her attention clearly elsewhere. I smiled at the back of her head. A cumulative report was a collated listing of an inpatient's every lab test result, X-ray interpretation, vital sign, pathology report and medication given since admission; it was updated daily and placed on a patient's chart. Marisa had been an in-patient. I had just figured out a back door to at least part of Marisa's chart.

"Bess, I need another favor. Show me how to pull up a patient's chart history number, and then, if you can, print out a cumulative report for me."

There must have been something in my tone, perhaps suppressed excitement, perhaps the pure greed I was feeling at the opportunity for classified information. Bess stopped, her fingers hovering over the keypad. Slowly she turned and looked at me, her bright brown eyes speculative.

"Off the record, Doc?"

Suddenly uncomfortable, I nodded. "If you don't mind."

Bess sat back in her chair. "Is this patient still in hospital?"

I shook my head, watching her eyes.

"I guess you'd rather not have anyone involved, or you'd just ask the supervisor to pull the chart for you."

Great. I had given myself away, and I had only just gotten started. And I couldn't think of a way to get what I wanted without Bess's help. I was too tired to play detective; my mind was like mush. "You might put it that way."

Bess shook her head. "In that case, I'd rather not know the patient's name. But you got a problem, Doc. You need a tech's password to get into that part of the system. You aren't cleared to acquire a cumulative on your own."

I raised my eyebrows again. "I'm not?"

"No one but lab has clearance to pull up a cumulative. Patient confidentiality. So if someone finds out about this, it's my hiney that'll be in a sling. You going to back me up that it was for you?"

I smiled then. "You mean will I take the rap for the evil deed?"

"That's what I mean."

"I promise not to take you down with me, Bess. I'll do my jail time alone."

Bess grinned. "Good. I'm too pretty to do time. Those sex-starved women behind bars would be all over me like white on rice.

"You can use the printer in chemistry if you don't mind baby-sitting it. It's temperamental, but it's private."

"That would be fine, Bess," I managed to say. I hadn't realized just how intuitive Bess was. Or just how obvious I was being. And I hadn't thought out the consequences of enlisting help from others in my search for Marisa's records. I could cost someone their job if I wasn't careful.

I also had an unpleasant feeling Bess knew that I was doing something behind Steven Braswell's back. Thankfully, Steven wasn't well liked, and there was every chance she would keep her interpretations to herself. At least for a time.

"It works like this, Doc," Bess said, pushing the computer keyboard over to me.

Minutes later, I had the satisfaction of hearing the chemistry printer start clattering away, contributing to the din of the place. And thanks to Amanda, I was holding Marisa's chemistry battery in my hands as well.

According to today's results, Marisa was relatively healthy. At least on paper. Excluding the elevated WBC count and a slightly elevated cholesterol, every value fell within normal ranges. Except for the test results on the clear fluid seeping from Marisa's left nostril, Marisa might have been a perfectly functioning woman. Those values changed everything.

It was indeed cerebral spinal fluid, the clear fluid that filled the spinal column and helped cushion the brain. It wasn't supposed to leak, and if the leak was caused by a bump on the head following a stroke, it had had plenty of time to close up naturally.

Propping my chin on my fist, I rested forward against the back of another lab stool. Surrounded and isolated by the irregular beeping and grinding of a dozen machines in the chemistry department, I fought to stay awake, holding the pages of lab reports in my hand. With unfocused eyes, I watched Marisa's cumulative report print steadily out, folding itself neatly on the floor at my feet, page after page.

I didn't know what was happening here, but something didn't add up.

Steven was having a breakdown of some sort. Eddie was accused of attempted rape and looked like a starvation victim. Marisa was leaking CSF.... I knew in my heart that whatever the reports at my feet actually said, something else was going on.

The post office was out of the way, but my bank drafts were due any day now, so I turned up Black Street, made a left onto Mariposa, bumped slowly across the railroad tracks that swerved through midtown DorCity and ended up on Main Street, parked at an angle to the slow traffic.

DorCity proper had been built in cotton-boom times, buildings constructed of red brick and fanciful white plaster trim work, big-paned windows in both storefronts and public buildings, and huge white columns like something pulled out of Tara. The county, with its pretty little signature town, had attracted textile mills by the dozen and ridden the boom time into the early seventies, when the textile bust had put a stop to the county's and DorCity's future hopes and dreams. In the bright light of January, DorCity looked a bit shabby, a worn and aging southern belle, unable to keep up with the times.

The town had received three face-lifts in the past two decades and was due for a nip and tuck. It looked as if the refurbishing would take place soon, courtesy of Hollywood. Local rumor mill had it that Harrison Ford's people had been through town scouting for a site to film his next blockbuster, and DorCity was high on the shortlist. *Chiefs* and *The Patriot* had both been filmed in and around the county and each time the town itself had been spiffed up for the camera. The city fathers were hoping for more spendthrift California executives to appreciate the charm of the place.

Like most small southern towns, there was still a predominately "black" section and a predominantly "white" section, the races divided by railway tracks and the topography. Until the mid-sixties, the whites had lived exclusively on the hillsides of DorCity from White Street on south, while the black community had lived on lowland from Black Street on north. With the exception of the Chadwicks, a wealthy and eccentric mixed-race family who broke all the accepted rules of society, there had been little crossing over between the racial sides of town in DorCity.

Forced busing had begun a change and the decimation of the textile industry had done the rest. Now there were African-American doctors, dentists, lawyers and even a mortician living in restored antebellum mansions on White Street, and wealthy white families living in new brick houses on land purchased from tired black farmers on the north side of town. The farmers received a good price on worn-out farmland needing more attention than they had energy left to give, and used the new funds to buy better housing and to send their youngsters to the better schools and universities.

There was a change, yes, but there was still a long way to go to create an equal-opportunity, nonsegregated society. Though I vote Republican, and tend to be conservative in both politics and finances, perhaps there is still a little of the liberal democrat buried in my soul. I see the difference in attitude and opportunity constantly in my work, with whites expecting success, however limited, and African-Americans—for the most part—expecting to be kicked when they are down. Martin Luther King, Jr. would have been disappointed in the slow speed of change, I'm sure.

My postbox was stuffed full, too much to bother carrying home. I piled the well-shuffled mass on the long, scarred table in the center of the icy room and went quickly to work sorting my mail. I was glad, now, of the cold temperature, as it helped hold off my need for sleep.

Ads, sales papers, pizza coupons and assorted trash went into the oversize can at one end of the battered table; bills, three letters, a thank-you note and a large brown envelope I stacked haphazardly and carried out to my car. I could go through them all later, after I caught a few Zs and studied Marisa's partial chart.

Dropping the mail in the front seat of my car, I walked across the street to the office of the *Dawkins Herald,* the DorCity general news, and picked up the slim stack waiting there for me. I managed small talk and a few smiles for Edith, the receptionist/book reviewer/lifestyles editor. Edith wore more hats than I could count, and had personally kept my papers together, all seven of the triweekly published news.

Bleary-eyed and fighting sleep, I headed home, stopping only twice along the way. The first stop was the bus station for a cup of the best homemade vegetable-beef soup ever made and a grilled cheese sandwich, and the second was to pick up the first three loads of my laundry. All were neatly folded and smelling wonderful, ready for the mattress and the pillows in my dank rental house. At least now I could sleep in underwear that had some elastic left in the waistband.

I didn't remember turning up my drive, pulling around back or unloading my little BMW. I didn't remember anything until my alarm woke me at 5:00 p.m., reminding me that there was a hospital up the road needing my attention and patients who wanted to be treated. Foolishly, I had slept away the afternoon, snoozing while Marisa's brain atrophied and my best friend in all the world slipped deeper into the nether-land of possibly permanent vegetation.

4

Delivery By Flashlight

It was fully dark when I reached Dawkins County Hospital, the low scudding clouds screening and exposing the moon, the wind fitful and cold with a damp bite. It was my practice to run at least once a day, and when working I took advantage of the hospital's Health Run, a two-and-a-half-mile-long dirt track with hurdles to the side, varying terrain, two picturesque footbridges over a bend of South Rocky Creek and a paved bicycle path that paralleled the route. In the more moderate seasons I might share the Health Run with half the county. In the heat of August or the cold of a Friday night in January, I pretty much had it all to myself.

Leaving the warmth of my car, I breathed deeply, quickly stretched my hamstrings and Achilles' and stepped onto the path. Sodium vapor lights lit the way, casting wide arcs of illumination through the bare branches of oak and maple, sweet gum and hickory that dotted the lane. Scrub cedar, pine and low-growing, aged evergreens were spots of darkness in the night, wrapping black shadows across the wide footpath.

Unlike my years in Ohio, when running alone at night was little more than a suicide wish, there was almost no random crime in Dawkins County. I was safe here, day or night.

I took my time warming up, my breath white puffs in the darkness, my soft-soled, light running shoes making solid thwacks on the winter-hard ground. Muscles that had stiffened in sleep began to loosen and warm. My heartbeat quickened to keep pace. I hadn't jogged in two weeks and my muscles were less flexible than I liked, hiking in the mountains working different muscle groups than running.

The Health Run encircled the hospital, skirting the woods and cow pasture down one side, paralleling the main road out front, weaving between parking lots and doctors' offices up the far side, to the back corner where South Rocky Creek bent in a wide sweeping curve past the First Presbyterian Church and its ancient cemetery. It made for a picturesque run, but I had always thought it a bit macabre that a graveyard should border hospital property. It couldn't have been a very soothing view for terminally ill patients in the north wing.

The moon broke through as I ran along beside the main road, a cold white light throwing my shadow before me, two pair of long muscular legs pumping. An ambulance slowed as it passed me, red and white lights strobing. The driver was Mick Ethridge, a kid still wet behind the ears but already infected with the near-manic addiction to adrenaline rush experienced by most emergency medical personnel.

Pounding along, I hit my stride and made the turn back toward the hospital. Mick waved as I neared the entrance to the E.R. He and his partner weren't in a big rush to unload the patient, the EMTs seeming almost bored. A routine run, then. Dawkins County had no taxi service, and many of the residents used the ambulance as a surrogate. Unpaid, of course, as most never bothered to open bills. I waved back.

The air was cold but not cold enough to actually make my skin ache. The night was still, but it was not the frozen silence of the really lung-burning cold I remembered from my last winter with John. I increased my speed, pushing thoughts and memories of my former fiancé to the back of my mind. Again. The fog of sleep began to dissipate, pounded out by my speed and the rhythmic pulse of my heart. My mind began to clear and sharpen. Images of John faded, to be replaced with the dull emptiness of Marisa's blue eyes. Body heating, I lengthened my stride. I had lost John, given up without a fight. I wasn't going to lose Marisa, too.

My feet pounded across the wooden footbridge, South Rocky gurgling below, the railed bike bridge a black ribbon beside me. Ahead, a branch lay across the path, jagged ends caught by moonlight. With a single bound I crossed to the paved bike path and ran across the second set of bridges. The bike path didn't have the satisfying hollow sound of the footbridge, but at least I didn't have to worry about slipping on loose bark or becoming entangled in shadowed branches.

Gravestone shadows reached toward me as I ran back into the moonlight—rounded, cross-shaped, one a Madonna, her shadow lying broken across my route. Without breaking stride I leaped back to the dirt course. One more turn and I would pass by my car, start on the second and last lap. I could see the BMW like a toy in the distance, shining in the glow of the security lamp. A second vehicle, a dark green Jeep, was parked beside it now. The parking lot was filling up with doctors making late rounds.

Sweat cooled my skin and chilled my scalp. My breath was loud and even, in through my icy nose, out through my mouth, over and over, my feet leaping through gravestone shadows.

A strangled moan echoed into the night. I jerked, missed a step, lost my rhythm and came down hard. The jar shocked its way up my spine. A second moan, more prolonged, resounded through the air. Panting breath, not my own. It came from the grave-yard.

Kids playing games. They had done the same thing on Halloween. I found my rhythm and increased my speed. I was a runner, not a jogger.

The muffled moan came again, softer. Pain-filled. Twisting and wordless. *Not kids, then....*

My hair, wet with a light sweat, lifted, scalp crawling. Eyes scanning, I swept the shadows for movement and spotted him. A big black dog, lying almost even with me, half on, half off a grave, head resting on an access road that serviced the cemetery. He was quivering in the moonlight, his moans weakening into high-pitched, desperate yelps. A white flea collar and chain caught the pale light. I slowed and swerved off the Health Run, my feet landing smoothly on the short grass between the headstones.

Small puddles of blackness moved on the ground

beside him...her. White and dark puppies, newborn, steamed in the night. Several of the dark shapes didn't move. Stepping between them, I knelt by the dog, hands moving slowly forward to touch her heaving side. She snapped. I jerked back, and nearly fell on a puppy beneath me.

"Easy, girl. Easy," I said softly. Her eyes, black and liquid, found mine. "Good girl. Sweet thing, you. Let me help you, girl. What's the matter? Hmm? You hit by a car and go into labor? You hurt?" I eased my hand back up to her side. This time she didn't snap, and the long-haired black tail slapped once on the grass as I stroked her. She whined, sniffing the cold air.

"Want your puppies? That what you're asking me? Hmm?" I gathered all the pups I could see and put them between her front paws where the tired dog could clean them. Immediately she separated two of the dark shapes and nosed them aside, concentrating her tongue on the five left to her. The two discarded pups didn't move. My hands moved across her, searching for injuries and damage, but there were none. She felt healthy.

"You picked a strange place to deliver a litter, girl," I said. And then I spotted the tire tracks, fresh on the grass where the driver had pulled off of the access road. A strange feeling washed through me, part dismay, part some other emotion I refused to name.

"Oh. I see," I said softly. "Got dumped, did you? Well, me, too, sort of." I slid my fingers through her hair, finding her ears, and rubbed a velvety one gently. Even in the cold it was warm.

The mother dog stiffened, whined and came up on her haunches. Long tremors ran down her body. White teeth gleamed in the darkness. Crouching, she moaned, long and dirgelike, took several steps and stopped. Suddenly she turned, moving in a half-dozen circles, snapping at the air. The moan quickly became a howl, a yelping screaming agony, and I knew she was in trouble.

I had seen Beca deliver her second litter, helped her with all twelve pups, even catching two as she dropped them, helping her clean the mucoid plugs from their noses. And not once in the three hours of hard labor had Beca made a sound like this. The hairs on the back of my neck stood straight up.

"Rhea? Rhea, where are you?"

A male voice, familiar in its anger, came out of the darkness. I stood, my thigh muscles cramped, knees stiff. I hadn't done a proper cooldown and I was sure I would regret it. "Over here," I shouted.

The dog was running now, fighting the pain, biting at the air, snapping at her tail, frantic and quick, yet never leaving the puppies wiggling on the ground at my feet. The sound of her struggle was frightening.

A beam of light bounced across the headstones. "Rhea?" The tone was urgent, on the edge of anger, which was perhaps the only reason I recognized it. I hadn't heard it in three months, since I'd made the decision to spend the last two weeks with John. "Rhea, where the hell are you?"

"I'm over here, Mark, and if you're coming in gun drawn like the cavalry, you can holster your cannon first. I'm—"

The dog growled, the sound menacing.

"Mark, stop. Stop! Stay where you are a minute. She's in labor and she can smell your hunting dogs. Stop!"

"I heard you. Jesus, woman, I'm not deaf."

"No, you're just rude as hell. It's all right, girl," I soothed. "It's all right. Come on back here, girl. It's okay. It's just a dumb cop who's rushing in where angels fear to tread."

"At least *I* brought a flashlight."

The dog was turning in tight circles beside me. The sounds of her labor were awful and there was blood. I didn't remember so much blood when Beca delivered. It shone in the moonlight, darker than her coat. Slowly, I bent and touched her. "Easy, girl. Easy. I won't leave you. That's a girl," I said dropping my tone lower. "Good girl." In the same voice I said, "Mark, can you hear me?"

"Yes."

"Toss me your flash."

"I've seen you catch. This is county property."

"Fine. Shut it off and roll it to me."

The light went out. In the darkness, the distinctive sound of heavy-duty plastic on earth and winter-crisp grass preceded the flash to me. I grabbed up the light, simultaneously pressing down on Beca...on the dog. She lay, giving way beneath my hand.

I thumbed on the flash, shined it at Mark. His face was set and fierce, either angry or pained. Or perhaps both. I'd had that effect on the man from the first time I set eyes on him. Of course, I was digging part of a branch out of his thigh then, and anger and pain were not entirely inappropriate.

I turned the flash on to the dog, lifted her tail and

parted the lips of her vulva. All of Beca's pups had been small and come out headfirst. If the paw I saw sticking out here was any indication, this puppy's daddy had been part Newfoundland, part Great Dane, part Saint Bernard. It was huge. A long loop of cord preceded the foot. The puppy appeared to be wrapped in it.

"Okay, girl. I know you don't want the smelly old man to be around your babies, but I need help to hold you still. That's right, I do.

"Mark," I said in the same calming tone, "move downwind slowly and come in behind me. I need you to hold the flash." The sound of boots on earth moved through the darkness.

"Good girl. Good girl." Mark and I spoke the words at the same moment. She quivered but didn't fight.

I felt more than saw Mark settle in beside me. He took the flash, his fingers warm where they brushed mine. Turning his wrist so the light was properly aimed, I stroked the dog again. "This is gonna hurt again, sweet thing. And I wish I had gloves. Mark, hold her.... Right," I said as his other hand settled on the dog's head. "She might snap."

"I'd snap, too, if you were ramming your hand up my, uh, backside," he said as he took a firm grip on the dog's muzzle.

I grinned in the darkness and risked one quick glance up at the man beside me. Still angry, but less so, his square jaw outthrust. Gently, speaking soothing nonsense, I parted the dog's vulva again and inserted my hand. She yelped and strained, fighting me. Mark dropped the flash and held her. The light went off but I didn't need it now. I was working blind. The yelping became a yowl. Mark cursed, struggling with the dog.

I needed forceps; the small body resisted. But I had strong hands and finally turned the puppy, rotating it once—I hoped in the right direction—and slid out my hand. The puppy came with it, bouncing to the pavement. It was the first time I noticed that we had worked our way onto the access road.

The dog stopped yelping and fell, rolling slightly to the side, breathing hard.

"Good girl. Good girl. She bite you?"

"Yeah, but she got the vest, not meat."

"Where's the nearest vet?" I asked, still smiling.

"Five miles or so up Rollins Creek Road. Doc Aycock has a new place. He's closed, but he and his wife live next door."

"How 'bout you pull your Jeep up here and load the dog up. Take her to him."

Mark stiffened. My grin spread. "Please?"

"What makes you think I'm in the Jeep?"

I sighed, ignored the question and duck-walked to the pile of puppies, gathered them up and ducked-walked back to the dog. The puppies were cold. The tired dog pulled them all up under her muzzle and dropped her head over them. She was too exhausted to survive the night in the cold, even without freezing puppies to care for. I pulled my sweatshirt over my head, cleaned my hand on the smooth outside and tucked the pups into the fleecy inside. The mother dog didn't seem to mind.

"I'll get the Jeep," Mark said finally.

"Thank you."

He stood and walked toward the hospital, his combat boots loud in the silence. When he reached the bike path, he paused, soles grinding. "You back for good or just to give notice?" The words were gruff, anger only partly masking uncertainty.

My smile faded. I stroked the dog, shivering in the cold without my insulated shirt. "I'm here for good," I said. "I won't be moving back to Charleston." Mark stood there, waiting. "I won't be going back to John. It's over."

"Your choice or his?"

"That's none of your business."

Mark laughed shortly. "No. I guess it isn't." His boots ground again, footsteps receding. I wasn't sure he'd return except that I still had the flashlight. County property. I found it on the ground and thumbed it back on to check the dog's eyes. Her pupils were equal and reactive, mobile black points in irises the color of raw honey or the shade of oak leaves in fall. Soft golden-brown. She panted up at me. Her gums were white. Human's gums showed white like that in cases of severe blood loss, shock, anemia. I was no vet, but I knew that if Mark didn't come back, she wouldn't make it. I tried to decide what I would do with her in that event.

Waiting, I stroked her coat. It was curly and soft, black as the night sky above us. Except for being dumped on the side of the road in a graveyard, she had been well cared for. "It's okay, girl. He'll be back. Even if he wouldn't come back for me, he'll come back for you. Mark has a thing for dogs. Especially big beauties like you."

Minutes later I saw headlights turn into the access

road, weaving through the cemetery. Gravestones brightened and vanished in shadow behind the lights. Even though I knew he'd be back, I was still relieved. After all, I *had* been a bit rude....

The Jeep halted beside us. Mark kept the engine running as he left the cab and opened the back hatch. He stayed busy there a few moments before joining us on the cold asphalt, handing me a box. Jack Daniel's, Black Label. Wordlessly, I lifted the sweatshirt and deposited the sleeping, blind pups inside. Mark took them, disappeared and returned with a folded blanket, which he opened out and rolled up halfway, placing it beside the dog. Together we scooted the tired mother onto the blanket and lifted her into the Jeep. She was still breathing, but her respirations were rapid and shallow.

"Mark? Thanks."

He grunted, slamming the hatch before walking to the driver's side. I followed, watched him climb in and reach for the door.

"Mark?"

He paused.

"I knew you were in the Jeep as soon as I heard your voice because I spotted the car parked next to mine when I crossed the creek." Mark said nothing and I shivered. I knew he saw, but he still didn't offer me the warmth of the cab. I could feel the heat dissipating into the night.

"Oh, all right. The breakup was mutual. John only wanted me if I was willing to move back to Charleston and join the family practice. I didn't go through three years of emergency medicine residency to treat

South-of-Broad, snot-nosed rich kids. And I don't care much for ultimatums,'' I added.

Mark grunted again, shut the door and drove off into the night. I wasn't sure, but the grunt sounded awfully like *"Good."*

As I watched the Jeep taillights recede, I felt that curious emotion seep through me, more slowly this time. The dismay I had identified earlier, and the alien emotion that felt strangely lonely.

Shivering horribly in the lightly insulated, long-sleeved T-shirt I wore for winter runs, I headed for the hospital. I was late. I knew because I still had Mark's flashlight, with which I checked my watch. Six-fifteen. Steven would be perturbed.

At my car I grabbed my bag and sprinted the last few yards to the ambulance airlock. The heat of the hospital hit me like a blow, miserable warmth crackling with static electricity. The E.R. had been redecorated in recent years in shades of gray, teal and white, but no one had considered adding a humidifier to the budget.

Running in the door, I dropped my duffel on the counter by the phone and winked at the nurses. Diane lifted a hand as she disappeared into the soiled utility room with an armful of dirty sheets. Ashlee glanced over her shoulder, as if apprehensive about something in a patient's room, before smiling back. She ducked her head just before Steven roared.

"Goddamn it, Rhea! It's not my job to cover for you when you decide to mosey in here half an hour late. I don't pay you to get here at half after, I pay you to get here on time!" Steven's face was red, that curious beet-red shade of the serious alcoholic or the unmedicated hypertensive. The rage, the high color and the expletives in front of patients were all unlike him.

Quick heat replaced the peculiar emotions inspired by touching the black dog. I smiled tightly at Steven and tuned him out, checking patients' charts on the counter. Though I never would have believed it as a child, there were benefits to having had an alcoholic, manic-depressive mother. I might react inside, but on the outside I knew I appeared calm and unconcerned. I could sleep through almost anything, too, if the need arose, thanks again to the drunken binges of my socialite-turned-drunk mother. Oh, the sweet memories of childhood. Deliberately I turned my back to Steven, giving him time to compose himself.

I had three patients. A laceration to the head that had been cleaned and was ready for 4-0 Ethilon, the synthetic monofilament best for stitches in a scalp; a kid with a cough and fever; and a kid with abdominal pain, who hadn't had a bowel movement in three days. I made a notation on the abdomen's chart for him to receive a flat and upright abdominal X-ray series, a CBC and a urine analysis. Standard stuff. Steven should have ordered the tests already. The patient had been in treatment room B for an hour.

A hand grabbed my wrist and jerked. I spun around and stumbled, catching a glimpse of Ashlee's shocked face as I fell into Steven. Bones ground beneath the pressure of his fingers. Instantly, my thumb went numb. Steven's dark blue eyes blazed down into mine. His voice roared in the stunned silence of the room. "You're not listening to me, bitch." The scent of alcohol and mints blasted my face.

Slowly, distinctly, I said, "Ashlee, call security, please."

Steven blanched, the unhealthy red vanishing into deathly white. I caught his eyes and held them; caught myself as he moved, stepped back, releasing me. Covering my wrist with the fingers of my other hand, I massaged the sore flesh and bones. The wrist didn't feel broken. And oddly enough, my smile was still in place.

"Cancel that order, Ashlee," I said softly. "Steven, if you ever so much as touch me again, I'll file assault charges on you. If you ever curse me again, I'll take it to hospital staff and the board with a formal complaint. If you ever raise your voice to me again in an unprofessional manner, I'll do the same. You have something to say to me, say it in private. Understand?"

Steven nodded, his color pasty white now with sharply defined blue veins at both temples. He looked ghastly. Slowly he pulled his eyes from mine and stared at his hand as if it had gone berserk and grabbed me of its own will. He opened his mouth to speak but no sound emerged.

"And, Steven, please try to remember that you don't pay me here. I'm under contract to the hospital, not you personally." Even more softly I added, "I'm sorry I was late. Go home to Marisa. She…" My throat closed up and tears threatened again, the second time in two days. "She needs you." The last two words were little more than whispers.

Steven looked from his hand to me, his eyes strangely hollow and bewildered. "I…I'm sorry, Rhea."

My smile slipped. I wondered if that was what he'd said to Dora Lynn, the X-ray tech he had hit. I wondered if that was what he said to Marisa each time a drop of spinal fluid dripped from her nose, untreated. *I'm sorry.* "Go home, Steven," I managed to say. "Go home."

Without another word, Dr. Braswell turned and walked from the room, his hand—the one that had grubbed me—held before him like a specimen of poisonous snake.

Ashlee slipped from behind the counter, took my injured wrist in her hand and probed it. Her fingers were warm and dry, the skin cracked and raw like that of most nurses, perpetually irritated by latex gloves, the talc inside them, vigorous hand washing with strong soap, and inadequate lotions. "It doesn't look broken. Do you want an X ray?"

I flexed the fingers and made a fist. There was only a little discomfort. "No," I said slowly, watching the wrist move. "It isn't broken." I smiled at her, the smile I had learned at my mother's knee, gracious and serene, as if I was unaware of Mama's brash rudeness and the constant smell of liquor on her breath as her addiction grew.

I didn't like the way memories of Mama were suddenly foremost in my mind. I shook them away and studied my hand.

"But there's blood," Ash said.

I looked at the fist I had made. Blood was dried into the cracks of flesh and ridged my nails in brown-red arcs. Dog blood.

"Yuck," I said succinctly. Ashlee laughed uncertainly. "It's only dog blood. I delivered puppies behind the hospital. It's why I was late.'' I glanced down at Ash, who was several inches shorter than I. ''Steven would have had a grand mal if he knew he'd grabbed it. Probably wash with Clorox for a week.'' Steven's incessant hand washing was sort of a hospital joke.

Ashlee laughed, a tinkling sound, very southern and very feminine. Very unlike my own rare boisterous laugh. ''I'll go wash up and put on scrubs. Back in five. Get me a tray out for the laceration and weigh the infant. Oh, and find out if the laceration has had a tetanus. If not, give him one. That'll make him think he's getting attention.''

''Yes, ma'am.''

I smiled again and picked up my bag, jogging down the halls to the call room designated as my home for the next six nights. I determined that by the time I reached the end of my work week, I would have dealt with Marisa's diagnosis and gotten help for her if the evidence demanded it. Steven was falling apart.

5

Powers That Be

I took care of the three patients left to me by Steven
and two more that came in while I stitched up the
lacerated scalp. The baby got a dose of the antibiotic
Rocephin and her mother was given strict orders to
see the county's only pediatrician first thing in the
morning. The abdomen turned out to be acute, sending the patient to surgery for an emergency appen-
dectomy. The next two patients got treated for gon-
orrhea. College kids who had shared the same
hooker. I ordered blood drawn for HIV testing and
RPRs—syphilis testing—swabbed them for chla-
mydia and generally scared them silly for not using
condoms. Some might have preached abstinence at
them but I figured they were way past that now and
that the lesson was best driven home by medical science.

The last words out of my mouth to them were,
"You can pick up the HIV test results on Monday
by showing picture IDs in medical records. If the
results are negative, you'll need to have the testing
repeated at the health department every six months
for the next two years. You could still die from this,

guys. Think about it." I even managed to hide my grin as they hobbled out the door into the cold night.

"The clap, two massive injections each—one in each cheek for balance—and an HIV scare, all delivered from a good-looking lady doctor who treated them like imbeciles. I bet today doesn't go down in their diaries as a fun day," Ashlee murmured as the door whisked shut behind them.

I nodded and let the grin loose. "Think I laid it on a bit strong?"

"Oh, no, Doc. You did just fine. And the health department will do the rest. When an STD counselor shows up at the front door of their mamas' houses next week, requesting the hooker's name and all previous sexual contacts, I bet those two boys'll be put on bread and water. Probably *never* see the family Mercedes again."

I raised my eyebrows. "From good homes?"

"Oh, Lordy yes. White gloves and garden clubs. The short one's mother plays the organ at the First Baptist Church. There'll be hell to pay for this, Doc." Ashlee's eyes glistened with merriment. Diane walked up at that moment and agreed, nodding her red head at Ashlee's final comment.

It seemed a good moment to ask so I jumped in with both feet. "Listen, Ash, Diane. I have no intention of reporting Steven Braswell and I hope no gossip will come from this department. His wife…well, you understand…" I let the words trail off expectantly.

"Gossip'll be all over the hospital by morning, Doc. Sorry, but housekeeping was cleaning the trauma room and they're long gone. As to Mrs. Bras-

well, we weren't working when they brought her in,
but we heard all about it. Pretty awful," Diane said.

I leaned an elbow on the counter and massaged
my wrist. It throbbed where Steven's hand had
twisted it. "Mrs. Braswell is my friend. Who was
working that morning? I was working with a temp
crew last night and no one seemed to know. I'd like
to hear about it firsthand."

Diane checked the logbook and compared it to the
employee schedule. "Zack and Anne. They'll be on
tomorrow night, Dr. Lynch. From 7:00 p.m. to
7:00 a.m. Ask Anne. She ran things when Dr. Braswell fell apart."

"Fell apart?" This was the first time I had heard
about Steven not dealing with Marisa's injury in the
first urgent moments.

"Uh-huh. Way I heard tell, he backed off and just
stood there like a man in a trance. Eyes wide, face
white as a sheet. Anne handled things until Mrs.
Braswell's medical doctor got there. Good proof
about what they say—doctors should never treat
themselves or their families. Anyway, Dr. Braswell
hasn't been himself since."

"So I noticed," I said wryly, looking at the
bruises on my wrist. They were strangely like the
bruises encircling Marisa's wrists. I slid my sleeve
down over them.

"You guys hear the latest gossip?"

Ashlee and I turned. Tricia, the night nursing supervisor, was moving quickly down the hallway,
hips swaying and shoes padding silently on the
newly waxed floor. "It seems Dr. Lynch and Dr.
Braswell got into a knock-down-drag-out and he hit

her a few times and cussed her out for being an hour late," Trish said. Ashlee laughed. I groaned.

"Housekeeping?" Diane asked.

"You got it. And it gets better every time I hear it. How about you filling me in so I can put a stop to it before we have rumors of Braswell strangling the entire E.R. crew and dancing over your naked corpses."

"Pretty picture, Trish," I said.

"Ain't it though."

I filled her in on the particulars and Trish sighed. "It's a shame, really, and him such a nice-looking man and all."

Ash laughed. "You wouldn't want a cold fish like him even if you could have him."

"I hear there's ways of warming up even the coldest piece of mackerel," Trish said archly. Trish was a woman my mama would have referred to as trash, Mama having stringent standards for everyone in the world but herself. Trish was a bleached blonde with light brown roots, big breasts in tight clothes and a magnetic personality. She was perpetually on the make, always looking for a man to fill up her life. And she usually did have three or four men dangling after her, most of them unsuitable to her high expectations.

Ugly, married, particularly stupid or overly bookish, sports fiends, poor men, overly religious ones, alcoholics, child abusers and deer hunters were all beneath her standards. In Dawkins County most men fell into at least one of her "no" categories.

"That's what you get by reading tabloids and listening to gossip. A willing suspension of disbelief,"

I said, stretching my Achilles' and hamstrings by pushing against the desk.

"*Cosmo* is *not* a tabloid. I'll have you know the latest exercise for slimming down saddlebags really works. Besides, my job security may depend on my knowing the latest gossip. What with the new doc-in-the-box company opening in the south of the county and stealing all the hospital's corporate business, things aren't exactly stable around here."

"A new clinic? I thought the county was having trouble attracting new doctors."

Ashlee shook her head. "Got to keep up with the times, Doc."

"So enlighten me."

"Some lawyer in town has put together a corporation to provide medical service down toward Lockerville," Diane said. "You want coffee, Doc?"

"Yes, please. A little on the strong side. Will it be twenty-four-hour service or just clinic hours?"

Diane shrugged and led the way into the break room, busying herself with grounds and filters and bottled water. Ashlee took over the narrative. "Twenty-four-hour service at the first one and plans to open a total of three over the next five years. The clinic near Lockerville opens next fall."

I settled into the tall-backed chair I habitually claimed when on duty. "What lawyer?" From spending summer vacations and school holidays in Dawkins County with Marisa and her parents when they were alive, and Marisa and her Aunt DeeDee once they passed on, I knew most of the local bigwigs.

"Mitchell Scoggins. We graduated in the same

high-school class?'' Trish said, her voice rising in the gossipy cadence that was peculiarly southern. "And Mitchell went to medical school before moving to prelaw. Mitch tried to pick me up when he and his wife were separated, so I know the whole boring story. His wife was hooked on 'ludes and benzo," she said, referring to quaaludes and benzodiazepine, one a street drug, the other the medical term for Valium. "Spent most days asleep on the couch. Anyway, I told him where he could put it. I don't do married men."

"He and his wife are back together again and they started this new business with outside financing to build doc-in-the-boxes all over Dawkins, Ford and Lancaster Counties," Ash said, clarifying it all for me. Sometimes the gossipy relationships went right over my head. "They call it Medicom Plus or something."

"And I heard that he stole all sorts of potential hospital profit. Word is he might have had inside information on the hospital's bid," Trish added, bleached eyebrows raised knowingly.

"Bid?" I asked.

Diane and I were looking back and forth between Ash and Trish. They were both long-term residents of the county, having lived here more years than I had been alive. Ashlee was a Chadwick, a member of the county's famous—or some say infamous—multiracial family, and was perhaps more accustomed to being the center of gossip than spreading it. The Chadwicks had been a cause of rumor for over a hundred years. Diane, like me, was a relative newcomer and not up on all the relationships and past peccadilloes of the county's more visible and well-known citizens.

"Yeah, they underbid the hospital to provide Sundown Chemical's medical services."

"I was gone a long time," I said. "Longer than I thought."

"Yeah. Things can move in this backwater town, Doc. You got to keep up with the latest news and reports," Trish said, snapping her fingers as if to illustrate the fast pace of rural living. "You want to know what's happening, you just ask me. I know it all."

It wasn't an idle boast. Trish—and most of the rural county where I now resided—lived on gossip. Which was why I knew about Sundown Chemical in the first place. Dawkins County had won the company's nationwide search for its new national headquarters and for two new chlorine plants. It had been unconfirmed rumor when I left for vacation. It seemed the rumor had been corroborated.

"Hospital was just over the Medicom bid, and it meant losing millions of steady income over the next ten years, what with the employment physicals and drug testing, on-the-job-injuries and workers' comp cases. Way I heard it, the PTBs are mighty pis—uh, upset at Medicom Plus underbidding them," Trish said.

"Excuse me. PTBs?"

"Powers that be," Ash said. "Hospital administration and the county council. Who wants coffee? I see feet moving under the door to the lobby so we better get it while we can."

"Who else besides Mitchell Scoggins and his wife are involved in the Medicom deal?" I asked.

The door to the lobby opened and a crying woman carrying a bloody child ran through. Both were screaming.

Trish shrugged as Diane ran for the trauma room and pressure pads. "Somebody with big bucks obviously. I've heard all kinds of talk about a big New York investor, or a conglomerate of some sort. I even heard it was some local people. Maybe the Roseboro family." The Roseboros owned the county's three funeral homes, having bought out all the competition.

Diane steered the woman into trauma. She was screaming about how her baby fell and went right through the glass-topped coffee table. Blood was spurting all over the trauma room, splattering the privacy curtains between the two beds. It looked as if a small artery had been severed. The woman could have stopped the bleeding at home before bringing the kid in here, but basic first aid wasn't well known in the more sparsely populated parts of the county. The woman's husband burst through the doors after her, swearing and stinking of day-old beer.

Over the sound of screaming and drunken raving, the rescue squad radio buzzed and squawked. "Dawkins County E.R., this is unit 351. Do you copy?" I reached for the mike to respond to the call. It was going to be a long night.

The patient brought in by the rescue squad was burly and bruised, dressed in torn, muddy jeans and a once-blue plaid flannel shirt. Carolina red clay had stained it and him a ruddy brown shade, obscuring any identifying marks like hair color or skin tone. I could tell that he was probably Caucasian, probably young—an assumption made from the Nike on his right foot and the sock with a hole on his left.

He was bloody and battered, as if he had been stomped on in a mud bog. And he was mean. Waving his fisted arms and shouting incoherently, he struggled against the Velcro restraints binding him to the lightweight, collapsible rescue stretcher.

Standing at the nurses' counter, I could observe both of my patients and not be in the way of the emergency personnel and RNs running for supplies, sterile 4×4s, IV kits. I didn't have to say anything; they knew what to do without me at this point. At the moment, I was unnecessary.

I watched as four EMTs—three men and a stocky woman—maneuvered the muddy male with only one shoe to the cardiac room. I would rather have had him in the trauma room, but a class-one urgent patient in with a child was never a good idea. At the moment, one patient per room was enough. There were five rooms, seven beds, and not enough nurses to go around. I called the desk out front and requested the switchboard operator hold all nonemergency calls and keep any nonemergency patients in the lobby until further notice.

The bleeding child was quickly stabilized, Diane moving with practiced economy, holding three pressure bandages in place on the child's leg and sealing off the arterial blood flow. As soon as the bleeding was under control, Diane used a Betadine solution to cleanse his more minor wounds. When he was no

longer at risk of bleeding out, Diane caught my eye
and nodded at her patient as if giving me permission
to handle the muddy combatant in the next room.
''I'll be a while in here, Doc.''

Satisfied with the child's treatment, I nodded and
wandered into the cardiac room. One of the EMTs
was swearing, shaking a gloved hand he had caught
in the steel ribs of the stretcher. Mud flew from his
elbow and splattered on the floor. I realized only then
that the entire rescue crew was as mud-splattered as
the patient...and that some of the gunk they wore in
wasn't really mud. A potent aroma began to fill the
E.R. as the latest arrivals warmed from the frigid
temps outside.

I wrinkled my nose. ''Yuck. You guys find him
in a sewer?''

The finger-shaker whooshed out a final curse.
''Sumbitch was wandering around a freaking cow
pasture in the middle of the freaking night.''

The patient roared and took a swipe at the air with
a massive fist. Three bodies ducked. The man was
powerful and out of control, a restraint loose at his
side. The female EMT landed across the arm and
held it in place with her body weight as one of the
men reattached the Velcro restraint. I looked for an
IV so I could order meds to calm him, but the only
evidence of a line were the fresh trails of blood leaking from the inside of his left arm at the AC—the
antecubital fossa vein.

''Manure?'' I asked as I placed the scent.

''Tons of it,'' the woman answered. ''And vomit.
He baptized the unit with it.''

''Let's cut his clothes off,'' I said, backing out of

the room. "IV. Five milligrams Valium push. And clean him off so I can see him." Valium might cloud my diagnosis, and wasn't the best medication to give a patient who had not yet been assessed, but I didn't have a choice. It was calm him down or possibly treat one of the EMTs for a broken arm.

Trish, her white uniform smeared beyond recognition, pulled out a pair of purple-handled shears and sighed. Sometimes I was exquisitely grateful not to be a nurse.

Ten minutes later the man was naked, tied to the bed with leather restraints at arm and leg, held down by two soiled sheets pulled across his waist and hips and tied to the E.R. stretcher's rails. One of the EMTs had shoved a Jelco—an IV needle—under the patient's skin at the right AC and opened the fluid wide, sitting atop him until the sedative worked. Trish was monitoring the effects of the Valium she had administered via a syringe attached to the line. The man was finally beginning to relax.

"We have an ID on him?" I asked as I reentered the room.

"No, Doc. Two kids camping out on the old Gibbons farm found him and made the call."

"Nothing in his pockets," Trish said, "but this."
This was a ten-milliliter syringe, its steel needle broken off to a quarter-inch length. Trish held it up between index and thumb, her hands heavily gloved in trauma-blue latex.

"You stick yourself?"

"No, ma'am."

"Bag it. And bag his clothes so we can breathe." The room stank so badly I couldn't even smell the disinfectants sprayed after the last rush of patients. "Any track marks on him?" I asked, referring to needle scarring left by a junkie's constant use of veins for illegal drugs.

"Not the kind you're referring to," Trish answered.

I cocked my head, but as no one was looking, my unasked question went unanswered as well. Crossing my arms over my chest, I stepped close and studied my formerly combative patient. He was at least six foot two, two hundred twenty pounds. His face oozed fresh blood from what looked like a severe beating. Trish passed me a pair of trauma gloves like her own and, without taking my eyes from the John Doe on the stretcher, I pulled them on. The heavy-duty, blue latex resisted and I snapped them in place with impatient fingers.

Gloved, I traced a dark purple bruise on the patient's calf. It was five inches long, elliptical, with a sharply delineated tip. There was another larger one on his thigh. Raising a hand over my head, I found the adjustable examination spotlight and pulled it into position, highlighting the leg. Turning the dial on the side of the lamp to high, I bent closer and studied the bruise. It was nasty, several hours old. Others were on his torso and up one side of his chest. Our John Doe was covered with the strange elliptical bruises. As if he had been beaten.

I looked up to ask and caught a glance from Trish to the female EMT. Janet, I thought her name was. Both looked amused. One of the men nudged the other and snickered in what sounded like good-old-boy fun, silently challenging me. Even Ashlee, who had been characteristically silent, was smiling, eyebrows raised in mock innocence.

I swallowed my question and returned to my study of the patient. The bruises were peculiar to me, but not to the crew. They hadn't called the cops, so he hadn't been beaten.... They knew something I didn't. Something I had missed.

"Doc?"

I looked up at Trish, who nodded at the heart monitor. There was suddenly no trace of humor in her expression. I followed her gaze and watched the lead-two line on the LED screen. A typical sinus rhythm wasn't displayed in glowing green. Instead, I was looking at a prolonged P-R interval in each heartbeat—an abnormality. At intervals the P wave disappeared. A few beats later, the P wave was back. The pattern repeated itself several times as I watched. It looked like a mild AV block, meaning the electrical impulse from the atrium to the ventricle was slow, resulting in an abnormal heart rhythm. His blood pressure was 195 over 140, pulse 95 and dropping slowly. His bruises might be a source of amusement, but he was in bad shape.

"Turn his IV down." I could give him procardia to control the AV block, or nitroglycerin...or I could just watch him for a while. A mild blockage was not a condition usually addressed by an E.R. doc. It was a long-term, chronic problem, not an emergency. "Get an EKG, some facial films, CBC, ETOH, chem seven, cath him for a UA and drug screen." It was a basic set of orders that would check him for traumatized kidneys, internal bleeding, infection and a variety of blood chemistries, including ethyl alcohol. The drinking variety.

John Doe's stomach muscles tightened and he retched. Ashlee turned his head to the side, but he had emptied his stomach contents long ago.

"Phenergan 25 IM," I added. Ashlee injected the medication that would suppress the man's nausea directly into his hip.

The earpieces of my stethoscope went into my ears and I moved directly over the man. Placing the bell on his chest between the fourth and fifth ribs, I listened to his heart, following the curve of ribs around to the left. Fast. Irregular. The man's lungs were slightly wet, the right one more so than the left. The right side of his rib cage was significantly more bruised than the left, the elliptical bruises overlapping and dark. There was an odd, faint sound to the right lung as he breathed, both wet and dry, as of sandpaper on wet rubber. "Get me a chest," I said softly, meaning a chest X ray.

The man mumbled. "What's your name?" I asked him. He didn't respond. "Do you know where you are?" Still unresponsive. He gagged again and moaned, trying to roll off the stretcher and pulling against his restraints. "You guys get anything from him?" I asked the EMTs.

"Not a thing. Just a lot of rambling."

"Mmm."

His pupils were equal and reactive, Babinski reflexes on feet equal. But the deep tendon reflexes on his right hand, arm and knee showed hyper-reflexia—faster and harder reflexes. His right hand was bruised, the flesh torn, the fourth finger—his ring finger—was turned at an oblique angle. "A right hand," I added to the list of orders.

The bruising extended itself from the man's chest down across the right side of his pelvis. "Might as well get a C-spine, LS, KUB and pelvis," I said, sounding disgusted. It was a lot of X rays, but with the patient unable to, or unwilling to, respond to me, I had to rely on diagnostic tools to do an assessment. The list of X rays would cover his back, abdomen and major organs. Trish grinned at me, amused at the overkill.

"EKG first, draw the blood second and rainbow him." *Rainbow him* meant for the lab to draw extra tubes of blood, tubes in all colors, in case I wanted additional tests run on the patient later. "Then the cath and last the X rays," I said, prioritizing my orders. I left as a tech attached electrodes to the patient's chest for the EKG. The child in the next room was surely ready for me by now.

"You want to give something for the blood pressure, Doc?" Trish asked.

"Nah. Just watch him. If he spikes or his pulse rate falls off, call me." With his injuries and his facial trauma, I didn't want to do anything that might cause him to crash. He could live with the high BP and the AV block, as neither condition was life threatening, but he might not make it if I screwed up and caused his pressure to bottom out.

The kid was perhaps five years old, all long legs and knobby joints, bright blue eyes wide with shock and fear. His skin was cold and clammy to the touch, his color slightly ashen. I took his pulse and watched his breathing, evaluating his possible blood loss. The symptoms I was seeing could be due to emotional or hemorragic shock.

From behind me the boy's drunken father growled, "I want to know when a doctor's gonna see my boy. We been waitin' over half an hour."

"Right now," I said simply. I was accustomed to patients and their families expecting a doctor to be male, assuming I was a nurse because I was a woman. To the patient I said, "My name is Dr. Rhea-Rhea. Who are you?"

The patient sniffed and blinked tears out of his eyes. "Cody. You're a girl."

I met his eyes and grinned. His pulse was 118 and slowing even as I held his wrist, but his respirations were far too fast and shallow. He had perhaps a dozen superficial lacerations. Five were deeper, and at least two would require stitches. "You never met a girl doctor?"

"Girls should stay home and take care of their kids, not run around behind their husband's back and get a job."

"Cody," his mother gasped.

I glanced up at her, then to Cody's dad, but I spoke to the child. "Well, I don't have kids or a husband, Cody. And even if I did, don't you think it's a good thing I'm here tonight to stop your bleeding and sew you up?"

Cody's dad snorted. I could smell the fumes from where I stood, but as if I might have missed some precious scent, the bandy-legged man moved closer and breathed up into my face. He was well-padded with fat that hung out over his belt and strained against his flannel shirt. The down-filled vest he wore was pulled back away from his gut, but I was certain it would never zip up over his paunch. He had given his son his blue eyes and was trying to give the boy his bad attitude as well.

"They ain't got no real doctors at this pissant hospital? I want the best for my boy, not some *woman*."

I smiled without taking my eyes from his, showing my teeth, but not my reaction to the sexism. The pulse beneath my fingers didn't jump at the tension suddenly in the room. Poor kid must be used to it. "And you are Mr....?" I left the question hanging in the air. If the man heard the cool threat in my voice, he didn't react, just sniffed and threw out his chin.

"Everett Neal. Cody's dad."

"Everett, how 'bout we step into the hall and discuss it?" I indicated the door, dropping Cody's small wrist.

Neal smiled as if he thought he had won a boxing round, but if he thought he had me cowed he was about to be disabused of that quaint notion. All I wanted was witnesses for what I intended to say, and for the witness not to be Cody. I followed Everett out into the hall, calling back over my shoulder to Diane, "Tetanus if he needs it, 4-0 Ethilon and Chromic," I said, asking for both the usual suture and for catgut, which would dissolve in the boy's leg. I knew I would have to perform a layered closure, sewing the deep tissue first and then the surface tissue.

"Might as well get some butterflies," I added. "And while you're at it, Diane, some stickers for Cody." Butterflies were like small, strong Band-

Aids. Put one on tightly and it would contract, pulling together the edges of cut flesh. Sort of a topical suture. Stickers were cartoon stick-ons that said, "I was a good boy in the E.R." or "I got stitches" over a cuddly teddy-bear character.

"And Diane, get me an H&H please. Fingerstick is fine." I wanted to make sure the boy had not lost too much blood.

I closed the door behind me, shutting Everett Neal off from his son. The smile I had worn for the patient disappeared, and though I didn't look up, I spotted a white-clad figure behind the nurses' desk. "Everett, I want you to wait in the lobby while I sew up your son." His mouth opened and his face changed color, but before he could speak I went on. "If you don't, I'll call 911 and have the deputies haul you in for drunk and disorderly."

Everett's fists balled up at his sides and the veins bulged out on his neck. If I hadn't been in danger, it would have been a real lesson in the result of soaring blood pressure. "Ain't no woman gonna send me out to the lobby so she can botch up my son."

Over Everett's shoulder, the figure behind the desk lifted the phone and punched in three numbers. It was Ashlee. Smart woman.

Everett took two steps toward me.

6

Foreign Body

I smiled again, and knew it wasn't a pretty sight. My job description didn't include an honest reaction to his prejudice—physical violence and verbal abuse of patients and their families were frowned upon— but that didn't mean I had to take it lying down, either. I leaned in over him and spoke softly, so only he and Ashlee could hear. "I'm the only doctor here, Everett. Now, you go sit down and let me do my job or spend the night in jail. It's up to you."

"I'll take my boy to Ford County. I don't want no second-rate doctor trying to sew him up," Everett said, making as if to shove his way past me into the trauma room.

I didn't budge. Though I wanted to ball up my fist and punch some sense into his empty head, I kept my hands on my hips. "Everett, you try to take that boy out of this E.R. without my permission, and I'll have the Department of Social Services on you so fast it'll make your head spin. You're so drunk you nearly let your kid bleed to death."

Everett paused and cocked his head. It wasn't much, but it was something. At least he was listening. I could hear his back molars grinding, however, and knew it wasn't over.

"That's child endangerment. And I'll bet you drove up here. That's DUI. I may be only a woman, but in here tonight I'm queen," I said softer still. "And if you make the slightest bit of trouble, I'll make your life a misery for weeks to come. You understand?"

Everett turned to me and looked up to meet my eyes. It was clear he didn't like looking up at a woman; his eyes narrowed. "I'll tell you what I understand." His eyes trailed down my body and back up with malignant interest, and when he continued he raised his voice. "You screw up my boy and I'll sue you and this hospital for every dime you got. That's what I understand. Bitch."

Okay, so he wasn't listening. And I had now been called bitch twice in as many hours. I was starting on a record.

At the desk, Ashlee turned a pale face from me to the ambulance airlock and sighed in relief. The doors pushed open and in walked two cops, sheriff's deputies, dressed in South Carolina's new combat black-and-gray fatigues.

"Now you move out of my way or I'll make sure you learn your place."

"Got a bit of trouble here, Doc?"

Everett whirled, rising on his toes, his fists flying out to his sides. A stifled sound, half fury, half groan, came from him and he turned to me, pulling back his fist. A deputy reached him, catching his arm, before Everett could make good his threat. He looked up over his shoulder and saw the face of the cop. A big black man with a shining shaved head and a smile that promised all sorts of fun. I shrank back against the door frame in delayed reaction and then slipped into the trauma room as an altercation broke out in the hallway behind me. I had a feeling Everett didn't like African-Americans any better than he did women.

I smiled at Cody's mom and shrugged. "You able to drive home alone?"

Her eyes closed in what could have been fear or sorrow or simply resignation. "Cops?"

I looked down at my patient. Cody was sleeping soundly, his sweaty head beneath his mom's hand. His dirty-blond hair was tangled in her fingers. "Yes, ma'am. I think he took a swipe at one of them. I don't think he'll be coming home with you tonight." I just hoped Everett slept off the booze and anger before he made bail.

While I was sewing, I had plenty of time to realize how little I was getting done on Marisa's case. She was vegetating and I was spending my time arguing with an abusive drunk because he'd stepped on a raw nerve. Stupid. I could have let Everett take the boy to Ford County.... I would have cleared up an hour of time for studying the paperwork on Marisa. And I still had an hour's work on the patient in the cardiac room.

Instead of paperwork, I pulled together layers of muscle and flesh and stitched up the laceration. And thought about the moaning child under my hands. He was so innocent and so at risk of being warped. Just as I had been at one time.

Risa and I had been seven the year we met, and

to this day it was the best year of my life. Better
even than my senior year of med school, when John
noticed me for the first time and began pursuing me
as if I fit into his parents' upper-class lifestyle. Better
even than the year I graduated medical school and
was accepted into my first choice of residency pro-
grams. Better even than that perfect summer when
John and I became engaged. Better because there
were no butterflies, no uncertainties, no hormonal
confusion, no stress, no self-doubt. No grown-up
angst. Just childhood perfection.

We had met at a creek that meandered through the
subdivision of Willowcroft. The creek bordered both
the former indigo-rice-cotton plantation still owned
by Risa's parents, and the back boundary of the
newer neighborhood where Mama had rented a
house.

Though fairly stable at the time of the move,
Mama had been drunk since, and groceries had run
out. Her next trust-fund check wasn't due to arrive
for a week. And it wasn't as though I could ask my
daddy for money, as he had died before I was born.
Even when Mama was sober, I was alone....

Hungry, angry at the world, I had carried every
rock, branch and construction remnant I could find
to the creek and hurled them in. I had built a fine
dam. Water had begun to swell and rise over the low
banks, flooding the low-lying empty lot near the
rental house where Mama snored in a pool of vomit
on the bathroom floor.

I don't know. Maybe I wanted to drown her.
Maybe I just wanted the attention that flooding an
entire neighborhood would bring. Maybe I just

wanted something to happen in my life. Anything. And so I built a really fine dam with junk and angry frustration.

Just as I dumped in an armful of wallboard scraps, I heard a voice. "Ugly."

I jerked, slinging mud. "What's ugly?" Looking around, spotting the perfect little girl watching me from the far bank, I was suddenly furious, the fire of too many of Mama's drunken binges and casual cruelties scorching me. *"Me?"*

"Nooooo," she said, the word melodic as a bird-call. "Not you. The dam." She shook her blond curls and sighed. "I like water that moves. When it moves it sparkles. Now it's just all muddy." She tilted her head and her hair caught the sun. "Water should move," she concluded.

I intended for the water to move all right, but not in the way she meant. Critically, I eyed the mass of tangled debris, wallboard, rocks, siding, brick and board, with limbs and branches pointing accusing fingers up to the sky. I had even heaved in a small broken window—glass, sash and all—found at the construction site down the road. She was right. It was ugly. I liked it.

"Want to share my picnic lunch?" she asked, holding up a brown paper sack. "I have PB&J, pimento cheese, potato chips and an apple. It's green."

I looked at the girl with the food. She was dressed the way my mother dressed me when she was sober. Pretty. Pink shorts, pink embroidered top, pink leather sandals. Like a doll. And her toenails were pink, too. Somebody let her paint her toenails....

I was wearing dirty green shorts, muddy sneakers

and one of Mama's favorite silk shirts. It had ripped when I threw in the broken window. I was figuring to rip it again before the day was over.

I looked back at the pink toes. The girl wasn't crossing over the muddy creek with those toes. Still, I hesitated. My stomach growled. "Is the apple sour?" I asked.

"It's a Granny Smith. It's supposed to be sour."

I didn't know what a Granny Smith was, but didn't say so. "My name is Rheane Rheaburn Lynch. Mama sometimes calls me Rhealyn. You can call me Rhea. My mama hates it when people call me Rhea," I said, the last sentence sounding mean.

"Pleased to make your acquaintance," she said politely, solemnly. "I'm Marisa Sto—" She stopped. "Marisa Carolyn Jacqueline Stowe," she amended. The perfect head tilted to the side and she smiled. It was a glittering smile. Only word for it. It glittered with mischief. "You can call me Risa. My mama will hate *that*."

We both grinned. I clambered over my makeshift dam to the food and the girl. To this day I can remember the crunch of that apple and the taste of the peanut butter and jelly. It was peach jam. I had never eaten peach jam, and it was wonderful.

After lunch, Risa took off her sandals and waded in with me. Together we tore down my dam. I never built another.

Carefully, I tied off the last stitch, patted Cody's head and smiled at his mom. She looked exhausted. It had taken four packets of silk and one of Chromic to complete the layered closure on Cody, and I left his mother with strict instructions for dealing with infection, blood loss and shock, just in case. I also instructed Diane to give the woman a quick first aid course in arresting bleeding. Technically the child needed a half liter of fluid to combat blood loss, but I hated to traumatize him further by starting an IV. His mom proved agreeable to forcing fluids instead.

When I walked out of the trauma room, I pointed a finger at Ashlee. "I owe you dinner."

She grinned and passed John Doe's lab and EKG reports over the counter to me. "I pick pizza. Can I call it in?"

"Help yourself. Make mine veggie." I studied the EKG. It was indeed AV block, but there was something strange about the pattern. Something I couldn't put my finger on. The man's urine drug screen was negative for all major categories of illegal drugs, opiates, amphetamines, cannabinoids, cocaine, barbiturates and benzodiazepine. His ETOH was up just enough for me to believe my John Doe had had a beer or two in the afternoon, but nothing recently. The CBC results were all within normal parameters, as was the chemistry panel, with the exception of the man's CO_2. It was up when I would have expected it to be low. I remembered he was breathing pretty hard with his struggles, which tended to decrease the carbon dioxide level in the bloodstream, not retain it.

Again odd… "X rays?"

"In the fracture room on the view-box. And Doc, Bev said to tell you she repeated the pelvic film. The foreign body is not an error."

"Ash, you're a doctor's dream."

"Pizza will get you everywhere," she said, covering the phone's mouthpiece with one hand. She had already dialed Pizza Hut. They delivered.

"Get enough for everybody," I said.

"Thanks, Doc. Will do."

The fracture room was dark, lit only by the rectangular view-box on the far wall. It was an intense light, throwing everything into harsh shadows and angles of brightness. The films hanging there were about what I expected. Broken fourth finger, two clean fractures that might not require surgery. Hairline fracture of his mandible, the kind prizefighters and barroom brawlers got from a right upper cut. C-spine and abdominal films nonremarkable. A small fracture of the left orbit, which meant he wouldn't be a keeper. He'd be flown out to the trauma center at Richland ASAP.

But it was the chest X ray that answered many of my questions, and the pelvic that raised new ones. He had three fractured ribs and beneath them was a small hemothorax—a pocket of blood that was seeping between the lung and its lining. It explained the high CO_2 and the rubbery sound I had heard in his chest. The bleeding might stop and the blood might reabsorb. Or it might keep seeping, forcing the lung to move, to close up, to deflate and collapse. I checked the time, knowing that I would need a repeat chest before the man could be flown out.

"Ash," I yelled.

"Too late, Doc. I already got four large pizzas on the way." She stuck her face in the door, and though I didn't turn to see the smile, I could hear it in her voice.

"I won't back out of the pizzas, I promise," I

said. "But get Russell on the phone and let's get a CAT scan on this guy's head. He's got a skull fracture. And get me a chest tube kit. I may not need it, but he's got a—"

"Kit's out on the tray beside his bed, Doc. Respiratory's available to assist at your convenience. Lab just drew a blood gas and the report will be back in a minute." I turned and saw a slightly chubby form outlined by the hall lights. She had changed clothes, the stained uniform dress replaced by a wrinkled purple scrub suit that bagged around her ankles.

"Ash, if I ever go into practice I will pay you a fortune to be my nurse."

"What, and give up all this?"

I laughed. "So what about the bruises on this guy? Pizza enough bribe for you to tell?"

"Hooves," she whispered. "Cattle hooves. Trish wanted to see if you could figure it out."

"You mean like in a cattle stampede?" I didn't mean to sound so incredulous.

"Ponderosa and Lonesome Dove, right here in Dawkins County. We got us a thriving cattle business in the county, both for tax breaks on land and for the profits. People make big money on cattle round here. I've seen bruises like that, but his are the worst, by far."

"I'm a city girl. Tell Trish I had to ask."

"I asked the deputies, when they were here, to do an ID check on him, see if anyone is missing."

"Um, good." I turned back to the films but the shadow in the doorway didn't move. "Mr. Everett Neal go peacefully?" I asked without turning my head.

"Not exactly. I think assault on an officer of the law was added to the drunk and disorderly you promised. He'll be in jail awhile. You really want to call in DSS?"

I shook my head no and sighed. Drunks and stampedes. "Jeeeeez."

The chest considerations momentarily handled, I concentrated on the pelvis X ray. A long, slender, white object appeared in the film. It was undoubtedly the foreign body mentioned by Bev to Ash, and it appeared to be buried in the man's buttocks.

Gathering the films under my left arm, I went back into the cardiac room. The EMTs had left while I was involved with Cody, and Trish stood guard over the man and his monitor. Ash was a silent figure at my back.

"Blood pressure stabilized at 165 over 130, Doc. And the AV block seems to be diminishing," Trish said, surprised. "He's now in a sinus rhythm."

Sinus meant normal, which was weird as heck. Blockages didn't just go away, at least not any I had ever heard of. I punched a button on the heart monitor and ran a strip of the rhythm to document the abnormality and the change. "Make sure you get all these on the chart. I want to make sure someone else sees this."

Holding the pelvic film up to the light again, I noted that the foreign body was indeed still there. "Turn him over." I stepped back and waited as the RNs used a pull-sheet to turn the patient. I directed the overhead light closer and bent over the man's buttocks. One of the bruises on his right buttock was different from the ones covering the rest of his body.

Instead of long and elliptical, this one was small and slightly pear-shaped, about one and half centimeters in diameter. It was centered with a puncture mark.

Fingers palpating gently, I pressed at the wound. There was something inside. I applied firm pressure at the sides from several directions, following the contours of the foreign body, until I was certain of its location with regard to bone.

"Ash, get me some forceps, please."

"Coming." Stiff paper rattled at the supply cabinet in the far corner. The room had fallen silent as I worked, the door to the hallway opening and closing as technicians of various kinds came and went. Ash held out an autoclave bag, fingers gripping the edges as she opened it. Reaching in, I took the forceps by the handles and worked them open and closed to loosen the movement.

I hadn't specified the type of forceps, but Ash had supplied a needle carrier, a thin, needle-nosed instrument perfect for the purpose I wanted. Ash was a doctor's idea of heaven. She could read minds. "Thanks," I mumbled, pleased, my eyes on the small wound.

Making a mound of the flesh and muscle around the bruise, I probed gently with the pointed forceps. They clicked on metal deep in the muscle. I widened the wound with the forceps' jaws, and after a moment, got a grip on the sliver of metal. Two tries later, I pulled the foreign body from his buttock.

I studied the bloody object clamped in the teeth of the forceps as I probed again at the wound with my left hand. It was clean. The foreign body hadn't fractured into several pieces; I had it all.

The metal was one and a quarter inches long with a sharp beveled end. The other end was bent and rough. "Ash, let me see the syringe you pulled out of his pocket."

The syringe, encased in a small freezer-type plastic bag, was placed in my left hand. I compared it to the broken needle in the forceps. The ends matched. I had assumed they would. Stepping away from the patient's bed, I said, "You can let him back down now. And thank you.

"Ash, how close is the nearest reference lab?"

"Charlotte," someone else answered.

"I want a stat gas chromatography or mass spectrophotography on the liquid left in this syringe. How soon can I get it?"

The same voice said, " A courier can pick it up in the morning. You can have the results by this time tomorrow. Maybe as early as 5:00 p.m."

I looked up and found Bess, the lab tech who had arranged for me to get Marisa's chart. I routinely worked with dozens of medical personnel at one time and often forgot to look at faces or remember names when in a triage or critical situation. "Hi, Bess. Take care of this for me?" I held out the bag.

"Yes, ma'am." She took it and held out an emesis basin for the broken-off needle and forceps. I dropped both into the plastic container.

"Watch the tip. Needle's broken off in the bag. You working over?" I asked her.

"Lucky me, pulling doubles today and tomorrow. I'll cap it," she said, referring back to the syringe.

"I should have known it was you getting me out of a warm bed to do a head scan."

I turned and met the dark brown eyes of Chris Russell, the radiologist who handled the CAT scans. "Hi, Chris. Yeah, I've been called a pain in the rear end a few times. I have a head for you. The skull series." I handed him the stack of films. "Man had nothing better to do than end up under the hooves of a cattle stampede."

"You're kidding."

"Nope. And he had a broken-off needle in his butt and a syringe in his pocket. UDS is negative, UA shows no blood, his blood pressure is up, but I don't want to give him anything here, not with all he could have going on. Oh. And did I mention his impossible on-again-off-again AV block?"

Chris looked down from the films he was holding up to the overhead light. "Guy been breaking mirrors all week?" Ash and Trish laughed dutifully. "Okay, let's get him to radiology."

The man on the bed mumbled, "Purple diving weed. Chicken purples."

I wandered over to him and watched curiously. "Chris, I may have to pick your brain sometime this week. Can I call you from home?"

"Anytime, Rhea. Or we can talk one morning before you leave."

I nodded, watching the John Doe being wheeled from the room. He called out as he was whisked down the hallway, "Hatchet! Bike hit!"

It was after ten when I finally got free and the E.R. emptied. Though I was comfortable with his treatment, I wasn't entirely satisfied with the diagnosis of the John Doe flown out to Richland Memorial, the state hospital. Of course, I didn't have to be. The moment he was in the air he was someone else's problem, not mine. My job as an E.R. doc was to "greet 'em, treat 'em and street 'em," to use an old euphemism. Say "howdy," treat his symptoms, get him stable and turn him over to someone else. Meatball medicine, fast and furious with no particular specialty except trauma, blood loss, gunshots, general violence and clinic work. The final diagnosis, surgery, or course of treatment was some other doc's responsibility, and if I had missed something, well, I missed it.

Yet... There was something about the John Doe that bothered me, and I couldn't put my finger on what. Perhaps it was the phrasing Chris had used when he discussed the man's closed head injury. "Guy got stepped on by a bull or something. Peculiar pattern to bleed, not consistent with typical traumatic head wounds, but..." He'd let the words hang off in space, unattached to anything. "Richland will repeat the tests in a couple days and we'll have a better picture. Call me if you get any more cowboys in tonight," he'd finished as he headed for home.

Blood-splattered and suffering from cramps following my aborted run, I needed a long, hot shower and a good stretch. I had X rays to pull and phone calls to make first, however. Trying to appear casual, I pulled Marisa's purloined cumulative record from my bag, copied down all the pertinent order numbers and walked to X-ray.

Beverly Akins was working and though she wasn't someone who owed me a favor, there were compensations to her being on duty. She was a slow-moving, hopelessly lazy female whose hospital nickname was "Sloth." Not like the deadly sin, but rather like the lethargic jungle creature who moved at such a sluggish rate of speed that mold actually grew on its long-haired coat.

I leaned over the half door into the X-ray office. "Beverly. Got a minute?"

Bev looked up. After a moment her eyes appeared to focus and she recognized me. Her eyebrows lifted in question. "What can I do for you?"

"I need to look over a patient's E.R. and admit films. I have all the numbers, but I hate to disturb you. If you'll point me in the right direction, I'll be glad to pull them myself."

Beverly thought about that for a time, took a breath and exhaled. Painstakingly, she lifted a hand and took the scrap of paper on which I had copied the numbers. With unhurried deliberation she studied it. One thorough minute later she lifted a nail and tapped one of the numbers. "The top ones look like accession numbers for individual X-ray orders." She paused, to recharge or breathe or for her heart to beat once or twice.

"Yes. They are," I said to encourage her.

"We file X rays by patient-history numbers so they're all in one place. This one on bottom looks like a history number. An old one. All the X rays would be stored under this number, in a single file." Bev pivoted in her desk chair, the sound of ungreased metal a prolonged squeak. After another moment, she pointed into the next room, down a dimly lit row of filing shelves filled with thousands of large brown folders. "Should be on that rack there about midway down. You can just leave the file when you're done and I'll put it back.''

"Thanks, Beverly," I said, already backing into the darkened room. I could take Bev the Sloth for short periods of time, but anything beyond five minutes or so and my heart rate began to slow. I was afraid of spontaneous bradycardia just from association with her. I didn't have time to flat-line; Marisa needed me. Unfortunately I wasn't done. I needed more from Beverly. Pausing, I said, "And I may need to go online to Duke later to confer with a specialist. Is there a manual I can follow or will I need your help?''

Slowly Beverly turned again and lifted an arm, index finger pointing. I wanted to shake her or slap her or maybe hook up a car battery to her for a jump start. But I knew from experience that complaining to Bev did no good. She moved no faster for the reprimand and then wasted more valuable time offering exquisitely prolonged explanations and apologies. I ground my teeth and waited, following her finger down a row of manuals lying on their sides on a narrow shelf. She pulled one out and paged it open to page seven, each page turning as if caught in a stop-action breeze. Finally, she handed me the book.

"It's all right here, Doc. Clear as a bell. And very user-friendly.''

"Thanks, Beverly, you've been a big help.''

"Anytime, Dr. Lynch. All you have to do is ask.''

I heard the majority of the comment from the film storage room as I searched for Marisa's patient-history number. Finding her file almost exactly where Bev had pointed, I beat a hasty retreat. Dealing with the slow-motion tech always had that effect on me, making me move that much faster, as if to make up for time wasted in her presence. I was just glad I wasn't her OB-GYN watching her deliver. I didn't think I could stand the suspense.

File in hand, I closeted myself in the small office used by the contract E.R. doctors. Steven Braswell and the E.R. doctor in charge of operations, Wallace Chadwick, had their own offices on the hallway closest to the emergency department. Dropping back in the velour-covered desk chair, propping my feet on the scarred wooden desk, I studied the CAT-scan films through the overhead light. I went through them twice. And then again, standing at the lighted view-box in the fracture room, films hung in a row, comparing them with the admitting diagnosis listed on the cumulative chart and the radiologist's interpretation of the CAT scan. A chill that had nothing to do with my aborted run past the graveyard settled into my stomach.

"Jesus," I said softly, not certain if I swore or prayed. "What have you done?"

7

Peculiar Pattern To Bleed

Sitting back at the desk, the overhead light off, the small room lighted by the white glow behind the films, I dialed a number from memory. It was near ten-thirty, but in med school Cam Reston had seldom hit the sack before 2:00 a.m. A real party boy.

"'Lo." The familiar voice was sleep-clogged. Soft jazz played in the background. The sound made me smile.

"I never thought I'd see the day when Cam Reston was asleep before midnight."

"Rhea?" Pleasure suffused his voice. "Rhea-Rhea Lynch?"

I leaned back in the padded desk chair and studied my feet. Cody's blood was smeared on my shoes. "How you doin', Cam?"

"This residency's about to kill me, Beautiful. I'd be through now if I had gone into E.R. medicine like you and John—" He stopped himself abruptly. John may have started out in emergency medicine, but he had abandoned his preference—and me—under family pressure.

"No time to party?" I asked lightly.

"No *energy* to party."

Cam was taking his residency at Duke University Medical Center, in neurosurgery, a seven-year program that would leave him one of the foremost surgeons in the country. It was a grueling endeavor involving surgery, study, long call-back hours and emergency calls. I didn't envy him the course of residency.

"Besides, I have a steady love life now, and frankly would rather spend the evenings with her."

There was the soft murmur of a female voice in the background under the strains of jazz saxophone. "*No...*Cam Reston, the playboy of med school, with one woman?"

"Devastating, isn't it? I get that kind of response from all my past loves. But I'm properly domesticated now and settled into a cozy love nest with the woman of my dreams."

"I was never one of your past loves," I said with a half smile.

"Yes, you were, I just never told you about us. How's John?"

I bit my lip. I had known this was coming. "John's fine. We aren't together anymore."

"Ahhh, Rhea, you need to talk?"

"I didn't call you up in the middle of the night to cry on your shoulder, Cam."

"You could. Anytime, Rhea."

I knew he meant it and the tension I had felt at the question slipped away from me. "Thanks, Cam. Actually I called for a favor of a different sort."

"Business, then, instead of pleasure," he said with mock grief. "I was hoping you were about to

proposition me. I always did have a thing for tall,
long-legged women. And I always wondered how
we'd be together.''

"This is the kinder, gentler, more domesticated
Cam?''

"Domesticated, yes. Dead, no. Never confuse the
two, Rhea.''

"I take it she got up and went to the bathroom or
something,'' I said wryly.

Cam laughed.

"So, back to my favor. I have a patient's chart I'd
like to fax you. And then I'd like to go online with
you and get your opinion on some films. I think
something's been missed.''

I told him the admitting diagnosis and gave him
a few particulars about the case without mentioning
the patient's name. Cam might have had an isolated
sexual attraction to this long-legged woman—as he
had for ninety percent of the female undergrads and
all of the female uppergrads—but his interest in Marisa had been anything but temporary or isolated. He
had wanted Marisa with a passion, and hearing Cam
say he was happy at last with another woman meant
he had come a long way. I didn't intend to injure his
newfound contentment.

Cumulative reports were not a permanent part of
a patient's chart, so I could remove Marisa's name
from hers with Wite-Out before I faxed it. I wanted
Cam Reston's best and finest attention to the details
of this case, not some hormone-and-emotion-steeped
trip down memory lane. Besides his unwavering interest in anything female, Cam had the finest diagnostic mind I had ever known. If there was as much

wrong with Marisa's diagnosis as I thought, Cam would find it.

"My fax number hasn't changed. You got it?"

"I have it," I said.

"Just send it on tonight and I'll look it over in the morning. When can I reach you on MODIS?"

"I go on duty at seven p' every night for the next six. I'll call you and set it up."

"And if you change your mind about us..." His voice trailed off suggestively.

"'Night, Cam," I said firmly, and set the receiver in its cradle. With the overhead light back on, I studied the manual for MODIS, the Medical Online Diagnostic Interface System. It was a new computerized setup whereby small rural hospitals in the state could send pictures of films online to Duke, Carolinas Medical in Charlotte or the medical university in Charleston, and speak with any specialist or diagnostician in real time. It consisted of a video camera, a lighted film view-box, a scanner, speakers, a microphone and the usual computer paraphernalia. But as Bev the Sloth had said, the system was very user-friendly.

The E.R. was empty when I checked in a moment later, and I took the films, Marisa's cumulative report and my blood-splattered self to the call room. I didn't get much sleep that night. Between clinic patients, I managed to grab a quick, hot shower that left my skin clean and pink, but far too dry. I had forgotten to pack the bottle of jojoba oil I usually kept in my overnight bag, and suffered for it.

I succeeded in obtaining Marisa's full chart from a willing and conspiratorial Trish, photocopied it and blotted out any mention of Marisa's name before faxing everything to Cam. I hoped he had a new roll of paper in his fax machine. It would take the whole thing.

Carrying piles of paperwork tucked under my arm, I returned Marisa's original chart. The copy I toted back and forth from the call room to the E.R., scratching my dry skin, studying the chart word for word, day by day, for Marisa's entire hospital stay.

Between patients, I rested and studied the films through the light over my bed, coming away with some serious concerns about my friend. A number of things in the cumulative and chart did not add up, from the original CAT-scan interpretations to the hospital symptoms and medical conclusions.

It looked as if Marisa had been admitted by Percy Shobani, over the indignant objections of her personal physician, Dr. Byars. Patients changed physicians all the time. When incapacitated, they were sometimes removed from their primary doctor's care by the family and another doctor brought in. It happened. There was nothing unreasonable in such a change.

But this situation seemed oddly out of sync with the usual justifications for the decision to bring in another physician. There had been no previous personality or professional conflicts between Steven and Douglas Byars, Marisa's M.D. There had been no problem with Douglas's previous treatment—at least not that I had heard, and in a hospital this size, I would have heard about anything untoward.

Percy had no specialty training that required he take over her care. And most strange of all…Steven

Braswell and Percy Shobani had been publicly antagonistic to one another for months. For Shobani to be called in as Marisa's physician made no sense at all.

The most common way for a physician to read the chart of another physician's patient was to simply read the doctor's "Notes" page and correlate the notes with the official diagnosis. I was going a lot further, digging a lot deeper. Comparing the test results and Marisa's symptoms, the nurses' notes and the medications given, with Braswell's and Shobani's course of treatment.

There were dozens of anomalies. Small things that didn't seem to add up.

When Marisa was admitted to the E.R. she had obvious trauma to the left orbit—the bones and soft tissue around the left eye. Her speech was erratic and senseless, strange words strung together with no sense to them. The initial lab work was ordered and a CAT scan scheduled. Dr. Russell, the county's only radiologist, was called in to perform and read the scan.

Steven ordered a CAT scan with contrast, the kind where dye is injected in the patient's veins and the scan performed while the dye circulates through the bloodstream, allowing the film to pick up greater detail and ease the diagnostic interpretation.

Dr. Russell suggested that a contrast be performed at a later date and instead did a basic unenhanced ten-millimeter slice/ten-millimeter spacing film, with multiple cuts. His reasoning was that if Marisa had had a non-bleed stroke, she could be TPA'd to dissolve any clot they might find. The contrast dye would interfere with the TPA treatment, and could always be performed at a later date if needed. *Sensible.*

TPA, trans-plasminogen activator, was a strong anticoagulant used to dissolve clots in the brain and heart, and was the most common method of treatment for hypertensive crises—non-bleed strokes—and myocardial infarction—heart attack. But if used incorrectly, or not monitored properly, or given in conjunction with other drugs, it could cause massive bleeds. There were documented cases of such incidents and the patients did not always pull through.

There were flaws to the scan ordered, things it couldn't pick up, but it was the most common head scan ordered and performed at any hospital. The rule of thumb was that a scan performed at ten-millimeter increments wouldn't pick up anything smaller than ten millimeters. You might see a shadow or part of something in one of the films or you might not. However, it was a basic order, and one I would have ordered had I been there myself.

The scan had been performed just above the orbital meatus axis, to preserve the eyes from the blast of radiation. *Everything in order to this point.*

Russell's preliminary report read:

Hemorrhagic changes noted in the frontal lobe. Some subarachnoid hemorrhage noted with accompanying subdural hemorrhage. Peculiar pattern to bleed suggesting trauma. Recommend further scans to orbit at axis of hard palate in one-millimeter increments.

I paused as I read this last. *Peculiar pattern to bleed...* It was almost verbatim the words uttered by Chris Russell about my John Doe. Frowning, I returned to Marisa's chart. There was no mention of a shattered bone from the sinus cavity, a bone that might have pierced the lining around Marisa's brain and allowed leakage of cerebral spinal fluid. The bone was something I had expected to see. Something I had *wanted* to see. It was a condition I could have arranged to have treated. It was possibly reversible. I closed my eyes.

By this time, Shobani had been called in on the case. His diagnosis read, "Typical subarachnoid and subdural hemorrhage." A CVA. Cerebral vascular accident. Stroke. There was no mention of the suggested CAT scan being done to the tissue and bone around Marisa's damaged eye—the *further scan to orbit at axis of hard palete.* No explanation of the *peculiar pattern to bleed.* There was no final report from Russell on his findings. And no mention of trauma in the final diagnosis....

I wondered where it was. I hadn't seen the final diagnosis in the cumulative report Bess had ordered up for me. It was missing. I wondered what Steven had been doing in the radiology department the night he supposedly hit the X-ray tech. I wondered if he had been looking for the final report....

I held the films up to the light and studied them one by one. Most M.D.'s would have missed the irregularity of the bleeds. For that matter, most E.R. doctors would have, too. But then, studying and interpreting scans was more an art than a science. There were dozens of types of CAT machines used in this country alone, each with its own personality and quirks.

I made a note to have Bev the Sloth look up the final report on the scan. I made a note to have Cam look at the *peculiar pattern to bleed* and wondered if I could find a way of bringing it up in conversation with Russell. The phrasing bothered me.

Other things bothered me as well. Specifically the timing. Marisa had been brought in just before 6:00 a.m., with Steven Braswell pulling my shift. If I had not left for vacation the previous day, I would have been on duty.

The phone beside my bed rang—Ashlee telling me I had a patient. I left the films scattered across my bed, gathered the chart beneath my left arm and walked down the halls lost in thought... I needed a table in the room. Always had. Maybe Trish could scrounge me up one to hold the reports. I'd have to crawl over it to get from door to bed but it might be worth it.

The patient was the next of a long night of trips back and forth to the E.R. It was clinic night and though I fought the feeling—because I was being paid to do the job—I always resented giving up sleep to see patients who had such silly complaints.

In the course of that long night I saw one insect bite. I don't know what the patient wanted me to do about it. It itched. So what? It wasn't a spider bite, it wasn't infected. "Live with it. It'll go away," I told him. The patient didn't like my lack of sympathy and didn't like the fact that I refused him a work excuse because of the bite. Tough.

I saw two colds that could have been treated with

OTCs—over the counter meds. Tylenol. Cough syrup. I gave them each both and sent them home.

There were two hysterical high-school girls who just found out their boyfriends had the clap and wanted treatment. I gave it to them and warned them about the dangers of HIV and herpes and syphilis. Scared them silly too, just as I had their boyfriends earlier. It would get worse when the STD counselor came by later in the week and talked to them and their mothers. I warned them about that. They left walking like the two boys had earlier that evening. As if in great pain.

There were two broken toes on a cowboy's left foot where a horse had stepped down hard and not tried to find earth first. I sent that one home with pain meds. I had suffered with a broken toe myself before. I had sympathy for *some* things.

I had a hysterical thirty-nine-year-old female with family problems and no teeth, her abusive husband waiting in the lobby. She refused to press charges, and in the state of South Carolina, I couldn't press them for her. I left her alone in the room for two hours to calm down and sent her back home with the louse. I had no choice.

In between, I read more of Marisa's chart and went to my car for the old newspapers I had picked up at the *Herald*.

According to the chart, the nurses on duty the day Marisa was admitted to intensive care listed a variety of symptoms that were never addressed by Shobani. The nurses' notes indicated that Marisa was unable to answer simple questions, was not oriented to person, place or time and was unable to follow simple commands, though she did retract from pain. Oddly, all her neuro-checks were normal—peculiar for a stroke victim—yet she was babbling and incoherent, suffering from acute anxiety, and the wound above her eye would not stop dripping a thin, serous, bloody fluid. She held on to the RN's hand and eventually had to be sedated.

Shobani ordered Haldol, a drug usually given to geriatric patients who suffered from anxiety. I couldn't understand why he had chosen Haldol. Ativan would have made more sense, and there were other medications he could have ordered to combat Marisa's panic. Drugs that would not have the possible side effects of Haldol, like plain old Valium. However, the medication did seem to calm Marisa, as the nurses were able to care for her afterward. I made another note to ask Cam. "Why Haldol? Any thoughts?"

Turning to the old newspapers I had brought to work, I read the stories about the attack on the teacher. They were full of hysterical rhetoric about the attempted rape, which had taken place in the parking lot after a game, as Bess had said. The articles were liberally interspersed with comments about the state of the nation, crime in general, the lax bail requirements and laws of parole that let violent criminals out too soon, to commit crimes again. Details of the parking-lot attack were sparse, offering little more than the basics I had learned from Bess in the laboratory. The name of the other youth in the attack had been omitted due to his age, but the name Eddie Braswell, *son of a distinguished local physician,* was prominent.

Without violating sealed juvenile police records, someone had leaked just enough to the press for broad claims of past problems to appear in print. Eddie's failed attempts at drug rehab, the number of arrests, a quote from a cop called to the Braswell home when Eddie disappeared for a week and came home stoned and beaten up, his car supposedly stolen. There was a "no comment" quote from a counselor when asked about violent tendencies. I wondered what "no comment" concealed. And I wondered why Marisa hadn't told me more about Eddie and his problems on the long phone calls we shared weekly. Had my life in residency in Ohio with John been so self-absorbed that there had been no room for such confidences? I returned to the charts.

Through the hours of that first day in ICU, Marisa's pulse rate had soared and dropped, her blood pressure following the same rocky course. Her temp went up to 101. Shobani did order a repeat CBC, which revealed Marisa's WBC count was higher than upon admission, with an increase of polys and bands, indicating infection. And although he ordered IV antibiotics, Percy Shobani did not order blood cultures. Percy had a thing about blood cultures, ordering them in cases where other M.D.'s would simply shotgun the patient and send them home—shotgun referring to one of several strong, wide-range antibiotics, not pellets to the torso.

Remembering Eddie's arrest, I went back through Marisa's chart yet again, looking for evidence of rape or indications that a rape exam had been done on her, but found nothing. No mention of either.

On the second day of Marisa's hospital stay, Steven made a note to restrict visitors. All visitors. Especially Eddie and Marisa's Aunt DeeDee, who worked in the hospital and was the only family Marisa had left in the world. I made a note to ask the RNs on duty that day why Eddie and DeeDee had been refused admittance to the unit.

I had a list of questions and no answers. And Marisa was continuing to vegetate. I could see her eyes every time I closed my own. And I had a mental image of Eddie Braswell and friend attacking Marisa. Hitting her. Bile rose in my throat.

Eddie had loved Marisa when she first married Steven. The summer after my junior year in medical school, I had spent a few weeks with Marisa and Steven at the Stowe farm, recalling the summers Marisa and I had tromped the fields, ridden horses, flirted with the country boys and learned esoteric lessons in wine tasting, horse husbandry, proper etiquette and gun handling from Miss DeeDee. Eddie had been so happy, his eyes glistening, long skinny legs flapping against a horse's sides as he followed Risa and me around the acres. He had followed Marisa like a lovesick puppy. What had gone wrong since? What had changed? How could he possibly have hurt Marisa?

According to Marisa's chart, it was only the next day that the swelling had started around Marisa's left orbit. It was only then that the bruises on Marisa's wrists and ankles had made it to the nurses' notes. *Wrists and ankles... Had Marisa been held down...?*

I had scanned the news reports of the assault on Eddie's teacher. None of the reports mentioned bruises on wrists and ankles. But I could check the E.R. logbook for the woman's name and have Trish pull the chart. I could look for mention of them in the doctor's notes...if I dared to pull another patient's chart without medical reason. Feeling brave or desperate, I called Trish and asked her to research the patient's name and pull the chart.

Toward dawn I caught a few catnaps, and even they were interrupted by uneasy dreams. They were dreams I had often as a child, where I was underwater trying to swim to shore. Weighted down, I couldn't reach surface and light and air, I could only fight the current and struggle to hold my breath. Then, as now, I would wake short of breath, gasping, drenched in sweat.

Even as a child I knew that the dreams were about my mother. About that sense of suffocation I experienced when she drank. The feeling I was losing ground in a relationship doomed from the start by personality conflict and then poisoned by alcohol.

In medical school the dream was a sign of stress, occurring near the end of a term when exams and papers were due. Now it was fear. Pure fear. My mother was dead. I had left John. I had no family anywhere except Marisa and perhaps her Aunt DeeDee.

Now I had lost Marisa. When I woke from the last dream of the night, pushing against the sheets as if they were the water holding me down from freedom and safety, I knew I was alone. Perhaps forever.

I checked my watch with Mark's flashlight and dropped my head back to the pillow. It was 5:30 a.m., and I was scheduled to work till seven.

Though I was exhausted from the dream, I rolled over and this time slept dreamlessly.

I jerked awake. Voices and the sound of an air compressor thumping outside the call room waked me. My spartan room had no window, surviving building and fire codes only because there were two exits, one into the call room and one through the shower bath into the hallway around the corner from the first one, just outside the surgery department. A hammer began pounding on the wall at my side, sending vibrations through my bed. By an unexpected ambient light I checked the time again. Six-forty. Someone wanted me up.

Groggy, I climbed from bed and pulled the clean but badly wrinkled scrub suit from my body, the second clean scrub in twelve hours. Some nights I went through as many as five. Without switching on the overhead, I dressed in the insulated T-shirt and sweatpants I had worn the night before. The heat came on overhead, blowing more dry air down on me. My skin ached from the parched breeze.

I ran a comb through my hair, what there was of it. When John and I separated the first time, I had moved to Dawkins and cut off my hair. Both actions were little more than childish rebellion. I could have stayed on in Charleston or moved to Savannah and worked close to home. I could have trimmed my long hair or worn it in a ponytail to get it out of my way. But I wanted a drastic change in my life, one that would mirror the drastic change in my emotional security.

So I moved near Marisa and away from John and

his family of misanthropic, controlling M.D.'s and their huge and successful family practice and cut my hair. Off. I now wore it in a pixie style, wash-and-wear. The black tendrils of hair looked good against my long, narrow face. I liked the look. Perhaps more so because John hated it. He had actually winced the first time he saw me after the breakup.

The only bad part of having such short hair was that when I slept hard, as I had the last hour of the night, it stood straight up on my head. I wet the black mess and slicked it down, tossed my few toiletries into the duffel and stripped the bed for housekeeping.

By the time I was ready to face the world, the noise outside my room was a raucous clamor of voices and power tools. In lab coat and running shoes, my stethoscope around my neck, I unlocked the door, stepped through the shower and stuck my head out into the surgery hallway. Bright lights, dust and confusion met my eyes. The partitioning walls were down, lying in heaps of busted plaster, strips of brittle wood, chips of broken terrazzo and dust.

A jackhammer resounded in what once was the orthopedic suite. The noise was enough to wake the dead, appropriate enough as the morgue door was now visible through a hole in the wall on the other side of the O.R. Sterile processing, the room that would contain the autoclave, was still being finished. Gray wallboard with lighter gray patches and strips was drying, cabinets were placed haphazardly around the room.

"Mornin', Doc. We wake ya?"

I shifted and focused on a man at a makeshift table

in the corner of the bright room. The table was constructed of two sawhorses overlaid with a big sheet of plywood, covered with rolled-up and tacked-down plans, a pair of leather work gloves, tools with plastic-coated handles and a Hardee's breakfast sack. Everything was coated in dust. The man in front of the dusty mess was clean by comparison, a short, wide, booted man in jeans and a plaid shirt turned up at the cuffs. Popeye forearms extended beyond the flannel shirt.

"Actually, yes," I said, yawning and sneezing all at once. "But I get off in—" I checked my watch again. I couldn't seem to keep up with the time this morning. "In five minutes, so I'm not complaining. When did all this start? And isn't this Saturday? Don't y'all have union rules or something?"

"Preliminary demolition started five days ago and finishes up today, so you missed the noisy part."

This wasn't noisy?

"And we have a contract with a firm finish date. We work seven out of seven till then. 'Course, tomorrow we start tearing out the plumbing and wiring, which might be a problem if you think you might want to use the toilet. Might not work."

That sounded like fun. I yawned again and nodded. The man had a plastic laminated name tag clipped to his collar. Matt Childers, job site supervisor.

"We're scheduled to finish up here in under a month and then start in on the general surgical suite up the hall, so we'll be a problem in the daytime through March. I'll leave word with the E.R. if it looks like you have to move for a few days. How many doctors use the call room anyway?''

"For the next few days, you're looking at her.''

He grinned, showing teeth meant for a much larger man. Or a small horse. He was good-looking in a rough-hewn sort of way. Unfortunately, he was god-awful cheerful for so early in the day. "Check with me in the mornings then and I'll upgrade you on any potential problems. Right now the only thing to keep in mind is that we've sealed off the general surgical suite at the end of the hallway and the only entry is from the south wing. Well, that and the problems with the plumbing and electrical systems.'' He grinned again. A man who loved his work even at 7:00 a.m. "Also, the locks are on backward in half a dozen rooms. Factory defect. If you go exploring and get turned around, just don't close any doors. The locks are automatic and you could get trapped.''

I nodded and stretched my shoulders, the stethoscope banging across my chest. Matt's eyes followed its progress. Typical. Of course, Matt's eyes came to just about chest level anyway, so he had a better excuse than most. "Thanks. I appreciate it,'' I said, remembering to be at least minimally courteous as I took myself and my stethoscope out of visual range.

I headed back toward the E.R., nodding to other doctors and nurses on the way. I wasn't generally a communicative person in the mornings after an all-nighter. The hospital started coming back to life at 4:00 a.m. every day, and it seemed as if I was the only one having trouble adjusting to the coming daylight. I had a long day ahead of me and no way to fill it except with Marisa's chart.

This was the day Marisa and I had planned to spend in Charlotte, buying out SouthPark Mall. Once upon a time I had hated the idea. Today I would have given my eyeteeth to be spending it with my friend.

I picked up a cup of coffee in the E.R. on the way through. No matter when it was made, hospital coffee always had the taste and consistency of tar. Fresh tar perhaps, but still tar. I spotted Ashlee over the rim of my foam cup. "He in?" I asked, meaning Steven Braswell.

She nodded and stretched her neck. "Came in ten minutes ago and locked himself in his office."

"Was he pleasant?"

"Didn't bite my head off at the shoulders, so I'd have to say yes. Pleasant for Dr. Braswell."

I picked up the chart Trish had left me. The patient Eddie and pal had assaulted—*allegedly* assaulted, I reminded myself—was Amelia Deere. I scanned the list of injuries, concentrating on bruises. There was no mention of ankle bruises, but both wrists, forearms, thighs and torso displayed bruising. I felt sick again, remembering Eddie's face in shadow the day I first saw Marisa. Why was he allowed in the same house with her? And then I recalled the door leading to the garage from Steven's office. Had Miss Essie even known he was in the house?

A male patient came in the lobby door, dripping blood and trailed by a white-faced kid. I headed out the airlock into the cold, dark morning. This patient was Steven's. My tour was over for the day.

The icy air hit me like a part of my dream, murky and damp and hard to breathe. I really missed my fleecy sweatshirt. But if I hurried and didn't stop at home to replace it, I might make it to Marisa's before the day nurse arrived. Shivering, I raced the few miles home, parked the car and jumped out. Locking my duffel in the passenger seat and carrying my little black bag, I jogged through the woods to Marisa's. I was in luck.

Essie met me at the back door, a vivid purple crocheted shawl around her shoulders, a starched housedress in brown-and-blue stripes crisp and neat beneath. "You come in out of the cold, Dr. Missy Rhea. That nurse done call and say she be late this mornin'."

I slipped past her into the warmth of the kitchen. Like the rest of the house, it was decorated to Marisa's tastes in shades of yellow and white with touches of rose. Feminine and lively, as Marisa once had been.

"I told you 'bout not wearin' a bra, Missy Rhea. You's poking out like them *Twin Peaks* Missy Marisa be watchin' on reruns last month. Never did like that show. It just a land of evil and misbehavin' come through the TV every day now."

I glanced down at my chest. I didn't have much down there to consider most days, but today she was right. I blamed the cold, but to Essie there were no excuses for looking like a harlot.

Essie always spoke her mind. Even when the comments were on an embarrassingly personal level. At such times I was simply Missy, not Doctor. Essie saved the Dr. Missy Rhea for less intimate comments.

"I'll remember, Miss Essie. I promise to put on one as soon as I get home."

"Shame on you, runnin' 'round like a boy or a harlot. The Good Book say you comin' to a bad end you poke out like that."

Essie was grumbling more than usual this morning, pulling at the fringe on her shawl, shuffling along in house slippers too big for her feet, a pair of bright purple socks hiding her ankles. The shawl-pulling was a sign of distress. The last time I had seen her like this was when Mr. Stowe, Marisa's father, lay dying. The sight of her fingers moving through the long yarn threads clenched at my heart.

"Miss Essie, what is it? Is Marisa...?"

Essie's eyes flashed black fire. "'Course it Marisa. My baby layin' there like a dead woman, Mr. Steven goin' crazy and not sleepin' and drinkin' hisself to death. And Miss DeeDee and Eddie Boy not allowed on the premises no more, and you neither accordin' to Mr. Steven, and you got to ask me somethin' *wrong?*"

I walked the two steps to Marisa's room. The door was shut. I put my palm on the raised panel. The wood was cool to the touch. "Steven's drinking?" I remembered the scent of alcohol on his breath the night before, half hidden beneath the breath mints.

"Done 'bout cleaned out the liquor cabinet in the den. Walkin' the halls every night talkin' to hisself and cryin'. Can't a body seem to get no sleep."

"And Eddie?" I asked.

"Him and Mr. Steven be arguin' and shoutin' and him just slam the door leavin'. Mr. Steven say don't let him back in. Done throwed his clothes in the driveway like some po' white trash family...." Essie trailed off, her fingers frantic in the fringe. "As if I can keep that po' boy out his own house."

"When did this take place, Miss Essie?"

"When he brung my baby home." She looked up slyly, her fingers stilling in the purple fringe. "You seed him when you come by that first time, didn't you? I let my boy in to get his things, things Mr. Steven didn't toss out and he be needin'. I takes care of my boy jist like I takes care of you and my baby."

I grinned at Essie. Lines of worry pulled down on her face, making deep crevices in the dark skin. Her eyes were fierce and sorrowful at once. "Can I see her?"

"She sleepin'. That 'bout all she do now. Sit and stare. Sleep. She eat, you put food in her mouth. She soil her diapers and make water through that piping they got in her privates." Essie looked up at me, brown eyes in yellow gelatinous orbs. "You save my baby, Dr. Missy Rhea? You save my Risa?"

I turned, put my arms around Essie and pulled her close, my black bag against her bony back. I wasn't demonstrative by nature, but I had always been able to hug Essie. "I have her chart and X rays, Miss Essie. I have another doctor in Duke University who's willing to take a look at her. I'm trying," I said, speaking down onto the gray head. "I'm trying."

"You got to hurry, Dr. Missy Rhea." Essie pulled back and looked up into my eyes. "She dyin'. I know it."

I had long ago learned to listen to the statements of people like Essie, old folk who know how to pray and knew how to grieve. They seemed to know things the rest of us didn't. Or couldn't. The aged seemed sometimes to sense death, like the scent of autumn on the air. Or winter. Or snow. Some doctors didn't listen to the words they spoke, believing in their own saving medical powers. I always listened.

"I may have to take Marisa to the hospital, Essie. For more tests. Some special CAT scans of her face bones that should have been done when she was in the hospital. But it'll have to be when Steven isn't around. And I could get into trouble, Miss Essie, treating Marisa against Steven's wishes. A lot of trouble. And if I move her away from this house when Steven is gone..." My voice trailed off as I watched the old eyes watch me. "It's considered kidnapping, Miss Essie. It's against the law. And I can't do it alone."

Essie grinned widely, exposing ill-fitting dentures of a blinding shade of white. "You tell me when and I'll help you. I carries her feets."

I chuckled, the sound a strange vibration in my chest. It seemed like days since I had laughed. "You got a deal, Miss Essie. We can share a prison cell together."

Essie laughed with me then, the sound rattling in her bony rib cage. "You need to come back, you keep watch with that little telescope Mr. John give to you. You see them yellow flowers in the kitchen window? The cloth ones Missy Risa give me for my birthday three year back?" She pointed to the vase of silk daffodils the sun touched with a golden glow. "I move 'em when the coast be clear. They gone, you know it safe for you to come."

I pictured Miss Essie, an aging, dark-skinned Miss Marple, playing spy games. "I'll watch for the flowers to be gone. It'll be our sign.

"Now, let me see her, Miss Essie. Please." Carefully, I set the fragile woman to one side and walked into Marisa's bedroom. She was lying in the bed on her side, pillows beneath her head and between her knees and another bracing her back so she wouldn't flop over. Marisa's face was slack in sleep, spittle drooling down her cheek. There were tissues beside the bed, and I took one, wiping her face. When I tossed it into the trash, it landed on a stack of other tissues, similarly folded. Essie had been keeping Marisa's face clean.

Marisa was breathing deeply, her cheeks blowing out with each breath. I checked her blood pressure and pulse, took her temp. Except for the temperature of nearly 100, everything was normal. I checked her reflexes, which were slightly slower on the right side this morning than previously. I made a note of all my observations. And then I looked at my friend, not as a doctor, but as my family. Essie was right. There was something different this morning. Some change I couldn't put my finger on except that she needed a bath.

Marisa stank. Her breath; her body, which had been always so fresh and lightly perfumed; her diapers, which needed to be changed... I knew Essie didn't have the strength to do it and I couldn't. If the RN arrived and Marisa was clean, she might thank Steven for changing his wife before he left for work in the morning. He would know DeeDee or I had been here, as no one else would volunteer to change her diapers.

For a reason I couldn't put my finger on, I lifted Marisa's nightgown, pulled down her diaper and looked at her buttocks. The smell was strong and rank, and liquid feces curdled in the cottony folds. The skin of her backside was pasty, winter white and slack from two weeks of no exercise. Across the left buttock was a scratch. Superficial and nearly healed, it was about six inches long.

My heart beating an irregular rhythm, I replaced the nightgown and pulled the sheet up over Marisa's body.

"Miss Essie, if she changes today, if she starts breathing with long slow pauses between breaths, if her pulse changes by slowing or becoming erratic, if she starts vomiting or her fever goes up, I want you to call me. You have a watch with a second hand?"

"I can't see the watch no more, Dr. Missy Rhea, not with these old eyes, but I know what normal be. I been taking care of this chile for enough years so's I know how *everything* suppose to be. I count in my head. I watch over my baby and I call you, Dr. Missy Rhea, anything changes. You got that fancy new car phone?"

"I have it." I heard a car pull up out front and checked my watch. Seven-thirty.

"You carry it with you all the time, you hear? And you go on now. That nurse be knockin' on the door and you got to be gone."

I hugged Essie and let myself out, sliding the back

door closed behind me. The sun was coming up, a golden ball of light, as I jogged back to my house through the leafless woods. A fear I couldn't suppress held my heart in its icy grasp.

8

Manners and Special Problems

A car was waiting in the drive at the back of my house as I came through the woods. It was a long, black Lincoln with tinted windows, its engine purring with the smooth precision of a well-maintained car. It looked like a pimpmobile, or the kind of car an upwardly mobile drug dealer might tool around in. But it wasn't a car used for illegal activities, though Marisa and I had teased its owner for years about the image it presented. It was Miss DeeDee.

I sighed. I had hoped to get to DeeDee's house this afternoon, making a socially correct visit to my benefactor and asking her about Marisa. The fact that DeeDee had beaten me to the punch meant I had waited too long. DeeDee was very strict about proper etiquette and insisted that Marisa and I adhere to all the old codes of deportment and conduct.

I owed DeeDee too much, both professionally and personally, to treat her other than with absolute propriety. I owed her my entire education, until I could pay off the loans she had underwritten.

I unlocked the BMW and bent in to retrieve my duffel, placed it on the ground and shivered, though the sun cast a pallid warmth onto my dark T-shirt. The Lincoln slipped into gear and eased forward, pulling to a stop. DeeDee stepped out into the cold. She was dressed in a Chanel two-piece knit skirt and top, the black fabric perfectly draped and accenting the pearls she habitually wore. They were family heirlooms, a twenty-seven-inch strand of impeccably matched pink pearls brought back from the Orient by Captain James Stowe, the family patriarch, in the early 1800s. I rarely saw DeeDee without them.

"You're back," she said as she reached me. Leaning down, I accepted the delicate kiss she placed on my cheek and kissed her back. DeeDee smelled like powder and Chanel No. 5. "Did you have an enjoyable trip, dear?"

"Yes. As well as the outcome allowed."

DeeDee made a tsking sound. "You and your young man have decided not to marry then?" She looked up at me with eyes so like Marisa's, blue and bright and not faded at all by the years.

"It looks like I will be remaining in Dawkins County until my contract expires, Miss DeeDee. And John will find some other female doctor to marry into the family business. I have no desire to do so." It was bluntly stated, and I could have tried to find more elegant phrasing, but I was tired. And I still carried the stink of my friend in my nostrils, which no amount of Chanel could overpower.

DeeDee lifted an eyebrow. She expected better than blunt crudity of me. And because she had done so much for me over the years, I took a deep breath and searched for the more proper forms of conversation she had taught me.

"I would invite you in, Miss DeeDee, but I haven't had a chance to clean up since I got home the night before last. Would you care to go somewhere and have a cup of coffee?"

"No, dear. I know you must be tired after a night in the E.R. I am on my way to the hospital for work and simply hoped to catch you on the way in." DeeDee tilted her perfectly coiffed head to the woods, and I followed her eyes, seeing bare gray branches scratching at low gray clouds. She knew Marisa and I visited back and forth through the path.

"Have you seen her?" Odd tone, full of pain.

"Yes. Just now," I said gently.

"He let you in?" Her voice was wounded. Tears gathered in her blue eyes, dampening the line of blue eye shadow.

"No. Miss Essie let me in. The nurse was late."

She turned her head away a moment, and to comfort her I said, "Can you see the kitchen window from your house, Miss DeeDee? Because if you can, Miss Essie is going to remove the yellow flowers when it is safe and we can slip in and see her...." I almost said "sneak in and see her," but Miss DeeDee often said no true lady ever went sneaking around anywhere. It was her foremost reason for criticizing the old TV show *Murder, She Wrote,* and Dick Van Dyke's show *Diagnosis Murder.* The hero or heroine was always skulking around—not the behavior of a person of culture.

"I can see if I stand in my guest bath. I'll watch for it." DeeDee patted my cold hand, her eyes still focused away from me, either to hide the depths of her misery or to stare through the woods and walls that separated her from Marisa. I felt a momentary pang, knowing no one had ever looked toward me with that intensity.

DeeDee didn't believe in wearing her heart on her sleeve, but her misery was impossible to miss. She took a deep breath and straightened her already ramrod shoulders. "How is she?"

I hated to tell DeeDee the truth. Although she had a nurse's degree and worked in the comptrollers office full-time at the hospital, it had been years since she'd practiced, and she was not accustomed to being with patients. And knowing that her beautiful Marisa was lying in her own excrement would have been too much for her. DeeDee didn't exactly deal with body effluents and the reality of illness. DeeDee dealt instead with money.

She had more money of her own than anyone should ever have to handle, and because she had parlayed three husbands' estates and her own immodest inheritance into a fortune, she had been offered the position of dealing with the hospital's profits. She had done very well by them, too, in the three years since she'd stopped traveling so much and accepted a permanent position. A position that let her spend time with Marisa, and lately with me.

She pursed her lips, eyebrows raised slightly. "Trying to decide how much to tell fragile old DeeDee?" she asked dryly. "Remember, dear, I worked for years in the state hospital, in every wing from the old tuberculosis ward to the mental ward. I may be out of practice, but I'm not a novice to blanch at the sight of blood or body wastes." Her eyes grew steely. "I *know* what a sick patient looks like."

I blinked and may have blushed slightly. I certainly felt warm all of a sudden. "I'm sorry. I do know better. Marisa's not doing well, Miss DeeDee. Not well at all." Dirt bikes sounded in the distance, a muted thunder.

DeeDee's eyes flashed blue fire. "That man is letting her lie there and die. You have to do something."

"Steven?"

"Yes, Steven. He—" She pressed her thin lips together as if to shut off the flow of words. DeeDee did that when she caught herself about to make an impolite remark; DeeDee was never anything but proper. "I have a concern about Steven and his treatment of Marisa since she was released from the hospital," she rephrased delicately. "The rumors of his mental instability are positively rampant. I had hoped when you came back you might…" She paused, seeking the words.

Finally she settled for, "I don't want her to die." DeeDee placed a gloved hand on my cold arm. "You *must* keep her alive. You *must.*"

"I'm doing what I can, Miss DeeDee," I said, covering her fingers with my own. "Why didn't you call me back from the mountains? Why did you wait until I came home?" It was a question that had been plaguing me since the first moment I discovered that Marisa had been injured.

"In the beginning I didn't think there was anything wrong with that Shobani person's course of treatment. And then I didn't know what to do. I'm the one Essie called when she discovered her, you know. Me. Not Steven. And I think Steven blames me for that. For the closeness between us all these years.''

I crossed my arms and fought the shivers. If DeeDee noticed the lack of bra in the cold, she didn't mention it. It wouldn't have been the polite thing to do. "No, I didn't know that.''

Dismissing the addict-socialist wife, DeeDee had investigated Steven, his marriage, family life, medical practice, income and family tree. Approving, she had taken the schoolgirl crush in hand, introduced Steven and Marisa in a proper social setting and presided over their courtship and wedding like some marriage broker of old. Steven treated her like his own mother. His refusal to allow DeeDee to see Marisa was part and parcel of his emotional crisis.

DeeDee checked her watch and tsked again. "Are you working tonight? I was planning on coming by to see you and getting a little something for my..." She paused carefully, a bit of color in her cheeks. "For my *problem*. It's acting up again. I could come by and bring you supper,'' she suggested. "Emily is making pot roast.'' It was DeeDee's way of both asking for help and saying we could talk then.

"I go on duty at seven. But you don't have to suffer till then, Miss DeeDee. I have some Bactrim in my bag now. Some samples a salesman left for us before I went on vacation.''

I pulled my medical bag to me and searched in the bottom for the individually wrapped capsules. DeeDee suffered from recurrent UTIs—bladder infections brought on by a tilted uterus and surgical complications she had not taken time to have corrected yet. I had urged the surgery on her for months but until she decided to allow a surgeon to cut on her again, I kept her supplied with antibiotics.

"You are such a sweet dear child," she said, taking the antibiotics I offered her. "And you tell all the E.R. nurses that dinner will be provided. They won't have to eat that disgusting food served to the hospital staff. Did you know that for lunch yesterday they served limp boiled cabbage simply swimming in butter, cornbread and beans, and hot dogs. At a *hospital*," she finished indignantly.

"I'll tell them. And thanks, Miss DeeDee. I am trying to help Marisa."

"I know you are, dear. Have a nice day," she called over her shoulder as she slipped back into the Lincoln, moving with the kind of grace that was inbred in southern women until the early sixties and has never been duplicated since.

Dirt bikes roared to life somewhere close and raced away. Moments later they flew over the path behind the house, the engines echoing down the creek bed as the well-tuned Lincoln backed down the curving length of the drive. It always amazed me that the delicate little woman could control the huge car with such precision. But back in my high-school days, DeeDee used to drive a dual-wheeled pickup truck, pulling a full-size, fully loaded Featherlite horse trailer back and forth from the horse farm in Kentucky to the winter stables in Dawkins. It seemed she hadn't lost her touch.

Shivering, goose bumps visible beneath the thin cloth of my T-shirt, I picked up my duffel and unlocked the house. Cold air hit me, slightly sour smelling. Mildew I expected, but I had thought I left the heat on. I really was going to have to clean up the place now that I knew I would be staying here. I turned on the hall light and picked my way through the camping equipment to a bare spot on the hardwood floor where I dropped both the duffel and the medical bag.

Outside, a horn tooted. Not a Lincoln deep-throated, dual-toned horn, but some new version, sharp and demanding. Which meant I didn't have to start cleaning right away after all. Pivoting in the cramped space, I went back into the cold, stopped, crossed my arms and shivered.

"What do you want?" It wasn't Aunt DeeDee, so I didn't have to use my manners. It was just some dumb old cop.

Mark grinned at me behind his aviator glasses. They were reflector glasses that wrapped around his head with slim, dark frames. My reflection was a skewed thin speck in the center of each lens.

"Good morning, Dr. Lynch. My, don't you look ravishing today."

"Stuff it, Mark. Aunt DeeDee isn't here. She just left, as I'm sure you happen to know. What did you do, park around the corner and wait until she drove off?"

"Guilty. I never did remember half of what the old bat taught when I took culture courses from her over Christmas vacations. Never could remember who to introduce first, the duke or his mother. Not that I ever met the duke or his mother. I can't see them vacationing in DorCity."

I hid a smile. It wasn't so cold with the house at my back and the breeze diverted. "Maybe the duke is a hunting freak and he wants you to take him deer hunting and run with your dogs."

"In that case I know what to do. I introduce the dog first."

I laughed and saw Mark's lips twitch up on both sides. He always could make me laugh, but this was the first time he had shown any real emotion except anger toward me since I told him I might be going back to John.

"You shipped out a John Doe last night."

I raised my eyebrows. I had long since given up being surprised at the speed of the rumor mill in Dawkins County. "Yeah. Trauma patient. Injured in what possibly was a stampede." I grinned at Mark's expression. It wasn't often I left him dumbfounded. "For real. The guy was covered in bruises shaped like cattle hooves. Nasty skull fracture."

"I got a missing-person's report this morning. Willie Evans, white, twenty-four years old. Local laborer, working on several cattle farms in the area part-time. His daddy's yelling and going on about how it's foul play and wants me to bring in every farmer in the county for interrogation."

"Drunk?"

"For the past twenty years, father and son both."

I shook my head. In Mark's glasses my dual heads swiveled back and forth at sharp angles. I told him about the syringe in John Doe's pocket, and the needle buried in his buttock. "Looked like a drug situation that went wrong somehow. Maybe on one of the farms he worked on at feeding time. He didn't have anything illegal in his system but the lab routinely holds the UDS sample for two weeks. If the reference lab turns up something in the syringe, I'll have his urine tested for the same substance. That's about the best I can do for you.''

Mark pushed at the bridge piece of his glasses and sighed. The puff of breath made an oval spot of condensation on the window top. ''Well, you were right about part of it. If your patient's Willie Evans, he was moving cattle from a recently sold farm pasture. Two and a half acres sold to a company called Medicom Plus. Ever heard of it?''

I shivered, as much from surprise as from cold. Medicom Plus was Mitchell Scoggins's company. The one that underbid the hospital for Sundown Chemical's medical business. I told Mark what little I knew, and even behind the mirrored glasses I could see him processing the information.

''Well, that helps, I guess. Here. This is yours.'' Mark held a piece of paper out to me. Since he didn't remember any of the deportment lessons taught by DeeDee, I didn't expect him to bring it to me. It would have meant opening the door of his Jeep and letting all the heat out. I stepped down the stairs and took the paper. At least the sunlight was still drab and he couldn't see the not-so-flat chest I had been hiding.

''What is this?''

''Vet bill.''

I remembered the dog in the graveyard, long silky hair under my fingers. ''This county doesn't have a humane society?''

"Nope. Just the survival of the strongest and the kindness of passing strangers."

"Why me? She's not my dog." My reflections in Mark's glasses were larger and shaped weirdly, big bodies and minuscule heads off to the sides.

Mark put his Jeep in gear, the engine sounding powerful and robust. The side window began to rise in my face. "She is now." The Jeep backed down my driveway, leaving me standing there holding the vet bill. I opened it and the total figure made me wince.

"Great. I don't want a dog." But part of me remembered the thump of tail and the warm wet of the black dog's tongue. And wanted her. Firmly, I pushed the thought away and went into the house, locking the door behind me.

The air was colder now than moments before. The heater was on full force, the vent along the wall blowing up between the camping supplies. I held out my hand. The air blowing up was warm yet the house was cold. "What…"

I moved through the house, the blackness of the hallway not quite as complete as usual. The scent of mildew not quite as strong.

I stubbed my toe and stopped. My television was on the floor at my feet, the screen broken out. As if someone had dropped it in the hallway.

I walked to the front room. The front door was open, the glass in the left pane broken out. My computer lay in the center of the room on its side, the screen of the monitor broken out as well. Chairs were turned over. The old, secondhand couch lent to me by DeeDee was on its back, cushions tossed around. Someone had been in my house.

A flush shot through me. *Someone might still be here.*

I whirled. Sprinted out the open front door into the cold. My heart beating like the jackhammer earlier. My breath hot in my throat. I was shaking, but not from the frigid air.

Mark's Jeep was turning down the road.

"Mark!" I shouted, surprised by the breath in my lungs. The sound reverberated through the bare limbs above me. I ran after the Jeep, feet flying. *"Maaaark!"*

The Jeep slowed. Mark lowered the window and started to grin until he saw my face. "Get in."

I raced around the Jeep and found the passenger door open, Mark still leaning across the seats, hand on the latch. I climbed in and pulled the door to. "Someone's been in my house. The front door was open when I went in just now."

"They still in the house?"

"I don't know."

Mark reached for his radio and called in the code. Replacing the handset, he eased the Jeep over to the side of the road and turned to me. "Tell me what you saw."

Quickly, I described the television and the computer and the mess of the front room. "But I remembered something just now. I heard dirt-bike engines close by when I got home. And then, maybe seven, eight minutes ago they came around the back of the house on the trail. Two of them, both red." I was shaking again and felt as if I had never been warm in my life.

"Riders?"

"Yes."

Mark laughed and I understood his question, feeling stupid. "They looked like males, but were both wearing helmets with face shields, one was red, the other black I think. And with heavy coats. I guess I could be wrong about the sex, come to think of it. All that padding."

Mark handed me a coat from the back seat. "You need some padding yourself. Here. You never heard of layers, woman?"

I could have been embarrassed at the oblique reference to my twin peaks, but the shock of the open front door and the sight of the damaged electronics was still fresh in my memory. I wrapped the coat, which was several sizes too large, around me. It was already warm, smelling like Mark. A hint of spicy aftershave and dog.

"When I saw you running after me, I thought you were returning stolen property," Mark said.

"What?"

"My flashlight. County property. You have it. Remember?"

I shuddered, sinking deeper into the warmth of the coat. "It's in the front seat of my car. Help yourself. And it was loaned to me by a county employee, not stolen," I added irritably. Mark laughed.

A marked car pulled alongside us; an officer I recognized leaned out the open window. "You make the call, Cap?"

"Yeah. Looks like the doctor might have walked

in on a B and E. Don't know for certain the house is empty, so as soon as 114 gets here we'll do a walk-through. I called for crime scene and— Here's 114. House number is 2172, the bungalow-style set off the road there.'' Mark pointed.

He turned off the engine and handed me the keys. "You get cold, you turn on the Jeep. And keep the jacket on. Your teeth are chattering.''

Mark left the cab, letting in a draft of cold air. Pulling my knees up to my chest, I snuggled into the down jacket. It was heavenly warm. Turning in the seat, I watched the cops approach and enter my house. They each moved in a bent-kneed crouch. Each had a gun drawn, held to the side, pointed at the earth.

9

Housebreaking and Puppies

Twenty minutes later Mark returned to the car, his lips slightly gray from the cold. I had the engine running and the heat on and he rubbed his hands together in front of the vent after dropping his flashlight into the glove box. "Well, they weren't inside but they trashed the place." He glanced at me from the corner of his mirrored glasses. "I don't suppose they brought the dust and mold with them and left them there."

I tucked my chin into the high collar of his coat. "I've been out of town," I said gruffly. More honestly, I added, "I'm not much of a housekeeper."

"No kidding. That why you never would ask me in after a date?"

"No. I never asked you in because I figured you wouldn't have settled for coffee and conversation," I surprised myself by saying.

"I know the meaning of no," he said softly.

"I wasn't sure I did," I said back just as softly.

The air in the cab was suddenly too warm and I wanted nothing more than to take back the last words I had spoken. And couldn't. I didn't look at Mark though I know he stared at me. "Did they take anything?"

"I don't know. It's your house. But there were some clean places in the dust, so I'd guess so. Crime scene is almost finished and you can go in and start looking around. I'll need a list of everything stolen, with serial numbers if you have them. Make two copies so you can turn one over to your insurance agent. You still using Selective?"

I nodded, glad Mark had the sense to let the conversation turn back to safer ground.

"I'll have Dan give you a call." Dan was Mark's brother, and the county's only independent insurance agent. I had all my insurance except my professional liability through his company.

"You think it was the bikers?"

"Could have been. We found tracks in the grass at the side of the house. You probably came in right after they left, just like you thought."

I nodded again, relaxing a tension I hadn't acknowledged. I hugged his coat around me. "I appreciate your telling me all this. And Mark?"

He turned the glasses to me.

"Two things. First, thank you for stopping when you heard me scream."

"You got a set of lungs on you, woman."

"And second, I really hate those glasses."

Mark grinned. "Get the front-door lock changed, and while you're at it, have the locksmith take a look at the back doors and the windows. The security system on that house hasn't been updated in twenty years."

"Needs insulation in the walls, too," I said. It was

the closest I had come to admitting I would be staying in Dawkins County for a while.

Mark nodded. "It does at that. Come on. I'll walk you home."

I noticed he had not removed the glasses and wondered if that was an indication of his feelings toward me or just plain stubbornness.

"By the way," he said casually, "now would be a great time to acquire a guard dog."

"You have any particular guard dog in mind?"

"I took a black mixed breed in to deliver puppies last night. Up at Doc Aycock's."

"I'll keep it in mind," I said as I opened the door and walked toward my house. A moment later, Mark joined me.

The house was worse than I had expected. A lamp was broken, the medicine cabinet had been ransacked. The clean clothes I had yet to put away were strewn across the bedroom floor. The shower door was hanging open and black mold was indistinguishable from the black fingerprint powder on the doorknobs and handles. Paper was scattered all over the place.

My CDs were gone, as was the small CD player and speakers I had bought recently. I hoped the kid bikers hated jazz and blues. I hoped Motown and soul and pop/rock from the sixties and seventies were not to their tastes at all, and that the theft would leave an unsatisfactory tang in each boy's mouth. I hoped that performers like Aretha Franklin, Etta James, George Benson, Carole King, Bread, Jimi Hendrix and James Taylor were recordings that their parents listened to, though I had no reason to suppose the bikers were young, except that most bikers in the county were.

My bed had been stripped of sheets, the mattress knocked to the floor. My kitchen had been searched and the locked silver box was lying on the floor. The silver John and I had purchased to begin our married life. I bent and lifted the case, placed it on the counter where I had placed my mail the day before. Silver tinkled inside.

The mail was gone. My computer discs were gone.

"So far only the CD player and speakers, which were small, my computer discs and a week's worth of mail seems to be missing." I looked into the hallway. The camping equipment was untouched. "But the computer and the TV are goners, I think."

Mark patted my shoulder. "Look at it this way. You lost a few valuables and learned a great lesson—you need better security and a dog. And you didn't lose your life learning it. Feel better?"

"Oh, just loads. Thank you so much."

The other cops were eavesdropping and grinning as they packed up. I ignored them, though I recognized most of them from being in the E.R. at one time or another. Cops and accident victims, cops and gunshot victims, cops and rape victims, cops and trouble. Which was the main reason that I had never encouraged Mark, my attraction to the man notwithstanding.

Cops were dangerous and lived dangerous lives, adrenaline junkies even worse than EMTs. Cops got shot at and shot at other people. And there were other ways of being injured on the job that had nothing to do with guns and flying bullets, which was how I had met Mark—after he fell down a hill in a winter ice storm. He had landed on the man he was chasing and broken two of the guy's ribs. Stabbed himself in the thigh with a broken branch at the same time.

"Thanks, y'all. I appreciate you checking the place out for me."

"Nothing to it, Doc. But next time, how about trying not to go inside in the first place. That's the way people get killed."

"I'll get the locks fixed today," I promised as I pulled Mark's coat off and handed it back.

"Don't believe a word she says, Jacobson. Dr. Lynch is more accustomed to saving lives and playing hero in the E.R., not following orders or protecting herself, or using the good sense God gave her. I'll bet she doesn't even have a gun."

"If I had a gun, the bad guys would have taken it," I said smugly.

Jacobson laughed. Mark glared at him and the uniformed cop ducked his head, taking the front steps into the yard.

"Every woman living alone should have a gun," Mark said stubbornly, walking to the door.

"I'm not buying a gun."

"No. But I'll bet you *will* get a dog." He grinned and slid on those awful glasses as he stepped down into the front yard, a big man who moved with an animal kind of grace. So unlike John....

I shut the front door behind him, turning the little single-cylinder dead bolt with my fingers. Leaning back against the door, I surveyed the house by the dull overhead light and what daylight made it

through the overgrown hedges out front. It was a
mess. And I hated housework. And I had so much
to do today for Marisa.... I had to study her chart so
I could talk to Cam intelligently, though I had never
been on his level, either diagnostically or intellec-
tually. Pushing away from the door, I heard a crinkling noise in my pocket and slid my hand inside.

The vet bill. I had no memory of stuffing it down
there. No memory except the panic I felt when I
realized my home had been violated. Maybe it *was*
time to get a dog. One with a deep bark and big
canine teeth. And puppies.

Before another thought, I was outside and in the
car, revving the engine down the drive. I studied the
directions to the vet's on the back of the bill and
made phone calls to the locksmith and a window-
repair shop on the way, then called Office Depot,
where I bought the computer that now lay in pieces
on the floor, hoping they could save my hard drive.
I drove like a maniac to Doc Aycock's and the dog
I had wanted last night even as I was saving her life.

An hour later I pulled out of the Wal-Mart parking
lot with a twenty-pound sack of dog food in the
trunk, a bottle of flea spray, a fresh flea collar and
two bowls. The black dog and her three living pups
were comfortably seated on the front passenger seat,
smelling up my car and making the windows steam
with heat.

I found myself driving one-handed, scratching the
big black dog behind the ears. She grinned up at me,
tongue lolling, golden-brown eyes happy. I wasn't

certain who was happiest, me or the dog, but made it a point not to look in the rearview to see my expression, fearing it would resemble the dog's so much I wouldn't recognize myself.

I *had* needed a dog, I realized, and had denied myself the pleasure, certain I would be back with John and Beca in Charleston, living the life we had promised ourselves back before John's uncle died and he was expected to join the family practice.

The black dog—I refused to call her Blackie or Lady or simply Dog—followed her pups and her new bag of food into the dark confines of my house. A strange dog in the house wasn't a good idea, especially as I had no idea of the level of her house training. But it wasn't as if the house was spotless or smelled any better than the dog did, so why should I care if she left a few accidents around while we were getting used to one another?

I tossed the sweatshirt I had given up to keep the puppies warm into the corner where I usually left my dirty clothes. Doc Aycock had saved it for me, but hadn't thought to rinse it out while the blood was still fresh. If the cleaners could get the bloodstains out I would be tickled pink. I really loved that shirt.

In the dining room at the front of the house were all the boxes I had used to move to Dawkins County. I had saved them, thinking I would be here only a few months. I had better sense now and chose the largest one for the black dog and her babies.

With a pair of surgical scissors I kept in my medical bag, I cut out a big hole, high enough for the dog to step through while still containing her pups, and placed the box in the nook between the kitchen and the hallway. Adding an old fleece blanket made the box safe, warm and cozy. The dog stepped in and sniffed her sleeping puppies, turned around twice and settled beside them. I loved the tongue-hanging smile she gave me.

I spent the next hour cleaning, stuffing debris into packing boxes from the dining room, adding to the list of things broken and missing. The mail was the only problem. Bills were all on draft, so I wouldn't miss anything there, but the last correspondences really bothered me.

I exchanged e-mail with several friends from med school and wrote several others who were not so computer literate as I. I hadn't bothered to check my e-mail when I came in from the mountains, and now had no way to do so. It was also time to hear from Theresa and Margaret, and perhaps time for a letter from Josh, though I hadn't noted any familiar return addresses in the stack of mail I brought home from the post office. I would have to write them all and tell them about the lost mail and that I would not be moving back to Charleston. I wasn't looking forward to their replies.

The computer still had its own box and packing Styrofoam, which I used to seal it up and place in the trunk of my car. With that done and a fairly clean trail blazed through the rest of the house, I felt justified in playing with the dogs before the window repairman and the locksmith arrived. While I fondled the pups and told the mother dog she was wonderful in the kind of baby talk only another dog lover could understand, I dialed the Realtor who had leased my house and told her I wanted to buy.

Like the dog, it was an impulse decision, but I had put my life on hold for the last year. It was time to try and live again and I had the feeling I would not regret the decisions I was making so seemingly blithely. As I discussed an offer on the house, I kept seeing Marisa's face as I had last seen it. Dried drool in the corner of her mouth. No life in the flaccid limbs.

Essie was right. I didn't have long to correct whatever Marisa's problem was. And no way did I think it was only the subdural and subarachnoid hemorrhage stated as the diagnosis. The CAT scan confirmed my suspicions. Though there were bleeds present in Marisa's brain, none of them together or separately were big enough to cause the total collapse I had seen this morning. There was something else going on.

My mind strayed to the John Doe, possibly Willie Evans, now under the care of a specialist at Richland Memorial. He, too, had bleeds that didn't fit the normal pattern. Bleeds caused by trauma? I wondered if Cam would mind looking at Doe-Evans films as well as Marisa's....

It was quiet in the house, the only sounds the ticking of the central heat and the sound of air in the vents. Soft dog sounds, the sucking noise of puppies nursing. The air warmed up around me and I dozed off sitting on the floor by the dogs' box, one arm draped inside, resting on the mother's back. The ar-

rival of the window-repair guy and the locksmith
woke me up.

They arrived together in separate vans, the window guy's van a battered, once-gray vehicle with a
bashed-out windshield, the locksmith's spanking
new, sparkling white. It was obvious which business
was most profitable.

While they worked, the dog and I toured the backyard where she sniffed every bush and tree, watered
every neglected flower bed and generally made herself at home. Once, while we stood in the sun, dirt
bikes whizzed by on the back line of the property
and she barked frantically, her ruff standing up and
her tail held at half-mast. The bikes were both blue,
not the red I remembered from this morning, but I
praised her nonetheless. If she hated dirt bikes, she
and I were going to get along quite well.

When the bikers were gone and she was certain
they weren't coming back, she left the edge of the
woods and came to me where I sat on the back steps,
climbed up with only her front paws until her head
was on a level with my face. Watching to see how
I would respond, she licked me thoroughly. I hated
it, frankly, but permitted it just this once as a part of
our bonding. Then I pushed her down, forced her to
roll over and held her there, to remind her I was boss.
She grunted up at me and wagged her tail against
the cracked concrete of the drive. We had established
a pecking order that suited us both. I named her Belle
on the spot.

Together we went back into the house and Belle
crawled into her box, waiting for me to be properly

impressed, once again, with her babies. I bent over and petted them all, one at a time.

"Yes, they are all just beautiful," I said. "And you did it all by yourself without the help of a husband, too, didn't you. I see that often in my line of work, Belle, yes I do. Some big old boy dog, or two, or three, just knocked you up and then took off." Belle's tail wagged hard and she licked my face. This time I pushed her huge head aside and scratched her ears. Belle didn't seem to mind.

Before the men left, I had receipts from each, new locks and a new window at the front door. I also held estimates for replacement of all the old windows and for a new security system. Owning my own home wasn't going to be cheap. I would have to consider costs of replacements and updating in my offer on the house.

Outside, the air had warmed into the low fifties and I felt like a run. I dressed in my jogging clothes, this time with a bra, to please Essie and DeeDee, and took off through the woods, following the same path that the dirt bikes did. I needed to clear my head and free up a few clogged brain cells to study Marisa's chart.

I broke a sweat quickly, my feet pounding over the hard-packed earth. The trail followed the road for a pace and I studied the houses I was intending to live among for the next few years. Starlight Lane. I liked the sound. Liked the old, bungalow-style houses with their gingerbread porches and long, deep windows and arching steep gables. Most of the houses had well-manicured lawns, even in the deep of winter, and I decided to hire a yard crew and have the exterior of the house painted if the deal went through.

I was passed by dirt bikers on the way home and one bike was red. It gave me the shivers, though both bikers waved and yelled as they passed.

When I got back home, the answering machine was blinking, one of the few things not damaged or removed by my burglars. It was Cam. He was furious that I had blotted out the name of the patient on the chart I had faxed him. He had solved his own dilemma and called the hospital, asking for medical records. He knew it was Marisa's chart.

I'm not afraid of much in life. Losing John didn't fill me with trepidation. Facing a future full of bills and uncertain relationships didn't really dismay me. Even the fact of my house being broken into hadn't affected me for long. Watching my mother change from socialite to hag as she drank herself to death had stolen all the fear of the future out of me. Anything life tossed my way, I figured I could deal with one way or another. Anything except losing Marisa or dealing with Cam Reston on the subject of Marisa.

Cam had spent premed darting from one woman's bed to another with near abandon. Until he set eyes on Marisa. When she had no interest in dating him, let alone letting him into her bed, Cam had reacted in a typically sophomoric, masculine fashion, getting roaring drunk and passing out on the sorority lawn. Marisa had ignored his antics, just as she ignored his constant phone calls, his flowers, his gifts and his desperate desire for her attention. And when Marisa met Dr. Steven Braswell in medical school, handsome, sophisticated as only an older man can be to a young woman, Cam's fate was sealed. Marisa never glanced his way again.

When Marisa dropped out of her second year of medical school to marry Steven, and informed us all she was both pregnant and blissfully happy, Cam had mourned her with a passion that bordered on the self-destructive. And now he knew Risa was in trouble with only his once-rival to care for her.

I dialed his beeper number slowly, and punched in my number. Then I sat down to wait. Or tried to. Waiting made me antsy, always had. The antsy feeling was the only reason the house of my youth was ever clean. While waiting on my mother to come home from one of her drunken binges with what ever man she would be bringing home, I cleaned and scrubbed. It was a sure thing Mama never would have. Perhaps that had some psychological impact on my hatred of cleaning now that I was grown and my mother was long dead.... I had never bothered to analyze it.

While I waited, I brewed up a pot of raspberry-flavored coffee and drank two cups with a blueberry bagel and cream cheese. Weird combination of flavors, but Belle and I loved it. She, eating dainty bites of bagel from my hand; me, taking less moderate bites and scattering crumbs.

When the phone rang, I picked it up, swallowed and took a deep breath. "Hello."

"Why the *hell* didn't you tell me this was Marisa?'' His voice was low, deadly soft with suppressed fury.

"Because I wanted you to be at your diagnostic best, not grieving over what's happened to her and therefore unable to see this as a puzzle,'' I said, my voice biting. At the sharp silence on the other end, I continued more gently. "That's what you called neurodiagnostic procedures. Remember? A puzzle? She needs you too much to have you emotionally involved in this, Cam.'' Before he could reply I continued.

"I know you said you had a lady in your life finally, but this is different. You were in love with Marisa. I didn't know how much of that feeling was left, and I couldn't risk you losing your sense of detachment.''

Belle, sensing discomfort in her human, padded in a large circle to the back door, the front door, and back to her puppies, searching for any problem best solved with big teeth and a little attitude. As she moved, she whuffed softly in dismay.

After a long moment, Cam sighed. There was anger in the sound still, but resignation too. "So I'm supposed to forgive you for not telling me about this? This chart says she was admitted over two weeks ago.''

"I was on vacation in the mountains. Marisa could have tracked me down, she knew where I was going, but hardly anyone else up here did. I just found out about Marisa day before yesterday. Thursday night when I came on. It took me this long to get the chart and the films.''

"You haven't been called in on consultation?"

"No. I'm an E.R. doc, not a neurosurgeon," I said, stating the obvious. "And *you* haven't been called in, either. Not officially.

"I want to make certain you understand my position on this, Cam. I'm *not* treating her. In fact, I'm not even supposed to be *seeing* her, but Essie let me in.

"Are you going to be able to be detached about this *patient?*" I went on. "Because if not, you'll have to find me someone else to help her. Someone who'll understand I'm doing everything under the table. On my own."

"I can do it." After a moment he said, "I should be there. I have a few days coming to me. I can fly up tomorrow afternoon."

Cam had a plane, a single-engine Cessna with two seats. He had taken up flying when Marisa dumped him—or rather, never had a second thought for him. Flying was a panacea for him, and I wondered if he saw the irony of the situation.

"Why don't you wait until you see the films on MODIS? You might not find a reason to come. There may not be anything wrong here, Cam. I may be just seeing shadows and ghosts where nothing really exists."

Belle padded back from her box and put her head on my knee. Soulful eyes questioned my distress and I rubbed her ears for comfort. My comfort, not hers.

"That happens when a doctor is personally involved in a case and loses his sense of detachment,"

I said. "I don't think we need more than one of us like that on this case."

"Okay. You're right. I'd only shoot the bastard."

"Who?" I asked, distracted by Belle.

"Steven Braswell. You can't tell me he's the right man to be responsible for her, damn it."

"Steven's falling apart. Literally. He attacked me in the E.R. last night. I had to threaten him with the police and hospital security."

"Really?"

"You don't have to sound so pleased."

Cam chuckled, his pique smoothed. "I'll be on duty and available for MODIS at any time after seven tonight. And I want to see the final diagnosis on the initial CT as well as the second CAT scan of her orbit."

"It wasn't taken, Cam. There is no second scan." I ignored the sound of his cursing. So much for better moods. "And I haven't been able to get a copy of the final report, but I will."

"I want a repeat scan of her head as soon as you can get it, Rhea. With contrast, one-millimeter slices this time so I can tell how much damage has been done. She really needs an MRI but I don't guess you have that in the wilds of Dawkins, do you?" It wasn't a question as much as an insult. Cam was reacting harshly. Not much better than Steven...

"No. We just now stopped using reusable Jelcos and having our OB patients deliver in the bushes out back."

In spite of himself, Cam snorted with repressed laughter. "Sorry."

"How important are these scans?" I asked him. "Will a delay in the diagnosis make a difference to her treatment?"

Cam breathed into the phone a moment before answering. "No. Not really. Frankly, the damage is done. Now we are looking at rehab and recovery time."

I couldn't think of anything to say.

"Shit!" he said explosively into my silence.

"I'll get the films, Cam. Somehow," I said softly.

"I'll be waiting."

Cam signed off and I fondled Belle's ears for a while until it was time for me to get ready for work. At least tonight I remembered to pack my jojoba oil.

10

Gunshots and MODIS

The emergency room was a typical Saturday-night madhouse when I got there, a patient with a gunshot wound to the chest in one room and a patient stabbed with an ice pick in the other room. The stabbing had resulted in cardiac tamponade, blood seeping into the layer of tissue that surrounds the heart, slowing and ultimately impairing its ability to beat.

There were three more injuries waiting in the lobby, various lacerations that I would be left to deal with, and a young man with a gunshot to the thigh. I triaged him in the lobby, determining that it was a clean in-and-out wound with no obvious swelling. As he had no loss of blood pressure, I left him sitting there, a dirty towel tied around his leg.

The gunshot to the chest was being flown out to Richland Memorial. The tamponade was being flown to Carolinas Medical Center in Charlotte. Blood was smeared down the hallways and into the trauma room, small puddles, bloody footprints. There was panic in the cardiac room and a trail of angry family members swearing the usual vengeance on one another and falling out in the halls. Falling out is rural

southern for fainting and fits of hysteria. It was a
term I had learned quickly in E.R. work.

I didn't have to deal with either level-one, acute-
care patient, as Steven was handling the tamponade
and Wallace Chadwick was dealing with the other.
It wasn't often I got to sit and watch either man
work, so I unwrapped a slice of gum and propped
myself against a wall out of the way. Ashlee, called
in to handle the flood of injuries, was assisting her
cousin, Wallace, and Percy Shobani. Trish assisted
Ash, and all worked with quiet efficiency, though
blood was smeared down the blue paper aprons they
wore and dried onto their gloves. There was a portable X-ray machine in the room, a respiratory therapist, a lab tech and two EMTs waiting to do CPR
or help act as muscle if required to move bodies. A
stone-faced cop leaned against the wall, a clipboard
in his hand, taking notes. It was Jacobson, the same
cop who had helped with the robbery investigation
at my house. He looked up and nodded when I came
in the room and managed to catch Ashlee at the same
time. She had slipped in a puddle of blood. I passed
the cop three sheets from the linen supply and helped
him spread them on the bloody floor for traction.
Breathlessly, Ash said thanks, handed Wallace a
chest-tube kit and answered the phone all at the same
time.

While Ashlee was pale-skinned and gray-eyed, her
cousin was a light-skinned African-American with
green eyes in the peculiar way of the Chadwick family lines. Wallace ran the E.R., working the daytime
split shifts with Steven, and it was nice to watch him
work, laughing, smiling and keeping everyone, in-

cluding the patient, calm and relaxed in the midst of the crisis.

In face mask and shield, Shobani assisted Wallace, handing him forceps and probes. He was quick and sure, peppering the room with short, English-accented phrases.

The situation in Steven's room was vastly different, with Steven growling out conflicting orders and then maligning the employee who followed his demands. He was hopelessly tangled in EKG leads, pulling them off his patient's chest while the lab tech worked around him to reposition them. He had a portable X-ray machine and Bev the Sloth in one corner, a respiratory therapist bagging the intubated patient to maintain sufficient O_2 levels, and a second lab tech drawing blood gases from a femoral artery. EMTs handed supplies and stood ready to perform CPR if required. The patient was ashen, his chest smeared with blood. It didn't look good, unless Steven pulled himself together and organized his team.

Zack and Anne worked across the patient, handing Steven fresh cardiac needles to try to draw off the blood that had collected around the patient's heart inside the pericardium, the sac that covered the heart and allowed to it beat for some eighty years with fluid ease. Steven's hands shook.

I slipped out and checked on the two family members who fell out in the hallways. Uniformed cops had pulled the two unceremoniously from the path of foot traffic and propped them against the walls.

One was a female in her forties who rolled her eyes up in her head when I checked her pupils, and protected her face from harm when I tried to drop her own arm across her. She was faking. I cracked an ammonia capsule under her nose and held it there until her eyes watered and she started coughing. Whispering, I told her to get out of the E.R. and if I saw her face again tonight I'd call the police and have her arrested for interfering with an emergency situation. It wasn't exactly polite or even a medically correct response, but I had always hated fakers.

The other patient was actually having a seizure and I had to draft a cop to help me get her onto a bed. An IV, two doses of Valium and a family member who admitted the patient hadn't been taking her prescription phenobarbital took care of that one. It wasn't often I had to start my own IVs, and I was out of practice. I left two bruises for the patient to remember me by.

At some point in the crazed hour, I overheard Steven and Percy in the break room, their voices filtering out into the hallway. Shamelessly, I left my patient and stepped across the hall to listen.

"I'll be gone two, three days," I heard Steven say. "It'll take that long to get my father settled in the nursing home. I have a nurse coming in to see Marisa every day, and if anything changes, she'll call you."

"And if she takes a turn for the worse?" Percy asked. His voice sounded stressed and tense. I maneuvered so I could see him through the crack at the hinges. His back was to me, but his shoulders were rigid, pulling at the fabric of his shirt.

"Just handle it," Steven spat. "Look. I don't *want* to be away now, but I put off this trip three times, thanks to Eddie's situation and Marisa's condition.

Dad can't wait any longer. Marisa isn't exactly going to suffer for my absence, now, is she?'' Steven's voice hardened as if he saw something in Shobani's face I couldn't. ''You handle it, Percy. Understand? *You* handle it.''

Without a reply, Shobani turned and moved toward the door. I whirled and returned to my patient, pushing another half cc of Valium.

The seizure patient took nearly an hour to stabilize, and by the time I was done, both emergency helicopters had taken off. Wallace had seen to the gunshot to the thigh and sent him home with a hipful of antibiotics and a tetanus. Steven was long gone. The lesser-laceration victims had decided there were too many cops in the E.R. and had vanished, and suddenly I had the place to myself.

Just me and the two RNs who had been on duty the night—morning—that Marisa had been brought in, Anne and Zack. And Marisa soon to be at home without Steven. I wondered how I could convince Percy Shobani to order a CAT scan or two on her....

Blood trailed through the hallways, the rooms were a mess, and a housekeeping employee dressed out in a blue paper apron, trauma gloves and shoe covers smeared bloody water with a mop, while another collected sheets and emptied garbage cans into biohazard bags. Anne was leaning against the cabinet watching the coffee machine trail out a thin stream of dark fluid, and Zack was resupplying the crash cart in the trauma room, dark-skinned hands moving in the harsh light. Both were quiet. I needed some time alone with them to talk before I went online with MODIS and Cam. I needed to ask some pointed questions, but not in front of witnesses.

I also needed a moment to consider what Steven Braswell had said to Percy. *"Thanks to Eddie's situation and Marisa's condition."* Had the two been separate in Steven's mind and tone, or conjoined, like some cause-and-effect Siamese twins? I waited, drawing no conclusions. It was nearly nine, and I couldn't think of a proper way to bring up my nosing into Marisa's medical condition.

Just as we were getting ready to sit down, in walked DeeDee, in starched jeans and a crisp white work shirt with a pair of thousand-dollar ostrich-skin boots she had bought in Las Vegas ten years back. She carried a huge blue metal roaster in both hands. "I know I'm late, but I heard on the scanner you people were too busy for dinner anyway," she called out as she entered the airlock doors. The scent of roasted meat filled the corridor and my mouth watered. Zack grinned, his dark eyes sparkling above a blinding smile, and took the metal roasting pan from her. "A beautiful woman and food. An angel from heaven."

"Hush, young man. You flirt like your daddy did back thirty years ago." But she pinked and smiled. Everyone knew and loved DeeDee. She was an institution in Dawkins County, and especially at the hospital where she had mothered the E.R. employees for all the years that Steven had worked rough hours. "Don't spill it, Zachary. There's homemade gravy in the bottom and carrots and potatoes out in the car. Hungry?"

"Always, Miss DeeDee. Your home cooking is

the one thing I miss about Dr. Braswell not working nights anymore." He looked up at me. "No offense, Dr. Lynch."

"None taken," I said. Dinner at DeeDee's was about the only home-cooked meals I had eaten as a child. My mother had relied on frozen dinners and fast food. "I just hope we get time to eat."

On the echo of my words the emergency scanner stuttered to life. "Dawkins County, this is unit 67. Do you read?"

We all groaned. An ambulance was inbound with a patient, only two minutes out. I could hear him raging in the background over the sound of sirens; the EMT on the radio was clearly stressed. Behind me, the police scanner crackled to life. It looked like a busy night ahead.

Familiar with the exigencies of the E.R., DeeDee tucked her gift-meal into the break-room fridge and stood to one side, out of the way. I put her and the potential meal out of my mind.

The patient was young, in his late twenties or early thirties, and he was raving. Nonsense talk full of profanities, wild laughter and jerky movements of arms and legs. I stood at the door of the trauma room watching as the EMTs put him on a stretcher and then were forced to secure his wrists and ankles with leather restraints. Except for the lack of mud, manure and hoofprints, this could be a repeat performance of last night.

I frowned watching the crew at work. I didn't have to give orders yet. Just listen, watch and wait while the RNs did the preliminary work.

I had learned early what most E.R. docs take years

to learn—the RNs run the E.R. The doctor is often just stage dressing, there to think and talk. The RNs do the actual work, and a good E.R. nurse could do a great deal of the thinking, too, if a doctor would just listen.

My initial impression of the patient was drug overdose. PCP or LSD. Or a combination of drugs, perhaps. Druggies seldom made it easy on us.

"Pressure 180 over 105."

"Pulse 120. Hooking up pulse-ox now." A pulse-ox was a small device that used light to measure the amount of oxygen in a patient's bloodstream. It snapped on the patient's left index finger and began to measure both pulse and oxygen in a matter of seconds. I watched it a moment. Normal.

"IV with, what, boys, D5?" Anne asked the EMTs. They nodded, breathing heavily. "D5, Doc," Anne said.

"Pupils equal and reactive," Zack said, "but we got some bleeding here."

I walked over and leaned across the patient, bending past the EMT, who sidled out of the way. "It was like that when we picked him up, Doc. Family said they came in and found him acting crazy."

"Bleeding?"

"Yeah. Right here." The EMT pushed back on the patient's straining head, avoiding the teeth that tried to bite. "Just under the eyebrow."

I pulled a penlight from my pocket and shined it at the man's left eye. "Pad." I held out my hand and a 4×4 gauze pad was placed there by someone. Patting at the wound, I was careful not to apply pressure as I removed the dried blood and fluid tangled in his brow hair and lashes. I froze.

It was a one-centimeter circular wound placed just below the supraorbital notch. Edges were sharply demarcated, and there was some swelling already. It was a strange wound. I had never seen anything quite like it.

Except at Marisa's just this morning...

I stepped back. *Marisa had been raving.... Marisa had bruises.* I leaned in again and pulled back the man's sleeves. No bruises. But there was a faint odor. I sniffed. Not alcohol. Some chemical, familiar as my days in medical school. My heart rate picked up speed.

"I want a stat drug screen and ETOH," I said, meaning a blood alcohol. "CBC, a seven, cath UA, and save all urine for possible later tests. Make sure the chain of custody is properly handled. No clerical errors. Get X-ray down here for a portable AP lateral skull series, and guys—" I looked up at the EMTs "—cut his clothes off for me and put them in something that will seal. Give them to me." If the EMTs thought it an odd request for me to want the patient's clothes, they didn't say so. They each pulled out a pair of surgical scissors and started cutting through the layers of clothing.

"And check his pockets for drug paraphernalia—needles and syringes." *The patient last night had a syringe in his pocket...* The thought intruded. I shook it off.

"Find out if he's got any allergies. If not, I want Ativan IV, two milligrams push, *now,* and tritrate up till he gets quiet. No more than six milligrams total though," I said to Zack as he started for the drug room. I turned to the venipuncture tech from the lab. "Tell whoever's on duty tonight to do the drug screen first and they can worry about controls later. I need those results now. Oh, and add a PCP to the standard six-drug testing panel."

"Yes, ma'am," she said.

Pushing Anne gently out of the way, I started on neuro-checks.

Pupils were equal and reactive, left and right reflexes equal on both sides, and his heart beat steadily, smoothly. His breathing passages were clear and equal. "Soon as you get him calm, I want blood pressures on both sides, lying down and sitting up, if you can," I said to no one in particular. I knew it would be done. "But right now, finish stripping him and let me take a look at his buttocks. See if there is a puncture wound from a recent injection. Possibly traumatic."

The EMTs pulled the patient's clothes off of him and bundled them up into a five-gallon plastic bag. The strange scent I had noticed was stronger as the clothes were waved through the air. "I want the sheets underneath him now and the ones from the ambulance stretcher put in separate bags and sealed," I directed.

"Do we know who he is?" I asked. "I want to talk with his family."

"He's got a mother outside, and a brother," one of the EMTs said. "They're filling out a chart."

I turned to Anne, who was getting ready to catheterize the patient. "Get them for me, will you please, as soon as you have that urine sample to the lab. Take the family to the office and see that there are chairs for both of them. Would you help out?" I asked the EMTs.

"What's going on, Doc?" one asked.

I had forgotten his name and discreetly checked his name badge. "Buzzy, I'm not sure, but last night we had another patient with similar symptoms." In a softer voice, I added, "Two weeks or so ago, two EMTs brought in a third patient just like this. Mrs. Braswell, Dr. Braswell's wife. I want you to find out which EMTs answered her call then and tell them that the cops may need to talk to them. Have them on hold, okay?"

He looked puzzled but agreed. I turned my eyes away for moment, fighting a peculiar pain in the pit of my stomach, as if something was in there, clawing its way out. *I had to be wrong... I had to.*

Anne took the urine to the lab on the run and Zack pushed two milligrams of Ativan into the IV lock, watching the patient to see if he would respond.

"Allergies?" I asked.

"None, according to his mother. Smokes a pack a day and drinks, though."

"Drugs?" Meaning the illegal type.

"Nothing they would admit to."

The patient was naked. I indicated he should be rolled away from me so I could view his buttocks. They were clear. No puncture wound. No bruise. No six-inch-long scratch.

I was unaccountably disappointed. I stepped back and the patient was returned to a supine position. He began to grow quiet as the meds worked their way into his system. Anne, back from the lab, replaced his restraints loosely. As she did, I checked the patient's upper arms. And found a recent puncture mark. No bruise, just a raised, hard spot centered with a puncture mark. I would not have noticed it had I not been looking specifically for it.

A portable X-ray machine hummed down the hallway.

"Check his pressure. Stop the Ativan. Give him a minute or two."

Zack pulled the needle from the plastic lock in the patient's IV line.

"How old is he?" I asked.

"Mid-twenties," Zack said. "Uh, twenty-four," he amended, looking at the chart on the bed.

I stepped back and watched as Bev the Sloth slowly positioned a metal film cassette beneath the patient's head. He fell silent while I watched, as the Ativan did its job and he relaxed against the restraints. Bev moved as if she might take root at any minute, but I knew the films would be perfect the first time. She was slow, but she was efficient.

I watched his eyes. Baby-doll eyes, back and forth, back and forth, slowly. A sign of some neurological problem. His chest rose and fell. I left the room.

Marisa's eyes had not done that.... Surely that was a good sign....

"His mother and brother are in the office, Dr. Lynch. The brother's ETOH." Which meant he had been drinking.

I checked the lead-two tracing of the heart monitor. AP wave appeared and then disappeared. Appeared again. The man was in mild, intermittent AV block. I wondered if it would self-convert as in my last odd patient.

"Thanks," I said, heading up the hall to the office the contract doctors used. The door was open a crack. "Come get me if there are any changes and call Russell. I'm probably going to want a head scan. Maybe two. And tell the lab to step on it with the drug screen. And don't forget to hold all urine and blood."

Zack nodded. I opened the door to the office and stepped inside.

The woman was in her early forties, with hair the shade of hickory, lightly streaked with gray. She was plump, wearing a red, down-filled coat that made her appear even larger, and jeans with loafers. She had sad eyes, wide with fright, brown, like her sons'. Both sons.

The boy beside her was in his early twenties with bloodshot eyes and a scraggly attempt at a beard. He stank of beer and body sweat, but he didn't seem angry, which was a blessing. I hated to throw the woman's son in jail while she was facing an emergency, but I would if the boy and the beer didn't mix well. I had done it before.

I introduced myself and asked the patient's name as well as the mother's. Raymond Abel was the man on the stretcher. The mother was Rebecca Abel.

"Mrs. Abel. Your son is evidencing some peculiar neurological changes," I started. Rebecca's eyes began to water. She twisted her hands in the pockets of her big coat. "It could be caused by any number of things from stroke to trauma to drug use. I need you to tell me honestly about any drug use Raymond might be involved in. I'm not a cop, and I frankly don't care about illegalities. I have no intention of reporting him to the cops if he *has* been using drugs. I just need to know what, if anything, he has been taking.''

The RN had asked the same question, but sometimes stories changed in a matter of moments when a grave picture began to emerge. I wanted to frighten them both enough to get the truth but not enough to make them difficult to handle. I needed them both strong and able to think rationally.

''Ray drinks too much. His daddy done the same. But both my boys stay off drugs, Doctor.'' She turned to the boy beside her. ''Lloyd, you know anything I should tell the doctor?''

Lloyd reddened and looked at the floor.

''I need to know. To help your brother,'' I said gently. ''Protecting him now won't help.''

Lloyd shrugged, his shoulders bony beneath a flannel shirt. ''He done some pot a few times, I don't think he does it anymore, Mama. He just tried it a few times.''

''That's all? Just marijuana?''

''Yeah. 'S'all. Sorry, Mama. He told me not to tell.''

Rebecca's sad eyes looked hollow as she stared at the boy beside her. He avoided her gaze.

''Will you tell me how you found Ray?'' I said. ''Everything he might have done today? Anyone he might have seen?''

Lloyd's eyes darted away. The boy knew something he didn't want Mama to know.

''Well, we come home about eight-thirty from the

store and Ray was standing in the middle of the living room kindly weaving," Rebecca said in the vernacular peculiar to the region, "like he'd been drinking. But I couldn't smell no alcohol on him, just something like he gets on him when he works on cars down to the shop. He works some at the McArdles Auto and Cycle Repair down to Biddles Street. You know it?" she asked.

"No, ma'am, I don't. But Ray works on cars? Was he doing that today?"

Rebecca looked to Lloyd for confirmation. The boy looked away again and mumbled something. Rebecca stood up and grabbed his chin in surprisingly strong fingers. I watched in fascination as she forced his face to hers. "You got something to say you say it now. If I find you didn't say it and it ends up hurting your brother, I'll deal with you later. And you won't like it." Her voice was low and forceful and I wouldn't want to be the one she was threatening. I had no doubt this woman always carried out a threat. Lloyd thought so, too.

He pulled his chin away and rubbed the reddened flesh with his fist. "Ray laid out today down to the shop. He played pool a while and then he and some buddies done went riding. I don't know where. And I don't know who he was out with, Mama. Honest. He don't always tell me everything. And he's been being awful quiet lately."

"Like he was the time he got in trouble?"

"Yes, ma'am. Sort a'."

Rebecca turned in her chair to face me. "My boys was raised without a daddy. I tanned their hides good when they needed it, yet and still they got into trouble a time or two. Ray fell in with a bad crowd and got drunk one night. The boys done robbed a store and beat up the clerk. Spent three years in jail. He's on parole. And if he's running with that crowd again, I'll call his parole officer myself if I can prove it."

I nodded. "Did he look as if he had fallen in the house? Was anything there indicative of a crime or a problem before you got home?"

"Place looked like it always does. Except the TV weren't on. Ray likes Vanna and watches *Wheel of Fortune* every day, even the reruns. And the TV weren't on."

"How long had he been there, before you got there?"

"Lloyd and me left to go to the store 'bout seven, so no more than a hour and a half."

"How did he get home? Did he drive himself?"

Rebecca and Lloyd looked at one another. Lloyd answered. "I didn't think about it, but his car was parked in the ditch, Mama. And Ray would never put his car in the ditch. He loves that car. Keeps it covered with a silk topper to keep the water and dust off. Painted and detailed it hisself," he finished, most of the last of it to me.

"So it's possible someone else drove him home and parked the car, or that he drove himself home but wasn't acting like himself at the time."

Mother and brother nodded, both sets of eyes wide now.

"Thanks. Will you wait in the waiting room, and I'll come talk to you soon. I have to get some tests back before I'll know what happened to Ray, but we're taking good care of him, Rebecca."

She took my hand and held it. Her fingers were icy. "Thanks, Doctor."

I followed the mother and son down the hallway, past the closed door where Anne and Zack were working on Raymond. The woman paused and put her hand up to the door as if to knock, but then opened her fist, placing the open hand against the steel fire door for a moment. Slowly then, she turned and followed her young son back to the waiting room. I was thankful to whomever had pulled the door to.

Anne opened the door and stuck out her head. She was blond and tall and had solemn blue eyes. "Doc, the X rays are in the fracture room on the view-box. CBC and seven are on the chart."

"Anything out of range?"

"No, ma'am."

"Thanks. How's he doing?"

"Quiet. Zack's monitoring him."

"How long on the UDS?" I asked, referring to the urine drug screen.

"Couple more minutes, Doc."

I nodded and pivoted on my left foot for the fracture room. The overhead light had been turned out and the view-box was the only illumination, a harsh white light shining through the films of the boy's head.

I studied them silently. I had ordered the AP lateral skull series in the hope that I would find the cause of the small wound in Ray's forehead. But I hadn't really expected to find a bullet, a shotgun pellet, some foreign body lodged there. And I had been right. There was nothing. The X rays were pretty much normal. Sighing, I turned and made my way back in to the light. In the trauma room, I asked Anne if Russell had called back. I was now certain I would need a set of CT scans.

"He's on the way, Dr. Lynch. He'll be here in about five minutes or so," she said. She was hooking an oxygen mask to Ray's face, two small cannulae inserted into his nostrils. I said nothing and went back to the unrevealing X rays, standing in the dark for the five minutes until Russell arrived. My eyes roved the contours of the boy's head, followed the shape of his mandibles and the wide openings of orbital bone. But not really seeing.

Just thinking of Marisa.

My fingertips itched, a feeling I had often in medical school when faced with a problem I was certain I understood but hadn't yet proved. And my stomach ached with a deep burning, acid on tender tissue. I knew what had happened to this patient. I was sure of it. And that meant I knew what had happened to Marisa.

The doorway darkened behind me and I turned. "Hey, Rhea. Anne said you would need me. What do you want?"

I told Chris Russell briefly about the patient, his lab results and the negative X rays, the way he had been found, the small wound above his eye. He stood beside me in the dark, little more than a shadow in street clothes, listening, asking a few pointed questions. Finally I said, "I want an unenhanced CT of the head, followed by a scan of his orbit at one-millimeter increments shot at oblique angles." I took a deep breath. "Pretty much the same series you would have done on Marisa Braswell if you'd been allowed to shoot them, except the angle I'm looking for is above the eye, not below.''

"What are you looking for, Rhea?" he asked softly.

After a moment I said, "A sign of a small hole created by a foreign object, moving from the supra-orbital notch up through the sinus cavity into the brain. Chris, I think this boy's been lobotomized.''

11

Fine Dinners and AV Block

Chris didn't ask the obvious question about Marisa. I didn't volunteer an opinion. After a moment he turned and left the fracture room, his shadow throwing a long band of darkness across me. Voices came from the hallway. Orders given in Chris's specific, low tone. Anne replying. The phone rang and Zack answered. A stretcher with a squealing wheel made its way up the hall, taking my latest patient for his CAT scan.

I heard it all but didn't react to it. I simply kept seeing Marisa's face, skin slack, drool accumulated on her chin, her eyes vacant. I felt cold and far too warm at once. Finally, I stepped from the blackness of the room to the hallway and stopped Bess on her way back to the lab. Her shoulders drooped, and her hair was hanging in strands. Back-to-back double shifts was a problem for all hospital employees, and with staff cutbacks was an increasingly recurring problem.

"Bess. Did we hear from the reference lab about the contents of that syringe?"

"Uh, just a minute, Doc. I'll check. I think I did

hear the fax working during supper. I forgot to look.''

A moment later Bess was back with a detailed report from the lab in Charlotte. They had isolated and identified a drug. Perhaps I should have reacted, felt some passion, some excitement at the possibility of a diagnosis of my cattle-bruised patient from the day before. Instead, the specter of Marisa's face hung in my memory, blocking out all lesser emotions as I scanned the page.

I skipped the chemical structure gobbledygook and focused on the chemical name at the bottom of the fax sheet. *Xylazine.* It meant nothing to me. It wasn't a common street drug. I wasn't familiar with the chemical composition as I finally studied it.

Pulling a PDR—a *Physician's Desk Reference*—from the shelves, I flipped through its two thousand-some pages until I found the listing. Xylazine. Common name Rompun. It was a sedative for large herbivores, used mostly for cattle. Its use in humans had been restricted as it caused several dangerous side effects. Among which were vomiting and mild AV block, which self-converted as the drug left the patient's system. ''Well, well, well,'' I said softly.

My patient of the night before had been found on a cattle farm. How convenient. Was someone borrowing the sedative and using it as a cheap designer drug? I looked up and found DeeDee sharing a hand of cards with Zack. She was beating him at some form of rummy, and had a stack of the poor man's pennies at her side. ''DeeDee.'' I walked over. ''Got a minute?''

"Of course, dear." She expertly folded her hand and pocketed her winnings.

Zack looked rueful. "Thought I had you this time, Miss DeeDee." He looked up at me. "I actually beat her about one game in five."

"Good odds for an amateur," I said, smiling. I didn't tell him I had once cleaned house playing cards with DeeDee. Wiped her out of pennies, nickels and dimes, too, in a memorable session in my senior year of high school. I had never repeated the performance, but I never let DeeDee forget it, either. I always hoped I'd beat her so soundly again, but never had.

"What can I do for you, dear?"

I held the PDR out to her. "You ever hear of Rompun? It's a sedative used primarily in cattle."

"Of course, Rhea, dear. Everyone uses Rompun. It's one of the least expensive and easily obtainable sedatives on the market." She looked up at me, her blue eyes wide and curious. "There isn't a farm in the county without it on a shelf somewhere. I even used it once or twice at the horse farm, though I prefer other medications for my horses. Why?"

I could rule out its being difficult to obtain. Thoughtfully, I closed the PDR with a finger inside to mark the page. "I had a patient with a syringe in his pocket. The reference lab in Charlotte tells me it held Rompun."

"Oh." DeeDee's eyes looked blank a moment. "Are you going to eat some dinner, Rhea, dear? I'll fix you a plate before I go if you like."

"Thanks, Miss DeeDee. Sounds good."

Distracted, I studied the details of Xylazine in the

PDR, carrying the book with me back to the desk. The details on Xylazine/Rompun's reactions in humans was sketchy at best. In low doses a patient would have the type of problems I was seeing—blood pressure fluctuations, AV block, vomiting. In higher doses the situation changed drastically. As little as ten milliliters could kill. Remembering the position of the needle broken off in Willie Evans's buttock, I didn't think he had administered the dose himself. Considering the extent of the needle trauma, I thought it likely he had resisted the injection....

After a moment, I lifted the phone and dialed the lab, asking for Bess when it was answered.

"Yes, ma'am?"

"Bess, you ever hear of a Liebermann test?"

"No, ma'am. But I can look it up."

"Good. If you can do it in our lab, I'd like one on the John Doe from last night. He's been identified as Willie Evans, by the way. And one on this patient, ah..." I checked his chart, having forgotten his name. "Raymond Abel."

"Will do, Doc."

We hung up the phone and I considered my next move. I had to get Marisa back into the hospital for more tests. Tonight. *Now.* But she wasn't my patient, and I couldn't exactly call up Shobani and demand her return. And according to Marisa's chart, she had never been in AV block. I had studied the EKG traces myself. No indication of Rompun side effects...

Interrupting my musings, a cop came in to be treated for a knife slice to the upper arm. It was Bobby Ray Shirley, good ol' boy with the ubiquitous beer gut and a shiny bald pate. The cut wasn't deep and didn't require stitches. I had Anne clean and Steri-Strip it and ordered a tetanus just to be safe. It wasn't a difficult wound to treat and I didn't have to focus on it, my mind returning to my other patients. My attention didn't center again on the cop until I heard Anne talking to him about a rape case in Ford County. A case that involved Eddie Braswell.

The sound of the name brought me back to the door. "Eddie Braswell?"

Bobby Ray looked up. "You know the daddy, too, I take it." I nodded. "His kid was out on bail. Took hisself to Ford County to find and rape a girl there. Old girlfriend. They got him locked up and this time his dear old *daddy* can't pull strings to get him loose." The accent on the word *daddy* was derisive.

"Steven Braswell pulled strings? To get Eddie out on bail after he assaulted his teacher?" I clarified. I wanted to be certain what I was hearing.

The tired cop winced at Anne's ministrations. "You got it. The doctor plays golf with the judge, is the way I hear it. Probably lets the judge play double mulligans and not count it. And now this little gal in Ford has to pay the price."

I nodded and left the room, wondering. *Was Marisa also paying the price for something Eddie did? And would this be the final blow causing Steven to fall apart...?*

A four-year-old kid was carried in with bilateral earaches, his face red and swollen with tears. His mother was not in much better shape herself. I treated the child, whose left eardrum was perforated, and referred him to a specialist in Ford County. He would probably need tubes in both ears, which meant surgery, and I wasn't certain about the extent of his hearing loss.

As the kid and mom left the building, Bess called me from the lab. "Yes," I said, taking the phone, "what have you got?"

"Two things. First, your drug screen is negative. Second, Liebermann testing is really easy, Doc, but you do know it's just a screening test, don't you?"

"Yeah, I know. Make my day and tell me both patients are positive."

Bess laughed. "Just count me as your personal genie in a bottle. Positive results on both Evans and Abel. Want I should send them both off to the reference lab for confirmation?"

"Please. And Bess, I know it's a lot of trouble, but would you send a courier and get it done tonight? I really need those results."

She sighed. "I'll call Mike and get him to set it up. The lab manager has to approve all courier requests right now, what with the patient census being so low and all."

"Thanks. I really do appreciate all you're doing for me. How are the kids? Making it through flu season okay?"

Her voice brightened. "Just fine. Missing their mommy, but I'll have tomorrow off. I thought I'd take them to the video store and let them pig out on Disney."

I laughed, seeing Marisa in my mind. She had been Snow White in the junior-high play. I had been a dwarf. *Doc*, oddly enough. If Bess heard the hollow tone of my laughter, she didn't comment. I hung up the phone.

Eighth grade had been my last year of private school. After that I had attended public school, as Mama alternately hoarded and drank away her last emotional and financial resources. Different schools had made a friendship with Marisa Stowe difficult, as she continued in the private prep schools that a young woman of her social standing was expected to attend. Yet we always found time and means to visit. We had managed.

"Zack. Where is that bag with Raymond's clothes in it?"

Zack got up from the break table and the cooling plate of food dished up by DeeDee and vanished into the soiled utility room.

"You should let that young man eat, Rhea. He's skinny as a rail. And you should eat, too. Your plate is getting cold."

"I am, Miss DeeDee. In just a minute."

"Uh-huh. I've heard that before. Well, you bring my broiler pan back tomorrow. And it had better be empty. Eat!" she commanded as she slid into her coat and walked out the door. My response was lost on the cold air that blasted in on her wake.

"Clothes, Dr. Lynch. Bag still sealed." He handed me three plastic bags, each containing one red bio-hazard bag. "Sheets from the stretcher." He pointed. "Sheets from the ambulance."

"Thanks." I placed all three on the countertop and opened the one with Raymond Abel's clothes. The scent that met my nose was unmistakable. I sealed up the bag again and reached once more for the phone.

The number was as familiar and fresh as my own; odd, as I hadn't dialed it in months.

The phone picked up. Music played in the background. I think it was Clint Black, singing about a lost love. "Yeeellow."

"Pink," I said automatically. He said nothing. "Or is it green tonight? I always did get the code mixed up." He didn't laugh. Flushed with embarrassment, I turned on my professional voice. "Look, Mark, sorry if I caught you at a bad time, but I have a problem with that John Doe you identified as Willie Evans."

"What." It wasn't a question exactly. More in the nature of a demand to tell all.

"It turns out he had a cattle sedative in his system. I think it's possible it was administered against his will."

The music disappeared from the background. "I'll be there in ten." The phone went dead.

"Nice talking to you, too." I hung the phone up, wondering if he had been alone or if he had to ditch some woman before he could leave. Mark was popular with the ladies in the county, having a steady job, a uniform, a devilishly good-looking, square-jawed face, green eyes, and the land and money he had inherited from his grandfather. After a moment, I shrugged and went to treat another patient, a sore throat and fever. I couldn't worry about some dumb cop's bad manners.

I was free when Mark came breezing into the E.R., wearing skintight jeans, a brown flannel shirt with a

T-shirt beneath, and lace-up boots. Trish was there as well and sighed softly. Mark had that effect on some women. I straightened my spine and, without a word, led him into my office.

Carefully, I left the door open as I went behind my desk. Mark pushed it to behind him. I ignored the shot of adrenaline through my system at the slight snicking sound of its closing. I expected him to be wearing a look of amusement when I turned to face him, but he was serious, green eyes steady and intent. I handed him the bag of Raymond Abel's clothes. "Sniff."

"Good evening to you, ma'am. My, don't you look just ravishing tonight."

An unwilling grin crossed my face. "Passed Miss DeeDee's car on the way in, did you?"

Mark grinned. "Guilty. But you do look good." He opened the bag and lifted it to his nose. A frown crossed his face. "What is it?"

I sat in the high-backed chair behind the desk and laced my fingers across my stomach. "I think it's chloroform. After I tell you what I know, you might want to have those clothes analyzed for trace chemicals. Have a seat."

I told Mark about the John Doe he had identified as Willie Evans. About the transient, self-converting AV block, the needle in his backside and the syringe in his pocket. About the chemical analyzed from the syringe. And then I told him about Raymond Abel and the similarity of the two men's heart tracings. "Both men have positive screening tests for a drug called Xylazine in their systems. I think, from the location of the needle marks and the trauma surrounding one of the injection sites, that both men were given the sedative by someone else. Possibly against their will." I took a deep breath. "And I think it's possible that both men were lobotomized."

I paused, waiting for some reaction from him. When there wasn't one and the silence between us lengthened, I asked. "You understand what I mean when I say lobotomized?"

"Not really." Mark's eyes slowly focused on me as he came back from some distant place in his own mind. He sat up in his chair. "Tell me about it."

"It is a surgical procedure. In the past—like twenty, thirty years ago—under some conditions— like severe, uncontrolled seizures or mental illness that could not be relieved by medication or therapy—a doctor might have recommended a lobotomy. The procedure was done under sedation and could be performed in one of three ways. Either the skull was opened and a small portion of the brain removed, or a sharp object was shoved up through the sinus cavity from beneath the eyebrow into the brain. In the third method, a similar instrument was shoved up through the nostril into the brain. The last kind of lobotomy can only be diagnosed with a CT scan, what we call a CAT scan. There are few physical indications that the surgery has been performed when the nostril has been used as the point of entry into the brain."

Mark's eyes narrowed.

"Lobotomies lost favor when the procedure left most patients unable to communicate, violent or abnormally passive. Some were catatonic." Marisa's vacant stare called to me. *Please God, let me be wrong...*

"Jeez. You doctors are more barbaric than some of the guys I try to put away. Sounds like something out of *Planet of the Apes*."

I nodded. I had seen the movie and the human character with the horrible scar over his temple. His eyes had been like Marisa's. Empty. I looked down at my hands. "I think it is possible that both men were given Xylazine and then lobotomized by the second method. I have tests being performed now on the patient brought in tonight. Raymond Abel, the patient I'm referring to, has a small, sharply demarcated...hole, I guess is the best way to say it...under his left brow bone. I'm getting ready to call Richland and ask to speak to Willie Evans's admitting doctor to see if he will order confirmatory tests, too."

I looked up. "You may have heard of Xylazine. It's used on cattle farms under the name of Rompun and was never intended for use by humans because of the side effects. Because tests are positive, you may have a series of injuries in this county."

"Series usually means more than two," he said slowly.

I had trouble finding air to speak. When the words came, they were low and without force. "I think Marisa might be one of three."

"Your friend?"

"When I came home, I discovered she had been diagnosed with a stroke. Anne and Zack, the RNs on duty with me tonight, were the crew working when she was brought in, but I haven't had a chance to question them about her. However, she has some striking similarities with the patient tonight. Willie Evans might share the same symptom—a hole at the supraorbital notch—'' I pointed up under my own eyebrow "—but he was traumatized by the cattle. If it is there, I missed it.''

"When will you know?"

"About my patient? In an hour or so. About Willie Evans, later tonight, if I can get the doctor up there to cooperate. About Marisa…she's not my patient." I paused. "Off the record?"

Mark nodded, his face grave.

"She has the same kind of hole. I slipped in to see her against her husband's wishes and treated her without his knowledge."

"I didn't hear that."

"Okay."

"And you are not to repeat it under any circumstances to anyone else. It did not happen. Understand?"

"Yeah." I looked back at my hands. "Thanks."

"Tell me what you know about Mitchell Scoggins."

I looked up in surprise at the non sequitur. "He's a lawyer. And according to rumor he is part of a corporation called Medicom Plus, building doc-in-the-boxes for the new chemical plants coming to town."

"That all you know?"

"I…yeah. Trish knows more about him. Apparently he tried to pick her up one night at a bar. You might ask her."

"Mitch has hit on most everything female in the county. But I'll ask. She working tonight?"

"That was her standing beside me when you came in tonight."

"Yeah?" Mark smiled, his green eyes twinkling. "When I see you, I don't tend to notice much else. I'll ask around, talk to them all. Let you know what I find out."

"Mark?"

He waited, eyes curious. I hadn't told him about Eddie...but then I didn't know anything, did I? Not really. Yet, Eddie was likely doing drugs, growing violent, striking out against women in sexually dominant ways. Had Marisa been his first victim?

"Can you find out something for me? Find out if Eddie Braswell was out of jail at the time of the attacks on Willie Evans and Raymond Abel...." My voice trailed off.

Mark nodded, his eyes slightly out of focus again as he processed my question in light of recent developments. His lips thinned in concentration. "Yeah. Yeah, I can do that," he said, though I didn't know if he was talking to himself or answering my question.

And suddenly his chair was empty. Mark was gone, leaving the door hanging open. I touched my cheek. It was hot with a blush I hoped he hadn't seen. Taking a moment to compose myself, I followed him into the hallway.

12

Bag Balm and Competition

Reaching the admitting doctor in Richland had been easy for once and, for once, a doctor in the huge hospital had been cooperative. He had immediately ordered a comparable CAT scan on Willie Evans to determine if a traumatic injury had taken place. And he was gratified to discover why his patient had converted from AV block to a perfectly normal sinus rhythm and normal blood pressure. He promised to contact me before morning with the scan's results. If I hadn't been so concerned about Marisa, I would have been overjoyed at the progress I was making on two difficult diagnoses.

Worried, I treated patients for two hours as the clock approached midnight. Mark questioned Trish, Anne and Zack about Marisa, Willie Evans, Raymond Abel and Mitchell Scoggins, calling each of the employees back to my office for a private discussion. He hadn't asked for its use and I hadn't complained at what might be termed his high-handedness. I wanted answers, and an infantile desire to defend my turf would not accomplish my goals.

As I worked, I tried to remember any gossip I had

heard in the last year about the lawyer, but it had gone in one ear and out the other. I wondered why Mark had asked about him....

"You got a minute?"

I looked up from the sink where I was washing my hands with antibacterial soap. The harsh soap stung my chapped hands and I had left my oil in my bag. I reached for the Bag Balm and smeared a generous portion of the greasy gel into my skin. Mark leaned against the door frame and watched. "You know what they use that stuff for?"

"To keep cow udders from chapping in winter," I said matter-of-factly. "It works on human hands too. Want a cup of coffee?"

"Sounds good."

He followed me into the break room, watched as I poured steaming coffee, and accepted a foam cup from me. The coffee was several hours old and smelled like burnt oil, but I drank it gratefully. I needed something to keep me going. I hadn't had a full night's sleep in days.

"Zack says there was blood coming from Marisa Braswell's eye the night she was brought in. Same kind of wound as your patient tonight."

I looked down at the cup I was holding. Tears made the surface of the coffee waver. I said nothing. I had been right. I wished to God I had been wrong. Mark continued.

"I had a subpoena delivered and asked Zack to pull her chart. There is no mention of that blood or that wound in the doctor's notes. No mention of some bruises on her wrists and ankles that both Zack and Anne told me about. And some bruises on her neck. Off the record, have you seen these bruises?''

I nodded, blinking back the tears. ''I have pictures of them. And she has a long healing scratch across her buttock that might have been made during an attempt to dose her with Rompun.''

Mark did not respond to my comment, but went on as if he hadn't heard me at all. ''Would that be odd? A doctor not writing up a wound or an injury like that. Not making note of bruises that might point to assault?''

''Not if he thought that the injuries occurred during restraint of the patient at the scene. Not if he was her husband and was so distraught that he was not thinking clearly.'' My face finally composed, I looked up at Mark. ''Steven was at the hospital for the twelve hours prior to Marisa's being brought in. He was working my shift. If he'd been at home he might have helped her sooner. Might have known she was in trouble. I think he was working under tremendous strain while he was treating his wife. So, no. I don't think it odd that anything might have been left out of his notes.

''My problem with Marisa is that her diagnosis was not revised during her stay, and the tests that might have confirmed or changed her diagnosis were not completed.''

''I need to talk to the EMTs who brought Marisa in the night of her stroke.'' Mark glanced at his watch. It was one of those bulky black plastic things worn by divers, lined all around with knobs for various functions. ''If the EMTs caused the bruising on her wrists and ankles...'' He stopped.

I gave him the EMTs' names and lifted the cooled coffee to my lips. It was tasteless and thick, like black mud, and I drank all of it. "You can call the ambulance dispatcher and tell him to have the EMTs meet you up at the law center at your convenience. I had them notified that they might be needed."

Mark's eyebrows lifted. "Why, thank you, Dr. Lynch. I would never have thought about that on my own."

I smiled slightly, watching the coffee dregs swirl around the uneven bottom of the cup. "Butting my way into your case?"

"My thought exactly."

"I'll keep out of it," I said.

Mark laughed and stood, tossing his empty cup into the open can at the back of the room. "Fat chance of your keeping that promise."

"It wasn't a promise, exactly."

"Rhea. I'll keep you informed. When you know something about the—" He broke off, his eyes falling on Chris Russell walking down the hallway from X-ray. "That the answers we're waiting on?"

Shaky from fear and the sudden burst of caffeine I had swallowed, I stood and walked to Chris. His lean face was grave. Without speaking, he led the way into the fracture room and flipped on the lighted view-box. With practiced ease, he shoved film after film up in the clips at the top. The dark contours of skull and brain came clear. Even I could make out the pattern of blood pooled between layers of tissue surrounding Raymond Abel's brain.

"Patient has a now-familiar, yet abnormal pattern to bleed suggesting some sort of trauma. Note the hemorrhagic changes in the frontal lobe, with both a subarachnoid hemorrhage and a subdural hemorrhage. I would have picked this up on a standard ten-millimeter scan with no problem. What we see with the one-millimeter scan is a bit more conclusive as to the type of trauma that caused the bleeds." Chris's voice was calm and reasoned, as precise as if he had rehearsed it word for word before walking down the hallway toward me.

"Note the dark cavity beginning just above the supraorbital notch and entering the sinus cavity here." He pointed to the round dark stain on one film. "It moves through the sinus cavity up through the dura mater and into the cortex, here. We have some beam hardening here and here—" he pointed to some dark and light areas in the cavity and in the area of the brain's lining "—which could be CSF or blood or even clots."

I said nothing. The silence seemed to ripple out in the small room.

"All this sounds vaguely interesting, but what does it mean? In plain English, please," Mark said. "Is this the lobotomy you were talking about?"

When Chris didn't answer, I said, "Yes. It is."

"Any way the man could have done this to himself? Injured himself like this?"

Chris turned and stared at Mark in the darkened room. "I don't see how. If he shot himself in an aborted suicide attempt, there would be some indication of burning around the entry hole. There would be an exit hole or some kind of pellet on his films. If he accidentally rammed something up his head in a fall, there would be tremendous trauma in getting himself off the object or the object would still be in place. There isn't. It isn't.'' Chris's face twisted in the strange light, half of his expression in darkness, half in harsh brightness. "This guy didn't get hurt while running with a pair of scissors in his hand.'' The sarcasm hung heavy in the air. I didn't turn, staring at the films hung on the box.

Mark said mildly, "I have to be sure, Doctor. And I don't have the medical terminology. I thank you for making it clear.''

Chris shrugged. "Yeah. Well.''

"This is what you would have seen in a similar scan of Marisa Braswell's orbit, isn't it?'' I asked.

"I don't know. I expected to see some sort of trauma that occurred after the stroke, as in a postictal fall. An orbital fracture of some sort. But with the similarity of the bleeds in Mrs. Braswell and the last two patients... I just don't know, Rhea.''

"Chris, I have a friend at Duke who wants to see these films. He's a neurosurgery resident, fourth year. Would you object if I get a second opinion on MODIS?''

"Would you object if I sit in?'' he asked.

I turned from the scans and smiled. "I'd appreciate it. Cam Reston tends to talk over my head sometimes. You can interpret for me.''

Mark snorted. "Glad I'm not the only one who needs interpretation. This guy's family here? I need to see the crime scene. Ask some questions.''

"Out front. Mother's name is Rebecca. She's with a younger son, name of Lloyd, and he's just a bit drunk. Or he was when I saw them two hours ago.

Let me bring them in and tell them about Raymond, then you can have them in my office.''

Mark raised an eyebrow. ''*My* case, remember?''

''Not till I've done *my* job. *My* E.R. Remember?''

Mark shrugged. ''Any objection to my sitting in on the conference, *Doctor?*''

''None whatsoever, *Captain.*''

Chris looked back and forth between us, a quizzical expression on his face. ''Am I missing something here?''

''Not really. Just establishing boundaries,'' I said. ''I'll be ready for MODIS in about ten minutes, Chris. And thanks for coming in tonight.''

''Lately when you're working, I think I live here at night,'' he grumbled.

Minutes later I was in my office with the Abels, the mother tired and wan, with deep circles like bruises beneath her eyes, the son nearly sober. The wait had been good for the kid, hard on the mother. Rebecca looked from me to Mark with red-rimmed eyes, the question clear in them.

''Sit down, Rebecca.'' I was pleased when Lloyd moved to stand behind his mother's chair and placed a hand on her shoulder. Rebecca would need a lot of support. I hoped her younger son would provide it. ''Ms. Abel, I asked Captain Stafford to sit in on our talk. It seems your son Raymond was assaulted.''

Lloyd's hand tightened on her shoulder.

''Rebecca, Raymond has received an injury to his brain. A trauma. The result of that trauma is a bleed inside his head next to his brain.'' I spoke slowly, watching her face. Her lips tightened as I spoke, and Lloyd's hand gripped the red down-filled coat.

"There is some brain damage, but at this time I don't know what the result will be in terms of impairment or loss of function. I want to fly Raymond to Duke Medical Center and put him under the care of a specialist there. Someone I know and trust. I know that is a long way from home, and if you would rather a hospital closer, or if your insurance won't pay for Duke, we can arrange that instead. But I would feel really good if he went to Duke. I think with the type of injury Ray has, Duke will offer him the best chance of improvement."

Rebecca waited, eyes boring hard into mine.

"They can do things there like neural imaging. A test called a positron emission tomography scan and an MRI—magnetic resonance imaging—could greatly improve his chance for fuller recovery. They have all these testing capabilities at Duke, but if that is too far away—"

"I got a sister lives not far from Raleigh," she interrupted. "I can stay with her while Ray is getting better."

I nodded. "Fine. I know a doctor there who will likely be willing to look at his case."

"You say he was assaulted. You mean like someone hit him on the head?"

I glanced at Mark. "Not exactly. Rebecca, it looks like someone put a spike or something up into Ray's head. Into his brain. That is what the bleeding under his eye was, the hole up into his brain. And now his brain is bleeding. I'm sorry, but now Captain Stafford is going to have to ask you some questions so he can try to find out who did this to Raymond."

"But I want to go with my son to the hospital."

"And you can. If you like, I will see if you can fly up with him on the helicopter. But it will take me quite a while to arrange transport, and then the helicopter from Duke has to make the trip here. In the meantime, you need to answer the officer's questions. Can you do that?"

Tears welled up in Rebecca Abel's eyes. I hated to force her to answer Mark's questions. It wouldn't be easy on her, not with her son in the next room, and the sense of helplessness she must surely be feeling.

"I know it's hard. I'm sorry." I glanced up at Mark. He was wearing his professional face, watching both mother and son. I knew he would consider the two closest to Raymond as primary suspects until someone better came along. But for Rebecca's sake I hoped he remembered the others with similar injuries and tried for a tie-in before he charged the wrong person. Quietly, I left the room.

13

Too Little Sleep and Kernig's Test

I went online with Cam at Duke just a little before 1:00 a.m. He was napping in the doctors' lounge, awaiting my call. Instantly awake, he instructed me in the use of the MODIS system, exchanged pleasantries with Chris Russell and began the information transfer. The Medical Online Diagnostic Interface System was a new procedure, still suffering the advent of bugs and problems that made the transfer of images slow and sometimes a bit unclear. It was 2:00 a.m. before the entire series of scans had transferred, both Marisa's, Willie Evans's and Raymond Abel's.

Cam was at his diagnostic best, chattering away with Chris about scan angles, targeted areas and density levels of the various soft tissues and fluids in each image. I mostly listened, able to follow, but intensely grateful that Chris was here to handle the technical part of the discussion. I sat near the door of the darkened room, slipping in and out as necessary, handling Raymond's progress, making arrangements for his transport to Duke Medical Center and giving orders to the RNs for patients who continued to trickle in as the night wore on.

I was in the MODIS room when Cam made his preliminary diagnosis. "Chris, I have to agree with you here," he said, his voice heavy. "Looks like an injury to the brain from invasive trauma of some sort." In layman's terms, my patient had been lobotomized.

I felt sick when I heard the official words. Sick for Raymond. Sick for Willie Evans. Sick for Marisa. Coffee that I had downed like water for hours rode uneasily on my stomach. I leaned my head against the wall of the MODIS room and wanted to cry. Instead, I informed Mark, drank more coffee and prepared for the helicopter transport to Duke. Once there, Raymond Abel would receive an MRI, repeat lab work, massive doses of antibiotics, medications to relieve possible swelling of his brain, perhaps even surgery if it might help. And then rehab to discover what was left of Raymond's memory, creative functions, verbal skills. All this was attention and treatment that had been denied Marisa. I wanted to strangle Steven and Shobani, who had refused Marisa the care she so desperately needed.

There was little I could do tonight for Marisa. Mark would have to determine if a crime had been committed on my friend. Steven would have to be convinced that she needed further treatment. I was out of the loop entirely unless something broke while Steven was out of town.

Willie Evans was being treated by another M.D. miles away in a hospital with better diagnostic equipment and technology than any I had available. Sick at heart, I phoned Richland Memorial's switchboard and had Willie Evans's doctor paged. He, too, had bad news. His patient's CT film displayed the same type of trauma as Raymond Abel's. I gave him Cam's number for future reference and put him on speakerphone with Cam and Chris.

Technical and neurosurgical lingo flowed around me. I sat and listened. I was an E.R. doc. A good one. During that golden hour following a traumatic accident when a patient's life hung in the balance, there were few better than I at making the right decisions and providing the proper course of treatment to save a patient's life. I had offers from prestigious hospitals all up and down the East Coast. I had offers of a fellowship at Johns Hopkins Trauma Center, which I had turned down to stay with John.

But in this conversation I had nothing to contribute, nothing to offer. I was little more than a practitioner of meatball medicine. It was the first time since my earliest days of residency that I had felt so ineffectual. I was…useless.

Cam would handle Raymond Abel's course of care from this point on. I could do little else for him.

Rising from the seat near the door, I found an empty office and sat in the dark, visions of Marisa as she used to be playing on the darkened walls. We were closer than sisters. And I couldn't help her.

Marisa had possibly—probably—saved me that day at the creek so many years ago. If she hadn't stopped me, I might have finished my dam, flooded the neighborhood, causing damage to property. I had stood on a cliff edge that day, poised between two worlds, between reason and striking out in anger, between looking for the good that life had to offer and punishing myself and my mother for her drinking and her neglect of me.

Without Risa, without other family to take me in, I might have eventually ended up in juvenile detention or in a foster home. She pulled me back from a brink that day, from a place I seldom acknowledged. And she had somehow kept me centered all these years after. I didn't know if I could do it without her. She was my family.

I put my head in my hands, fighting to breathe, fighting against the pain in my throat, hot tears burning their way past my fingers until I finally retrieved enough control to wash my face and go back to work.

A little after 4:00 a.m., after Mark and Chris had gone home, after I had my emotions under better control, after even more coffee to keep me alert and rattle my nerves, Raymond's helicopter finally arrived. Rebecca had made arrangements for a place to stay, sent her younger son home to pack bags for her and Raymond, and was ready to make the flight to Raleigh, North Carolina. We had no patients. Except for the RNs and the flight crew, I had the place to myself.

Anne and Zack exchanged equipment, transferring hospital EKG leads, oxygen cannulae, blood pressure monitors and IV poles for the ones brought by the Duke team. Trish made fresh coffee for the crew, filled their thermos and visited with us as we made Raymond flight-ready. I didn't fool myself that she did it for altruistic reasons. She hung around being helpful so she could flirt with the male RN in his khaki flight suit and combat boots. However, her presence made things move faster, and suddenly Raymond was out the door and Rebecca was in my arms, giving me a fierce hug that left me winded.

"Thank you, Doctor. I'll let you know how he does. And I'll bring Raymond by when we get him back home so you can see how you done saved my boy."

I smiled down at Rebecca's tear-stained face and hugged her back. I didn't know how much I had done to save her son or if she'd be grateful to me in the end. "You be careful now. I'll be thinking about Ray."

"Thanks, Doctor." With one last squeeze of my lower ribs, she was gone, running across the tarmac to the chopper, bulky red coat bouncing with each stride.

My stomach crawled as the helicopter began its preflight procedures and the big rotors began to turn. A faint electrical whine filled the air, a high-pitched vibration I could feel even through the observation windows of the E.R. patient lounge. My feeling of uselessness grew as the chopper rose into the air, taking Raymond to Cam Reston. Wind whipped the bare limbs of the maple trees planted beside the hospital drive, tossed the frozen leaves of the magnolias near the ICU wing. And Raymond Abel was gone. The silence that settled around me was acute. The fire truck, ambulance and security vehicles waiting for the helicopter to depart turned off their red and blue flashing lights and pulled away from the hospital. Darkness descended. I stared at the reflection of my face in the window. I was pale and needed to put on a few pounds. I hadn't been eating well since my return to DorCity.

I had a few hours to sleep before the jackhammers started up. With a single wave to the RNs, I headed to my call room. My skin burned with exhaustion and dry heat. Caffeine trembled in my fingers and muscles. "I'll be in the shower, guys. And then the bed. Life or death only. You disturb me for a sore throat and I'll skin you alive."

"Will do, Doc," Zack said, lying through his teeth. He had a job to do and would call me for a hangnail if one came in the door. But it was a nice sentiment.

Locking both bathroom doors, I stood beneath a scalding spray and let water beat the exhaustion from my skin until it actually ached. Unscented jojoba oil eased the rest of my discomfort and I thought I might make it to the bed before I fell asleep. I did. I hit the switch, throwing the room into darkness, and rested one knee on the cover as I leaned down to pull at the sheets. My mobile phone rang.

I said something for which my mother would have rinsed out my mouth. And then several more some-things as I fumbled in the dark for the light switch. It wasn't the E.R. They would have used the room phone. With my luck it would be a wrong number. On the fourth ring I found the light switch and the flip phone and answered.

"What."

"Dr. Missy Rhea, I hate to disturb you. I know it late and all."

"Miss Essie?" Suddenly I was wide-awake.

"It's Missy Risa. She burning up."

My hands began to shake. "How bad?"

"I took her temperature with that new digital thermometer the nurse done lef' and I can read it with my magnifying glass. It 104.9 and I know that too high for my baby. What you want me to do?"

"Call for an ambulance, Miss Essie. I'll meet you at the E.R."

"I done that, Dr. Missy Rhea. You want I should keep her warm till they get here?"

"No, Miss Essie. Strip her down. Get cool tap water and put wet towels on her skin. And pack her bag. She may be here awhile."

"You think I should call that doctor? That Englishman? Shobani?"

"Not just yet. I'll call him if need be."

"Good. I see you in few minutes, Dr. Missy Rhea." The phone clicked off in my ear. I flipped it shut and tossed it in my bag.

I looked longingly at the bed and finally dropped onto it. *Just five minutes. If I could get just five minutes.*

I got nearly half an hour and felt horrible for it. I was so groggy when Anne called me from the E.R. that I felt like I did the time John and I went to New York. We caught a red-eye from Chicago after pulling twenty-four-hour shifts and landed in the city at dawn. Instead of checking in and making up for lost sleep, we dropped off our baggage at the Gramercy Park Hotel and hit the streets. We walked to Union Square for breakfast and ate at a little sidewalk café as we people-watched. We walked from there up Fifth Avenue and shopped our way up to the Empire State Building. By the time night fell we were zombies. It took the rest of the week to recuperate. I felt like that now as I jogged back to the E.R. A zombie. I didn't have a week to catch up on sleep.

Marisa was silent and immobile on her stretcher. There was an IV hanging on her left side supplying her with D5WSS—distilled water, salt and dextrose. The blood pressure monitor read 159 over 130, her pulse raced at 122. Too high. Both too high. Her breath came fast in little puffs at twenty-eight times a minute. Shivers racked her body. Her temp was 105.2.

Without asking me for an order, Anne and Zack had continued with the wet-towel treatment. A lab tech stood at Marisa's side drawing blood cultures and a rainbow of tubes for tests.

"Get me a CBC, a seven, a cath UA with culture, and draw for a DIC workup just in case." The DIC would test various parts of the blood coagulation cycle. As the tech withdrew his needle, I leaned in and listened to Marisa's chest. "Her lungs are wet. Get me a chest. And ABGs. Sorry," I said to the tech. ABGs were arterial blood gases. With them, I could evaluate how well Marisa was exchanging carbon dioxide for oxygen. If I had been here sooner, I might have saved the tech some work and Marisa a needle stick.

"How many blood cultures did you get?"

"Just one set. Want me to draw another set when I get the gases?"

I looked over at him. It was Macintosh Spivey, a short, rotund black man who worked the lab on third shift with only the help of a single venipuncture tech—when she bothered to show up at all, that is. "Yes. Thanks, Mac. You working alone tonight?"

"Yeah," he sighed. "Lita's baby is sick again. Sickest kid I ever heard tell of."

"They need to get you some dependable help."

"Hell," he said as he attempted an Allen's test on Marisa's left wrist. "They'd have to pay someone a real salary. You know they won't do that.

"She's got poor peripheral pulse in this arm. Let me check the other one."

The Allen's test had been negative. That meant that Marisa had only one major artery feeding her hand. The brachial artery that comes down the arm is supposed to branch off into smaller arteries by the time it reaches the wrist. In Marisa, the branching was too small or nonexistent. A traumatic or difficult needle stick in that artery could create a clot and occlude circulation. The chances were small, but I didn't want to risk it.

"Thanks, Mac. You are the only one I ever see doing that. All the other techs just find a pulse and jab."

"None of the others have ever seen a hand fall off. In the service, I saw this guy with only one hand? You know. Lost it when an RT did a piss-poor job and no Allen's test. I know better. This wrist is good." He paused, then, "Zack. Can I get you to put the blood pressure cuff on her other arm? Thanks. ABGs in a sec, Doc."

"What's her temp, now?"

"It's 105.6."

"Let's get some ice. Pack her down and pack the saline in ice while you're at it. Rocephin two grams

IV, and prepare an ice saline enema. We're going to pack her and flush out every body cavity. We got her meds?''

"Here you go, Dr. Missy Rhea. I know to bring every one.''

I turned and found Miss Essie at my elbow. I hadn't noticed her. "Thanks, Miss Essie.'' I took the bag but found little that would relate to the condition Marisa was in. A vial of Ampicillin, half-empty. A vial of pain meds, unused. A vial of Tylenol with codeine, and packs of birth control pills dating back to August. "Has she been taking the Ampicillin?''

"No, ma'am. That Englishman done say she don't have to take it no more.''

"Temp 105.9, Doc. It's skyrocketing. Want a Tylenol suppository?''

"Hmm. Not yet. Spread her legs and bag her with ice. Under her arms too. Around her neck and head, wrists. Keep her wet. And start the enema. And start an ice saline douche. Move it, people. Someone get me Shobani's phone number.''

I stepped to the break-room coffee machine and poured a cup. I didn't need it, but my hands were shaking and I had to stay busy or break into tears. Marisa was dying. I had done nothing to help her and my best friend in the world was dying. I drank back the coffee; it landed hard on my stomach and curdled there. I hadn't eaten the meal Miss DeeDee had left, and was beginning to regret the empty stomach.

"ABGs, Doc.'' Mac handed me the printout from the IL, the machine used to run arterial samples. In many hospitals, the respiratory therapy department drew and ran the blood gases, often on a POC—a point of care—blood gas instrument. Here it was the responsibility of the lab to draw and run the test. It wasn't faster, but I did benefit by not having to wait on a computer printout in times of crisis. I was simply handed the original machine values, often in as little as two minutes.

Marisa's pH was 7.258, her PCO_2 was 26, and her PO_2 was 145. She was blowing off too much CO_2, hyperventilating, causing her oxygen level to rise. She was acidotic, her blood pH too low and her oxygen level too high. Not life-threatening, but not good. This was something I could deal with. Calmer, I walked back into the cardiac room and ordered the oxygen turned off and Marisa fitted with a rebreather mask. "What's her temp?"

"Settled at 105.9. Rocephin's going."

"Let's give her some bicarb to bring her pH back up." I checked the cardiac monitor again. Unchanged. "Let me do a neuro-check." The RNs stepped out of the way and I reran the series of tests on Marisa that I had performed in my first and second secretive exams. She was hyperreflexive down her entire right side, a change I didn't like at all. Mentally, I began putting together a preliminary diagnosis and course of treatment.

If Marisa had been lobotomized like Willie Evans and Raymond Abel, and if she was still dripping CSF from her nose, she likely had an open wound from her nasal passages to her brain. If CSF was leaking out, then bacteria had a way in through the same passageway to her brain. Marisa might have meningitis, a bacterial inflammation of the meninges of her brain. Marisa had responded to pain only hours before....

"I want her sitting up for a Kernig's test." This meant placing the patient in an upright fetal position to test pressure on the brain. Zack raised the head of the bed to a ninety-degree angle so Marisa was upright from the hips up. I pulled Marisa's legs up, bending them at the knees and pushing them into her chest. Then, slowly, I pushed her head down toward her knees, putting a strain on her neck. Marisa moaned in pain, sounding like a child. I eased off the pressure and let her legs slide back to the bed. The Kernig's test indicated I was right, and that Marisa might indeed have meningitis, most likely caused by some common bacteria residing in Marisa's sinuses. Something simple, perhaps even staph epi., or a yeast.

I had a choice. I could do an LP—a lumbar puncture—putting a long spinal needle into a space between Marisa's vertebrae to draw off spinal fluid for confirmatory testing, or I could simply depend on the Rocephin to do its job. If I did the LP, I would be opening another passageway into Marisa that nature never intended, with the possible side effects of the LP itself, if it wasn't done right. If I didn't do the LP, and Shobani took over her care, he could discontinue the Rocephin as unnecessary because I hadn't done the test and confirmed the diagnosis. I stared at Marisa. She was flushed and her forehead was wrinkled in obvious pain.

The RNs had hooked a pulse-oximeter to Marisa's left index finger. It read an oxygen saturation level of ninety-nine percent. As I watched, the level dropped off to ninety-eight percent. The rebreather mask was working. Eventually her own breathing would correct her acidosis.

"Get me an LP tray and notify the lab we have a CSF on the way."

"Temp is down to 105.1, Dr. Lynch."

"Good. Discontinue the ice while we do the LP. I don't want her shivering."

"Shobani's home number, Dr. Lynch." Anne slid a scrap of paper into my pocket. I nodded my thanks and stood back as the nurses pulled bags and unisize gloves filled with crushed ice away from Marisa. My friend was exposed, lying naked on the stretcher, pale mottled skin shining bright beneath the hot overhead lights. I resisted the impulse to cover her. I was Marisa's doctor now. Not her friend.

Anne and Zack gathered equipment for the LP, including sterile cloth drapes, the lumbar puncture kit with its three-and-a-half-inch-long needle, sterile bandages. Together they turned my patient. As they worked, I washed. Using a sterile scrub brush, I scrubbed for the requisite five minutes under scalding water. The skin on my hands turned a lobster pink and went from aching to agony in seconds. The extreme heat and strong surgical soap on my chapped hands combined with my aggressive use of the plastic bristles would leave me in misery. I didn't care.

I dried on sterile towels provided by Zack and gloved in sterile size six and a half surgical gloves. "Tell the switchboard to hold all nonemergency calls. And put all the in-house lines on hold."

"Yes, ma'am," said Anne.

"She ready?"

"I have her on her left side, ready to be placed in fetal position," Zack said.

"Let's do it then."

Anne and Zack had put Marisa on her side and positioned the overhead light so it shone on Marisa's spine. Working together, they pulled Marisa's knees up to her chest and pulled her head down close to her knees. The position again put strain on the spine, increasing the internal pressure of the fluid in the spine and around the brain. It was painful, but it stabilized a patient quickly and easily for the procedure.

Her back had been scrubbed with a surgical scrub mixture of Betadine and alcohol, and was a ghastly shade of orange brown. While Zack held the patient's head, Anne, also wearing sterile gloves, opened and spread the E.R.'s sterile cloth surgical drapes. Two went across her back, above and below the site used for an LP, one went beneath her, and one went directly over the puncture site. This one had a hole in the center, about three inches round. The hole was placed directly over the fourth and fifth lumbar vertebrae.

Anne opened the kit and laid out the four sterile vials, uncapped the long needle and held it for me. I took it in steady fingers and bent over my patient. Palpating the site, I found the exact spot I wanted and took three deep breaths. Exhaling and holding the last one, I inserted the needle.

The skin resisted, as did the underlying soft tissue and the cartilage surrounding the disc. It was a rubbery, tearing sensation that never felt quite the way

I expected it to. And then I was in. Cerebral spinal fluid dripped out the end of the needle.

I held my left hand out to Anne and she placed in it an opened, clear plastic vial. I held the vial under the steady dripping and captured a milliliter or so before handing it back. She replaced it with another vial, capping the first one. Moving with the ease of practice, we collected a total of about five milliliters of the CSF in the four vials before I withdrew the needle and applied pressure to the puncture site.

I stood up, easing the pressure on my own back. "Let me see it."

Anne held up one of the vials. The fluid should have been clear, the color and consistency of water. Instead, it was milky, as if someone had poured a drop of cream in each vial. My diagnosis was confirmed. No other doctor would be coming in and changing Marisa's course of treatment.

"I want a stat gram stain, C-and-S, cell count and diff. And tell Mac to concentrate on the gram stain first. I want to know what I'm treating.

"Thanks, y'all. You made that easy. What's her temp now?"

"It's 104.7 and dropping," Zack said.

"Hold her flat for a full half hour. Monitor her temp and blood pressure and bolus her with normal saline—500 cc's. If her temp starts back up, you can resume the ice after the thirty minutes, otherwise, just keep on with the towels till we get her down to 103.5. Then you can give that Tylenol suppository and call in Chris. Offer him my apologies and tell him we have another head scan, same parameters as the last one he did for me. When we get the results of that we'll call her doctor.''

"You her doctor now."

I looked over at Miss Essie. I had again forgotten her presence. If I had thought about her, I would have moved her to the hallway or the E.R. lobby to wait out the procedure. Instead, she had been offered a full view of the LP.

"I'm an E.R. doctor, Miss Essie. I can't treat Marisa when she's admitted.''

"You treating her now. So you just keep her in the E.R.''

I grinned. I intended to do just that for as long as I could. But Adam Hoffman was relieving me at 7:00 a.m., and Marisa would have to be on the floor by then at the latest. "Come on, Miss Essie. Let's get some coffee.''

"You drink so much that stuff it a wonder you ain't black as me.''

"True. I drink too much of it." I lifted the frail woman by the upper arm and turned her to the doorway.

"And don't eat enough to keep a bird alive."

"True again." I shuffled with her into the hallway.

"And live in a pigsty.''

I laughed, guiding Miss Essie to the break room and the tall-backed chair I usually saved for myself. I sat her in it and poured coffee for us both. Then I closed the door to the hallway, shutting us in privacy. As we drank, I explained to Miss Essie what I had discovered about Marisa's condition. I explained to her what I thought had been done to her to cause that condition. I spoke slowly and carefully, explaining in layman's terms what had most likely happened on the night Marisa had first been discovered, what had been left undone in regards to her treatment, and what I wanted to see happen next in regards to Marisa's treatment, recovery and rehabilitation.

For any other patient's family, and under other conditions, I might have waited until I had the full diagnosis in hand, in case I was wrong. But I knew my diagnosis would prove to be the same for Marisa as for Raymond Abel. I knew it in the tingling of my fingertips. In the part of me that made me a good E.R. physician. In that part-intuition, part-training, part-experience, part-gift-from-God that helped me graduate at the top of my class, that extra something that couldn't be explained or quantified, but simply was. Marisa had been lobotomized. And I wouldn't keep that from Miss Essie any longer.

14

CTs and Sexual Harassment

Chris, tired and bleary-eyed, his thinning hair standing up on one side of his head, came back to the hospital without complaint. He didn't like putting Marisa into the CT chamber with her temperature so high, and only agreed to the scan when I volunteered to stay with her throughout the procedure. Because she was unable to respond, we had to strap her down and stabilize the position of her head, wrap her in warm blankets to prevent shivering and sedate her mildly to keep her calm.

All of the actions necessary to perform the CAT scan would cause her temp to rise again, but I had no choice. To diagnose Marisa, it was now or never. As soon as I called in Shobani, I would lose control of her care.

While we were stabilizing my patient for the extended X ray, the results of the stat gram stain came back. Mac had discovered two organisms on the smear of Marisa's spinal fluid. I told him to work up both organisms, and to work up all organisms isolated from the blood cultures. If Marisa had an open passageway into her brain, there could be anything in her system. Even multiple opportunistic organisms. Satisfied that I had done all the lab tests I could, I prepped Marisa for her CAT scan.

The CT chamber is a gray-painted, cold room with blank walls and no seating, no posters, nothing to relieve the monotony. The table on which the patient reclines is white, as is the Hula Hoop-shaped gantry overhead. The table moves lengthwise through the hoop of the gantry, increment by increment, as the beam of X rays shoots around the gantry into the patient, taking a circular picture. One millimeter increments meant the table holding Marisa would move one millimeter at a time, giving Chris a hundred and twenty "cuts" to view for his diagnosis.

After I strapped Marisa down and helped place sandbags around her head for stability, I put on a lead apron. The heavy metal provided me with less protection than I would have liked, but was better than nothing. In school, one of the X-ray techs gave us an enlightening demonstration, taking X rays of various items placed beneath a lead apron. The film picked up almost everything hidden beneath the shielding. Still, I wore the weighty thing, my elbows propped on the table by Marisa's feet to take some of the weight from my back.

I kept my hands on her arches, my eyes on her body and face, evaluating through my skin, through my vision, through any sense I had that might give me an edge on Marisa's diagnosis. Her feet were cold, the toenails blue, the fragile bones tiny as birds' wings beneath my fingers. The pulse points of the plantar arteries fluttered unsteadily beneath my palms. Her lids were bluish, closed over her eyes, hiding the brighter blue of iris. The faint stench of sickness rose from her body.

She lay still and unmoving throughout the test, and I might as well have stayed in the E.R., I was so useless. Yet, I stayed in place for the full seventeen minutes it took to perform the CAT scan just in case. Or perhaps it was just an excuse to touch Marisa, to watch her face as she slept, to assure myself she was still alive, and might live, and *please God let me be wrong about her diagnosis....*

The room was cold, kept at sixty-seven to sixty-eight degrees for the sake of the electronics and the computer boards. Toward the end of the scan, both Marisa and I started to shiver. I was tired and miserable and my back was in spasms from the uncomfortable position I had assumed. Marisa's temp was probably going back up. I squeezed her feet to keep her calm, to convince her I was still with her. And when the test was over, I wasted no time in moving Marisa from the CT table back to her stretcher.

I rolled her back to the E.R., the IV on its pole swaying with the motion of the stretcher. She was pale and could have been sleeping. Or she could have been comatose. Or catatonic. I couldn't believe the Marisa I had known for so many years was gone forever. There had to be something I could do for her.

It was close to 6:00 a.m., and the deadline for turning Marisa over to Shobani was drawing near. I had asked Chris to speed up the preliminary report on this CT, and also for the final report of Marisa's original CAT scan. When he gave them to me I would have no choice but to call Shobani. Only Marisa's critical state had allowed me to treat her this long without notifying her husband and calling in her personal physician. I was treading on ethical lines I had never thought I would need to cross.

I turned Marisa over to the RNs and studied her CBC and chemistry results. Marisa's white count was up to 28.7, or 28,700. About 20,000 too high. It showed a strong shift to the left, indicating bacterial infection. Her glucose was up, a reaction to the septicemia, and her venous CO_2 was low, correlating with the arterial blood gas results. Marisa was a very sick patient. As we say in E.R. lingo, she was a keeper. We would be admitting her to the hospital for inpatient treatment; she was sick enough to be admitted to ICU.

Many hospitals have more than one ICU. One for cardiac patients, one for trauma patients, and sometimes one for critical postsurgical and medical patients. At Dawkins County Hospital, there was one ICU and the RNs who staffed it cared for all types of critical patients who were not in need of being treated at a major medical center.

If Marisa's CT film came back resembling those of the men, she would need the type of care provided only by a top-notch neurosurgical specialist in the best neurological unit in the country. However, she was too sick to be shipped anywhere today. The septicemia had to be dealt with first, then her other problems. I had to admit to a feeling of satisfaction in keeping her at Dawkins. She would be close by where I could care for her. And perhaps find out what had happened to her.

The cell count and differential run on the spinal

fluid correlated with what Mac had discovered on the gram stain—a bacterial infection of Marisa's meninges. So far, everything fit with the diagnosis I had made.

It was with a feeling of trepidation that I watched Chris Russell make his exhausted way down the hall. His thin shoulders drooped, his face was creased with lines that had not been present hours earlier. He had put in eight to ten hours on the previous day, stayed up all night to deal with my CAT scans, and now, with no sleep, would have to work an eight-to-ten-hour day. I was slightly ashamed but had to admit that I would have called him in again had I needed to do it all over. He held the twelve-by-fourteen-inch sheets of film, each containing ten shots of the inside of Marisa's head, in his hand.

As had become our routine, I followed him unspeaking into the fracture room and watched as he flipped on the view-box lights. He shoved the scans into the clip at the top and cleared his voice.

"Marisa Braswell's new scan shows an old bleed. You can pick up the presence of dissolving clots from the variance in shading, and what we call beam hardening. Fresh blood is bright on a scan, because it has a higher density than the old blood we see on this scan." His voice was tired, sounding hollow in the dark room. "Some shading right here—" he pointed with a finger "—indicates the meningitis you already diagnosed, and of course we have the dark area left by the foreign instrument that caused the injury. The lobotomy."

Though I had expected it, though I had known it was coming, it was still a shock. Hearing the words drained all the strength from my legs and I sat down quickly on the stretcher at my back. Chris's diagnosis meant that the Marisa I had known was perhaps gone forever. I shivered.

"Whoever did this—" Chris stopped.

"Knew what they were doing," I finished for him.

"Yeah. That, too. But they could have done it differently. They could have gone in through the nostril. It would have left fewer diagnostic clues. And they could have probed higher into the cavity. Marisa's bleeds are far less profuse than the bleeds of the two other men. She actually has less trauma from the original attack. The blood left in the brain has poisoned the brain matter itself, but there wasn't that much blood to begin with. Whoever did this to Mrs. Braswell was...the word that comes to mind is *tentative*. Less than thorough."

"From the method of the procedure, do you think whoever did this wanted to be caught?"

Chris shrugged. "Or was hesitant. Too cautious and economical to do a comprehensive job of it. Of course, she has been—what, two weeks?—without proper treatment. The results could be worse for her than for the others. What now?"

"Now, I call the officer back and tell him he has three patients with the same diagnosis. You go back over all the CAT scans of the heads you have done in the past few months and tell me if there are any more that we missed." I stared at the small, dark cavity that had been rammed up into Marisa's brain and wanted to scream. "And while you start your search, I call her husband and her doctor."

"You're going to call the cops before you call her husband?"

I nodded slowly.

"He was on duty for over ten hours before she was brought in. He couldn't have done it. It isn't possible." Chris was speaking of Steven.

"I know. But Eddie Braswell was picked up in Ford County tonight. He raped an old girlfriend there. I'd like to know if he had an ice pick in his possession when he did it," I said.

Silently, we stared at the scans lined up so neatly on the view-box, the light casting weird shadows into the room. Chris finally turned and walked out, leaving me with the evidence of an attack on Marisa. When I had myself under control, I, too, left the room. I had phone calls to make.

Mark was at the hospital by six-thirty, driving through the dark, arriving with the rain. It was miserable weather out, cold and wet, and his mood matched the ambience. Surly and uncommunicative. When I got through to him, Mark had told me to hold off calling anyone else until he got to the hospital, and so it was only after he arrived that I called Shobani and told him about his patient. The call was made on the speakerphone in my office, with Mark at attention, listening. I was glad I had a witness.

Percy Shobani was coldly angry that I hadn't notified him the moment his patient was brought in, and informed me he would be at the hospital in minutes. She was not to be admitted without his approval. She was not to be moved. She was not to receive treatment. She was to be left entirely untouched. To say his voice was livid with disapproval would be an understatement. For Percy Shobani, the grand old-world-gentleman of Dawkins County Hospital, this was tantamount to a temper tantrum.

When I told him I had followed standard treatment procedure and his own standing orders regarding E.R. patients and the notification process, he hung up on me.

Amazed, I replaced the receiver and stared at my hand on the beige plastic. "Approval?" I repeated. "Left untreated? *Untouched*? If you think she's going back home with a systemic infection, meningitis and a lobotomy, think again, Bozo." I looked up at Mark. "I *will* admit her to this hospital even if it means calling a judge to have her declared a ward of the court."

He grinned. "I love feisty women. It has something to do with sparks in the air and in their eyes."

"That kind of statement could be construed as sexual harassment."

"Construe away."

"You staying for the call to Steven?"

"Absolutely. I have a question. Would a person have to have some type of medical background to perform this type of assault?"

I shrugged. "You can find out how to do this procedure in the movies, on television, in the library, probably any ten-year-old could learn how on the Internet. Nothing is sacred anymore. Oh, by the way, I asked Chris Russell to search through all the head scans from the past few months to see if there had been any more cases like this we might have overlooked. And I'd like to know if Eddie Braswell used an ice pick in his assaults. It might explain Marisa's injury.''

Mark stood, lifting his hip from the corner of my desk where he had parked himself during the conversation to Shobani. "My case, remember?"

There was a sudden roaring in my head. The sound of anger, or of my blood starting to boil. "*I'm* the doctor. You want to tell me you would have figured out that there was something going wrong in this county without my help? You want to tell me you would have diagnosed three lobotomy assaults in less than twenty-four hours all by yourself? You want to figure out the rest without my help?''

I stood up and leaned over the desk separating us. "Marisa is *my* friend. Every one of these patients belongs to *me* or belonged to me at one time. *My* case. And don't you forget it. You want to tell me you would have thought to ask Chris to look for more missed diagnoses?''

Mark's eyes had narrowed as I spoke. "Eventually. When's the last time you got any sleep?''

I stopped. Closed my mouth on the retort I was about to make. We were glaring at each other like two dogs fighting over a juicy bone. We always did this. Found overlapping territory and came at one another with claws extended and fangs bared. Tennis, handball at the club in Ford County, jogging together. I took a deep breath, eased a hip to the desktop. Any excuse for no-holds-barred competition.

Mark could make my involvement in Marisa's future care easier or more difficult from a legal point of view. In fact, Mark might have a big say in Marisa's entire life for the foreseeable future. I bit my lips together.

After a moment of silence I grudgingly said, "You have a point." More stiffly, I added, "I am a doctor. I will act on my patients' urgent medical needs first and inform you later. To be fair, I will go so far as to speak to you about ideas I have regarding my patients and possible avenues of medical inquiry into the physical cause of their injuries."

Mark grinned at my stilted tone and words. I wanted to slap him, which was childish and stupid but still a nearly overwhelming desire. I shoved my hand into my lab-coat pocket. Marisa needed me here, not locked up in jail for assault on an officer.

"However, if I have any ideas that might help your investigation," I added, "I will turn them over to you instead of acting on them alone."

"Good idea."

"Will you keep me informed on anything regarding Marisa from a legal point of view."

"No."

I stood up slowly.

"That's the official answer," he continued. "Off the record, yes. I'll tell you what I know when I know it. I will not inform you of guesses, probabilities, possibilities or gut reactions that may not pan out. Now. Will you show me the pictures you took of the bruises on Marisa's arms and ankles? Off the record."

"Yes." I wasn't certain who had gotten the best out of this deal, but Mark seemed mollified and I was suddenly too tired to care. "I have to check on my patient. Shobani will be here shortly."

"I'll wait at the desk. I want to be present when you inform him of the nature of his patient's injury. I want to see his face."

"You don't think Percy Shobani is involved in this, do you? Dapper little Percy?"

"Right now, I think everyone is a possible suspect. Even you."

"Thanks. Just what I needed to hear." I moved to the door of my office. Mark followed in my wake.

"Couple more questions," he said. "If her husband and her doctor knew she had been assaulted, did she receive proper care for the type of injury?"

"No. She should have been flown out to a neurotrauma center."

"I'm not familiar with the law on this point. Is a doctor legally allowed to permit his patient to vegetate?"

I turned and looked at Mark, his face lit by the overhead lights. Choosing my words carefully, I said, "There is no law that governs the method of care given a patient in a particular medical situation. To create such a law would be to tie a doctor's hands, legislate medical care, which is half art anyway. So, yes. A doctor can allow his patient to receive less than adequate care. There are checks and balances in place to protect a patient, but the court system is the most effective of these. Unless a patient's closest relative becomes involved with the level of care, there is little to regulate a specific situation."

"However, if a *husband* allows a *wife* to get like that...like Marisa..." Mark's words trailed off. He was thinking along lines I didn't want to consider.

"I would think...it would be a case of spousal neglect. Not foul play."

"But I have some legal maneuvering room here to force Shobani to talk to me."

"Not much," I said. "Patient confidentiality."

"Unless Shobani is part of the neglect. And that neglect led to Marisa's nearly dying." Mark smiled. "Sometimes a legal case is all in the way it is presented. Which is why I don't want you getting in the way of my case."

I walked down the hall and looked back over my shoulder at him. "I'll be circumspect. I'll not step on your toes. I promise." I ignored the snort of disbelief he aimed my way. I was brought up to be a lady even in the face of barbarians. A true lady was a lady no matter what. My mother said so.

As Mark studied the photos of Marisa's bruises, Percy Shobani breezed in the ambulance airlock and up to the E.R. front desk. He took the chart I held out to him and turned his back on me. It was a deliberate cut. The kind I had read about in Regency romance novels as a teen.

My eyebrows went up. I crossed my arms over my chest. And from somewhere in the deep part of me that my mother never managed to tame with constant harping on manners or eradicate with her drunken binges, laughter bubbled up. It was inappropriate and improper, but I was just too tired to care. Shobani's head lifted at the sound. Mark came up behind me. I laughed for a full three seconds before the sound shut itself off.

"She was assaulted prior to admission two weeks

ago,'' I said into the shocked silence. ''Your chart notes from the time of admission make no mention of that. Neither do your follow-up notes. You did not follow through with further diagnostic procedures that were recommended by Dr. Russell. There is no reason for such an oversight or explanation for such a decision in your notes.'' My laughter had dissipated, replaced with a cold anger. ''Would you care to tell me *why* you decided not to follow up on Mrs. Braswell's diagnosis?''

I was having emotional swings from stress and lack of sleep. I was not myself. Had I been, I would never have attacked another physician so publicly. Later, when I had a chance to review my actions, I would be ashamed. For now, I was simply angry.

Shobani slowly turned to me. I could not read his expression. His eyes were cold, his emotions concealed. Dark brown eyes met mine. From the corners of my vision I saw Anne and Zack close themselves into the break room and shut the door. Cowardice? Or courtesy? Fighting for some degree of professionalism, I stepped around the desk and faced my colleague. Mark followed. He had done that a lot in the last few days.

''Marisa Braswell is one of at least three patients who were lobotomized in this county in the last two weeks. I realize it was easy to overlook; however, your course of treatment failed to discover her problem. I have ordered her admitted to ICU in your name and under your care.''

Shobani's frown deepened. Small, thin lines formed between his eyebrows. His eyes slid away from mine and something in his expression let me know he was angry. I went on.

"In my professional opinion, Marisa is suffering from cephaledema in conjunction with the lobotomy and the meningitis. It's up to you to determine at what point you might want to administer solu-medrol or some combination of meds to bring the swelling in her brain down. But she is stabilizing nicely. I suggest no delay."

"Your friend is the wife of a colleague, Dr. Lynch." Shobani rose to his full height and stared at me. "The course of treatment decided upon by me and approved by her husband is none of your concern. If you persist in attempting to take over her care, I shall deliver you to the medical staff of this hospital for a reprimand and possible dismissal." Shobani slammed Marisa's chart on the desk. "Have I made myself quite clear? This—is—my—patient," he said distinctly.

"You ignored a criminal assault and gave faulty care to a patient. I can prove it. Take me to the board, buster, and I will expose you to them. I will tell them everything."

Shobani blanched, stepped back as though preparing for a blow. His reaction was unexpected.

Leaning in, I capitalized on his withdrawal. "I have turned this situation over to the police. I did not intend to notify the board or partake in Marisa's course of care, however, due to your current disposition and approach toward this patient, from this point on, I will be monitoring her condition. If you don't like it, help yourself, *take* it to the medical staff or the board." I stepped in again, invading his personal space, my anger rising like half-time fireworks. "But be assured, if Marisa Braswell does not receive treatment which I think is proper and adequate to her condition, her aunt and I will find a judge and have her removed from your care."

I was hot, shaking as if I had run too hard and too far on too little food. I could feel muscles jumping in the skin of my face. Shobani backed away from me, a fast half shuffle.

Mark stepped in front and stood between Shobani and me, his body acting like a shield. "I'm Captain Stafford. I'm the officer responsible for the investigation of these cases. Could I have a word with you, Doctor?"

Slowly, Shobani moved his eyes from me to Mark. He trailed his gaze down the cop's body and back up in deliberate insult. Mark smiled. It was not a pretty sight.

"Perhaps we could use Dr. Lynch's office?"

"Help yourself," I said shortly. And I turned and walked away.

15

Catnaps and Hard Hats

Mark stayed in my office for nearly half an hour. Past the time when Dr. Hoffman came in to relieve me. Way past time when I should have been off the clock and on the way home. I was not a salaried employee, and did not draw overtime. However, I was paid for every hour I was on the clock at rates that neared a hundred dollars an hour. Hoffman was paid the same rate. I couldn't stay on the clock and I couldn't leave Marisa until her husband had been notified and Marisa was in a bed in ICU. With any other patient, I would have spelled out Marisa's situation to the doctor relieving me and left her in his care. But not Marisa.

I clocked out and waited for Mark and Shobani in the break room, eating Miss DeeDee's dinner cold, right out of the broiler pan. I was utterly famished. Miss DeeDee said she wanted the pan back empty. I accomplished that for her single-handedly. The meal was delectable, full of flavor and protein and vegetables that I needed hours ago and had denied myself to care for Marisa.

My stomach swelled and the sick feeling I had

carried around all night began to ease. I had Marisa in the hospital and diagnosed. I had a chance to monitor her treatment. I could help. Finally, I could help my friend.

While I ate, I called Cam and promised him a MODIS of Marisa's CAT scan. He had pulled an all-nighter, too, and sounded as exhausted as I felt, listening to my description of our friend with only an occasional curse word to mark the narrative.

As I spoke to him, I placed my hand on her old chart, my copy of the original from her first admission, the one I had acquired by less than ethical means and kept in my possession since. The questions I had asked upon reading it were finally being answered.

Cam had information of his own to share. Raymond Abel had just been admitted and placed under the care of one of his colleagues. Surgery to relieve the pressure on his brain was a distinct possibility. Free to fly up and monitor Marisa, Cam could leave in less than twenty-four hours and would make the flight sooner if possible. I was too tired to try to dissuade him. And frankly, I knew I could use all the help I could get in treating Marisa. It looked as though I might have to fight Shobani, Steven and the entire board.

After I rang off from Cam, I called the hospital administrator's secretary, Abigail Staton, at home and asked the proper procedure for granting Cam temporary privileges to practice at Dawkins. Mildly amused, she reminded me it was Sunday, and I apologized for disturbing her on a weekend.

Rather than sleeping in, Abigail was getting ready for church, but took the time to explain the procedure to me. It wasn't as involved as I had feared and I gave her the basics on Cam Reston so she could start on the paperwork first thing Monday morning. Final approval rested in the hands of this year's chief of medical staff, Wallace Chadwick. I knew Wallace would approve Cam's application. He would probably try to get Cam to cover weekends in the E.R., as well....

Once off the phone, I rested my head on the tall-backed seat and closed my eyes. Exhaustion clawed at my eyelids like sandpaper, crawled beneath my skin like snakes, hissed against my eardrums, roared in my mind. I was so tired I could die.

Mark woke me up near 8:00 a.m. In one of those strange quirks of the human body, this time I felt wonderful upon waking, the catnap having restored me with a burst of energy and clarity of thinking. The effect was entirely artificial and would not last, but while it did, I went with it. I sat up and nodded to Mark and Shobani.

"Dr. Shobani has been informed of the legal ramifications of this case, both as they now stand and as they might develop."

Which meant Mark had lied through his teeth to get Shobani to cooperate. Good. I smiled at Mark in gratitude. He winked back.

"He has agreed to allow you to monitor his patient's progress and will inform Mrs. Braswell's husband of his decision. He also will cooperate with the police department on this investigation. All this in return for your promise not to go to the board about any misconduct which you have discovered on his part to date or any which you might discover regarding this particular patient in the future. Do we have an agreement?''

''No.''

Shobani looked at me, his full lips pressed tightly together, expression shuttered. Mark frowned. I might be about to undo all he had accomplished in the hour in my office.

''I will, however, agree to discuss with Dr. Shobani evidence of any problems that I might uncover and listen to his side of things before I take any action. Agreed?''

After a slight hesitation, Percy Shobani nodded his plump face. ''I won't say it is a *stellar* arrangement, far from splendid, but it is *agreeable*.'' Mark relaxed.

''I'm not trying to take your patient away, Percy. And I'm not trying to cause you problems.''

Shobani nodded, but his face was troubled.

''She's all yours,'' I said, referring to Marisa. ''You going to call Steven this morning?''

''I attempted to do so from your office. He had left his suite. I have messaged him at the hotel and his father's nursing home. Per his prior statements to me, I should not admit Mrs. Braswell. However, under the circumstances—'' he glanced quickly at Mark ''—I will admit her to an ICU bed without his knowledge. And I will continue to attempt to communicate with him until he is apprised of the situation.''

"She's your patient. I overheard Steven Braswell giving you permission to treat his wife. You have a witness, if you need one."

Shobani's eyes widened fractionally before he glanced away. "Thank you, Dr. Lynch. However, it was Dr. Braswell's intention that his wife not be admitted to this hospital again. I do not think he will be pleased."

"Tough."

Percy Shobani smiled sadly. Mark nodded in approval.

"I have to get some sleep," I said. "I'll be in my call room and then back home as fast as I can drive there. See you tonight, Percy. Night, Mark. Or morning." I lifted Marisa's old chart and carried it with me down the hall.

The call room was hot and stuffy when I opened the door. And my duffel was on the bed, not on the floor where I'd left it. I stopped in the doorway and studied the room. I was certain I had left the duffel on the floor. I had risen from the bed and taken off for the E.R. without touching anything but my lab coat and watch. I hadn't moved the duffel.

Nothing else was misplaced. I walked into the room and checked the bag. Nothing was missing. I tossed Marisa's chart from her previous admission into the duffel, shouldered the bag and walked back to the construction site. There were no jackhammers this morning. No saws. Instead, a plumber and an electrician stood in a hole in the floor, heads and upper chests above floor level. They were handing down conduit and PVC piping, one chewing on a cheekful of tobacco.

"You guys see anyone go into the call room down the hall in the last few minutes?" I asked.

The men looked at one another and shrugged with their mouths, lips turning down in exaggerated frowns. "No. Sorry, lady," the one with the tobacco plug said. Then he spit a long brown spew into a stained foam cup. I ignored my stomach's gyrations and looked away.

"Where's Matt?" I asked, remembering the toothy job site supervisor of the day before.

"Down the hall, Nurse. You got to wear a hard hat, though."

"Doctor. Not nurse. Where are the hats?"

They pointed. I had to step over the nasty cup to get to the stack of hats. Swallowing nausea that threatened to overwhelm me, I walked to the pile of hard hats, placed a yellow plastic one on my head and wandered down the hallway. My stomach settled as I moved away from the men standing in the hole in the floor. Chewing tobacco sometimes had that effect on me and I was glad to be away from it. I studied the renovations around me.

There was wallboard up where only yesterday there had been none. Holes in the floor where only yesterday there had been tile. There was both construction and destruction all around me. Dust hung in the air like smoke. It looked like a disjointed way of doing things, but then I knew next to nothing about construction.

Small hospitals were disappearing all over the

country at an astonishing rate, gobbled up by the big conglomerates or simply going bankrupt as Medicare and Medicaid pay out less and less, politicians continue to wrangle over and then duck the health-care and insurance issues, and costs continue to rise. Yet, by dint of good management, Dawkins had avoided the snare that captured other less fortunate hospitals. Grants for expansion had come at all the right times, and though there had been lean years, Dawkins was currently operating in the black. As I watched for Matt, I wondered what corporation grant or government agency was funding the current surgical expansion.

Boxes stood piled in the doorway to a new surgical suite, and Matt stood in conversation just beyond, a set of plans held in one hand, the other propped on a hip. The worker beside him wore muddy jeans and boots and had left a trail of red-mud footprints through the white wallboard dust.

I waited, ignoring the conversation about water pressure PSI and drainage of waste products, spending the few minutes looking through the boxes that blocked the doorway. They were full of surgical equipment, the specialized pieces used by orthopedic surgeons. There were a dozen chisels, several Downing and McKeever cartilage knives, a Krull Acetabular knife, a lovely set of Bunnell tendon strippers and four custom-made mallets, all lying open, unsterilized and covered with a fine layer of dust. I tried my hand on the mallets and discovered their grips were of a larger diameter than usual, and were carved in a rougher pattern to make gripping with bloody gloves easier. I liked the feel of the larger handles and hefted a Meyerding mallet to check for balance.

"Those yours?"

I looked up at Matt and smiled. "Nope. But I like the feel of them." I placed the mallet back in the packing box.

"They were delivered yesterday 'bout noon and I didn't know where to dump 'em. They look like some stuff I might use in my line of work." Matt grinned a big toothy grin and I was reminded again of a mule.

"Bone surgery has its parallels to remodeling work," I said wryly. "Speaking of which, you didn't happen to see anyone go in my call room, did you?"

"Nope," he said, echoing me. His round eyes narrowed. "Something missing?"

"Not that I can see, but I sometimes leave a chart or two lying around and I wouldn't like to break patient confidentiality by accident." It was only a partial lie. I couldn't explain away the uneasiness I had felt at seeing my duffel on the bed. My house had been ransacked. Had my call room been invaded? The feeling of nausea returned.

"I've worked with these guys for two years now, and trust my men, but I'll ask around. Make sure they know the call room is off-limits without my approval."

"If anyone saw someone in there I'd appreciate a description," I said, trying for a light tone. Apparently I didn't entirely succeed.

Matt propped a foot on the stack of surgical equipment delivery boxes and stuck a toothpick between his teeth. "What's going on, Doc?"

"I'm not sure *anything* is going on. I may just be so tired I'm seeing bad guys everywhere. I'd appreciate your keeping your eyes open, though," I said as I edged around Matt, past the boxes and out the doorway. Matt's eyes had found my chest again and I didn't relish the inspection.

"Sure thing. You getting off work now?"

"Yeah. Long night," I said as I stepped into the room beyond. I banged my ankle on a box getting past him and Matt seemed to find my pain amusing.

"Watch yourself, there, Doc," he said, laughing. "Before you go, you might like to know that you might not have electricity in the call room tonight. If you got a minute, I'll show you the breaker boxes and you can flip on your lights if I forget 'em when I leave. And if the toilet don't flush, just push the handle a few times and it should go on down eventually if you don't use too much paper. Come on, I'll show you."

"Wonderful. Just flippin' wonderful," I murmured under my breath as I followed him through the dusty suite, limping slightly. He talked as we moved and I could hear the amusement in his voice. It was only marginally better than having him focus on my chest.

"You got hot water in your suite today, but cold may be a problem. Tomorrow everything may be reversed and you might have only cold water. But I'll try to move the boxes out of your way. And we'll keep an eye on your room."

I could hear condescension in his voice as well as the laughter, but didn't care. If he thought I was a klutz and a little paranoid, well, at least he'd look out for me. It was the macho thing to do, after all.

I got a crash course in the operation of a breaker box, and an introduction to several workers in hard hats and muddy shoes. By 8:30 a.m., I could turn on all the lights in the surgical suite, and was convinced that none of the workers had seen anyone go into my room. Paranoid klutz—with the bruised ankle and amused construction workers to prove it—that was me. I was so tired, I didn't even care.

Off the clock and free to do as I wished, I wandered outside to Shobani's office, trying to track down the wonder boy of Dawkins County Hospital. The lights were on in the semidetached office only yards from the E.R. entrance, nurses moved from room to room in the back, but no one came when I knocked. I stood in the freezing rain with sleet pelting down on my shorn head and sliding beneath my collar to melt on my too-hot, too-dry skin.

Through the window, ornately gilded, stamped and embossed Oxford diplomas and certificates caught the light from the overhead fluorescent lights. The less impressive board certificates in half a dozen specialties acted as anchors. The man was entirely too accredited. The entire wall was taken up by testimonials to Shobani's medical prowess.

I had never even framed mine. Rheane Rheaburn Lynch, M.D., had displayed no paper proof of her accomplishments. Perhaps that was in deference to Mama's refined, pre-manic-depressive, pre-alcoholic abusive illness. Perhaps not. Either way, I had left the medical school diplomas in storage and so had no wall of parchment.

Jealous? I pushed the thought away as ludicrous and went back into the E.R. in search of Shobani. I found him standing in ICU at the foot of Marisa's bed, his full lower lip caught in his teeth. I followed his eye as he watched her monitors, the steady sinus rhythm of her EKG lead, the unblinking light of normal blood pressure, pulse, and O_2 saturation levels. All so normal. I checked the fluids going in to Marisa's IV. Rocephin was still going, as were the fluids I had ordered from the E.R.

"I say, I have changed nothing, Dr. Lynch."

I didn't react to the caustic tone. Just dropped my arm from the IV pole and turned. I met his eyes, held them and waited. The sounds of the RNs out in the hallway were muted. A housekeeping cart squeaked down the hallway, one wheel out of line with the others. Percy looked away from me.

"It was...nothing more than simple courtesy," he said finally.

"What was?"

"Allowing Steven to...treat his wife. It happens quite often, though perhaps you have yet to practice enough years to know that fact." When I didn't respond, he continued as if educating me in the realities of medical life. "Doctors often treat family members—it happens all the time—and other doctors sign the notes and orders. It wasn't unscrupulous or unethical on my part. Simply a courtesy."

"And if Steven made a mistake?"

After a moment, Percy looked up at me. "I do quite agree that it was an error on my part to follow her course of care so shallowly. I should have...looked deeper perhaps. Hindsight and all that."

I nodded. "Perhaps. I hope you will rectify that oversight now. Meanwhile, Cam Reston, a personal friend of the Braswells, and a fourth-year neurosurgical resident, is flying up today. He'll be here by dark and he's agreed to oversee Marisa's case and to liaise with the medical doctors at Richland Memorial and Duke regarding the two similar cases as they need. And then if Marisa needs transporting, Cam will handle the details of flying her to Duke."

Shobani swallowed and looked away. Sleet pounded on the window glass beyond his gaze. He swallowed again. "Steven...Dr. Braswell...would not permit his wife to receive treatment by another doctor, nor would he allow her to be transported out. Only in the case of life or death does he intend her to receive treatment at any facility."

I watched the face of the man before me, not the weather outside. Stress showed in every line and pore. He was sweating and swallowing profusely, when I had never seen him in any condition but overriding calm and self-confident. "Why did Steven choose you as Marisa's doctor?" I asked softly. "Her own physician was just as capable, and Marisa had never seen you professionally before. You have no board specialties in any branch of neurology. And Steven did not really like you. That was common knowledge."

A strange expression darted across Shobani's face and was gone. Without a word, he turned and walked into the hallway. His shoes echoed hollowly down the hall.

I stared unseeing at Marisa's face on the plump white pillows. What had I seen? *Fear? Panic? Dread?* What did Percy Shobani know about Marisa's condition? Had he known it from the beginning...and done nothing?

I reached out and touched Marisa's foot. It was ice cold beneath the blanket. Cold as death. Blinking back tears of exhaustion, I resettled my duffel straps on one shoulder, left my best friend and went home.

16

Clean Windows and Hunters

I was so exhausted I felt drunk as I climbed into my car. Sleet followed me all the way home from the hospital, but seemed to dissipate as I wended my way up my drive. On the horizon, a faint warm glow prophesied the end of the current wet weather. The storm front was clearing, and warmer temps were hovering over the treetops.

I parked my little toy car and climbed wearily from the driver's seat. A breeze shoved me toward the door of the house, a hint of warmth in its push. Typical South Carolina weather, miserable one day, lovely the next. Sometimes changing from hour to hour, minute to minute.

Inside the house, Belle barked frantically. It was her barking that alerted me to my visitor; if my dog had been silent, I might have passed right by the young girl on my steps and never seen her. Instead, I stopped at the sight of her. She was African-American, dark-skinned and petite, small as all the white-gloved debutantes I had grown up with and towered over and never resembled at all. Her hair was lacquered up in curls like a hat, with braids and beads and a clip of gold balls like a hat pin to set it all off. She shivered in jeans and a sweater, and a look of pure irritation had settled her full lips in a pout.

"You always this late gettin' home?"

"Some days." I stopped in the drive, hugging my black bag to my chest with one hand and Marisa's old chart with the other. "Who are you?"

"Arlana. Mama Essie sent me. Said you live in pigsty worse than any she ever seen and said I was to clean it up for you today, seein' as how they wasn't havin' church. But I ain't no maid." Her lips thinned. "I'm a nurse. Or I will be in a few years, soon as I finish school."

"Why aren't they having church?" I asked, curious. I had never known Marisa to miss a Sunday. Until today.

"We meet on the first and third Sundays. Traveling preacher. It'll cost you forty bucks to get your house clean."

I managed not to smile. "There's a two-year waiting list at Ford Technical College. That where you intend to go?"

"Yeah. I'm taking my academics there now and start on nursing courses eighteen months from now. Can we do this inside, or do you just like to see me shiver?"

"How are you related to Miss Essie?"

"I'm her great-granddaughter. I won't steal your stuff if that's what you're thinking."

"I wasn't thinking that at all," I said mildly. I selected my house key by feel and moved to open the door. "Come on in, then. You know how to make coffee?"

"Mama Essie taught me. How to grind the beans and all. I hate the stuff myself, but I know how to make it strong the way you like it."

"How do you like dogs?"

"Better than cats."

I pushed open the door. Belle bolted past my legs and into the yard, sniffing once at Arlana on the way past. She found a spot and relieved herself for so long that I felt guilty for having left her unattended all night. I would have to have a doggy door installed right away. Arlana followed me inside.

"Jeez Louise," she said.

I had the feeling she was sorry she had set her price at forty dollars. The smell of dog and mildew hit me like a hammer and I almost felt sorry for her seeing the place for the first time. Before she had a chance to change her mind I said, "Cleaning supplies are under the sink, vacuum cleaner and bags are in the hall closet, mop is hanging on the wall behind the back door. Forty bucks cash and the place is clean, right?"

Arlana looked around in awe. "Mama Essie say this place be bad, but I bet she ain't been here in while. 'Cause she be fallin' out if she see a place this dirty."

I laughed and called Belle to me. The large mixed-breed pushed her nose into the crack of the door to open it and wormed her way on in. Panting and waggling her entire body instead of just her tail, she inspected us both and went straight to her puppies, counting them with her nose, sniffing to check the health and condition of each. Satisfied, she came to me and barked once.

It was a demand so familiar tears came to my eyes. Beca had done the same thing when it was time for a walk or dinner or a treat. To cover my reaction, I filled her bowls and found her leash, busying my hands and my mind. I had never been the weepy sort, and blamed my teary state on exhaustion. "Belle and I will be back in about twenty minutes," I said. "Then I'll hit the sack while you clean. You can get the bedroom and bath after I get up, if you don't mind."

Arlana sighed. "What am I supposed to call you?"

"I'm Rhea, and this is Belle." I met the black eyes of Essie's great-granddaughter. "Pleased to make your acquaintance."

Arlana laughed and I had no idea why, but I laughed with her. The sound of our laughter flowed out the door behind me as Belle and I went on a slow jog. She was a huge animal, her head coming to my hip, but she was well behaved on the leash and easy to handle, stopping only twice to relieve herself again and three more times to sniff a tree or a bush. Some redneck deadbeat had dumped her because he didn't want puppies or the dog who was dying to having them. His loss. My gain.

Belle was sore from her delivery so we didn't go far, but I felt refreshed nonetheless. The warm breeze melted the path to mush beneath our feet, and ice that had started to form on the branches and electric lines broke and fell in tinkling sounds all around us. And no dirt bikes sounded in the distance.

I was ready for sleep as soon we hit the drive, but took time to stretch out my legs and back muscles and to speak to Arlana before finding my bed. After that, there was nothing, not even the memory of dreams.

At 4:00 p.m. I woke, feeling groggy and bleary, eyes like sandpaper grinding against my lids, heart beating against my chest in panic. A dull terror, like some nightmare-ridden phantom, crouched in the back of my mind. I found the phone and dialed the hospital, asked for ICU and checked on Marisa. Her temp was down to 101.2 and she was sleeping soundly. *Alive. Still alive.*

I gave orders that no one was to visit Marisa except Miss DeeDee and Miss Essie. It was something I should have done before I left. Someone had injured Marisa, and I didn't know who. She had to be protected.

That accomplished, I asked after the lab reports on the cultures of CSF. The organisms responsible for Marisa's meningitis were *Staphylococcus epidermidis* and *Klebsiella pneumoniae*. Staph was opportunistic at all times, and I assumed the Kleb was opportunistic in this instance. Both organisms were sensitive to Rocephin, and I didn't need to amend the chart orders.

The charge nurse informed me that Cam had phoned in from the airport for a lift to the hospital. In my exhaustion, I hadn't considered what the lack of a taxi-cab service would mean to his transportation needs, but the head nurse of the ICU had gone to pick him up, saving me the trip and Cam a wait.

I wondered if I would be expected to provide a home away from home for Cam during his stay.... If so, I would need to buy a pull-out couch or a bed for the guest room. Far easier to put Cam up in the Comfort Inn. With that information passed along for Cam, and my fears for Marisa relieved, I hung up, rolled over and out of bed.

Standing in the dusty darkness of my room I wondered fully for the first time.... *Who hurt Marisa? And why? Eddie Braswell? If so, what did he have in common with the two men with similar wounds?*

Under the door a black nose sniffed, Belle blowing to let me know she was there and that she knew I was awake. ''Time for a run, girl?'' She whuffed softly.

Arlana was in the front room and didn't hear me emerge. I slipped a leash on Belle and left without speaking. It was guilt that prompted me to slither away. Dust hung like a cloud in the air, windows I had never seen through sparkled, their dry-rotted drapery in piles on the floor. The kitchen positively gleamed...and I had no idea the floor was white. I had thought it a pale tan. I would owe a great deal more than forty dollars for this cleaning job. And Arlana would deserve it.

Belle and I made the run a little faster and a little farther this time, the big dog stretching out beside me, tongue lolling in happy release. She was pleased to be out of the house, too. The day had warmed to the mid-sixties and the bowl of blue sky above was so bright it burned my eyes. Gorgeous day, Carolina blue, and I had missed days like this living in Ohio. Winter there was unremitting cold and icy and bleak…and the Carolinas were a constant surprise of day-to-day weather changes. Marisa had loved days like this.

Back at the house, I unleashed Belle and found Arlana. She had covered her lacquered hair with a scarf to protect it from the dust, and had rolled up her sleeves. She scowled when she saw me, but before she could speak, I said, "This job is worth twice what I promised you. Will eighty bucks pay for the clean windows and the aggravation?"

The scowl softened. "Make it ninety and I'll dance at your wedding."

I considered the black scum on the bathroom tile and agreed. Arlana hadn't seen the worst room in the house yet. I was getting off light. "Help me pull down the drapes in my bedroom and I'll do the windows there."

"How you gonna sleep in the morning with it light and all?"

"No problem. I could sleep anywhere. It's one thing you learn in residency—to sleep when you can. Period."

Together, we pulled down the dust-laden drapes and piled them all in my car. I would have them cleaned if they were not too far gone to rot. Window treatments were a long way off financially for me. The wood casings around the windows were wide and carved, the way they made them in the old days, by hand. They needed a coat of paint, but just cleaning made them gleam. The glass in them wavered, hand-blown panes with small bubbles and imperfections that the window-replacement specialist wanted to destroy. I didn't know how I could bear to part with them, seeing them clean. I used a whole roll of brown paper on one window, and loved the way the irregular glass panes felt beneath my hands. Arlana vacuumed and mopped the floor behind me as I polished, then went back to the front windows, leaving me alone. A half hour passed in pleasant mindless labor.

During a break when I drank my first cup of coffee for the day, I approached Arlana with an idea. "Arlana, did you know I paid my way through medical school by being a housekeeper?"

Arlana lifted her eyebrows, looked slowly from one end of the house to the other and said, "For who? A blind deaf-mute who can't smell?"

I grinned. "Nope. For Miss DeeDee Stowe. And I did a bang-up job, too. Which is probably why I'm such a slob now, 'cause I always hated housework."

In the distance a dirt bike roared, its engine sputtering. Belle barked once to warn it away from her territory, then the engine died, still far off. I relaxed my crushing hold on my mug. Belle returned to her pups.

"I noticed." Arlana put a hand on her slim hip. "This the dirtiest place I ever did see."

I returned my attention to the conversation at hand. "So how are you paying your way through tech school?"

"Not as your maid."

"How about as my housekeeper? General cleaning only, no windows after today, except once a year," I amended, "and you work two days a week, for forty bucks a week. And I agree to guarantee your student loans."

Arlana's eyes narrowed. "This because I'm black? You think because I'm black I need to work as a maid?"

"No. I think because you're a woman you're starting out with the deck stacked against you and you could work at Hardee's or McDonald's or waiting tables or you could work for me and set your own hours. I need the help and it's my guess you could use the loan guarantee. We got a deal?"

"I'll think about it. But it'll be sixty a week if I say yes, not no measly forty."

I smiled at her stance, half tough-street-smarts, half consideration. "Good. Let me know. I'll get back to the windows."

I carried my coffee mug back to my bedroom, all dusted and clean now, with one floor-to-ceiling window shining. I stopped in the doorway and admired my work. I had never noticed the wood slats of the hardwood floors. It looked like hickory stained a rich golden-brown. Beautiful wood.

Something *snapped*, and the mug in my hand exploded. The newly cleaned window imploded. Scalding coffee drenched me. An instant later, a gunshot cracked, echoing.

"Hunters!" I screamed as I hit the floor. "Get down!" Silence settled around the house. My heart tried to slow to a normal rate. Calm descended around me. I had landed in the coffee and on a sharp shard of my mug. I thought I might be bleeding. "Arlana, you okay?"

"This why I hate living so close to the woods," she shouted back. "You get killed in your own backyard. They gone?"

I lifted myself out of the cooling coffee and looked out the long window. The glass I had cleaned was shattered. I came to my knees. A man stood at the edge of the woods. He held a gun, pointed at the house. At me.

He fired, the rifle bucking up in his arms. I dropped. Glass cut into my side. Shattered above me. Hailed down over me. Ribbons of needle-sharp window, cutting the skin of my hands, wrapped around my head. The rifle fired again, sharp and booming at once. Deadly. Not a hunter with an accidental shot... *He was firing at me....*

"Stay down!" I screamed, huddling against the floor. Belle barked like a demon in the hallway. *"Arlana, stay down!"*

Two more shots seemed to come on top of one another. Glass was all over me. A dirt bike roared. Belle stood in the doorway, teeth bared, barking deep in her throat. I rolled to the bed and pulled the phone to the floor. Dialed 911. Screaming at Arlana. At Belle. "Arlana! Are you all right? Belle, stay! *Stay!* Arlanaaa!"

"You got lungs like one of them opera singers, woman. I'm fine. Your dog fine. We all fine. You ever shut up you hear we all fine."

"Nine-one-one. What is the nature of your emergency?"

"My house is being shot at!" I screamed. "Get me some help!"

The first cruiser arrived followed by most of the marked sheriff's cars in the county. I stayed put at the bottom of the window talking hysterically to the

911 operator until I heard the first siren, and then rolled quickly through the glass to the doorway and into the hall. I was covered with glass and blood, and Belle tried to lick away the horror, her tail between her legs as if she had done wrong. I had to hold her back to get to the door, one bleeding hand tangled in her new collar. She wanted forgiveness and she wanted to attack. She barked furiously.

Jacobson met me at the back door and stopped, eyes wide at the sight of so much blood on me. "It's just glass. I wasn't shot. But he got away. Dirt bike." I pointed the direction he had taken. My hand was shaking.

"Jesus, Doc. You come sit down." Jacobson pushed Belle out of the way and pulled me into the house. Sat me in a kitchen chair. I babbled as we moved.

"But he got away. He was shooting at me. At my house. At my dog. He was shooting. Shooting. At *me*."

"How many?"

"Lots of them. Dozens of them."

"He shot six times. Maybe seven. Rifle, not shotgun," Arlana said, standing in the doorway looking cool, the dust scarf gone and her sleeves rolled back down to her wrists.

"How many men?" More sirens came up the drive, down the street.

"One," I said. "Dressed in camouflage fatigues, on a dirt bike. Red. Red dirt bike. Red helmet. Running on too rich a gas mixture. It spluttered. He was *shooting at me!*" My house was full of cops dressed in black military fatigues. Four. Five. I was safe. I was safe. "He was shooting at me. At *me*."

"Calm down, Rhea. You alive. I'm alive. Dog's alive. He missed," Arlana said, and she shrugged.

I stopped at her summary. Laughter bubbled up in the space where all the words had been. Sharp barks of laughter, hysterical, combustible, out of control. Belle climbed onto my lap and curled on my thighs, her face in mine. Glass ground into my legs beneath her. "Ouch. Belle. Get down. Ouch. Oh, damn. I'm bleeding like a stuck pig."

"Yeah, you got glass all over you." Arlana pushed the cops away and pulled me to my feet, dumping the dog to the floor. "We get you cleaned up and then you talk to the cops. You bleeding all over my clean floor. You boys go on out back and look for clues or something."

Mark stepped in the doorway. His face was set and pale. I had never seen him so…angry. "He get away?" he asked Jacobson.

"Long gone. I was two blocks away. Hit the siren as soon as I heard the first shot. He was gone by the time I got here."

"You stick closer from now on."

"You want me to park in her backyard, Cap?"

"You boys take it outside," Arlana said. "'Specially if you goin' to argue among yourselves. Git! I'll get Rhea cleaned up and then you can argue with her all you want. Go on, boys. It too pretty to play inside."

I laughed again, letting Arlana lead me down the hallway to my bathroom by the hand. Like a child who'd bumped her knee at play. She closed the door on the men's voices, sat me on the toilet and pulled the clothes from my body. Glass tinkled all around me. Belle snuffed at the door and ran to her pups. Then back to the door, toenails scratching on the hall floor. She was frantic, unable to decide who needed guarding most, the pups or me. Suddenly I started crying.

"Yeah, I cried, too, first time someone shot at me. Then I got mad. You just go ahead and cry, but do it in the shower. You don't want the good-lookin' cop hear you cry. Damn. This the most filthy shower stall I ever see. You catch something you climb in that thing. But you a doctor, you can write you'self a prescription for it. You expect me to clean this thing the price just went up to a hundred dollars for the day, all this mildew and mold. Mama Essie have a conniption she see this."

Turning on the shower water, she stood me beneath it, talking all the while to cover the sound of my sobs. Glass and water fell in a torrent around me. Blood sluiced down, watery and crimson.

"You move your feet and I'll never get all the slivers out of your soles," Arlana said. "Stay still. Here. Shampoo. Soap. Don't need a rag. Just your hands, so you can feel where the glass is. Pull out the slivers. Jesus, a bullet got in here. Look, a fresh hole in the tile. Something else I got to clean."

The sobs subsided and I laughed again, this time at the picture of the young girl—who couldn't have been more than nineteen—caring for me, talking ninety miles a minute to cover the fact of her own hysteria. Finally the laughter faded. Hot water washed away the blood and the suds and the glass.

It sparkled on the mildewed tile beneath my feet. I rested my head against the wall.

"I have hydrogen peroxide in the medicine chest. And flip-flops under the bed for my feet. I can't get out of here barefoot."

Arlana vanished and returned with the rubber thongs, shocking pink and turquoise. A lavender jogging suit was in her other hand, and scraps of white that looked like underthings. She turned off the water and stepped into the shower stall with me. Poured hydrogen peroxide over me. I gasped at the icy splash and the instant pain.

"Here. Give me that." I took the bottle and poured a generous handful into my cupped hand. Carefully, I rinsed the exposed flesh of my hands, face and neck, letting the bubbles sting my cuts clean.

"How long since you had a tetanus?"

I laughed again, the sound almost normal this time. "I'm a doctor, remember? This the way you deal with being shot at? Being tough and taking care of everybody else?"

"Beats crying my eyes out."

I pulled a towel from the laundry basket in the corner and applied pressure to the open wounds. "So how many times have you been shot at?"

"Three. First time was in middle school. Friend of mine, DeWayne Lee, failed a test and pulled a gun. Shot the teacher. I was standing right beside her. She lived, but I never did get all the blood out of my favorite sweater. Second time was two months ago, down to the place where I stay. Drive-by shooting. Third time was today." Arlana looked up at me and pointed. "You still bleeding right there."

I took a deep breath. I had never been shot at. I had been safe all my life, or as safe as homes South-of-Broad and all the benefits of my mother's trust fund could make me. I took another breath, calming myself. Mother drank away all the money, digging into the principle and leaving me destitute by the time I was ready for college. Of course, she was dead by then. But I was safe still, under the protection of Miss DeeDee and her guarantee of my student loans.

I took a final breath and reached for the clothes. "Thank you."

"What for?"

"For pulling me out of there before I made a fool of myself."

"Too late." She grinned. "You beat me to the punch. But I did get you away before you made a *total* fool of yourself."

"Gee, thanks."

Arlana laughed. "Dry your hair. Put on some makeup. That big cop what came in last likes you, I could tell. And you look like shit, girl."

I sighed. "Yeah. Well. Thanks anyway." I pulled on the panties and bra and the jogging suit, found socks and sneakers and crunched glass as I moved. I was ready in ten minutes, with a bit of lipstick and my hair mostly dry.

I opened the door to my room and surveyed the damage. A cool breeze was blowing through the shattered windows. Glass sparkled in the late-afternoon sun, picking up rays on the bedspread, on the floor, in the far corners of the room. I could smell someone's wood smoke on the winter air. It was a mess.

There were three undamaged panes of glass in the window I had cleaned…the others were gone. Of the window that was still dirty, I was lucky. All the panes were gone. At least I wouldn't have to clean them. And now I wouldn't have to agonize about losing the antique panes. They were beyond repair.

Suddenly I stopped, seeing the woods beyond the broken glass. The dirt bike had taken off in the direction of Marisa's house. Was I in danger now? For helping Marisa? For discovering the lobotomies? For bringing in the police?

I squared my shoulders and went to the back door. If Arlana could find a way to deal with violence, then so could I. I took Belle with me on the leash to face the officers in my house and yard. Like my dog, I was subdued, but thanks to Arlana I was at least no longer hysterical.

17

A Fine-Looking Man and Old Hymns

It was nearly dark when I got to the hospital. Night comes early from November through March in the Carolinas, and I needed a run I was too afraid to take in my own backyard. The Health Run was well lighted, surrounded by people and cars and activities. I would be safe here. I laced on my shoes and started walking, stretching as I moved.

The day was still balmy, and though the cooler temps of night had taken over, my breath made no puffs of condensation as I moved. The air was still and silent. I increased my pace, soles slapping on the hard ground.

As I passed Shobani's office a shadow crossed in front of the window. Shobani, moving furniture. I slowed and watched as I passed from window to window. He was taking down blinds, removing framed prints from the walls, pulling his diplomas, awards and accreditations down. Time for a paint job perhaps. I returned my pace to normal and moved across the parking lot, letting my mind return to the scene at my house.

The cops had stayed at my place after I left, pick-

ing up shiny brass cartridges from the winter-bare
ground, walking around with their heads down, turning over leaves I had not bothered to rake up in the
fall, searching for clues. Mark had promised to nail
plywood over the holes where my windows had
been.

Arlana had agreed to finish cleaning my house,
even the shattered glass and bathroom tile that lay
all over. When I left, she was stripping the bed and
vacuuming the mattress to gather up any microscopic
shards of glass that might make sleeping there dangerous. I entered the woods at the back of the hospital and breathed deeply to erase the sudden tension
at my abrupt isolation. I was safe here. No one knew
I was running here. I pounded on.

The house would be livable when I returned in the
morning, but I didn't know if I could stay there now.
Didn't know if I wanted to live in a house that had
not offered better protection.... As I ran, I wondered
if it was too late to withdraw my offer to buy.

A shadow darted from a tree. I dodged and
crouched in the instant before I identified the shape.
Owl. Hunting at dusk. Straightening, I gritted my
teeth and ran on. The heroines in the novels Marisa
always read would laugh at my case of nerves, my
ducking at shadows. But I was afraid. For myself
and for Marisa.

In the brush, a small animal screamed. I increased
my pace running far too fast, considering the short
warm-up. I could get cramps, but I didn't care. The
next sodium vapor lamp was yards ahead. I sprinted
the distance, blowing hard in the still night.

There were no dirt bike engines. No sign of anyone with a gun pointed my way. I was safe. And yet, I still increased my speed. Not until I was again horizontal with the E.R. on the best lighted part of the run did I slow down. I could feel the cramps in my calves and shins and forced my speed even slower. No one knew I was here. No one knew I was running. No one knew I'd be stupid enough to do so.

I laughed at my logic and settled into a steady pace that pulled the cramps from my muscles and deepened my breathing. I could feel the worry, the fear, blow out with each breath. I could do this. I could make this run.

I relaxed, letting the pace beat the tension from me. Feeling myself loosen with each step, each yard I covered. I was able finally to think rationally about the whole experience.

The man with the gun… He should have hit me. He had a bead on me through the broken window. He fired before I dropped to the floor. He shouldn't have missed from that distance. Why had he? Bad shot? Or deliberate miss?

Before I left for the hospital, Mark had told me to be careful. His investigation indicated an increasing level of violence, that conclusion not based solely on the attack on me. He had proof that Marisa had been held down while she was lobotomized. The bruises on her ankles and wrists had been present when the EMTs arrived to take her to the hospital on the morning she was discovered injured. The news was not new to me—I had already drawn that conclusion. I wanted to put a guard on Marisa…. Mark wanted to put a guard on me. And perhaps, for Marisa's sake, it would be wiser if I didn't run again until she was better. As long as I was safe myself, I could protect my friend.

I didn't finish my usual five miles, but slowed at a bit more than four and turned in to the ICU wing. The window at the nurses' desk was lighted, with familiar figures sitting there. That meant that from another angle Marisa would be visible as well. I stretched my legs, picturing the window of Marisa's room, placing the position a dirt bike would need for a shooter to take her in his sights.

I grabbed my duffel from the trunk of my car, stuffed Marisa's old chart under the edge of the trunk cover and ran for the building. Without a proper cooldown, I tapped on the window at the RNs heads and motioned them to the fire door nearest. They let me in to the heat and the smells of the ward—deodorized cleanser, baby powder, alcohol, feces, the ammoniacal scent of old urine.

"Gave me a fright there, Dr. Lynch."

I looked at the nurse and smiled. "Sorry, Gloris. How is everyone tonight?"

"Feeling fat. I guess if I would run with you every night I'd lose the extra fifty. You're skinny as a rail. 'Course, I'd have to give up pizza and beer, and my husband would have a fit."

"There is a downside," I agreed as we walked down the hall to Marisa's room. "Has Dr. Reston checked in today?"

"That man? Best-looking thing I ever saw. He's got the nurses all up the hallway bowing and scraping. If I was a few years younger I'd join 'em. They think he's God's gift to the fair sex."

"So does he."

"I gathered that, too," she said, laughing and patting her mound of bleached, teased hair. "But he *is* fine."

I slowed as Marisa's bed came into view. There was someone standing there. Beside her. Holding a pillow before him, an end in each hand.

Eddie.

Heat blossomed in my limbs, exploded in rage. I threw myself into the room, diving for Eddie. He glanced up, met my eyes, stumbled back, dropping the pillow.

A nurse rose from the floor holding a liter measure filled with urine. She jerked, urine splashing over her gloved hand. Sliding, I stopped at the sight of her.

"What? What?" she said, holding the wet hand out. Urine dripped from her fingers. The room was oddly silent, all eyes on me.

"What is *he* doing here?" I demanded, lowering my hands. They were curled into claws. Turning to Eddie, I said, "I thought you were in jail!"

"B...b-b-bond," he stuttered, his eyes wide, shocked. Full of fear...

Fear of me? I took a deep breath. Uncurled my hands. "I left orders that no one was to see this patient," I ground out, not taking my eyes from Eddie. "And that meant Eddie Braswell, too. Eddie Braswell especially," I said softly, watching his eyes, so hollowed, so lost, skin raccoon-circled, black beneath the pinpoint pupils. He blinked, his gaze slipping from me to Marisa. She was little more than a small mound on the bed. I thought he might cry as he watched her, but whether his tears were from sorrow or guilt I couldn't tell.

"But he's her son," the nurse holding the urine said.

I ignored her. "If you come back," I whispered, "I'll have the police here so fast your head will spin. Now get out of here."

Eddie spun and ran. He was so skinny his bones might have rattled, but he was filled with manic energy, drug induced, his skin as pale as his stepmother's.

"Dr. Lynch?" the nurse said uncertainly.

"Eddie isn't her son. And he raped a girl in Ford County," Gloris said.

The nurse hissed softly. "He seemed so nice...." Shocked, she looked from me to the liter measure in her hand, turned slowly and poured it down the sink drain. "So nice..."

I took a breath. My second in what seemed like hours. Adrenaline pounded in my temples, thrummed in my blood. There was nothing I could do. Nothing.

"How's Mrs. Braswell doing?" I managed to ask. Stepping to Marisa's feet, I gauged the distance from her bed to the window, feeling hyperalert, hypersensitive, to any possible danger. My fingers tingled lightly. Any shooter would have to be awfully tall to target her from the ground. The other nurse left the room, shaking her head.

"Her temp is down to a hundred and hasn't spiked in over four hours," Gloris reported. "BP and vital signs stable. Dr. Reston is ordering all kinds of medications we don't usually keep on hand, and driving the pharmacy crazy, but it all seems to be working. He's down to the kitchen with one or another of the nurses getting a snack before they close. And I'm sorry, Dr. Lynch. I passed along the order about no visitors—''

I cut her off with a gesture. ''I'll go join them. But first, I want Marisa Braswell's blinds kept closed after dusk. Completely closed. Put up a sign so no one forgets. And close all the other patients' window blinds, too.''

''Well, I guess. If you say so.'' Her full lips pursed in puzzlement.

''Mrs. Braswell was assaulted, Gloris. I don't want anyone to finish what they started.''

''Someone hit her?'' Gloris asked as she turned the small knob closing the blinds.

''Something like that.'' I was surprised the hospital grapevine hadn't passed along the entire story by now. ''And if Marisa's window is the only one they can't see through, then they know where she is by the process of elimination. Any phone calls that want to know what room she is in are to be referred to me. I don't want any information given out about her condition unless you personally know the person you are talking to. Okay?''

''Yes, ma'am. I'll pass it along to the other RNs and to the other shifts. Poor little thing. And she was so pretty, too....''

''Yes. She was,'' I said softly, studying my friend. ''Gloris, do you know why Marisa, Mrs. Braswell, had restricted-visitor requirements when she was in here before?''

''Lord, yes. That child would get riled at the slightest thing. Kept the other patients up all night with her screaming and ranting. Seemed especially bad when family came by. Only person Dr. Braswell would let in was the preacher. He seemed to calm her down considerable.''

I nodded, oddly relieved. Perhaps Steven *hadn't* been worried that Eddie would hurt his wife. Perhaps there were reasons why Steven had done all he could to keep his wife here in Dawkins County instead of sending her to a neuro-trauma center. I frowned. *Perhaps Marisa hadn't really been assaulted.... Perhaps all my fears were worthless.... Perhaps cows could fly.... Fat chance.*

''Well, were you ever going to call me and tell me about my niece?''

I whirled and caught my breath.

Miss DeeDee stood by the door in an ice-blue Chanel suit, pearls swinging, reading glasses perched on top of her head. Her face wore a forbidding expression. ''Or are you going to try to keep me from my baby, too? I had to find out from the day's admissions listings that one of my own was in this hospital.''

''Oh, Miss DeeDee. I'm so sorry. I—''

''Don't you let her bamboozle you, Dr. Lynch. As per your orders, I contacted Miss DeeDee first thing this morning—after we had Mrs. Braswell stabilized—and told her all about her niece.''

''My orders...''

''Yes, ma'am. And though she won't admit to it in a million years, Miss DeeDee thought you were just the sweetest thing to let her know. She told me so.''

''Gloris, I'm so glad you remembered,'' I said. Had I written such an order?

Gloris turned, stepped from the room. And winked at me.

I grinned, understanding. It was nice to have friends.

"You could have told me yourself." DeeDee smoothed her polished nails back with the thumb of her other hand.

I put an arm around her thin shoulders and squeezed gently. "I really am sorry, Miss DeeDee. But it was nice of Gloris to take care of it for me."

"I was right about Steven, wasn't I? He wasn't giving her proper care...."

I said nothing, and the astute older woman scanned my face. "I know you can't say so, but he didn't take care of her. I know it. He let her get worse and worse at home where no one could tell that he was neglecting her."

I looked away, focusing on Marisa's face. The bruises were fading, I could have sworn that the swelling around her eye was decreasing. And someone had washed her hair. Cam Reston's orders, no doubt. I wondered if he had washed it himself. It was the kind of thing Cam might do.

She *had* been beautiful. I wanted her to be so again.

"I'm going to take her away from him," DeeDee said softly. Her face was stricken, *old*-looking. I had never thought of DeeDee as being older.... Never. She was *Miss DeeDee*. An icon. Never changing.

"I have friends in this state," she continued, her voice low and implacable. "Legislators. Judges. Steven won't keep me from my last living relative. I'm going to take her away from him. Marisa needs me, not that coldhearted automaton she married. For all we know, he did this to her...."

The thought was an icy shock to my senses. I let my arm fall from her shoulders. "He was at work for nearly twelve hours before Miss Essie found her. There wasn't time for Steven to be the one who..." My voice trailed off. I didn't want to think it. Not Steven. Not Marisa's own husband. Yet, the thought had been voiced more than once, even in my own mind....

Mark's voice spoke in my memory. *Everyone's a suspect. Even you.*

"I know all about the logistics. But something in my mind says...he did it," DeeDee whispered.

"Go home. Have supper. Get a shower. I promise to call if there is any change."

Miss DeeDee looked up at me, straightened her spine, lifted an eyebrow and said, "And you might want to write the order for Gloris to call me about Marisa before it slips your mind again."

"Ouch."

"I'm older and wiser, dear. Never try to pull one over on Miss DeeDee."

"I'll remember that."

"I doubt it, dear. I doubt it." DeeDee walked from the room, her silk slip swishing softly, her Italian-made shoes tapping gently. A lady who would never retreat. And who always had to have the last word.

Marisa's eyes slowly opened. They stared at the clock hanging beside the sink, its second hand ticking silently. "Toy box," she said, her lips moving slowly.

I leaned in and took her hand, my fingers automatically checking her pulse, fingering her IV. Her skin was cool to the touch.

"Purple running mountain marshmallow..." She took a deep breath. "S...s...spin dirty banana..."

I lifted Marisa's hand to my cheek and suddenly I was singing softly. "'On a hill far away... Stood an old rugged cross... The emblem of suffering and shame...'"

Marisa sighed and closed her eyes. As I sang, she found sleep again, her face peaceful.

Cam was sitting with Miss Essie and three nurses, regaling them with some anecdote from his boyhood. I think it was the one where his uncle taught him to fish and Cam discovered that he had to thread a fishhook with a wriggling worm. It wasn't a funny story, but when Cam told it women always laughed. Women generally did pretty much whatever Cam wanted.

I loaded a tray with salad fixings, homemade soup and corn bread—typical Sunday-night supper at Dawkins County Hospital—grabbed a Coke and joined the group. It was an E.R. doctor's perk that I didn't have to pay for the food. I ate for fifteen minutes, concentrating on the crunch of lettuce, the squish of meat and veggies, and the satisfying fat content of the corn bread. The kitchen staff made it the old-fashioned way, with lots of bacon grease and bacon cracklings, and just a pinch of sugar. It was heavenly.

When I wiped my mouth after my last bite, I thought I had been polite long enough. I had sat around listening to Cam flirt and cajole for too many years to find his current session the least amusing. Besides, he hadn't even noticed when I walked up.

"Cam. Can we talk?"

Cam looked up and grinned, his five-thousand-dollar orthodontia work gleaming. "Rhea-Rhea! The girl of my dreams..." He rose and leaned past a young nurse, grabbed my arms.

"Let's keep it that way, okay, Cam," I said as I pushed away his hands and dodged his lips. "You haven't changed one whit since the first time I saw you."

"It was love at first sight."

"Yeah. With the girl walking with me. I remember like it was the nineties. Which it was," I finished dryly. "Would you ladies excuse us? Dr. Reston and I need to discuss a patient, and this is the only time I have. Stop it, Cam." I pushed his face away as he tried again to kiss me.

The RNs left, one even giggling, a sound I have hated since my youth. A grown woman should never giggle, titter or simper. Laughter, discreet laughter, was acceptable. And then I hated myself for thinking that way, for the dictum on giggling was Mama's, and I seldom did anything Mama had demanded. I stood and got another Coke. "Want one?" I asked him as the carbonated drink bubbled out over the ice.

"That would be nice." Cam grinned, a shock of black hair falling over his forehead, his black eyes glinting. The dimples that had swamped the moral imperatives of uncounted debutantes and led to the man's reputation as a Don Juan peeked at me from olive skin brushed with a perfect five o'clock shadow. Gloris was right—he was fine, indeed.

"Consider it a professional courtesy," I said wryly, "not a member of your current harem doing you service."

Cam laughed, watching me return to the table. "I maybe didn't grow up, Rhea, but you did. You finally grew into those spectacular legs."

I shook my head. "Marisa. Let's talk about Marisa."

"She's much less cyanotic, heart and breath rate are stabilized, and she seemed to be responding to the meds you started her on in the E.R., as well as the two meds I had brought in by courier, Shalatrin and Comisolulin. Something new we're using in a study of traumatic injuries." He smiled. "This hospital is the back side of the earth, though, let me tell you. You don't have access to anything."

"More labs than you would imagine, the fastest blood gases this side of Oz, Bozo, and nurses who actually give a flip about patient care."

Cam ignored my comment. "Right side hemiplegia, decreased since her original admission according to her admitting physician—who is not happy that I am here, by the way. She hasn't regained consciousness, however, which I regard as a bad sign."

"She woke up about twenty minutes ago. Talked to the clock over the bed. Went back to sleep."

"Yessss!" Cam jumped to his feet.

"Sit down, flyboy. I'm not through with my Coke. And you need to hear the rest." I told him about the attack on my home, omitting tiny details such as my crying jag and the time I spent crouched in terror under my window screaming into the phone at the 911 operator. And then I told him the things Mark had learned during the course of the day and shared with me before I left for work.

"Mark says the state crime lab has already identified the substance on my third patient's clothing as chloroform. So whoever is responsible for performing the lobotomies is evolving his technique. He's getting better. So far as we know, Marisa was the first victim, and Marisa did not receive the sedative Xylazine to calm her. She was held down, physically restrained during her...ordeal."

Cam's face twisted. His black eyes narrowed, anger in their dark depths twisted with pity and revulsion.

I fought for control of my own expression, tried to banish the freeze-frame view I had of Marisa struggling with her assailants. I thought I could hear her screams as if in my memory. "In Marisa's case, there is some discrepancy in the original EMT reports and in the one that was finally filed. The original report mentions the bruising on Marisa's ankles and wrists. The final report is missing that information.

"The second victim did receive a sedative. Xylazine, which kept him calm, but also put him in AV block. The third victim was injected with Xylazine and also dosed with chloroform. Physical restraint in the last two cases did not appear to occur.

"We don't know why any of it has happened. Mark is trying to tie all three people together, but so far no luck. And you need to know about Eddie Braswell." I told him about Marisa's stepson and the assaults on females in the other counties. "I saw him when I first got back from vacation. He was horribly emaciated, like he had AIDS or weight loss from severe drug use. I haven't been able to find out if he used an ice pick or something similar to subdue any of the victims, and I'm worried about Marisa's safety.

"I just caught him in her room, standing over her with a pillow in his hands like he was going to smother her." Cam started to rise and I took his arm. "He wasn't doing anything, there was a nurse with him, but I had a bad moment, thinking I had let him have access to her. I ran him off. And I doubt he'll be back," I added ruefully. "I scared him pretty badly. May have scared the nurses, too, come to think of it."

"Got riled, did you? I'd like to have seen that."

I snorted softly, and attended to the last of my soup.

"Really," he teased. "I'll bet you look something when you get mad, eyes flashing, all that rigid composure wiped away. I've never seen you like that." After a moment he said, "You were always so controlled, the ice maiden..."

I ignored him.

"Okay. Be that way," he sighed.

I grinned into the bowl.

"I'll be staying in the room with Marisa tomorrow," Cam said, his voice businesslike again, his eyes still on me. "I can catch a nap in the evenings when you come in to work. That way one of us will always be here."

I nodded and told him about closing all the window blinds on the ICU floor. "I'm thinking about hiring a bodyguard for her until we can find a way to fly her out to Duke."

"I am perfectly capable of defending Marisa," Cam said softly, his eyes black as jet.

I ignored the deeper meaning—the almost husbandly protection—hidden in the dark depths and said simply, "You still taking that karate stuff?" I asked him.

"Tae kwon do and tai chi. I teach now, actually. On Thursdays and Saturdays."

"Okaaay." I had a hard time envisioning Cam in white pj's with a black belt tied around his waist. "Don't use it on Steven, okay?"

Cam laughed, eyes turning devilish. "I'll check in with you before I leave for the hotel. By the way, I didn't plan to stay with you, but it would have been nice to be asked." He leaned in close, eyes fastened on my mouth. "I would have helped you forget all about John."

I choked on my Coke and fought the blush that rose on my skin. Damn Cam Reston for being such a charmer. "Don't forget, my house got aerated this afternoon. Be glad you had a place to stay."

18

Old Mail and Suspects

That night in the E.R. I saw a few patients who really needed my care, and a round dozen who could have treated themselves with OTCs and let me sleep. The only bright spots in the night were the hot shower I took, the jojoba oil I slathered on my chapped and abraded skin afterward, the four-hour nap I caught between 2:00 and 6:00 a.m., and the time I spent sitting at Marisa's bedside. She never again regained consciousness, but there was a visible difference in her that went beyond mere medicine. I could tell just by looking at her that she was going to live.

Monday, 7:00 a.m., I greeted a freshly shaved Cam, instructed him to go by Abigail Staton's office for proper hospital-privilege papers, put off his teasing and pretended to be unaffected by the big hug he made sure to give me right in front of the nurses' desk. Climbing into my car, I drove home. The days were getting longer again, and it was almost light when I let Belle out for her morning business. The camping supplies I had left piled in the hallway since my return had been stacked neatly. Belle and I didn't

have to step across and over the knapsack, the bag
of metal dishes and cooking pans, and the leftover
tins of food that had spilled out from somewhere.
The floor beneath the supplies was gleaming clean
and the tins of food were stacked on the kitchen
counter.

Belle wanted to go for a run, but settled for a game
of ear-tug, where she dodged my hands and I tried
to touch her ears. Then I tossed her a rubber toy
Arlana had left on the counter and Belle obligingly
brought it back. She was a well-trained animal with
such a look of love in her eyes it was almost impossible for me to imagine the kind of person who
had put her out to die.

It was only after we were done playing that I saw
the envelope.

It was on the counter in plain sight, a yellow sticky
note on its nine-by-twelve tan front that said simply:
*I found this on the floor under all your camping stuff.
I put the food in the cabinets. I'll take you up on the
offer of the housekeeper job. But I am not a maid.
Arlana. P.S. You owe me for yesterday.*

I pulled off the sticky note and tossed it in the
trash. I had never seen the envelope before. I must
have come in that first day and dumped my camping
supplies on it in the dark hallway. It had lain there
hidden.

My name was on the front in a clean, looping
script. *Rhea-Rhea.* It was Marisa's flowing penman-
ship. A cold chill swept through me. My breathing
sped up. I watched as my hands slowly lifted the
envelope and opened it.

Inside there was a letter and a packet of photographs. I read the rambling letter, eyes on the familiar script, fingers tracing the letters, tears running down my cheeks.

Dear Rhea-Rhea,

There is so much to tell you and I wish you were here. I feel like my heart is breaking in two and I can't tell Aunt DeeDee just yet. She would be devastated. And I don't know what to do. I feel so lost.... I just don't understand how all this could happen.

Steven is having an affair. I noticed things were changing between us, and though I didn't tell you, I hired a detective to, well, to check up on Steven. I think I will just die. Perhaps I am dying right now....

Oh, aren't I sounding silly... If you were here you would slap me on the arm and tell me to cheer up, that things could get worse. But I'm not sure that's possible.

Steven is sleeping with a respiratory technician named Sarah. She is very pretty. Dark hair and blue eyes. And I hate her...I just hate her. I am putting the pictures and the detective's report together with my letter to you. I will make no decisions until you come home and we can talk, but I think I must leave him. I can't stand to live with him and love him so much and know I am not enough for him.

I know divorce will be a mess with all this evidence and with the constrictions on my trust fund.... I am just so sick. I can't stop crying. Please call me as soon as you get in from your

*trip. I need to talk. Perhaps I will call Aunt
DeeDee after all. I simply can't stand all this,
especially now. My life should have been wonderful—I had such exciting news—and now
this....*

Love,
Risa

I placed the letter on the kitchen cabinet and slid
onto a tall stool at the bar. I had cried more in the
last few days than in all of my entire adult life, and
now the tears flowed like a river of pain. Marisa,
alone. And Steven... "*Damn* him. *Damn him!*" I
whispered.

And then Miss DeeDee's words came back to me.
"*For all we know, he did this to her...*" And Mark's
words... "*Right now, I think everyone is a possible
suspect....*"

The cold had enveloped me. Belle, worried, had
curled up on my feet as I read the letter, and now
sat beside me, her head pressed against my leg. I
rubbed her behind the ears, tall pointed ears with tips
that fell forward, long silky hair. She licked my
hand.

If everyone was a suspect...and the assailant had
medical training...and Steven was at work and could
not have attacked Marisa... Then perhaps Sarah...

I didn't know the woman well. I skimmed the investigator's report. Ty Yarborough was his name,
and he worked out of an office in Ford County. He
had followed Steven for ten days and had a listing
of hotels, times and dates, and a collection of photographs. Even an audiotape of the illicit lovers talk-

ing over lunch. The tape was one of the micro kind, and was in with the photographs.

I flipped through the pictures, saw Steven touching the woman as he led her from a car to a hotel room. Steven and the woman sitting at a table in the Varsity Restaurant in Ford County, heads close. Steven and the woman—Sarah, I reminded myself—walking hand in hand on the beach, dressed for the cold. Steven laughing—such a rare sight—his eyes looking down into Sarah's. This photo had fingerprints all around the edges. It must have caused Marisa particular pain.

My tears had dried. Steven or Sarah... Sarah or Steven...

I dialed Mark's pager number from memory. I had never been good with numbers—words and associations and names were my strength. But with Mark, I seemed to remember well. He called me back within five minutes, which I took to grind beans and brew a fresh pot of coffee. Dark roast, Colombian, very strong. When I told him about Arlana's find, he hung up without a word and was at my house in another ten. The law enforcement center was farther away than that.

I didn't ask him where he'd called from or how fast he had driven. I just poured him a cup of coffee, added two sugars and two creams the way he liked it, and microwaved him a bagel. I watched his face as he drank the coffee and picked at the bagel, his eyes on Ty Yarborough's report.

Square-jawed, skin tanned and finely wrinkled at his moss-green eyes and around his mouth, he sat and studied. His hair was thinning just a bit at the crown. His hands were square and strong-looking, nails blunt and trimmed close to the quick. He looked tired, circles beneath his eyes.

With a shock I realized another reason why I had refused to move back to Charleston with John. It was this face I saw so often in my dreams. These eyes laughing down into mine, flashing green fire. I had been missing Mark....

He looked up, eyes cold. "Tell me again where you got this."

I blinked, banishing the image, and explained about the camping equipment, the housecleaning, and Arlana. And as I talked, my eyes kept dropping to his lips. They softened as I spoke and finally he smiled. "You *don't* keep a very clean house."

"I can afford a maid. A housekeeper," I corrected.

Mark settled back against the kitchen stool, drinking his coffee. He took a bite of bagel and chewed. When he swallowed, he asked, "Do you remember anything more about Medicom Plus and Mitchell Scoggins?"

I poured another cup of coffee for myself, thinking. This was the third time Mark had asked me about the company and its president. Though Mark was thorough, he wasn't dense. In his mind there had to be some connection. "I don't remember anything more than I told you at the hospital. Unlike you, I didn't live here growing up, remember? I just spent a few summer vacations here. Why?"

Mark toyed with his mug and I topped off his coffee, passing him the cream and sugar. I waited as he sorted through what he wanted to tell me, what he could tell me, and what he had to tell me. I wasn't an impatient person. Medical school and residency had knocked all impatience out of me. You couldn't hurry healing.

Mark added cream and sugar to his coffee, stirred with little tinkling sounds of spoon against stone-ware. "Mitchell Scoggins is Steven's lawyer. He also has employed Raymond Abel as a part-time yard worker, clearing limbs from a storm, raking leaves, that sort of thing."

Mark sipped and looked up at me. His green eyes were amused. "Willie Evans was arrested a year ago on possession of marijuana. Mitch got Willie off on a technicality. Mitchell is a link for all three of our victims."

"And Eddie Braswell?"

Mark grinned. "He put in a few hours for two local cattle farmers, working for a temp labor agency. The same agency that employed Raymond Abel. We even believe that Eddie worked with Ray on at least one farm..." He paused for effect, and to irritate me. "...and at Mitchell Scoggins's place. Scoggins, who is now the kid's lawyer."

I tried to place Mitchell, and found only a blurry place in memory. Had he come to Marisa's Christmas party last year? Had John and I met the man?

I stared at Mark's eyes, let mine slip to his lips again and then away. "Mitchell was a premed student before he switched to law," I said slowly, trying to remember who had told me that. Trish? "It's possible he had the basic know-how to lobotomize someone. It's possible."

"What is Sarah's last name? I saw it somewhere

in here,'' he said as he flipped back through the investigator's report.

"Gibbons," I said softly as connections were made in my brain between the name and one of my patients. "Sarah Gibbons."

"Willie Evans was found on Gibbons' Farms. Frank Gibbons owns it. Is that Sarah's husband or maybe her father?"

"Could be," I said. Suddenly I stood and moved from the kitchen bar where we sat. I opened cabinets to see where Arlana had put my dishes, and found them, plain white dishes stacked neatly on shelves lined with shelf paper, bright design of grapes, apples, lemons and passion fruit on a background of feathers and swirls. I checked the refrigerator and discovered it clean, black mold wiped from the rubber seals. I searched the kitchen randomly, something to keep my hands busy, my mind from screaming with loss of control. I bent and looked in the oven. I had never used it, but it was clean, too. I had to give Arlana a big tip. As I moved, Mark talked.

"Willie was helping Mr. Gibbons move cattle from the land because it had been sold to Medicom Plus. Mitchell intended to build one of the Medicom Plus buildings," Mark said, ruminating.

I closed the oven and returned to the bar, but my feet still needed to move and I wanted to *do* something. Run, perhaps. A good five-mile run with Belle. She was ready, or would be soon. "Who are the chief investors in Medicom Plus? I mean besides Mitchell."

"I have someone working on that now."

"I'll see to it that Sarah Gibbons no longer has

access to Marisa in the hospital and I'll let you know if anything looks suspicious.''

"Don't play Agatha Christie with me." He smiled, lips moving up at both corners.

I stilled my restless movements and swallowed. "Your case. My patient. I understand the boundaries."

"Do you?"

I had the feeling we had somehow strayed to unstable ground and I looked away from him. From his mouth.

"Mitchell Scoggins and Medicom Plus and Steven's little girlfriend are at the heart of all this mess. Somehow."

"I offered to let you know if something happened at the hospital."

"And I'll remember my part of the bargain and let you know what I discover about Mitchell and Medicom Plus. Is that what you're driving at?"

I smiled and reached for my cold coffee. Suddenly Mark's arms were around me, pulling me onto his lap. His lips were against my hair, pressed to my temple. "You take care of yourself. No heroics," he whispered.

I nodded and stopped myself from returning his embrace. Instead, I pressed my face close to his, mouth down so he couldn't kiss me. Or perhaps so I couldn't kiss him. "I'll be careful. You, too."

He slid me to my feet and walked me to the back door, one arm around my shoulders. The envelope with Marisa's letter and the photographs was beneath the other. It was only then that I realized the letter was evidence. That I wouldn't be able to keep it. My throat closed up.

"I'm glad you came home, Rhea."

"Me, too. Can…can I get the letter back someday? It's the last thing I have of…" I couldn't finish the sentence.

Mark opened the door and stepped down on the drive, holding my hand. His felt warm and dry, the skin tough. "I'll see you get it back. Meantime, get your windows fixed."

"Not just yet. I think I'll wait a few days. See what happens. Bad guys can't see through plywood."

Mark grinned. "Maybe that's smart. Call 911 if there's any problem here. Jacobson is staying close by your house, patrolling within a couple of miles at all times when he's on duty. At night, I can see across and I'm keeping an eye on the place."

I smiled and looked down at our hands. "Thanks."

A car pulled up, powerful engine purring, black paint shining in the sunlight. Miss DeeDee peered through the windshield.

"Jeez, one minute faster and I'd have missed her," Mark said under his breath, dropping my hand.

"Mind your manners," I said, laughing.

"I have to or she calls my mother and tells her I was rude." Louder, he said, "Good morning, Miss DeeDee. You're looking lovely."

"Good morning, Captain Stafford. Thank you. It's good to see you. How is your mother? I haven't seen Clarissa in ages."

I grinned, watching Mark squirm his way through

the small talk and finally make his way to the Jeep he had parked beside my BMW.

"Such a nice man. Reminds me of my Theodore, my third husband. Is that coffee I smell?"

"Oh, yes," I said, remembering my own manners. "Would you come in, Miss DeeDee? I have a freshly brewed pot and bagels and cream cheese."

"Just the coffee, dear. My, you've cleaned up your house. Essie told me she was sending Arlana over. Such a bright child," she said as she settled at the bar. "You need a proper table, dear. I have an extra one with four chairs in my attic if you are interested. A very pretty walnut table inlaid with maple and something else, I forget what, circa 1894, I believe. In fact, it is the very table Theodore and I ate from when we were married. My only true love match, you know," she said confidentially. "Your Mark reminds me of him in many ways."

I poured coffee for DeeDee and surreptitiously checked my watch. She was late for work, which meant she was interested in something besides my love life. And I needed to call the hospital and leave orders that Sarah Gibbons was not to be allowed near Marisa.

With old-fashioned southern grace, DeeDee chatted awhile before she got down to business, covering the unseasonably warm weather, my new car and the state of the nation under the new president. Finally she asked, "How did that nice Reston man come to be working on Marisa? I haven't seen him since he was a lovesick puppy trailing around after my niece."

I explained Cam's presence at the hospital, aware

that I had better do a more thorough job in explaining Marisa's treatment to DeeDee. If she tried to use the courts to take Marisa away from Steven, I would be right in the middle of the controversy. I didn't look forward to the possibility. I explained in detail everything I could, and then added my most recent find—the envelope detailing Steven's adultery. It was evident from the expression on DeeDee's face that Marisa had not told her about the affair.

She blanched at the news, sitting with coffee cup in hand, eyes staring out the kitchen window at the western horizon, the fingers of her left hand pressed against her mouth. She was dressed today in a pale pink Chanel suit, the fabric bringing out a warm tone in the Stowe pearls. Her blue eyes were troubled.

Slowly she returned the cup to the stoneware saucer. At last she said, "So Risa would have left him. Very soon, it seems."

"Perhaps."

"He would never have let her leave, you know."

"No?" I said softly.

"It was a matter of the trust fund."

I remembered the fund Marisa had mentioned in her letter to me. I poured more coffee, my fingertips tingling in urgency. This was important, I *knew* it. I wanted to urge DeeDee to continue, but any input on my part might be construed as being nosy, a major crime against etiquette in DeeDee's eyes. I set the coffeepot down and waited, watching DeeDee as she sipped and thought, her eyes hollow-looking and far away.

"When Risa turns thirty-five, the trust left to her reaches maturity and she will receive control of the principle. By then it should be valued at well over three million dollars. If she and Steven were divorced or she died without issue, he would have access to nothing. If she were disabled, he would have full control. The trust is convoluted, but you see, it is to Steven's benefit to have a disabled wife.''

"*If* she was about to divorce him..."

"Steven might have done this to her for the money."

"And if you take her away from him..."

"I would become responsible for the trust as well as for Marisa. It isn't something I relish, but there are advisers I can call in if necessary. I would simply have to find the time to manage Marisa's trust as well as my own funds." DeeDee peered at me over the rim of her cup, then smiled as she lowered it. "Life is so...strange. Isn't it, dear Rhea?"

"Yes, ma'am. It is." I didn't quite know what to make of DeeDee's mood. I had expected anger—she held to a rigorous creed of right and wrong and had a notorious temper. She believed that a woman of breeding had a right to a temper in certain circumstances and was honor-bound to express it, albeit in a dainty and ladylike manner. I had seen her unleash this temper more than once over the years, and a queen could not have expressed more stately rage. But this reaction wasn't anger, was more in the nature of exhaustion or...grief. I put my hand over hers and squeezed.

DeeDee smiled sadly. "Thank you, dear. But I want you to be careful. Let the police handle this investigation. You are too valuable to me to get caught in the center of something unsavory. I don't

want both of my girls to be..." She paused and
looked again out the window, returning the pressure
of my fingers. "Be discreet, Rhea, dear. Please."

I was warmed through by the tenderness in
DeeDee's gaze. This was the only family that had
ever mattered to me. DeeDee and Marisa. "I'll be
careful. And there is something you can do to help
Marisa, Miss DeeDee. Marisa's original EMT report
has been filed in the computer, and it is different in
a few particulars from the original. Bruises on her
wrists and ankles are missing from the computer version. Could the computer have been tampered
with?"

Miss DeeDee brightened, her blue eyes sparkling
like gems. "That it could. And if they left a trail, I
might be able to backtrack it to its source. Then we'd
have them, wouldn't we." I nodded and Miss
DeeDee hugged me hard. "Thank you, dear. It does
me good to be able to do something for Marisa right
now, even if it turns out to be a simple clerical error." She raised her hand and patted my cheek as
she took her leave.

After DeeDee left, her huge black sedan purring
like a big cat, I made the call to the hospital, re-
stricting Sarah Gibbons from access to Marisa, spoke
with Cam to explain why, and talked to Mark. I told
him about the trust fund and the impact Marisa's
moribund state might have on Steven's finances. Finally I hit the sack, crawling beneath the covers fully
dressed.

I slept hard, my mind tossing in stormlike night-
mares, images swamping me: Marisa fighting
Steven, her hands in fists, defensive. Marisa lying in

her own excrement. DeeDee in a Chanel suit, head cocked to one side, her eyes gentle. Shobani marking in Marisa's chart. Mark's hands reaching for mine. Dark cattle stampeding. Mark playing with his dogs, a hunting rifle at his side. DeeDee on horseback, dressed in work clothes, diamonds flashing. Marisa as a teen, playing cards and sipping wine, looking very grown-up, a glint of amusement in her eyes…laughing at something I said. Cam drunk on the lawn at school, crying for Marisa. Shobani's blank office walls. A man with a gun firing at me. And the man was Mark.

Twice I woke in a cold sweat and forced the images away. Yet they returned each time I closed my eyes.

I woke at 5:00 p.m., to the sound of someone banging on my back door. It was Arlana, standing in the Monday twilight, pointing at my car. "Your tires are slashed. All four. Someone sure be pissed off at you."

I was groggy from too much sleep, the perpetual jet lag I experienced from working seven days on, seven days off, on the graveyard shift. Yet, even with sleep clutching at my mind, I felt a frisson of fear leap through my veins. I knew what it meant. *Back away. Back off. Don't look into the attack on Marisa.*

I shut my eyes on the sight of the defaced car, forced the panic out with a long breath and sighed. I held the door open for Arlana to enter and called Mark. Then, with surprisingly steady fingers I dialed a mechanic and requested they pick up my car and put on four new tires if the ones on the BMW couldn't be saved, let Belle out to do her evening business and wrote Arlana a check. The activity brought a measure of calm.

I figured for the mold, the inches of dust, the newly cleaned windows that glistened even now with scarlet sunlight, and the aggravation of being shot at, a hundred and fifty dollars was a fair price. Arlana thought so, too, and offered me a ride to work in her old junker. For free.

We made and shared a pot of hot chocolate as we waited for the cops and the tow-lift truck, Arlana chatting about the destruction of the day before, the expense of replacing four tires and the possibility of who had done both deeds. Considering she had been shot at, she was remarkably unconcerned about the attacks.

Her nonchalant attitude about the shooting and the tire slashing helped me keep everything in perspective. I was still alive. I could fix the tires. Why get all bent out of shape about it?

Mark was a little less indifferent about the damage to my car, raging at Jacobson—who had checked my house and the grounds before going off duty—shouting at me for sleeping through the attack and scolding Belle for not waking me up when someone was in the backyard. He made a right-size fool of himself, to Jacobson's amusement and Arlana's unconcealed delight.

Belle, however, was horribly shamed without knowing why, standing with her back bowed, her tail between her legs. I stroked her ears as Mark raved, telling her I didn't expect her to have X-ray vision and that seeing through the plywood covering the window openings and the brick veneer of the house was not her job. She was a little mollified and brought me a puppy to admire.

This one was yellow, a large female, and though Belle was pleased with all of her progeny, I had noted a marked preference for this one. "She's a pretty pup. You did a good job," I said softly. Mark simply groaned, shut up and banged out of the house. Apparently he thought I wasn't listening. Jacobson, standing there in street clothes, laughed and followed Mark into the dark.

"That man got a thing for you, Rhea. In fact, I'd say he's hot for you. You ever...you know..." Arlana waggled her shoulders suggestively, her tweezed eyebrows arched.

"No, we never..." I waggled my shoulders back at her.

"Well, maybe you should."

"Well, maybe you should just mind your own business," I said, fighting both a grin and a blush.

"Only if you let me decorate your bedroom."

"Do what?" I hadn't followed the segue. In fact, I didn't think there had been one.

"Decorate your bedroom. I can have new drapes made with blackout lining, a bedspread with a contrast bed-skirt, and reupholster that chair in the corner to tie it all together. I'll handle it as part of my housekeeping chores."

"And how much is this going to cost me?"

"I'll bring you swatches and a price list tomorrow."

"Is this the cost of the ride to the hospital? Because I can't afford it."

Arlana snorted. "You a doctor. You can afford whatever you want to afford."

"Arlana, just take me to the hospital. And I'll look at your swatches and the price list. I like white. Tone on tone, and no ruffles."

Arlana peeked out at the Jeep still parked in my yard, emergency blue lights flashing. "Uh-huh. I noticed."

19

Traps and Babies

It was after six when I walked into ICU, the windows dark between the closed slats of the blinds. DeeDee, dressed in jeans and work shirt and smelling faintly of horses, was at the desk teaching two nurses and Cam Reston how to play rummy. Her hands flashed as she shuffled cards, diamonds sparkling in the harsh light, contrasting with the work clothes of a successful horse breeder. It was the only time I ever saw DeeDee without the Stowe pearls, when she wore jeans and work shirt. As for the diamonds, she wore them all the time, even when working, except when she cleaned a stallion's sheath. Then they rested in her breast pocket. I hadn't remembered seeing them this morning, an indication of my own exhaustion. Tonight, it was DeeDee who looked tired.

As they played, DeeDee was giving a running commentary of the best family-owned vineyards in the south of France. I recognized a vintner's name or two from my own days as DeeDee's protégé, and smiled at the old memory of Marisa and me, sitting with DeeDee on the side porch of her Charleston home, sampling wines and learning the terminology of tasting. Smoky. Tart. Fruity. Well-aged.

John and I had always kept wine on hand, my preferences always winning out over John's, as I had the best nose for wine. Testament to DeeDee's rigorous training.

I stepped into Marisa's room. She was conscious and alert, eyes roving from clock to the evening news on television to the doorway to the shuttered window. She couldn't see the nurses' desk from her vantage point, so activity there didn't draw her eye. I wondered if it would.

Marisa looked at me, eyes on the stethoscope around my neck, but she didn't look at my face. I pushed my disappointment away. It was too soon, perhaps.

I checked her pulse, felt her skin for temperature, elasticity, fluid beneath the skin. Her right pupil was normal, and the left constricted just a bit when I flashed a penlight into it. That was a great sign. It was possible the optic nerve had not been permanently injured by the pressure to her eye. Marisa might not be blind in that eye.

As I listened to Marisa's chest, the hallway exploded with sound. Cursing. A chair overturning. Marisa jerked.

Steven raged into the room, shouting, arms waving. Calling for Percy Shobani. Demanding a nurse attend him. Spittle flew from his lips. He kicked at the table holding fluids and nursing supplies, sending it flying into the wall. Plastic bottles shot into the air and landed with squishy thuds. And then he saw me standing beside Marisa.

Lethal silence settled over the room like a cloud of poisonous gas. Steven's color, already red, went purple. His eyes constricted to pinpoints.

"You bitch. You did this. You put my wife in danger."

The next instant was a blur. Steven moved toward me. Cam was suddenly there, an arm up to block a blow I hadn't seen coming. Nurses were shouting. DeeDee tugged at Steven's other arm to pull him around. I backed up fast, hitting the wall, accidentally pressing into the code light. Alarms went off, the sound of a soft klaxon at the nurses' desk, and over the loudspeaker, "Code 99, ICU. Code 99, ICU. Code 99, ICU..."

And Marisa screaming. "Sharp pain sharp pain pain pain bright pain sharp..."

Mark stood in the doorway, legs braced as he pulled Steven back and shoved him against the wall. Handcuffs flashed as he secured Steven's wrists, and Steven struggled, shouting profanities. The room filled up with medical personnel responding to the Code 99—a cardiac or respiratory arrest. Uniformed officers gathered in the hallway. Mark shoved Steven out of Marisa's room and into a storage room. Marisa continued to wail. Cam followed Mark, DeeDee on his heels. I followed them all, leaving the mess in Marisa's room to unravel itself.

"You have the right to remain silent. You have the right to—"

"I know my damn rights. I want a lawyer. I'll see you up on charges for this, you son of a bitch."

"Why did you let Marisa almost die?" Cam shouted over the other voices. His fists were clenched, teeth bared white. For the first time, I saw Cam Reston as a dangerous man. "Why didn't you report the assault?"

"She was fine when I left."

"She was dying when you left, you ass," DeeDee said.

"Why don't you give old Mitch a call," Mark said, smiling like a fiend. "You want a lawyer, I want to hear what Mitchell Scoggins has to say about all this. We'll kill two birds with one phone call."

And suddenly Mark was shoving Steven down the hall before him, still reading him his rights. The door whooshed closed on the supply room. Cam moved to follow and I blocked his way, arms out, holding him back. His body hit mine, hard and hot. "No. No, you can't." Cam shoved toward me. "Leave it in Mark's hands. Stop, Cam. Stop. Mark can handle it. He's playing with Steven. You understand? Playing with him like a cat with a mouse. You can't get in the way."

Cam stopped, his head above my shoulder, his breath fast in my ear, a bellows of anger and hostility. Corded chest muscles bunched in contact with my hands. Slowly, the animosity leeched out of him, blew away on his breath. He rested his head on my shoulder. A moment later I felt his tears through my lab coat. With a single sob, Cam collapsed against me.

I waved DeeDee out of the room. Her eyes were wide and frightened, but I couldn't comfort them both. "See to Marisa," I commanded over Cam's shoulder. DeeDee left without a word.

I slid my arms around Cam's chest, holding him

as he cried. The sobs were wild and shaking, as savage as his previous anger. I held him tight, as a mother might a child. Or as a friend might.

His hair was silky and fine, with tangles around the nape where it had grown too long. His neck muscles, bunched and angry, relaxed and loosened beneath my fingertips. He breathed deeply and sobbed, and I absorbed the misery, the lost love, the pain as I held him, my eyes on stainless-steel mesh shelving and linen, yet seeing nothing.

Long minutes later, he pushed himself away from me and turned to the far wall. His arms went up around his head, pressed to the plaster. I relaxed against the wall at my back and waited.

"I never seem to do this except with you."

I said nothing in response to his comment.

"The last time I cried was when Marisa married that son of a bitch. And I cried on your shoulder then, too, I think."

I nodded, though he couldn't see me. "So that makes me what? A sister confessor?"

Cam laughed, the sound magnified in the crook of his arm. "A friend."

"I'll settle for that."

"My best friend." Slowly Cam turned from the wall, his eyes red-rimmed, his face blotchy. "I remember how much I liked you in med school. Remember that I could talk to you like no other person on the face of the earth."

"I was a geek. Talking from guys I could get."

"You were beautiful and unapproachable. Still are. And maybe that's why I—" he took a deep breath "—like you so much. Love you so much," he corrected, his mouth turning down slightly with the admission. "I can talk to you because I know you aren't interested in going to bed with me."

Oh, I'm interested, Cam. Always was, John notwithstanding. Just...not as one of many... But I didn't say it. Wisdom keeping me silent. I smiled instead and let him think what he might.

Cam smiled. "Okay, Oh-Enigmatic-One. Can I get out of here now?"

"Wipe your nose first."

Cam dragged his sleeve across his face and grinned, a snotty-nosed little boy, charming and unrepentant and utterly irresistible. I shook my head.

"Come on, Cam. Let's go see what happened in the real world."

Outside, DeeDee waited in the hallway, her arms crossed over her chest, blue eyes blazing. Before either of us could speak she said, "I just found out that the night Marisa was injured, Steven could not be found for forty-five minutes. He wasn't in the hospital."

"How do you know?" Cam and I said together.

"Zack and Anne. They had a patient about four o'clock in the morning. Steven had been up all night and had only gone to bed in the last hour. When they called him he didn't answer and they thought he was in the shower, but he didn't answer fifteen minutes later. And they couldn't find him in ICU or PCU. The security guard was looking for him. It took forty-five minutes before he could be located."

It was a common enough problem—a lot of floor space, a doctor who couldn't sleep and went rambling.... Yet, this night of all nights? "And where was he when he was found?" I asked.

"He...he came in through the doctors' parking entrance," she whispered, her fingers twisting her rings around and around. "He came in from outside."

"We have to tell Mark," I said, moving for the nurses' desk and the phone.

"He knows."

I stopped and looked carefully at DeeDee. Tears sparkled in her eyes, brighter than the diamonds on her hands. Her expression was fierce, almost gleeful, as if she had caught Steven in a trap of her own making. Then her expression changed.

"They told him in one of the interviews he held with them. He's known for some time now. You didn't know, dear?"

"No." I turned and walked toward the E.R. "I didn't know." Mark hadn't told me. All the promises to let me know what he knew, and he hadn't told me. We had talked about Steven's alibi. We had discussed Steven's whereabouts the night of Marisa's injury. We had decided together that Steven had not hurt his wife. And now this. Steven had called Mark a son of a bitch. At the moment I didn't disagree.

My emotions were churned up, flighty and uncertain. Undependable. The presence of Cam, Mark not telling me what he knew, my tires getting slashed, my house getting shot at. *Me* getting shot at. John gone. And Marisa... Dear God, Marisa.

I passed through X-ray on the way to the E.R., and stopped short halfway through, my hands clenched into balls. Sheriff Gaskins was standing in the doorway to Chris's office, his back to me, hands braced on either side of his head, his body leaning into the room. He was laughing, a political sound, too boisterous, too hearty. In South Carolina, the sheriff is the highest elected law-enforcement official in a county. A political being through and through.

I had seen him in the hospital following the murder of a prominent citizen, and after a near riot touched off by the death of a local football hero under suspicious circumstances. Two times in over twelve months I had seen him, and here he stood, cowboy boots shined and hat pushed back on his head, laughing that laugh. The one that won him the election the first time he ran back in 1988, and still kept him in office.

I leaned past him and spotted Dora Lynn in a chair beside Chris. The hospital's lawyer stood beside her, a hand on her shoulder. The sheriff's visit was official.... And it had to do with Steven. My blood started a slow boil. I could feel the skin of my palms break beneath my nails.

"Well," Sheriff Gaskins said, scratching under an armpit, "from the wife's reaction when she saw him, we think we have him, but it's still gonna be a bugger to prove, him a prominent citizen and all, and her a vegetable all laid up in that bed. But we 'preciate all your help, Chris, Dora, in providing us with this information...."

The one-sided conversation continued behind me as I turned around and walked back to the ICU. Steaming. Furious. Mad as hell. Mad at Mark. He should have told me. He had the chance. He should have told *me* Steven was the one. I'd have saved him the bother of an arrest. I'd have killed Marisa's husband myself.

I didn't think just then of Eddie standing over Marisa, a pillow in his hands. Didn't remember until later what a distraught father might do to protect his son.

I stopped at the open door to Marisa's room. Cam was standing at the foot of her bed, his hands on her feet, holding her much as I had done earlier. Percy Shobani sat in the room's one comfortable chair, writing in Marisa's chart. She lay relaxed, her body flaccid, her face muscles slack. Too slack, too enervated, utterly diminished. A cold dread went through me, settling in my palms and breasts and the pads of my feet. It looked like a horrible setback. My eyes filled with tears and the anger I had nursed flooded away.

"Marisa?"

My alarm must have been evident, for Cam quickly stepped to the doorway, putting an arm around my shoulders. "I had to give her a sedative. We couldn't calm her. I gave her Ativan, one milligram, the lowest dosage I thought might work. It knocked her out, but I think she's fine. Her reflexes are still improving. It's all right, Rhea. Really."

I buried my head in Cam's shoulder and sobbed once, loosing in an instant the dregs of anger, of fear, the sound lost in the starched cotton. *She was alive.* I had to remember that. Marisa was still alive. I took a deep breath.

Cam stroked my head as I had his only moments earlier and my tears turned to laughter. We were a pair, Cam and I, weepy as schoolgirls. My laughter was only a short sound, definitely not a giggle, as I raised my head and wiped my wet left eye. "Sorry," I said.

Cam bent and looked into my eyes before continuing, his face inches from mine. "I also ordered soft restraints for the next day or so. She really lost it when Steven came in here—" Cam stopped when I tensed at the mention of Steven's name. "We have to talk about it, Rhea," he said softly. "For the baby's sake."

In a single jerk I pulled away and stood straight, staring at Marisa, understanding suddenly what her letter had meant. *Especially now....* "Baby. She's pregnant," I breathed. It wasn't a question. I pulled back the sheets covering Marisa's wasted body. Gently, I probed her abdomen just above her pubic bone, then deeper, higher in her abdominal cavity. And there it was. A lump not much bigger than my fist. I pulled the stethoscope from my neck where it always rested and put the earpieces in my ear, the bell against Marisa's...baby. It had a heartbeat all its own. Fast. Fluttery.

I couldn't help it. I laughed with delight. *A baby...* It would complicate Marisa's treatment, perhaps already had. And I didn't know why I hadn't detected the baby myself on my earlier exams of Marisa, except I hadn't expected a baby, hadn't looked for one. I considered the medications I had administered and none would adversely affect the child.... *A baby...* Its heart beat true and strong beneath the bell of my stethoscope.

"We just discovered the baby, about half an hour before Steven came in." Cam said, a smile in his voice. "I'd say she's about three, three and a half months along. I've ordered Sustacal to beef her up. And I called for a consult with her OB-GYN in Ford County. I'm hoping he'll make a house call to see her, as he doesn't practice here.''

"Something can be arranged," I said, taking Marisa's hand in mine. *A baby...* "Michelle Geiger could handle the delivery."

"I have heard a rumor," Percy Shobani said, his eyes on the chart in his lap, "claiming that Steven did not intend to renew his contract with the hospital when it is up in May. That he will be employed instead as full-time director of Medicom Plus."

Cam and I moved between Shobani and Marisa, the gesture automatic, protective. Perhaps a bit silly. But then, Percy had been Marisa's doctor for weeks after her attack. And he didn't notice she was pregnant?

I made a mental note to go over Marisa's new admission chart carefully. I hadn't studied it word for word as I had planned, and she had been hospitalized for two days. It was checking up on Shobani, it was technically unethical, but I didn't trust the man. Instinct said he was involved in Marisa's injury on some level, though I didn't know what that meant. Why Shobani? Why did Steven pick him to be Marisa's doctor?

Knowing Cam would keep an eye on Marisa, I left the two men and went to work, avoiding the X-ray department and taking another route to the E.R. Discovering the baby had taken the edge off my emotions and I felt calmer, steadier, more in control. Not like an overcharged rocket about to blast into space. I had work to do. And I could hate Mark for not telling me about Steven later.

20

Lies By Omission and Mulligans

A cold front blew in the night Steven spent in jail being questioned by police, his attorney at his side. We had heavy rain and falling temperatures with ice or snow as part of the five-day forecast. Locals knew not to pay attention to the warnings till they saw the white stuff falling. Forecasts were particularly difficult in an area halfway between the Appalachian Mountains and the Atlantic coast. Weather in the piedmont was always uncertain. But at least one thing was always well established—traffic in the E.R. was slow on days when the weather changed. Tomorrow would be a different matter entirely if the cold front held. The maxim proved true, the E.R. was devoid of patients almost all night and I slept like the proverbial log for six hours.

At 7:00 a.m. my re-tired car was waiting in the doctors' parking lot, my keys were at the switchboard, and I was ready to go home. The cold outside had meant extra-dry heat inside, and my skin crackled with pain and static electricity, though I had oiled up to prevent the discomfort. My hair stood up on end. I shocked myself opening my car door. It took thirteen minutes to defrost my windshield, heat the interior and get myself waked enough to make the drive.

It was a miserable Tuesday morning. I would be so glad when my seven days "on" were over. I may have just gotten back from a vacation, but I was now anything but rested.

When I got home, Mark's Jeep was waiting in the driveway. The fury that had dissipated upon hearing that Marisa was pregnant flared up fresh and potent.

I got out, pulling my starched lab coat with me, and banging my black doctor's bag on my knees. Before I could speak he said, "Who licked the red off your candy?"

I lifted my head and met his eyes. "Are you addressing me?"

"Oops. I guess you figured out that I set Steven up."

I wanted to say "No shit," but kept my mouth closed and unlocked my back door, letting a desperate Belle out into the cold. I really did have to get a doggy door installed. And new windows...

"I couldn't tell you. You would never have let me use Marisa to set Steven up. And I had to see her face when she saw him for the first time, just on the off chance that she might respond to him. I'll bet you never saw the camera your friend Cam Reston and I set up in Marisa's room. That guy is a genius with electronics."

No. I hadn't seen the camera. And Cam hadn't seen fit to tell me about it, either. The fact that we hadn't had time to chitchat, or that Cam perhaps thought Mark had told me already made no difference. I was now angry at both men.

I called Belle to me and went inside, shutting the door in Mark's face. He came in right behind me, bringing cold air and my keys and smiling in a way that begged to be slapped off. I had left the keys in the door. *Freudian?* I banished the psychobabble. I did not want Mark in my home.

He grabbed me as I put fresh water in Belle's bowl, causing me to slosh the water over the countertop. Mark took the bowl and set it aside, then put his arms around me. "I told Cam it was your idea. The camera, I mean. But I needed your face on film, too, reacting to Steven."

When I said nothing, he sighed. "Isn't the silent treatment a little childish?"

"It's better than slapping you. Perhaps you have a camera set up in here to catch me assaulting an officer of the law." He was right. I was acting childish. And I didn't particularly like him telling me so. "You used me. You lied to me."

"I did not lie to you."

"By omission. You lied. You were here at this house. Talking to me. Thirty minutes later you were at the hospital arresting Steven."

I pushed out of his arms and refilled Belle's bowl, placed it on the floor. Still with my back to him, I went to the puppy box. It was getting a little aromatic. The paper needed to be changed. I balled it up while Mark watched.

"I screwed up."

The admission surprised me. Slowly I stood, stinking paper in my hands.

"I should have told you. I'm sorry. It's this thing we always do. This competition thing. Like we're trying to one-up one another. And I don't like it. I think it's because we have unfinished business between us."

"What kind of unfinished business?"

"This kind." He crossed the kitchen, took me in his arms and kissed me. The puppy paper crinkled between us, crushed by our chests. The stench rose. I dropped the paper and sighed into his mouth.

It wasn't the way to end an argument. It settled nothing. It was just as childish in its own way as slapping him or giving him the silent treatment. But it felt so good. I let him hold me. I held him back. And the kiss stretched out until his hands were on my skin beneath my T-shirt, cold and stroking, and I had to pull away or lose myself in him. I moved back just a fraction and Mark dropped his hands but he stayed close, his face near mine.

"I really am sorry," he said. I nodded and stepped back another step. "I came here to tell you about Ty Yarborough. He's dead."

I sat quickly on a kitchen stool, my hands flat on the countertop.

"While you were out of town we found an unidentified body in Prosperity Creek near where it crosses under I-77. It was male, about six foot two, and had been in the water about a week. We sent it to Newberry for a forensic postmortem." Mark lifted my face with his thumb under my chin. His eyes were serious, troubled.

"It was identified this—yesterday—morning. Sorry. I've been so long without decent sleep that

I'm getting mixed up on the days of the week. It turns out to be Marisa's investigator. He was killed by a sharp object being rammed up into his head. His wrists and ankles had ligature marks. It means he was killed about the same time Marisa was assaulted. And he had a heart attack. I asked for a test on Xylazine, but it wasn't present. If it was ever there, it might have broken down in the time he spent in the water. Or he might have lived long enough for it to break down in his body before he died. We just don't know. Rhea?''

"I'm okay. Steven did this? Killed this man?"

"He could have. He had motive. Three million dollars' worth of motive. He had the expertise. He had the time. And he had the ability."

I buried my face in my hands. "That's the one thing that bothers me about all this."

"What?"

I couldn't believe I was about to say it. I couldn't believe I was about to defend Steven. "He had too *much* ability. If he wanted to get away with this— with everything—all he had to do was perform the lobotomies another way. Go up through the nose, into the sinuses, instead of through the supraorbital notch. I might never have noticed the drop of CSF in Marisa's nostril if there hadn't been the other thing. The circular hole below her brow. He's just too smart to be so stupid. It's why I keep coming back to Eddie." I looked at Mark and waited. He had on his cop face, noncommittal, unemotional, hard as stone.

Mark stared at me. Finally he said, "I have a warrant for the old chart on Marisa. The one from when she was first admitted to the hospital two weeks ago." He unzipped his coat and pulled a folded sheet from his pocket. Placed it on the counter by my hands.

"I only have a copy. But you're welcome to it if you want. Save you a trip to the medical records department."

I turned and walked to my car, the cold biting into my skin. I still had my coat on, the keys now in my pocket. I opened the trunk where I had placed Marisa's chart and pulled back the floor covering. The chart was gone. Someone had been in my trunk, which meant that someone had somehow gotten my keys.... I fought away a shiver, not sure if it was exhaustion, the cold, or fear. I closed the trunk slowly.

'It's gone," I said dully. "Sorry. You'll have to go by the hospital after all."

Mark's eyes flickered once and then steadied. He didn't even seem surprised. "Steven refused to explain why he couldn't be found on the night of his wife's assault. He has been uncooperative, to say the least. But we haven't been able to hold him, Rhea. Mitchell Scoggins somehow got the ear of Judge Burgess and he was released from custody before the first twenty-four hours were even up."

He led me back inside the house and pushed the door closed behind me. "I think that with the death of the P.I. who was looking into the state of his marriage, we have enough to bring Steven in again, and this time we'll charge him. I don't think there's much question that he's involved in this situation with Medicom Plus and Marisa's assault."

I looked down at my hands. I was twisting them together, fingers interlacing and shaking. I automatically stilled them, placing them palm down on the countertop. "How long will he be in jail?"

"He's got money. He can probably make bond less than an hour after he's charged. And I don't think it likely Judge Burgess will consider Braswell a flight risk. I hear that he and Steven make up a regular foursome at the Dawkins Downs Country Club. Golf," he snorted derisively.

"I understand Steven gives double mulligans, which makes him a popular player. Can you keep him away from Marisa?"

"Yeah. We'll see she has protection in the form of a security guard." Mark helped me up onto my tall stool as if my legs weren't perfectly able. At the moment perhaps they weren't. "This is getting complicated, Rhea. And dangerous. Can you go stay with family or friends for a few days?"

I snapped up my head. "No. My friend is here. I will *not* leave Marisa." In the depths of my mind I could hear myself ask, *Where would I go? My best friends are here. All the others have scattered to the four winds and the rest were friends of John and me. Couples. And there never has been a family except for Marisa and DeeDee.*

Mark took a deep breath. "Then I want you to have a guard, too. For the twelve hours a day you aren't at the hospital."

I was rested enough to laugh. "I haven't had a baby-sitter since I was ten. Forget it, Mark." I rocked off the tall stool and rinsed the coffeepot for fresh brew. I ground beans, choosing raspberry-cream flavor, and put the pot on. Mark talked as I worked, trying to convince me.

"His name is Reuben. Like the sandwich. He's a retired cop and he's bored out of his mind. He volunteers part time at the sheriff's department and he wants the job. He'll do it for free."

"No."

Mark pushed the on button on the coffeemaker and pulled me into his arms. I hadn't seen him cross the room. He kissed me soundly, bending me back in his arms. "Yes. I insist."

"No." But his lips were full and warm and slid across mine with increasing pressure and expanding warmth. "I don't need a caretaker."

Mark pulled me close to his body. I could feel his heat, his sudden need of me. "Please," he whispered. "I'd feel so much better if you did."

"Cheater," I whispered back, the words lost in the heat of his mouth. My knees weakened. His arms were supporting my weight.

"Say yes. I'll treat you to a French dinner at the Silver Criquet in Charlotte. Say yes." His tongue touched mine.

"Yes?"

"Thank you," he breathed. I had no idea why he said that, and didn't care. Wrapping my arms around his neck, I pulled his head closer to mine.

"You two finally got together, I see."

I jerked as if to move away, but Mark held me close, twisting to the back doorway. His hand was on his weapon at his hip. Breath blew out in quick gasps as I shoved Mark's arms away.

Arlana grinned at us. "I should leave, right?

'Cause the whole house is clean now and you two might need all that dust-free floor space, way you was groping each other."

Grinning, Mark released me and walked to the back door. He made a motion as if tipping a hat to Arlana. "The house does look right nice, Miss Arlana. And that new deputy, Malcom Haskins, was asking after you. He saw you when we were doing the clean-up work after the shooting here and he thought you were fine, fine, fine. Wanted to know where you lived, if you were seeing anyone, that sort of thing."

I steadied my knees and slid to the floor from the kitchen stool that again supported most of my weight. Standing, I wiped my mouth on the back of my hand. *Damn.* What had I just agreed to? Mark Stafford was a no-count sneak. *With wonderfully soft lips....* I stood straight and banished the traitor from my mind. I would not be talked into a bodyguard.

"You tell Malcom I'll be going to church on Sunday. He want to meet with me he can show up to the Church of the Holy Spirit and Tongues of Flame right 'bout 10:00 a.m. for the services. If my mama like the way he look, I might consider seeing him." Arlana looked over at me. "My mama, she got the sight. She can look at a man, tell if he good for nothing or not." Arlana looked back at Mark, her eyebrows arching coquettishly. "And she *liiiike* what she see when she look at this man right *here,* yes she do," she singsonged. "You got you a good one, Rhea, girl. Mama say so."

"Reuben will be here before nine this morning. He likes his coffee black and thick as syrup."

"This the bodyguard you gettin' for Rhea? Miss Essie be talking about it when I stop at her place this morning. I let him in, he come before I leave."

"No bodyguard," I insisted.

"Miss Essie say you taking the bodyguard so don't be making a fuss, Rhea. Come on, Mark, I walk you to your car and you tell me what he look like, this sandwich man, so I let in the right one."

Arlana hooked her arm through Mark's and led him to the back door, chitchatting about Malcom and his views of holy-rolling religion. She called it "spirit fired," and Mark gave her his entire attention. Didn't even say goodbye to me. The cheat.

A bodyguard. My hands loosened from an unconscious clench and I walked back to my room. I hated the thought. Yet…it would be nice to feel safe. To *be* safe. I hadn't felt easy in days. As much as I loved Marisa, I didn't want to end up like her…. Fully clothed, I settled into my bed and slept, the comforter pulled around me like arms.

When I woke just before noon, it was to the sound of the phone ringing softly beside my bed. I kept the ringer turned down, hating to be startled from sleep. "Yeah?"

"Rhea? It's Mark." His voice sounded coarse and grainy, the way mine did when sleep was a catch-as-catch-can affair and not the hours-at-a-time-luxury I had just enjoyed. "You awake?"

"Sort of." I yawned hugely.

"We have an alibi for Steven. It's a bit shaky, but it fits."

I sat up in bed, pulling the covers up over my shoulders. "Tell me."

"We charged Steven with the assault on his wife about ten this morning. Sarah Gibbons came forward less than an hour later and claimed she was with Steven during the time the E.R. was trying to find him. She claims they had a tryst in the respiratory therapy department. And we have a nurse who saw them emerge from there afterward."

"There is an outside door, a fire door from the RT department. I use it sometimes when we have a code in the nursing center and I want to make it there fast."

Mark sighed and I could hear his weariness through the phone lines. "I'll check it out. But it doesn't look good unless we charge the girl with accessory before and after the fact. I don't think the charges will stick. A grand jury will laugh us out of the courtroom. And Steven has good alibis for the time frame of the other two assaults on Willie Evans and Raymond Abel. We're checking on Eddie's whereabouts at the times of the assaults. You might have been right about him all along."

I pulled the covers tighter around me. A draft had found its way into the room past the plywood Mark had nailed to the glassless windows. My room was icy. I could hear sleet beating against the wood. It seemed the warm weather had been just a teaser between storms, and miserable temps were here again.

"I'll keep you informed, Rhea, but you be careful. And please let me know if you have any more thoughts on this situation. Hear?" His voice was laced with tension and something that sounded strangely like tenderness.

"I hear. Thanks, Mark." I placed the receiver

back in its cradle. What had Mark called it, this thing between us? Unfinished business? I fought my way out of the twisted covers and took a hot shower. The bathroom tile was beige, the fixtures sparkling white. I thought the whole place was pink.... There were a lot of things I hadn't known, it seemed, and a lot of thinking to do about it all.

Refreshed and warm, I closed off my cold bedroom and joined Arlana and my baby-sitter, Reuben, at the kitchen counter. They were eating fresh Krispy Kreme doughnuts—typical cop diet—and drinking spice tea. My kitchen smelled like a bakery. I nodded to them both, poured myself a cup and joined them. "I'm your charge," I said. "Rhea Lynch."

"And I'm your protection." Reuben stood and shook my hand. He stood six foot three, probably two hundred and fifty pounds, most of them around his waist. He was florid-faced with bloodshot hazel eyes and a receding hairline. But he carried a cop utility belt with a radio and .38 policeman's special, so I figured he was the real thing. When he grinned, perfect dentures glistened at me. "Mark thinks an awful lot of you, ma'am."

"I been tellin' Reuben 'bout your romance with the cop."

I sighed. "It's not much of a romance."

"Uh-huh. I know what I saw this morning. They got a thing, trust me," she said to Reuben. "Now, I got these swatches for your bedroom, and a price estimate. You want to hear 'bout this or what?"

We spent a cozy afternoon eating doughnuts and drinking spice tea. Reuben had given up coffee after he retired and favored cocoa or tea as substitutes. I picked out a taupe, cream and mauve pattern of satin stripes for the bed-skirt and chair, a similarly hued floral for the comforter and footstool, and solid cream for the drapery. We argued over the cost, played a few hands of rummy—which I won—and argued again over the cost. And though I couldn't afford it, Arlana talked me into redoing the entire bedroom at once. My gold card was going to be maxed out before we even got to the living-room swatches. But at least I had a housekeeper-cum-decorator I could trust. And I quite liked the idea of Miss Essie's family blending in with mine on this level. It was comfortable. Reassuring. Like having my own personal protection service was.

Late that Tuesday afternoon, I made some phone calls to the hospital to check on Marisa—who was following movement with her eyes. She had even made eye contact once or twice with Cam. He was ecstatic. DeeDee was another matter entirely. Steven was out on bail and she was livid with anger. Cam's presence at Marisa's bedside was not enough, and she could not believe that Mark had let *that man* out of jail. She was impossible to calm and I made a mental note to visit her as soon as possible.

One benefit of having Reuben around was that my daily runs could be resumed. Though he said it was a bad idea, I was itching to get out and pound off some energy. Perhaps it was the mild threat that I'd go alone that cinched the deal, but whatever it was, eventually Reuben conceded.

As the cop wasn't in shape to follow me through the trails at the back of the house, our arrangement had to be a bit more high-tech. Ignoring Belle's pleading eyes I drove to the hospital, Reuben in tow in his brand-new, tiny Chrysler. I would have to take the dog with me on my next run. She was getting cabin fever tending to the pups.

The steady icy rain let up on the drive, and a black sky pushed its way through the clouds. I was dressed for the cold in my Chicago inner wear—silk long johns—and a heavy wool sweater under a light-weight parka. I stretched before the run, doing the full fifteen-minute warm-up, and when I started on the Health Run on hospital grounds, Reuben was right beside me on the bike path in his little car. The wheels just stayed on the narrow paved roadway. Reuben toasted me with his cup of spice tea and followed along on the path parallel to mine, lights off to keep the glare from blinding me to icy spots on the pathway. I hated to admit that I liked the man. I especially hated to admit that Mark had been right about my safety and protection.

The ground of the running path was saturated, making footing less than sure. I ran ahead of Reuben's car, my legs beating strongly into a hard run, lungs a steady rhythm, like my heart. It was a perfect time to run. No one but a crazy person would be out in this cold weather. The break in the freezing rain would not hold out long. I loved it.

Water in ditches to the side of the paths was over-flowing. Ice made a lacy network of coruscating crystal on the banks of the ditches, along the tops of branches, smoothed over the few remaining leaves. The path was slippery in spots, and I was careful to set each foot down precisely, moving my weight forward evenly.

As we approached the creek, the sound of the water was boisterous, clamorous. The noise of my breath was lost beneath it. The wind had come up, fierce in the trees, banging the ice-laden branches into one another with drumlike echoes. The breeze slapped against my face wetly. I increased my pace to fight off the growing cold and to beat the next spatter of rain back to the warmth of the hospital.

I was too late. I ran into the cold rain as if into a wall; it stung my face raw, as bad as any Ohio night. I would be drenched. My leggings were wet through already, and the skin of my thighs was numb. Miserable idea, this run, though I would never admit it.

The noise of the creek hid the sound of Reuben's engine. I glanced back to see him grinning broadly, hidden beneath the pouring rain but for a few reflections of light off the black paint of his car and his new dentures. He toasted me again with his travel cup and I cursed all cops roundly. Know-it-alls, every one of them.

I could see the water just ahead, a boiling black serpent with a frothy mane tumbling under the bridges. My feet hit the wooden bridge. On the far side a light glimmered. A faint hum of engine noise starting up. There was no time to react.

Suddenly a dirt bike was there on the path before me. And then another, both black as blood in the wet and the dark. They skidded to a stop. Both riders pulled handguns and pointed them my way. Behind me Reuben hit the bright lights on his little car and the sudden glare blinded the men before me.

They fired wildly.

"Get down!"

I dropped to the bridge decking. Breath slammed from my lungs. Shots came from both sides, from Reuben and from the dirt-bikers. A barrage of sound louder than the flood beneath me. I clung to the wooden bridge, fingernails digging into the wet oak. A round hit the bridge planking in front of my nose, showering me with splinters and grit. I had nowhere to go. A fierce pain hit my arm, dazzling agony. I was hit.

With no thoughts at all I rolled to the edge of the bridge and over the side. The cold of South Rocky Creek extinguished the pain in my arm. Icy water rolled me over and under. Utter blackness held me prisoner. *I couldn't breathe.* I gagged and water forced its way into my mouth, a cold wet fist at the back of my throat. I swallowed the muddy water. Fighting my way to the surface, I took a desperate breath and flailed my arms. The water tumbled me along. I was under the second bridge, its supports dark above me.

My fingers were numb. Hands losing the ability to move. Hypothermia. The extremities were the first to go. If I didn't grab something now, I might never have the chance.

Kudzu trailed into the water from above, leafless and brittle. I grabbed hopelessly at the vines, catching a long tangled bunch in one arm. Twisted the vines around me and let the force of the water hold the tendrils in place. Singly they would not have held me, but together they were doing the job. Over my head, the bridges thundered with footsteps. Then silence.

21

Hypothermia and Trachs

I was growing light-headed, the vines slipping from around my arms. The water battered me against the steep bank, against bridge supports. I gulped water every time a wave came downstream. I had lost all sense of feeling in my arms and legs. It was hard to breathe. I had no clear idea of what I was doing in the water, memory wiped by the intense cold. I was dying.

From somewhere there were sirens, and light bounced over my head, illuminating the naked trees and brush, brightening the churning water. I drank more water and vomited it back up again, retching horribly. It was then I heard my name called. And again.

I was too weak to respond. Finally I managed a croak, a pale lifeless sound. But someone heard.

"She's here. In the water."

"I see her! She alive."

And another voice. "Rope. We need rope. Get the rescue squad."

But there wasn't time. I understood that, if nothing else. I would be cold beyond caring and ready for death in seconds. The kudzu slipped and I drifted a few feet downstream before the vines caught me again.

And then there was Mark's voice, blazing in fury. At me. "Goddamn it, Rhea. You can't do anything right. Can't look after yourself for a single minute. I should strangle you! I may strangle you! Jesus, this water's cold."

He had me in his arms, the movement of his limbs against mine a pain beyond compare. Pain. Pain was good, wasn't it? A good sign that I could feel pain....

I was up from the water, lifted by strong hands, Mark behind me, his teeth chattering. Mine were long past that reflex. I was dumped on the tarmac in the glare of a car's lights, black night and falling rain all around me. *Shooters. On dirt bikes.*

I tried to sit up and couldn't. Around me voices shouted.

"We got ambulances coming."

"We can't wait. Get him into a car."

Mark slogged past my field of vision and fell to his knees. A body was resting on the asphalt, struggling. Reuben. I could see the blood in the beams of the cop's flashlights. He'd been shot. I forced myself upright, rolled to my hands and knees, took a deep breath and vomited all over the rain-pelted ground.

I crawled on elbows and knees to the body on the ground. "Let me sh...see."

I don't know how they heard the words, so breathy I sounded, but a beam of light landed on Reuben. He had a single entry wound on the left side of his neck, flowing bright crimson. Flowing, not spurting. That was important but it was a moment before I could recollect why. The artery feeding his brain wasn't severed. Only a vein. A big one. And there were air bubbles in the blood. Reuben gurgled and the bubbles foamed out. On the right side of his neck was a larger hole. Exit wound. Very little bleeding.

I returned my gaze to the entry wound. Reuben was drowning on his own blood. He needed a tracheotomy. I looked up, met Mark's gaze. "I need knife. A f-firm piece of tubing. Tape."

Ever practical, Mark pulled a Swiss Army Knife from his pocket. "I don't have any tubing."

"Cut it from the car...engine," I said, my lips thick, numb.

Mark's eyes opened wide in surprise and he grinned before shouting the order for someone to cut a length of tubing from the car. "What kind of tape."

"Electrical? Or sshumm...some..." The name failed me. "That bright shiny schtuff...stuff to hold pipes together. Or windows shut." My words slurred; I didn't like that thought.

"Duct tape."

"Whatever." I fell to the side, my strength spent. I watched Reuben trying to breathe, his skin stark white in the harsh light. Blood was flowing faster, it seemed to me. He gagged, blowing blood all over. An ambulance sounded in the distance.

"Okay. Tape. Tubing. Knife." Mark laid them all out in front of my face.

"Sit me up. Open...knife. T-t-tape it to my hand," I said, forcing the pronunciation through frozen lips. I was stuttering, my teeth starting to clack.

"What?"

"Do it. Don't have much time." Rain sliced through the night, something heard and seen, but I couldn't feel it where it pelted down on me.

Mark did as he was told. I couldn't feel his hands on mine. A bad sign. I was still losing body heat. And so was Mark. He was gripped by horrid shivering.

"Sh...sit me up. Shine...light...Reuben's neck." Someone lifted me. Someone else shined the flashlight beam on the grisly bloody mess that was my baby-sitter's neck. "Good. Now. I'm gonna make an...incision in...skin. And then a second one, deeper. After the first cut, someone...will have to pull the lips of skin apart so I can sh...see." I forced the words clear, my mouth moving as if it belonged to someone else.

"The second incision..." The world darkened, spinning crazily. Gasping, I bent forward on numb hands, trying to keep from passing out. From far away, I heard my voice droning between shallow breaths, "...will push frew...through cartilage." A slow roar seemed to build in my head, cresting and falling back. "When...I do that—" I turned my head on my neck, glanced up at Mark "—you shhhove the tubing into R-R-Reuben's airway. We won't have but a sec or two. My hands're too numb...to do a good job of it. Then you tape...tube into place. Here goes."

In the background I heard someone swear. Or perhaps pray. I couldn't feel the knife in my hand or skin beneath the blade. I had to work by sight alone and my eyes were full of creek water and mud, forming overlapping coronas of glare.

Twisting my hand, I slit the skin, jaggedly. Not a neat slice at all. It would leave a nasty scar. I did better my first year of gross anatomy. A bright red line of blood appeared. Mark reached past me and pulled the lips of the cut apart. Whiter cartilage showed beneath. Angling the knife perpendicular to the first cut, I pushed harder. The cartilage resisted. I twisted the knife point in and was through. Mark moved behind me and shoved a piece of black plastic through the hole.

"Sh...sh...see can you hear air movin' in and out." My words were garbled.

Mark's head obscured my sight. "I hear it."

"Tape tubing...in place. Get him to the E.R. And Mark?"

He looked at me, green eyes grinning devilishly, black night like a sinister halo around him.

"I'm dying."

"Serves you right."

"No. Li'erally. I can...not...feel my arms or legs." Suddenly I couldn't swallow. Could no longer speak.

Mark picked me up bodily and carried me through the rain. Toward light and heat and people. I sighed against his chest. And only then remembered that I too had been hit by the shooter's bullets.

22

Hot Baths and Shadows

I came to in the physical therapy department, sitting fully clothed in an old-fashioned, stainless-steel Low-Boy whirlpool, the kind used for burn patients who were having their wounds debrided. The water was scalding. Burning me. I opened my mouth to scream, but a moan was the only sound to pass my lips. I struggled weakly to get out of the tub, but a hand pressed down on my shoulder.

"You're not being burned to death, Dr. Lynch. Water temp is only eighty-six degrees. It just feels hot."

I looked up into the amused face above me. Viewing it from the bottom, it had a grotesque appearance, whiskers in need of a shave. The face grinned, growing a double chin for a moment, and then he was gone. I seldom had a reason to come to the PT department. I didn't know anyone in here. And then the memory of the shooters and my wild dive into South Rocky Creek came back. Black snatches of memory, bone cold and wet, bloody and terrifying.

Tiredness seeped into my marrow, lethargy like none I had ever experienced. Fighting the need to crawl from the water, or scream with the pins-and-needles agony of nerve endings coming back to life, I forced myself to stay beneath the surface. Eighty-six degrees felt like a hundred and fifty. The level of pain increased. I was being burned to death, I knew it. Tears slid down my face.

After a moment, I lifted my hand. Instead of being scalded, with skin dripping from my bones, my hand was blue. The blue of icy-cold, near-death hypothermia. I dropped my hand back into the swirling water.

Mark, stripped to the skin and wrapped in a heated blanket, lay on a wheeled stretcher beside me. He was shivering uncontrollably, and as I watched he grinned. It was that devil-may-care smile that I sometimes saw in my dreams. I frowned at him.

"You look like hell," he said.

"Thank you ever so much. How's Reuben?" My tongue felt thick and I still slurred. Even talking took more energy than I possessed.

"Alive, last time I saw him. Looks like someone from *Star Trek* with that black tube coming from his throat, but at least he was breathing."

"Thank you for coming into the water after me. I was really…" I remembered being tumbled by the water, blackness all around me. The relief when I caught the kudzu, and the feel of the vines slipping from my arms. Remembered being too cold to grab them again. I caught my breath. "…losing it."

"My pleasure."

I looked back up at him and tried to smile, but my facial muscles were still paralyzed from the dip into near-death waters. I had a feeling I might dream about the waters rolling over me for some time to come. My childhood nightmare come true.

"Rhea."

I looked back into his eyes.

"You are in real danger. You know something, or someone thinks you know something, about this case. They tried to get it back when they ransacked your house. Tried again when they stole the chart from your car. Now they just want you dead."

Too tired to argue, I simply nodded.

"No more runs. No more being alone at any time. I have guards coming to stay with you. Twenty-four hours a day till this thing is resolved."

"Private guards?" My voice croaked. My mother would have had a conniption if she heard me. At his nod I said, "I can't afford them."

"We can worry about that later."

Too tired to argue, I nodded and rested my head back against the stainless-steel, raised neck of the old tub and closed my eyes. When I woke again, I was in my call room wrapped in heated blankets, naked as the day my mother bore me.

I didn't remember being stripped and carried to my call room, but I remembered being cold. Colder than ever before in my life. I was now wracked with shivering as my body heated back to normal temperature. Being dumped in a hot tub wasn't standard medical treatment for hypothermic patients, but it had done the trick, and perhaps faster than normal. I hadn't been in the icy water long enough to cool my core temp down to danger levels, so the fast reheat was effective.

"You wake now. You eat."

I rolled within the blankets and faced the doorway. Miss Essie was wrapped in a similar blanket, sitting in a rocking chair, her knitting in her lap. Static electricity had the fine threads of yarn standing out like a 1970s afro on her knees. Putting aside the knitting, Miss Essie stood and came the two steps to my bed.

"I got you a pot of hot cocoa and two of my best homemade drop biscuits with honey. I done made one of them policemans go to the house for it and it here just in time. Roll over and sit you up in that bed, Missy Rhea."

I rolled again and sat, shaken by another terrific spasm of shivers. I took the cocoa in shaking hands and sipped. It was heaven on earth, I knew it. Ambrosia. Food for the gods, and I told Miss Essie so. She smiled and nodded and agreed with me, pushing a plate of rewarmed biscuits drizzled with honey at me. I ate, finished off both biscuits and the entire pot of cocoa, feeling a bit of strength return to my limbs with every bite.

When I was done, Miss Essie passed me a warm, wet rag and told me to clean myself up. "Arlana done gone to your house and brung you back some clothes. You done lost your shoes in the creek, but she got you some like enough to them. She say you got three pair of these ugly things in you closet. Waste is what I be sayin'." She shook her head at the vagaries of the young.

Fortified, I stood and dropped the blankets, dressed in the small clothes brought by Arlana, and then in the jeans, T-shirt and sweatshirt. I couldn't work in these, but I could get warm in them. Dressed, I pulled the blankets back over me and checked my watch. It was nearly seven, time for me to be on duty.

As if reading my mind, Essie said, "That Dr. Wallace Chadwick, he be stayin' until you warmed up enough. I tol' him I let him know when you ready." Essie laughed, liking the temporary power she was wielding over the medical staff. I could see her bullying the E.R. crew out of all the blankets in the warmer.

A knock sounded at the door and Mark stuck his head in. "She awake yet?"

"You young peoples. So impatient. And nex' time, you knock and then just stand there. I tell you if it all right for you to come in. Don' know who done taught you manners, boy, but I bet you she 'shamed to her bones, she be seein' the way you actin'."

"I can only hope, Miss Essie. I can only hope."

I laughed through chattering teeth at the direct inference to Miss DeeDee, and Miss Essie looked from Mark to me and back again, shaking her head. "Say what you got to say, boy. She still cold."

"I just wanted to tell Rhea that Reuben is doing fine. They flew him out to a specialist, some kind of vein surgeon."

"V-v-v-vascular surgeon," I supplied, making the assumption. Clenching my teeth, I forced the chattering away.

"Whatever. And one of the attackers was hit. We followed a blood trail from the bridge into the woods before the rain washed it out. We're notifying every clinic and hospital within fifty square miles to be on the lookout for a gunshot victim."

At his words, I remembered the stinging pain from the shot in my own arm. I reached up and felt, my fingers coming away sticky. "I got hit too," I said.

"That not no bullet what made you bleed, girl. That Dr. Wallace done pull out a splinter from you arm while you was sleepin'. He see blood in the water you was bathin' in, when you got warm enough again to bleed from it. Pull him out a stick of wood mus' be half a foot long. It bleed through the bandage?" She peered closely at my arm. "We git him to fix it when we git to the E.R. You see. You be just fine."

During Miss Essie's monologue, Mark had leaned against the door frame and watched me, a smile I didn't try to interpret on his face. At this slight pause in Essie's string of words, he inserted a few of his own. "I sent a squad car to find Steven and Mitchell Scoggins right after the attack on you and Reuben. Neither man can be found. Mitch's secretary says he took the whole afternoon off, following a civil court case in Columbia that got canceled. Settled out of court. And Eddie Braswell is missing. Again."

I nodded, draining the last dregs of cocoa from my foam cup. The heat was on full blast in my room, and my skin already ached from the dryness. I needed fluids and asked for the water bottle I saw by Miss Essie's chair.

"That Dr. Wallace done say you be needin' it, he sho did. But you can stop lookin' for my Eddie. He didn't have nothin' to do with my Marisa. Nothin'."

I opened the bottle and drank the tasteless water. A flash of memory from the depths of the creek set me coughing. It was a wretched feeling, as if my lungs were being turned inside out. I knew I had swallowed some water, presumably getting some into my lungs as well. I'd have to get some antibiotics to ward off pneumonia or bronchitis. While I tried to calm my coughing, Mark added to my misery.

"The sheriff approved you a deputy as court protection. It seems you might be our star witness and that someone wants you out of the picture." One corner of his mouth quirked up. "So you get protected by Dawkins's finest at no charge to you. Ma'am." He made a motion as if tipping his hat to the local schoolmarm, though his head was bare.

I nodded at him, unable to curtsy and not interested in trying. "I'm grateful. I admit I need a babysitter."

"I know."

I glared at him, but he continued. "Sarah Gibbons was on tonight's schedule, and when I went to talk to her, she had blood splattered on her shoes. A good bit of it."

I nodded again to show I was listening between wracking coughs.

"She says her first patient of the evening had TB. She claims he was coughing up parts of lung tissue and that's how she got blood on her. Is that possible?"

I nodded again, and managed to speak softly between rounds of coughing. "Perfectly reasonable. Dawkins has a lot TB and most patients don't continue with the full six-month round of meds to cure it." I paused and swallowed down another attack. It passed and I could speak again. "They take the medication till they feel better and then stop. Next time they get a cold or virus, any little thing, they get the TB again, full-blown. And they sometimes lose their lungs. Cough actual tissue up on the bed. I've seen it."

Mark nodded. "Okay. I still want to see the patient, verify with someone else on the floor that she was actually with him."

"Wear a mask," I said with a small smile. "And you better hurry. Patients that far along in the disease don't last long."

"People don't die of TB," Mark informed me. A look of confusion crossed his face. "Do they?"

"Welcome to the plagues of the twenty-first century."

"That the truth, it is, it is. These the last days. They be plagues and wars and rumors of wars. I know." Miss Essie nodded her head and took up her knitting. "I know."

"I'll be around tonight, if you need me."

I smiled again at Mark and nodded, unable to find breath for more. He closed the door and left me with Miss Essie. My duffel and black bag were on the floor, and I didn't ask who had retrieved them from my car. I stripped again and slathered jojoba oil all over me, working the miracle oil into the cracks and crevices of my skin.

My hands, injured by the shards of glass earlier were tender and irritated. New abrasions over the knuckles, which I didn't remember getting, had bled freely and clotted over.

I could feel a trickle of blood down my arm as I worked, and opened my medical bag, insisting Miss

Essie help me rebandage it. I had no intention of stripping in the E.R. for Wallace to attend me. I had my pride. In the mirror over the sink, I could tell it was a nasty gash, but it had been professionally cleaned and Steri-Stripped. A good job, except that I probably needed stitches. Wallace might not have known that it was so deep and would continue to bleed, not if he had seen me soon after I was retrieved from the creek.

Re-dressed, I pulled on my starched lab coat—my last one until I made a trip to the cleaners again—and made my way slowly down the hallways. The weather had held, and I expected a busy night. I wondered if the injured shooter would be dumb enough to seek treatment in my E.R. tonight. I could only hope. I caught a reflection of my smile in the darkened windows of a file room. It wasn't a pretty sight.

I stopped in ICU to see Marisa. She was sitting up in bed, eyes closed, face serene. I stopped at the sight. Serenity. It had been missing from her face since I'd returned from the mountains. She had been blank. Empty. Not lively and lovely and full of joy. Not serene. And I knew suddenly that serenity had described Marisa, always.

Even when she lost her child to SIDS, when her parents died, when she miscarried her second child near to term… She had been serene. She had grieved, of course, soul-deep anguish. Yet she had never lost that sense of peaceful repose until an attacker took it away from her with a steel instrument. I still wondered what weapon he had used, but knew that Mark would not tell me. He was feeling territorial. Was it an ice pick as I had imagined? The dimensions were right. They were easy to come by—every one had an ice pick....

Cam came up behind me and wrapped his arms around me, holding me close. There was a time when I would have given all I had to have him hold me like this. Now I was just grateful for the body warmth. I knew that the change came from inside me...and was due to a certain pair of green eyes.

"She's doing better. I've done all I can here, Rhea. By tomorrow, she'll be stable enough to fly out of here and to a *real* hospital where she can get real treatment by real doctors."

I elbowed him in the solar plexus. Air whuffed out of him, but he kept his arms around me. "Admit it. This wasn't the backwater you expected, was it?" I asked.

"I'll admit I've never had lab work and X rays completed so fast. I'll admit the nurses all seem to have teeth and none so far have chewed tobacco or dipped snuff in my presence. I'll admit the local hotel has new king-size beds and an adequate whirlpool in the room. I'll admit the local vineyard was a surprise. I slipped away for a few hours and took a tour, bought a few bottles to take back home with me. And the steaks are almost as good as the ones in Texas."

"I am stunned and amazed at such high praise," I said. But I had had trouble following his comments. My brain was reacting to the cold by shutting down whatever parts it deemed unnecessary. Like the ability to reason.

"You should be. I am being very gracious and kind."

I laughed. He was warm, a furnace at my back. I sighed.

"I'll also admit I've enjoyed seeing you again. Let's get together more often. I don't have many woman friends, Rhea. And you're special. To me."

"I'll let you and your lady friend stay at my place anytime," I offered. "As soon as I can afford to buy a guest bed, that is." And then the meaning of what Cam was really saying sank in. "But I guess you do need to take Marisa away...."

"Soon. I'll let you know. I promise not to surprise you with a done deed."

"Just keep an eye on her. Okay? Till you're ready to fly her out."

"Don't worry. Miss DeeDee is staying with her at night, and I'll stay with her by day, till the bad guys are behind bars. Your boyfriend says he'll have them soon."

"Not my boyfriend." When I shook my head, my hair made static electricity on his shirt. I could hear it crackle as I moved.

"Uh-huh. I've seen the way he looks at you. And seen the way you look back. If lust could scorch..."

I elbowed him again, harder this time and pulled away. "I have to go to work."

Cam grinned that charming crooked smile. The one that had haunted my dreams until I met John. And for long after, if I was honest with myself. "Take care, Rhea-Rhea."

I smiled my good-nights. I wasn't ready to say goodbye. When I got to the E.R., Jacobson was sitting in the break room, drinking coffee, his uniform pulling at the arm seams. He didn't look comfortable or happy, and I knew he had family he would rather be with tonight. "You're my shadow?" I asked.

He grimaced a moment, and finally smiled. "'At's me. Favor owed to the captain. He's a persuasive guy, our captain. Isn't that right, Dr. Chadwick?"

Wallace nodded, his face a parody of suffering. "Persuaded me to work over, and considering that Pearl has a roast duck in the oven, that was quite a favor," he said, green eyes smiling in his dark face.

"I owe you," I said.

"Don't worry. You'll pay. First thing in the morning when I come in to work after eight."

"Bring in a fourth of that duck and you can wait till nine."

"No, thank you. That duck is all mine." Wallace hung his lab coat on the back of the break-room door and pulled on a heavy leather jacket as he spoke. Minutes later, he was gone, leaving only a blast of frigid air to mark his passing. Pearl was a gourmet cook with years of cooking school behind her in Paris, New York and Tokyo. Or someplace equally as fine.

My mind had turned to mush, and I was glad to see Ashlee was in attendance as one of my RNs tonight. I would need the backup and the support both, if I was to keep from killing someone in the next few hours.

I envied Wallace the jacket as well as the elegant meal. Fresh chills swept through me as my body continued to adapt a normal temperature. It was going to be a miserable night.

23

Chills and Antibiotics

Between patients I stayed wrapped up in a heated blanket, huddling in the corner behind the break-room door to avoid breezes. It was baby night, with ninety percent of the patients under the age of two. A persistent cough, irritability, fever, diarrhea, refusing to eat, inability to keep down liquids—all were symptoms I saw in the first two hours after I clocked in. I had a feeling that my immune system had taken a dip in the creek with me, and that I would soon have most, if not all, of the viruses I came in contact with. Lovely thought.

I mostly listened to my nurses and let them tell me if the babies were really sick enough to need me or not. None were, except for the unmedicated five-month-old with a fever of 106.2. I dealt with the medical problem, surprised that one part of my mind was still functioning well.

The only adult I saw before 10:00 p.m. that Tuesday night was Miss DeeDee. She showed up in the E.R. wearing jeans and rubber boots, a cowhide coat fringed all around and a flannel shirt. And she still looked as if she'd just stepped from a fashion magazine. It was the breeding. I hated to agree with Mama on anything, but this time she would have been right. It was impossible for DeeDee Stowe to look anything but stylish.

Her UTI was no better and she wanted something stronger to treat the bladder infection. Wrapped in a fresh blanket, certain I could feel a fever coming on already, I insisted she had to give me a specimen and make out a chart just like a real patient. "I'm sorry, Miss DeeDee, if the meds aren't working, you have to let me see what is causing it this time. You need a cath UA and a C-and-S." Before she could respond, I continued, "But I'll let you slide on the cath, if you'll do a bang-up clean-catch."

It was negotiation at its finest, and I was proud that my brain worked well enough to consider the permutations of the situation. Perhaps I was getting better. But I was still so cold.... DeeDee wanted to skip all the preliminaries. I was letting her avoid the most uncomfortable and embarrassing part—having a tube inserted into her bladder. Miss DeeDee, no fool, lowered her brow and pressed her lips together. She knew what I was doing.

"I will accede to your request, under protest," she said, her chin in the air. "But I think you are acting like a bully."

"I'm acting like a doctor."

"Precisely," she said as she snatched the sterile urine-cup kit from my hand and marched to the employee bathroom. "I was married to enough of them to know." She paused. "And why are you wrapped in a blanket? It is too hot in here already." Piercing blue eyes swept over me. "What is wrong, dear? Are you sick?"

"No, ma'am. Just cold." I decided to explain. It would save longer explanations later, and a good bit of pain right now, if the sympathy factor worked. I pulled the blanket closer around me. "I took a dip in South Rocky Creek this evening during my run."

"You deserve to be cold, then," she said before I could elaborate. "Foolish, is what I say."

Jacobson snickered, but thankfully, no one else heard. A riled Miss DeeDee I could do without tonight, and the UTI seemed to be making her irritable. I let the rest of the story go until another time.

It took her longer than I thought it should have to collect the urine, but eventually DeeDee came back with the specimen. It was cloudy, just as I expected, and she sat down in my break-room chair to await the results instead of in a treatment room like a regular patient. I wasn't about to tell her different. I even allowed the E.R. secretary to come to the back to take down her vital information and make out a chart. I wasn't feeling strong enough to make waves. Not with DeeDee.

The urinalysis came back positive for bacteria, but negative for WBCs, which was a bit strange. It meant her body was not even *attempting* to fight off the infection. I didn't like it one bit, but with all the stress she had been under for the last two weeks, I wasn't really surprised.

Sitting across from her, a fresh hot blanket wrapped around me again, I said, "Miss DeeDee, I'm shotgunning you with the big guns this time." I handed her some new antibiotics, samples I had collected from Steven's office while I waited on her to collect the urine. "Ciprofloxin."

She looked at the dosage and smiled. "Less like a shotgun, more like a cannon. This should do the trick. If you need me, I'll be in ICU for a while, sitting with Marisa."

"Mark said he was putting a guard on her, Miss DeeDee, so don't be surprised."

"It's about time someone did something for the poor child. I keep telling that officer that Steven is going to kill her right under our noses."

And with that final comment, Miss DeeDee turned on her heel and walked down the hallway. Three steps later, she whirled and came back, kissed my cold cheek with dry lips and said thank-you. That was Miss DeeDee. Courtly to the end.

Work and diapered patients were steady until nearly 2:00 a.m. when Mark came in looking damp, cold and tired beyond words. He leaned on the counter and propped himself up with his elbows, as if without them he would slide right to the floor. On the counter he placed a single sheet of fax paper with small, smeared typing on the front.

"You recognize any of these?" he asked, yawning. I could count the molars in the back of his throat and tell he still had his tonsils.

"Good morning to you, too, Mark. Did you ever get warm?"

"Oh. Is it morning already?" He tried to focus on the clock over the copy machine and couldn't. Instead, he looked at his watch. "So it is. Morning." His green eyes were bloodshot; a day or two of stubble scruffed his cheeks. "And no. I'm still shivering. But it was worth it. Now you owe me."

About to offer him my sincere thanks for saving my life, I clamped down on the words. "Idiot," I said instead. Mark laughed, appreciating my insult. I took the list and looked it over. It was a catalog of the investors for Medicom Plus. A chill having nothing to do with icy water slid over me. These were the investors Mark kept coming back to. Had one of them hurt Marisa? But what about Eddie?

"They're listed by most heavily invested at the top, to least invested at the bottom, though I don't have exact numbers yet. Friday morning for that. At least. If it's not next week."

Taking the list with me, I went for a new blanket, refolding the cool one around my shoulders and replacing it in the heater. If I used a new one every time I changed, I would run out in an hour. I just hoped the nursing supervisor didn't catch me at it. It wasn't exactly sanitary.

Steven and Marisa were prime investors, their company, Braswell Inc., right at the top. Below that were Procall Systems, Devonshire Investors, Frank Gibbons—whom we'd learned was Sarah's father—and a half-dozen others. Two looked familiar, but I couldn't place them.

"They could be cattle breeders or preachers, butchers or funeral directors. I don't get the principals in each company till Friday. In fact, I get nothing until Friday. You recognize them? Maybe unsuccessfully treat a family member? Maybe give me reason to tie you in with all this?"

I looked up from the list. "You mean, did I kill anyone here? Is that what you mean?"

"Now don't get riled." Mark leaned closer in and looked hard at me. "Jesus, you look tired. Why don't you go get some sleep?"

"Go get some sleep yourself," I said, pushing the paper back across the counter to him. "And no. Nothing rings a bell."

"Nothing at all?" he persisted. "You okay? Rhea, you're a little pale. Except your cheeks. You sick?"

I sat on the nurse's chair behind the desk and looked up at him for a long moment. A fresh shiver gripped me and my legs were weak. "No. I'm not all right," I finally admitted. "I think the dip in the creek took a bit out of me. I'm having trouble thinking straight."

"Isn't that dangerous? I mean, you're a doctor."

I couldn't have explained it, but that struck me as funny and I started laughing. And then couldn't stop. What was it I had thought about Miss DeeDee? Stress… It could do strange things to a person. I laughed for a long moment as my eyes filled up with tears and one slipped down my cheek.

Mark came around the desk and took my hand as the laughter finally waned. Jacobson came over from the break room and watched with interest as if we were the next segment on a popular romantic comedy. Perhaps we were.

"I don't like the fact that Sarah Gibbons's father is on the list, Rhea. You be careful. And by the way, we still haven't found Steven and Mitch. I told you earlier, remember?" I nodded and he continued. "And Eddie Braswell's still on the lam. He's dangerous, Rhea, no matter what Miss Essie says. Out of control.''

"Well, that's just lovely. I'll have Ashlee alert security for teenage visitors.''

"My case, remember? I'll alert security, such as it is. They don't even carry guns, do they?''

"Nope," I said. "Just their wit and resourcefulness.''

Mark snorted. If Miss DeeDee had heard him she would have rapped his knuckles. "Rhea, if you remember anything about these names—anything— you call me at home. Wake me up.'' He looked over at Jacobson. "You keep an eye out tonight. I got to get some sleep.'' And with that, Mark, one of Dawkins County's finest, lumbered away and out the door. Cold air blasted in, setting off another bout of shivering. Ten minutes later, I went to my call room, Jacobson on my heels like a faithful old hound.

I pulled an upholstered chair out of a vacant patient's room and set it up outside my door for Jacobson, alerted the RNs on the medical floor nearest that he would be spending the night and might want to bum coffee, handed him a blanket and went to my room. It was hot as blazes in there, and for once I was grateful for the blasting, dry heat.

I stripped for the third time that night, dropped my clothes and running shoes into the corner and stood under a blast of water, letting it roar down over me like a tropical squall. My skin pinked instantly, aching like a body-size wound. I didn't envy the true victims of hypothermia, the ones whose core temp had dropped into the danger zone and who had to receive medical treatment to survive. Warming for them must be agony.

I stayed beneath the water for nearly a quarter of an hour, my head leaned into the far tiled wall, eyes closed as images of the last few days wisped through my mind like ghosts, insubstantial as shadows. Nightmare reflections, some of them. Marisa as I first saw her, lying in bed. The sight of her in the E.R. when I thought she was dying. The memory of her face when she saw Steven come into her room and started screaming, *"Bright sharp pain pain pain…"*

I turned around in the shower flow and allowed the too-hot water to parboil my back for a while, Marisa's fear part of my own. *"Bright sharp pain pain…"* The shocked faces all around her. Nurses. Two respiratory therapists. Sarah? Had she been there? Cam. DeeDee. Mark's glee… *"Bright sharp pain pain pain…"*

I soaped my hair, hating the exhaustion that pulled my arms back down. The false exhaustion of hypothermia. *"Sharp pain…"* I lowered my arms, running the remembered sequence of events back through my mind. And again. "No…" I whispered. I rinsed my hair. "Nah…" I played it back yet again, uncertain of the order of the arrivals. Steven…his face twisted with fury…. I relaxed. Mark knew what he was doing. Mark had it all on tape. My brain simply wasn't functioning yet.

I finally felt warm and turned off the water, toweled down to my ankles and stopped. The water hadn't drained…. I swirled around the drain with my toe. A feeble suction rewarded me and then stopped. "Great." I pushed open the shower door and was met with the sight of more water, an inch deep all over the bathroom, and draining down through both doors. The hallway would be running with water, and my room would be wet. At least I wouldn't have to contend with dry heat all night, not with this mess. I wondered if housekeeping had anyone on duty this time of night.

Sitting on the toilet seat, I oiled my skin again, dressed in fresh scrubs—short-sleeved, thin and not near warm enough—and tossed my wet clothes into the sink. Cleaning out the supplies from my last clean lab coat, I stuffed my rubber reflex hammer, my scissors and a roll of mints into the breast pocket of my scrub top and hung the stethoscope around my neck. My wet running shoes I tucked under an arm. They were for the nearest heating vent.

Dressed, I unlocked the hallway door and glanced out. Water, water everywhere. Leaving the door unlocked for housekeeping, I turned, waded through the chilled water from my shower and unlocked the door to my call room. I paused in the doorway.

The light was off. I was certain I had left it on. Fear zinged through me like an electric shock.

A hand reached out of the blackness and gripped my arm. I stared at it an instant. *Hairy knuckles. Rough skin.*

Without thinking, I jerked my arm down. His fingers slid across my oil-slick skin and off. Whirling, I slammed the door and cut the lights. Fumbled for the latch. Puny little thing. Metal hook and eye. Movement in the room behind me. A body hit the door. My heart rammed into my throat.

Barefoot, I ran for the hallway door, out into the

hallway. To my left was Jacobson, slumped in the chair I had found for him. Bright blood showed in the overhead lights, trickling from his head. *Venous. Still alive.*

The door to my room opened by his head. A man emerged. Looking left, away from me. *Big. Dark clothes. Lab coat, several sizes too small, pulling at his shoulders.*

I turned right and sprinted for the surgery department. *Too slow. Muscles ice-water stiff. Moving like in a dream, a nightmare, where the monsters have fangs and claws...*

Behind me I heard cursing, the sound of water splashing as someone fell in the shower room. More than one, then. *How many?* My wet feet froze on the tile, then on exposed concrete as I rounded the corner.

My heart beat an irregular tattoo. I couldn't find my breath. Cold on my feet. Burning cold pain. I had an irrational desire to laugh when I realized I still had my wet running shoes beneath an arm.

The hallways were dark, lit only by a rare overhead. But not dark enough.

I spun through sterile processing, a new autoclave hulking in the center of the room, wrapped in packing and thick tape. Dodging cabinets like black obstacles in a track-and-field game, I ran out the far side. Pausing only a second, I shut the door behind me, bare feet aching but silent on the icy floor. My fingers fumbled in the darkness. There was no lock.

The words of Matt came back, toothily amused. *"The locks are on backward in half a dozen rooms. Factory defect. If you go exploring and get turned around, just don't close any doors. The locks are automatic and you could get trapped.''*

I ran back through the corridor and paused. At least one man was in the room. I could hear him fumbling with the lock. He cursed. In the darkened half-finished hallway, I saw no one. A cold sweat trickled down my spine. Quietly, I leaned in and gripped the door to sterile processing. Shut it. The lock snicked shut. A shadow covered my hand, head-shaped.

"Stop!" A man's voice, hoarse. "You come with us! Or Marisa dies."

I looked back, met the eyes. Brown eyes in a flushed face. Bandage soaked with dried blood on one shoulder, ill-fitting lab coat hanging off the other. *Gun in his good hand...*

I spun, a perfect pirouette, and ran for the blackness. No heat in the new part of the building. Had I known that? My feet were cramping. Each step a shattering throb.

Lights came on behind me. In the distance, a woman's scream. My mind couldn't fathom why. I was here, in danger. *Here.*

I ducked into an unfinished surgical suite and out the other side. Shadows and light made odd splotches on the walls. Black equipment was scattered across the floor, invisible as I ran. If my bare foot hit one in the dark...

I was like ice all over. My heart a pained flutter. More lights behind me. *Where were the breaker boxes?*

"There she is!" Hoarse voice, calling to another. *How many...?*

I dashed into a last room and doubled back though a hole in the wall, squeezing through metal framework. And spotted the breaker boxes. In the cold I pulled the ring that opened the metal door and began hitting off all the switches. They were stiff, new. They resisted, loud echoing clicks. Ten. Fifteen. Twenty-five. Blackness fell around me. Thirty.

"Shit!" Resonant in the black night. One of them stumbled. They were close. Cursing. Two? Three? More?

I pulled the ring of the second box and felt my way down the rows of breakers. In the distance, more lights began to flick off. Voices in the background raised in complaint. I was affecting other floors. *Good. Call for help.* A siren went off down a far hall. *Alarm bell?*

I stood in the blackness, breathing like a damaged racehorse. Movement in the rooms to the left. And to the right, farther down. Two of them then... At least.

I sat on the frigid floor and untied the wet laces on my shoes. Somehow I had held on to the running shoes. The leather was warm from my underarm as I pulled them on. The warmth was like a gift from heaven. Not for long, though. Cold began to seep through as soon as I stood. I had to get help soon.

From the breaker box I could move one of two ways. And then I remembered the hole in the floor. The hole where the two men were standing... Was it still there? I moved slowly down the hallway, away from the sound of the men, fingers on the unfinished wall to guide me.

24

Rock of Ages and Steinmann Pins

I stubbed my cold toes twice in the gloom, moving as silently as I could, cursing under my breath with pain. Gasping. The sounds magnified in the blackness.

Long hallway. Cross over. Doorway? There it was.... I passed through and moved right. Grit on the floor made sliding steps an advertisement. I lifted and placed each foot carefully. If I fell through the hole instead of entering deliberately, I might never get out alive.

Finally, my foot found a raised...something. Less than an inch high, it was wide and long. I bent and felt with my fingers. Not plywood. Metal. Icy metal with a cold breeze blowing up around the corners.

I slid my hands along it till I felt a section that wasn't flat with the floor. Slipped my fingers between the floor and the metal. Lifted. Nothing happened. No give. Not even a groan. I braced my knees and lifted again. The metal shifted up only a fraction of an inch. I dropped it. Dust blew up in the cold air, choking.

It was flat iron, a quarter of an inch thick. No one

was going to fall through or get trapped by climbing in the hole. And I couldn't get in.

"Damn," I whispered. Great time for safety precautions. Whatever happened to poor job performance and slack workers. It would take more muscles than God ever gave me to get the metal off the hole in the floor.

I slipped through into another room, keeping moving, as much to generate body heat as to find a hiding place. I could call out. Perhaps the nurses in the distant wing would hear me. Or perhaps the men would find me more quickly. The alarm bell in the far hall had gone silent. It would be no help to me.

I could double back. Find an outer door, a fire exit. I hadn't noticed any on my earlier jaunts into this unfinished maze, but surely fire codes insisted that they be operational even at this stage of construction.

In the darkness, my foot slammed into an obstruction. I went down with a woof of pent-up air, a silent scream. The pain spiraled up and through me, stealing my breath and my heartbeat, claiming my blood, all of it pooled in the wounded toes, pounding with torment.

I found a breath, half sob, the sound quickly choked off. Water from my still-wet hair dripped off and landed with a loud splat on the floor. I gripped my wounded foot and cried silently, curled on the dusty floor. My shoulders were wet from the shower water that still dripped from my head. My left foot was a frozen block of screaming agony, my fingers wrapped around it.

A soft sound. Scraping. Someone was here. In this room with me.

I stood, balancing myself with a hand on the boxes I had run into.

Soft footsteps. One. Two. Three. Grit grinding beneath his soles. He was alone. Just one man.

The boxes shifted beneath my weight. A soft sliding. The footsteps stopped.

I could hear breathing. See nothing.

Suddenly I pictured the boxes piled in a doorway. Pain then, too, the first time I stood here, my shin abraded by unexpected contact. The boxes of orthopedic surgical instruments. Heavy. Steel. I slid a hand in.

Metal like a brand of ice touched my fingertips. Slowly, moving like the glacier I was becoming, I slipped my hand in among the instruments.

A footstep. I could hear his breathing. Smell the garlic of his breath. I blocked out the awareness of him. Of his warmth, so close I could feel it.

A different box this time. Not the same one I had explored last time. No time to find that one. Lessons from a lifetime ago came back. Me as a medical student being grilled on the instruments and their uses.

McKeever cartilage knives, small blades to trim or slice through cartilage, so sharp I felt nothing though I slid my hand along an edge. Too small to be effective against an attacker.

Bunnell tendon strippers. Used to strip the tough tendons of their sheathlike coverings. Useless to me.

Footsteps. Closer, then away. Then closer again.

Shivering had set in and I was quaking like a seizure patient. The urge to cry had died. I prayed instead, mindless phrases running through my mind.

Rock of ages, cleft for me… Let me hide myself in Thee…. Marisa's hymn. Marisa who had been attacked. Where was God? Why should I pray? But I did.

Sticky-handled osteotomies… Bone chisels with my blood coating them… The gash on my hand from the McKeever knife was bleeding profusely.

A T-handled corkscrew. Forceps.

Something sharp. Pointed. A Steinmann pin. I gripped it. If I pulled it out and something slid in the box… I took the chance. Pulled.

It was silent, resting in my palm. I gripped the thin, nine-inch-long pin with its dual-bladed ends. One end was capped with rubber. One end was solid steel, a point so sharp it would pierce bone with ease.

The capped end I centered in my palm. My skin was sticky with my blood. The sharp end of the Steinmann pin aimed out, its shaft secured between my first and middle fingers. A weapon worthy of a hunter.

With my other hand I searched the box again, came away with a bone mallet—a blunt-headed hammer. Five pounds of surgical stainless steel, it had a crosshatched handle for holding in bloody hands, a steel pipe filled in with solid steel. Its business end had two heads, each one-and-a-half inches in diameter.

I hefted it in my right hand. Twelve inches long, lightweight, nicely balanced. I stood to a crouch and listened for my assailant.

He was moving away from me again. I slid my foot along the floor, a deliberate, slow-soft sound. He paused and came my way again, moving toward my left side. I gripped the Steinmann pin, stepped away from the boxes to give me maneuvering room, left foot back. Regulated my breathing.

I was standing in a bent-kneed crouch when I saw him. A black shape, capped by white, the lab coat shining in the darkness. An irregular shadow. Half light, half night. Four feet away, he came on.

I pivoted my weight to my left foot. Waited. Three feet away. Two. Garlic breath, short and puffed. He was out of shape. Or injured. Or afraid.

With a single motion I shifted my weight forward and thrust out, low and fast. The Steinmann pin connected and slid through. Cloth and flesh, crisp then rubbery. I shoved it in, the palm of my hand making contact with his clothing.

A gush of blood. Simultaneous scream. Animal howl of misery, girlish-high. I grinned in the darkness and stepped away, empty left hand held above my head like a banner of war, hammer held at my side. Moving through the night to the doorway, I listened for the other one.

I knew where he was. *Knew* it. He was running toward the agonized screams of the injured man hitting the floor behind me. Softer-than-soft sounds of rubber-soled shoes. Softer breathing, controlled and certain. A thinker, this one. Letting the minions take the first charge, the cowardly way of craven commanders throughout history.

He came on. More cautious now as he recognized the screams of the injured man. *It wasn't the woman screaming. So where was she?* I understood his confusion. His uncertainty. I waited.

He was on the other side of the doorway. Listening. I held my breath, counted my heartbeats, fast and unsure, full of pain. Pain like fire in my limbs, like a burning coal in my chest.

He moved. Blackness framed in the doorway. No lab coat on this one to give his position away in the dark of night. Black clothes. Eyes like holes in a skull.

I lifted an arm. Brought it down. Hard.

I felt the crack more than heard it. The bone-hard crunch, the give of flesh. He said a single word, softly. "Ohhhh." And fell.

He landed with a series of sounds. Thump. Thump-thump-thump. Thump. And lay at my feet. No breath sounds. But then, I couldn't hear over the screaming of the one behind me, his howls suddenly loud in my ears, the resonance washing over me like waves over a small child at the beach. I felt tumbled, tossed, lost in the blackness.

I stepped over the man and slipped away, a dark shadow moving silently. Of course, I could have bellowed like a bull and not given myself away over the yowling of the man pinned with a Steinmann.

I slipped away in the darkness, finding a shadowed doorway and cutting inside. In a corner stood a makeshift carpenter's table, lit by a dull glow from a window. I bent and crawled beneath. With two walls at my back, I squatted. Creek-cold had seeped into my bones, making them ache.

I had left the Steinmann pin inside one man. I was down to one weapon. Hefting the mallet, I checked my grip. Waited. And listened. There were sounds in the darkness. Sirens far off. I wrapped my arms around my knees, the mallet head against my forehead, and closed my eyes.

25

Evidence and Cobwebs

When the lights came back on I lifted my head. There were people nearby. I could hear them talking, hear the sound of many feet. Hear the sound of radios crackling.

With difficulty, I crawled from between the angled legs of sawhorses and stood. I finally recognized the sound in the background, the sirens I had been hearing. Somewhere in the building a fire alarm had gone off when I turned off the breakers. The sirens were the sound of fire trucks and police pulling up to the building. Help had arrived.

Mark called, his voice bouncing in the empty construction site. He was shouting for me, a tone of desperation in his voice. I called out to him.

A man in a firefighter's yellow and gray coat found me first. Then an orderly in white, carrying a fire extinguisher.

"Lady? You all right?" asked the first.

"Dr. Lynch, what are you doing here?" asked the orderly.

"Rhea!" Mark blew into the room, scattering the other men, and stopped at the sight of the mallet in my right hand. His eyes swept down me, pausing at various places. Looking at bloodstains, I realized as I followed his gaze. My blood from my left hand. Blood from the man I had struck with the Steinmann pin.

Delicately, he lifted the bone mallet from my hand and placed it on the plywood table at my back. Then he slid out of his unzipped down jacket and placed it around my shoulders. Furnace-like heat burned its way into my skin, so delicious I groaned.

"We have two men in here who need a doctor," he said, watching my eyes, his own questioning and uncertain. "Can you...are you able to check them out?"

I nodded, too tired to speak, and followed him back to the men I had injured.

The room where the two lay was filled with medical employees improperly dressed for the cold. Fire extinguishers were placed around the room as if they had been set down haphazardly so the nurses could attend to the injured. Firefighters tromped from room to room, grumbling about improperly wired breakers, and I gathered that I had set off a fire alarm when I tripped the second box.

A man in black clothing was lying facedown in the doorway. His head was bleeding. I stepped across him and bent, assisting someone—I didn't look to see who I helped—to turn him. He was breathing. Moaning. I couldn't find the emotion to care that he was still alive. I didn't know him. Didn't know why he had attacked me.

"Get him to E.R. If his vitals are okay get a skull series. Call Chris in and get a head scan."

"Right, Doc."

I looked up into Ashlee's face. She smiled at me. "Good thing this happened so close to your call room, huh?" she said. "And we got another one with a head wound in E.R., waiting for you. No hurry. Cop fell out of his chair and busted his head. Ward secretary found him lying in the floor outside your room. Must have fallen asleep."

I understood then that Ash had no idea that Jacobson had most likely been hit by the man she was helping. No idea that the men had attacked me or that I was involved in any way. No one understood but Mark. The way he had taken the mallet. Gingerly. As if it was evidence...

A nurse ran past me carrying an armload of supplies and I trailed her to the man in the far corner. Blood was smeared into the concrete beneath him and still seeped from the wound in his groin. He met my eyes and looked away, licking his lips. Suffering in his glance, and fear. He needed a doctor and there was only me. Cobwebs that had frozen in my mind began to clear.

I grinned grimly and knelt beside him. My knees popped, a sound like firecrackers in the cold. He flinched. I pushed against his clothing, studying the knot above the wound I had made. The Steinmann pin shone bright with blood, and was twisted with his clothes. During my run, I had managed to retain both the stethoscope around my neck and my surgical scissors, which I pulled from my pocket. With careful movements I cut away his jeans and the lab coat that had made him visible in the darkness.

"Nasty wound," I said conversationally. His face blanched.

"It looks like the pin went into the nexus where the nerve and artery and vein all come together in this one small place." I tapped the pin and he flinched again, moaned with pain. "I'll bet it hurts like hell," I said softly, leaning in, smiling.

"Oh Jesus," he gasped.

"Good time to pray. You need it."

"I...I want to talk to the cops. Now!" he shouted. "I want to talk to the cops now!"

"Well, I suppose that could be arranged, but not till I'm done with you. Now, be still or I'll tap the pin again." He shut up, gasping in and out, hyperventilating, his eyes wide, ringed with white and terror.

"Someone call for a cop?" Mark asked at my back.

Without turning, I said, "Yeah, he did. But you have to wait. And you shut up," I said to my patient.

"Fine by me." I could hear the grin in Mark's voice. He wasn't precisely enjoying the man's torment but he would use it to acquire a confession later. I knew how his mind worked, and I remembered a time when I had hated the callous insensitivity of the policeman's psyche. Not now. Mark's boots stepped to the side, giving me privacy with the man on the floor. He moaned softly.

"You're still alive," I said to him, "and so I assume the pin missed your artery. Quarter of an inch to the inside and you might be dead by now." He groaned again, his eyes on Mark over my shoulder. "Nicked the vein, looks like, but it's clotted off.

We'll get an X ray and see how deep this goes. Might need a surgeon to remove it or I might do it myself in the E.R.'' Pulling the stethoscope from my neck I listened to his lungs work, his heart beat. The sounds of a frightened bird I might have held in my palm.

"Ash, clean this wound, please. Then pack it and get me a picture. H and H to see if he lost too much blood. UA to see if it nicked the bladder. If he can't void, cath him."

The man groaned yet again and I smiled into his eyes, lowered my voice. "Did you injure Marisa Braswell?" I tapped the pin. It quivered. He jerked. His face was whiter than the lab coat he wore. "Did you help shove a pin like this up into her brain?" I leaned in, my face close to his. "Did you hold her down while Steven Braswell, or Eddie, or Mitchell Scoggins lobotomized her? Because if you did, you better get protection from that cop back there. You're gonna need it. You're gonna need it real bad." I stood, turned and walked away from the pleading eyes and the stench of fear.

At Mark's side, I slid out of the down coat and handed it to him. "Thanks." It was clear he understood that I was not referring strictly to the coat.

He nodded his head. "We'll have to talk."

"Anytime."

"Right now, let's go get you warm."

I nodded and didn't refuse the warmth when he placed the coat back around my shoulders.

"There was a man locked in a room just ahead. I'll give you one guess who it is."

"Eddie Braswell," I said, remembering the sound

of his voice from the hallway outside Marisa's room.
Was it only days ago?

"Bingo. He was screaming about information he
has on his daddy and Mitchell Scoggins. Said he
wanted a deal. Said he has something even bigger
he can share with us. What he calls 'other information.' He had a fresh gunshot wound to his shoulder.
Bandaged and cleaned, but infected already. Sounds
like he's our shooter. Had these in his pocket. You
know what they are?''

He placed a box of pills in my hand. They were
individually wrapped samples of a medication. I
turned them in my hand. And felt a flush rocket up
from the pit of my stomach, warming me. "Antibiotics."

"Thanks. No, keep the coat," he said as I once
again handed it to him.

"I'm fine," I said, my voice sounding far away
and thin. I forced his coat on him as if the touch of
it scorched my hand. "I'll be in the E.R. if you need
me. I have patients." I smiled at him, a sickly smile,
and turned away, heading for the lights at the far end
of the hallway. In one hand was the antibiotics. I
slipped them into a pocket of my scrub pants.

"Stay warm. And take care of Jacobson before
you see to this other scum. His wife is going to eat
my liver out as it is."

I had forgotten about Jacobson. The picture of his
matted hair, bleeding head, came back to me freshly.
He was still alive, then.

As I walked back toward my room, the heat increased, thawing my flesh. I needed clean dry shoes,
but I had none—only a fresh pair of white socks in

my duffel. Better than nothing. I smiled and nodded
to the medical personnel returning to the floors carrying fire extinguishers. Smiled and nodded to others
who were pushing stretchers into the construction
site. Smiled and nodded to someone who asked me
a question, though I didn't really hear the words or
pay attention to what she wanted.

I went into my call room. Found the socks and sat
on the bed to pull them onto my feet. My hands fell
idle. I understood now. Understood so many things.

Several of the companies that formed Medicom
Plus's investors had looked familiar. Now I knew
why. The lobotomies had been performed in a semi-
professional manner. Now I knew why.

And a germ of an idea began to form in the dark
and frigid depths of my mind that would explain why
all of it had been done. The ultimate reasoning. The
ultimate motive.

Slowly I pulled the socks over my cold toes. They
were miserable. I was miserable. But I didn't think
I would ever be warm again anyway, so I didn't try
to warm myself. There was no point.

In my sock feet I left the room, abandoning filthy
shoes on the rumpled bed. As I pulled the door to, I
caught a glimpse of myself in the tilted mirror over
the sink. I was wet, blood-streaked, wearing a thin
purple scrub suit, thick white socks and little else. I
was wrinkled and slightly blue with cold. Breast
pocket full of implements, stethoscope—the doctor's
constant companion—around my neck. A fool who
had believed in illusions.

I walked the halls, feeling the warmth bake the ice

particles out of my flesh, and as I walked, I put it all together.

Marisa was alive, breathing easily beneath a mound of blankets, a spot of drool on the pillowcase, bruises on her face healing. I checked her temp—normal. Checked her pulse and BP—normal. Everything normal. I could look at her, at the tone of her skin, the elasticity of it, the firmness of it, and tell she would survive. And I understood that she was intended to survive all along.

"She isn't to be left alone tonight," I instructed the nurse. "Not for a moment. Not with family, not with anyone."

"But, Dr. Lynch, we have four other patients and only three nurses tonight. I can't sit in here with her and ignore my other patients."

I looked down at the petite nurse, barely out of her teens, the kind of woman my mother had intended me to be, blond and delicate as a butterfly. I had fooled her, growing tall and gawky and dark as the stranger who sired me and then had the bad grace to die before I was born.

"Marisa Braswell is in danger tonight," I said mildly. "All of you are."

The nurse, whose name I couldn't remember for the moment, raised worried eyes to me, eyebrows lifted in alarm. "Why?"

I laughed shortly. There were no good reasons why. Not really. Not for all this. All these people injured. All this horror. And here, looking worried and fragile, was another one I was responsible for protecting. I just hoped that I did a better job protecting her than I had done with Marisa.

"Call Cameron Reston at the Comfort Inn and tell him to come stay with her. Tell him I said it's urgent. Have him call me in the E.R. as soon as he gets here. Meanwhile, you sit in that chair. Don't let anyone into this room. *No one*. Understand?"

"Yes, ma'am."

"Call security if you have to. But keep everyone out. Respiratory, nurses, lab, family. No one is to be allowed in here."

"Yes, ma'am."

I turned without smiling and left the department. I stopped at a supply cart and rummaged around for a pair of paper foot covers, the kind worn in surgery and into the rooms of patients who had seriously compromised immune systems. They offered a little warmth to my cold feet, so I pulled on another pair and continued to the E.R., the paper making little crumple-swishing sounds with each step.

The floors were deserted, the halls empty of visitors. All employees not urgently needed for immediate patient care were down in the construction site assisting or gawking, leaving it tranquil here in the rest of the hospital. In the connecting hallways the overhead lights were set on nighttime energy-saving settings, every third one lit. Dim. Peaceful. Falsely so.

I had nearly reached X-ray when I heard the boots, a rapid tappity-tapping as she ran. I recognized the sound, recognized the gait, and slowed for her, giving her time to catch up. DeeDee, a single strand of hair out of place, breathless, caught up with me in a darkened stretch of hall. Her fingers were ringless again, pale pink nails shining ashen in the wan light.

"Are you all right, dear? I just heard. They said you had been attacked again. What is going on, Rhea dear?" She placed one hand delicately on my arm, stopping us both, then withdrew her fingers. "What have you gotten yourself into?"

I told her about the men who had been waiting in the call room for me. About the attack that led into the construction site and the men I had disabled there. "One of the men was Eddie Braswell. As I left, he was implicating Steven and Mitchell Scoggins."

DeeDee stopped, her face corpse-pale in the murk. Her lips parted, blue eyes wide, appearing grayish and dull. Her hands were still, clasped lightly before her chest, poised even when anxious.

"And then he said he had something else with which to deal. I think it has something to do with Medicom Plus. Mark has them all in custody." I didn't mention that the men in custody were likely already in the E.R. waiting for treatment before going to jail.

DeeDee gasped, lifting her clasped hands to her lips. "Thank God it's finally over. I have been so terrified for Marisa and you. My two girls."

"Miss DeeDee." I stopped and looked down at her, so dainty, so elegant even in jeans and boots, without her jewelry. It was the breeding. Centuries of careful genetic selection, the best blue bloods marrying and begetting children on the daughters of other blue bloods. The estates, the property, the money passing from parent to child in generational affluence, an insulated, closed, protected society. It had resulted in this woman. Miss DeeDee Stowe of the Charleston Stowes.

"Who will take care of Marisa if Steven is found guilty of complicity in the assault on her?" I asked carefully.

"I will, Rhea dear. I will have that responsibility and that pleasure."

It was impossible to miss the delight in the colorless eyes, even in the somber light.

"And you will then have control of Marisa's trust fund...if Marisa is pronounced permanently disabled and incompetent?" I clarified.

"Well, if we must speak of *money*," she said as if the word were tainted, "yes."

I reached into the pants pocket of my wrinkled purple scrub suit. Tossed DeeDee the antibiotics. In reflex, she caught them, hands clasped around the box. "Ciprofloxacin," I said. "In samples. Eddie had these in his pocket. Your bladder infection had been responding to the Bactrim all along, hadn't it?"

DeeDee sighed, tilting her head into shadow. "Oh my. What a mess."

"You didn't need these for yourself, but rather to treat a gunshot wound one of your men received when they attacked me on the Health Run. Reuben shot one of them. I'm pretty sure it was Eddie."

DeeDee sighed again, the sound filled with real anguish.

"Eddie used to work at the farm with you when he was a kid, didn't he? Back when you owned the whole thing instead of being just a partner. He used to follow you around like a little lost puppy, mucking out stalls, feeding horses, exercising a few to take the work off the grooms. You were...buddies with Eddie. Weren't you?''

When she didn't answer, I continued. "Miss DeeDee, what would you have done if Marisa had come to you with her proof of Steven's infidelity?''

The smooth lips turned up, though I could no longer see her eyes at all. "I would have flown her to Reno for a divorce. No woman deserves to be deceived, my dear.''

Softly I said, "And then you would have lobotomized her anyway, to get at her trust fund. Am I right?''

The pink lips turned up higher.

"But you didn't know. So you hurt her and put the suspicion on Steven. And you killed the private investigator because you thought he was looking into your financial situation and the situation with Medicom.'' The words poured out of me like a contaminated stream spilling filth. "You stole financial information about the hospital's bid to provide medical services for the chemical company's employees. You had opportunity, you had access to the computer... You are one of Medicom's principal investors.''

"Oh no, dear. I could never kill anyone. The investigator was simply smaller than he looked all bundled up in winter clothing, which caused me to miscalculate the dosage. The sedative was too much for him.'' Her eyes came back into the light, placid eyes of purest blue turned glacial gray by the near darkness. "His death was an accident.'' She smiled gently. "I always did say you were the brightest little thing. Far more intelligent than Marisa, though I like her best of all my relatives. And I did so want to direct Medicom.''

It was bizarre, this calm, controlled chat in the dim corridors of the hospital. But considering the words were with Miss DeeDee, there was no other way for the conversation to go at all. And, I was beginning to understand, to put it all together. ''You've been selling off property for years, not so you could retire, but so you could gamble. You are dead broke. You lost it all.''

''Not at Vegas, dear. Nothing so vulgar as that.'' She shook her head, amused. ''On the stock market, over a period of years. It was an accident....''

''If Steven was in jail, and Marisa dependent on you, you would have control of the trust fund and of Medicom. But you had to get rid of all the people who helped you with Marisa.... Raymond Abel and Willie Evans worked as farm laborers.'' I looked down at DeeDee. ''They must have worked for you, too. But the men tonight...''

''Hired help, all but poor Eddie. I would have paid off the other two and dealt with Eddie myself. Then things would have come together so neatly.... Now it is all such a mess. And so terribly unfair.''

DeeDee turned and walked toward the hallway's end. I walked silently beside her. I could feel the cold now, colder than death in the long bones of my legs and the frozen pads of my feet. ''I have to tell Mark, Miss DeeDee.''

DeeDee smiled at me sadly and lifted one hand. A single hissing and a blast of wet hit my face. Burning, liquid flame. I screamed and gagged, covered my head, turning away. *Pepper spray...* I hit the floor, unable to draw breath, my skin on fire.

Hands on my arms pulled my hands away, pulled me across the floor, cold tile beneath me. *Incredible strength in her petite body...* I fought back, clawing my arm where her hands had been. Clawing at the air where DeeDee should have been. A door closed. I gagged, wiping at my eyes. The burning worsened. I could see nothing through my tears.

A sharp cracking sound, as of a single-dose vial of liquid medication being opened.

My throat was scalded. My sinuses blistered. I was sure of it. And I was blind.

Then the smell hit me. Chloroform. Acrid and sweet. A cloth pressed to my face, shoving between my fighting hands.

I hit out. Connected with flesh. Rolled. Things fell around me with a clatter. Mops and brooms, sour with wet. I was in a housekeeping supply closet. Being burned to death. I gagged again. Struck out, hitting only air.

A sharp pain hit me in the back, low down on my buttock. And I knew she was giving me a shot of Xylazine.

She. Not Miss DeeDee, but this other one... This madwoman I never knew.

I rolled, pulled away from the needle. Fighting for my life. For my mind. Kicking out, I screamed. The room was small. I hit the wall with my head, hard. Saw stars in my pepper-spray tears.

The doctor's equipment hit my chest.... *The scissors...*

I spun to my knees and pulled at the pocket with

desperate fingers. The cloth ripped. My fingers found the rounded, circle-shaped handles of the scissors and I hit out, again and again aiming for the movement I could see in the wavering of my tears. Hit nothing.

A peculiar lethargy began in my deltoids and the long muscles of my legs. I paused. Licked my lips. My heart pounded, fast and pained. Hands reached out of the tears and gripped my wrist, ripped away the scissors.

I grabbed the hand holding my wrist. Twisted down. She was strong, but small. I forced her to her knees. With a whipping motion, I wrapped the stethoscope around her neck, dropped her wrist and pulled on both ends.

26

PVCs and Phenergan

The fatigue blasted up and out from my core as the drug took effect. Hanging on to the stethoscope, I pulled the ends. And pulled. Strangling DeeDee.... Crying at the fact that I was killing my friend, and at what she wanted to do to me. Her body beside me began to soften, to relax, to give way. Pulling against the stethoscope, DeeDee settled slowly to the floor.

I dropped her. Felt her slide through my arms, and down to the tile. Loud breath roared in my ears, my own, like a violent surf. I fell beside her. With my hands, I tried to find her pulse, but got tangled in her hair, which had fallen in the struggle.

I was so tired. Slowly, I gave up my search for her carotid. Resting my hands beside her, I listened to my own heartbeat resounding in my ears. An irregular rhythm but normal for me. The erratic beat of occasional PVCs—pre-ventricular contractions—the sound I heard when running without warming up properly, not yet AV block.... I laughed. The sound was thin and shaky.

My elbows wanted to give way, to slip to the floor, to find sleep. I fought the urge and raised up. The door was a brown stain on the white of the walls. I found it with my hands and then the knob. Turned it. The door gave before my weight as I fell out into the hallway.

Behind me I heard rustling. The sound of hard breathing. Retching. Weeping. DeeDee was waking. I hadn't killed her after all. I crawled from the doorway across the hall into a darkened room. Around a corner. Beneath a desk. And fell. Blackness like fine lace covered my face, blocking out the watery and wavering world.

I woke to a different realm. White. Unbearably white. Groaning, I closed my eyes, turned to the side and vomited.

"It's okay, Dr. Rhea. You barf all you want to," a soft voice said.

"I don't want to," I whispered back. But I vomited again even as I spoke.

"Dr. Chadwick had me give you some Phenergan, so that nausea will pass in a minute. We're giving you something to counteract the sedative that woman gave you, too. You hold on, and you'll feel better in a few minutes." Ashlee's voice this time.

The memories came flooding back on another wave of nausea. I lifted my hand. It weighed a hundred pounds. Heavy. My fingers didn't want to move. With effort, I touched my face beneath my left eye. No wound. I had gotten away in time.

"She awake?" It was Mark's voice. I had heard that tone several times recently. Filled with concern. Tender.

"Keep him away from me," I mumbled. I didn't

want Mark to smell vomit on me. Foolish, perhaps, but then I wasn't exactly myself at the moment. I rolled away. "Keep him away from me."

"He's going, Rhea," Wallace said. "Hold still and we'll wash this pepper spray off. You'll feel better in no time."

"I better," I mumbled, "or I'll sue."

"Jump on the legal bandwagon. Strike it rich with a lawsuit. Join the crowd at the prosperity watering hole."

"Wallace?"

"Yes, Dr. Lynch."

"Shut up."

He chuckled. It was the last sound I heard before a deluge of water washed over me. The pepper-spray agony eased. A miracle. I hadn't even been aware how badly I was still hurting until the pain was gone. And then once again, sleep claimed me.

I woke a dozen times throughout the night as one nurse or another checked my pulse, my blood pressure, my temperature. I was given several injections, was bolused at least once as a medication was injected through the IV line on one wrist, and I didn't even bother to discover what was being given to me. I couldn't open my eyes. The pepper spray was gone, but my skin and my eyeballs felt scalded.

In excited voices, the nurses told me that I was in ICU, one room down from Marisa, and was the hero of the day. State law-enforcement investigators were crawling all over the hospital, getting in the way of medical personnel and generally making pests of themselves. The local cops were not happy to be sharing turf, and the RNs were enjoying the floor

show as male egos and male backbiting took prec-
edence over saving lives. I couldn't have cared less.

Cam was constantly at my bedside, stroking my
hair, helping me brush my teeth, putting cold com-
presses on my face, keeping the state investigators
away from me. I held his hand while I cried, and he
held me when I vomited. It was a miserable night
made worse when Mark came in to ask me questions.
Cam allowed him in, though he forced Mark to keep
his distance and sat holding my hand throughout the
interview.

The tender tone was gone from Mark's voice. He
was coldly professional and coolly polite. Called me
ma'am. I hated it. Cam seemed to find it all wildly
amusing. According to Cam, Mark was jealous—
which I didn't believe in a million years—and angry
that he wasn't in on the fight that brought DeeDee
down—which I did believe. Either way, his abrupt
change in attitude made me sicker than I ever
thought possible. I just wanted it all to end.

By morning, DeeDee had been charged in the
death of the private investigator, Ty Yarborough, and
in the assaults on Marisa, Raymond Abel, Willie
Evans and me. State and federal charges were pend-
ing on her involvement in the Medicom Plus bid-
fixing scandal. Steven and Mitchell Scoggins were
up to their necks in hot water; their offices had been
invaded and all their papers taken as evidence.

As DeeDee had said, it was all such a mess....

27

Therapists and Federal Crimes

It was spring, or seemed like it. In the Carolinas the worst of winter lasted only six weeks, and a false early spring always came in mid-February. Temps were in the high sixties, precocious bees buzzed over the dormant grass and birds sang a chorus in the trees overhead. Belle sat in her box, her last puppy curled into her side, asleep. All the other pups had been given away, much to Belle's obvious and vociferous disapproval.

I leaned over and checked both dogs, making sure that they were warm. The box was lined with newspaper and a blanket, but the ground was cold beneath it. I pulled the box inches closer to my chair, across the crisp winter grass.

Belle lifted her head at that moment and licked my hand, propping her massive jaw on the edge of the box to see if anything had changed in the world. My dog had discovered a peculiar interest in Marisa in the two days that my friend had been home, and Belle's dark eyes settled on her now.

Marisa sat beside me in a padded chaise lawn chair, her pale limbs encased in a thick pale pink sweatsuit, her bright blue eyes serenely surveying the warm winter scene. She had been home for two days, a respite from rehabilitation. Weeks ago, Cam had performed surgery on her at Duke, or rather, had assisted another surgeon. They had gone in and removed a stubborn clot that was supposedly keeping Marisa from relearning speech. I hadn't seen any marked improvement in her verbal communication skills, however, though Cam assured me that Marisa could—might—regain much of what she had lost when her aunt lobotomized her. I was beginning to think Cam's optimism was founded on baseless hope, not reality. However, I assisted county speech therapists and physical therapists and home-care nurses each time they came to the house to work with Marisa. I hadn't given up. I never would.

I leaned over and touched her cheek. Marisa tilted her head and met my eyes, smiling. She looked down at the book in my hands. It could have been a silent encouragement for me to continue, or it could have meant nothing. Her nonverbal communication skills were becoming more acute as she learned to point to things she wanted. However, I didn't know how much she understood from the words I spoke or read aloud. I turned the page and continued reading aloud the Tamar Myers novel Marisa had been reading before she was injured.

The words flowed from the page through my lips, a story of an antiques dealer who found a body in her shop. Amusing, light. Marisa's expression never changed as the plot twisted and wove. But then, her expression hadn't changed when I told her about

Steven, either. I wasn't certain she could react to anything anymore.

Marisa's husband was out on bond, charged with several federal crimes of a white-collar nature, blackmail, and attempted manslaughter of his wife through willful neglect. Though it had been passive on his part, he had indeed been allowing his wife to vegetate, hoping she would die so that he could collect on the two-million-dollar policy he had purchased on her life. Though her death would have cost him the trust fund, the insurance would have made up for the loss.

All I told Marisa was that Steven was gone and would not be coming back. She smiled at me as I spoke, a vacuous, tranquil smile.

The police had discovered all they needed to know regarding Steven's intentions for his wife from Percy Shobani. Percy was no longer practicing in Dawkins County, and I found that I missed his pompous, overbearing ways. He wouldn't be back. Although a certified physician, the awards and diplomas on Shobani's office wall had been bogus. He had never attended Oxford, but had been trained in a small, backwater medical facility on the Jamaican islands. A medical school known for practically selling diplomas. Having discovered the lies in Shobani's past, Steven had been blackmailing him, forcing the hapless man to watch Marisa die, with Shobani's name on the medical reports. I didn't bother telling Marisa any of this. She wouldn't have understood.

Essie walked across the grass, bright red house shoes peeking out from a long housedress. She carried a tray of hot stew in bowls, and a pitcher of iced tea. I closed the book and touched Marisa, pointing to Essie. As usual, she smiled.

I had tried everything to break through the void in Marisa's mind. I had sung her favorite hymns until I knew every verse by heart, played the local Christian radio station for hours, read to her till my voice gave out. She still hadn't spoken, or even made the attempt, and I desperately wanted her to be able to speak. I wanted to tell her about the baby growing inside her that would be born in the summer. I wanted to tell her about the house I was buying. The man I was considering dating. About the fact that I had applied to become the executor of her trust fund, asking that I be allowed to care for her. I wanted her to look at me and *know* me. I wanted to ask her if I was doing the right things for her.... I wanted a lot that I might never have.

I moved so that I could help Marisa eat if needed, though she was perfectly capable, rehabilitation having made fast advances in some areas of her recovery. Essie settled the tray close to her charge, poured a glass of tea and sat heavily in the chair I had pulled up for her. "Mr. Mark be coming for lunch. That man crazy 'bout you."

I said nothing, placing the spoon where Marisa could reach it and pouring my own tea. Essie made tea the old-fashioned, southern way, dark and wickedly sweet with cane sugar, and I drank gallons of it when I was here.

"When you goin' to let that man off your hook and tell him you goin' out with him? He be just like that dog there, all pantin' after you. Come here, Belle, I got you a treat. That right, girl. Sit. Um-hum. That a piece of roast beef I saved out from the stew. Good girl. Now go back to your puppy so we peoples can talk.''

Belle obeyed, black tail wagging. I had told Essie not to feed the dog table scraps, but she ignored me and went her own way as always. Belle stepped back into her box and fixed her gaze on Marisa, her head at an angle. She hadn't approached the woman yet, but the dog's curiosity was apparent and I knew it wouldn't be long before Belle went to Marisa and demanded that they make friends.

''You not goin' to talk about your man?''

''He's not my man. Yet.'' I took a sip of cold tea and grinned at Essie over the glass rim. ''But I told him I would consider dating him when he found a home for the last puppy. I would guess that's why he's coming for lunch. To give me the good news that he found her a home.''

''You likes him, do you?''

''I like him.''

''Hmm, Arlana say you two goin' to get married. Arlana got the sight, you know.''

''Arlana has a vivid imagination is what Arlana has. And a bad habit of spending all my money on upholstery fabric and window treatments.'' I watched as Marisa took a spoonful of stew and closed her eyes with a smile. It could have been pleasure. It could have been that the steam from the stew was getting in her eyes. ''And besides, Arlana says it's you who have the sight.''

''She got talent, my girl do,'' Essie agreed, nodding with satisfaction. ''I read in the mornin' paper that Mr. Steven and Mr. Mitchell is being charged with bribin' Miss DeeDee to provide them with confidential financial hospital information. Paper say that how they got the bid from the chemical company. That true?''

''Looks like it, Miss Essie.''

''This a coil a trouble, it is. Just a coil a trouble.''

I nodded and ate the homemade stew, thick with vegetables and potatoes and bite-size chunks of meat. Before Marisa was injured, the chunks of veggies and meat would have been larger. Now, in fear that her precious baby would choke, Miss Essie cut the pieces smaller, making them easier to swallow.

Belle stood in her box and started whining, her eyes on Marisa, distress in every twitch of her tail. I patted the dog's head and scratched beneath her ears. ''It's all right, girl. That's just Marisa, my friend.''

Without removing her eyes from Marisa, Belle stepped from the box and walked the few paces to the chaise. Whining, moving slowly, Belle placed her head on Marisa's lap, her tail swaying with anticipation. Marisa took another spoonful of soup. And another. Belle barked once, a sharp playful sound. Her tail wagged harder and her paws pounced on the cold ground. Marisa ignored her request for attention.

''She can't play with you, girl,'' I said softly. ''I don't think she even hears you.'' Marisa had once loved animals, especially dogs. Now she didn't even notice them. I blinked rapidly and breathed deeply, forcing my grief away and my own attention back to the stew, which was delicious.

After a few moments, Belle turned and looked at me, her large yellow-brown eyes soulful and confused. She stepped back into her box and sat, the last yellow puppy between her front paws.

Out front, the deep purr of a Jeep engine sounded.

"You man be here."

I didn't bother to correct Essie.

Belle moved again, bending down and lifting the puppy in her teeth. Carefully, she stepped from the box and approached Marisa. Holding the pup, she sat before Marisa, eyes intent. I put down my spoon, watching. Marisa continued to eat.

Belle stood and walked closer, lifted up on her hind paws and, balancing precariously, leaned over Marisa's lap. Slowly she lowered her head and sat the sleepy pup on Marisa's thighs.

Marisa stopped, her empty spoon halfway to the bowl. She looked down at the wriggling puppy. With the spoon still held high, she raised her left hand and touched the puppy. The yellow ball of fluff turned belly-up and kicked at the warm hand. Stretching, the dog yawned, little pink tongue distending long.

Marisa laughed.

Slowly, careful to avoid distracting her, I leaned over and took the spoon from her nerveless hand. She laughed again, and placed both hands on the puppy. Petted it. Gently scratched the rounded tummy.

Belle sat by the chair, her eyes moving from her pup to the laughing face above. She made a little whuff sound.

Marisa looked up at the dog and back to the puppy, laughed again, the tinkling sound I hadn't heard in weeks. It was a reaction.... The first Marisa had made since the night in the hospital when she saw Miss DeeDee in ICU, standing just beyond Steven. Tears flooded my eyes. Essie whispered, "Praise the Lord...."

Marisa stroked the pup. After a moment she looked at Belle and said distinctly, "Pretty yellow puppy. Pretty pretty yellow puppy."